A Knight and a Spy 1412

Other books by Simon Fairfax

Medieval Series

A Knight and a Spy 1410
A Knight and a Spy 1411
A Knight and a Spy 1412

Deal Series

A Deadly Deal
A Deal Too Far
A Deal With The Devil
A Deal on Ice

A Knight and a Spy 1412

1412

Simon Fairfax

Published by Corinium Associates Ltd

A CIP catalogue of this book is available from the British Library.

Front Cover Design: More Visual Ltd.

ISBN: 978-1-999 6551-81

simonfairfaxauthor@gmail.com

www.simonfairfax.com

Map of journeys

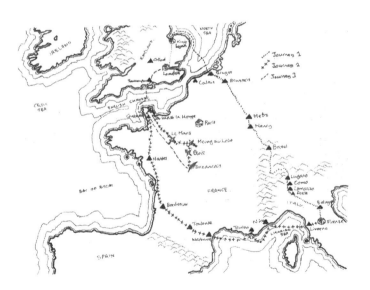

Part I

WINTER

The courts of England and France

Chapter One

Langburnestrate, London: early January

The lithe figure knelt upon the intricately woven carpet laid over the cold tiles, the mellow light thrown by the candles casting his upturned face into shadows that danced across the planes of his handsome visage. His slate-grey eyes were wide with expectation, mutely beseeching a reply to the words he had spoken in a whisper.

The room was heated against the cold winter night by a roaring fire in the carved fireplace that spat and hissed, as orange tongues of flame greedily consumed the oak logs that had been laid in the grate. Despite this, the man was cold – chilled not by the frost outside but by fear. His mouth was dry, and his lips tingled as adrenaline surged through his veins. A sheen of perspiration beaded his forehead under his dark curls.

He had faced death many times in his young life as an assassin, but now the erect figure before him would decide his fate, and with words soon to be uttered, he would gain his heart's desire or be humbled and slain as he knelt in supplication. Time seemed to slow, and all he could hear was the beating of his heart in his ears, before a rustle of silk preceded the reply he was expecting and dreading in equal measure.

"*Caro mio, certo, certo,* with all my heart I wish it so."

A smile broke out across Cristoforo's face: "*Vero? E vero? Oh, cara mia!*"

He rose to his feet in an effortless movement as though propelled by a spring, and embraced Alessandria, unable to contain his emotions. Tears of joy lined his face while the contessa cried into the nape of his neck. Eventually they broke apart, pushing each other back gently to arm's length and into focus. Gulping in deep breaths, they examined each other in minute detail, half expecting to see a change in their appearance after such a life-changing moment.

"What do we do now?" Cristoforo asked. "Our families are far away in *Firenze* and Bologna. Do we travel before or after our wedding? Will your uncle or father agree? *Oh Dio*, what have I done?"

The contessa was more practical in such matters than Cristoforo, and for once took charge. "Let us think carefully, *con calma.* We must plan, for there is much to consider. My uncle Filippo will give his blessing, of that I am sure. As for my papa, you must ask his permission. The tradition is sacrosanct for both me and my family."

At this point fear crept back into Cristoforo's mind as he interrupted the contessa's thoughts.

"But your father is il Conte degli Felicini. Will he grant the hand in marriage of his daughter to a *contidini assassinato* when you are part of the *arti maggiori* of Florence? Never in a million years, surely! What are we to do?"

"You must have faith in me and my ability to influence my papa. If he desires my happiness and wants to see grandchildren, then he will agree to my cause. Marriages may be arranged, but not for la Contessa Alessandria della Felicini!" she retorted. "I have two brothers, yet I am his only daughter, and I shall wrap him around my finger, *e bene*? Be not afeared. What gives me greater cause for concern is my dowry. For this we must travel to *Firenze* and claim it before the *Parte Guelfa*."

"They and the *Gonfaloniere* rule *Firenze,* but will you receive justice from them?"

"I will. I will have my way as well as my inheritance." At which she stamped her foot in impatience, cursing the ruling oligarchy of the *Parte Guelfa* for all they had done to harm her family and its birthright.

"As you say, *cara*. But beware, there lies peril not only on our arrival in *Firenze*, but also on the journey. The Duke of Burgundy still suspects your complicity in the firing of the cathedral at Saint Omer, and is ever watchful of you passing through his lands or those of France. He is a vindictive man with a long memory," he warned her.

"Then how are we to achieve our aims? I am not patient in this matter and wish us to be wed, for my heart yearns for you to stand at my side as my husband," she explained.

"I will think on't and find a solution. Mayhap Jamie can find a way to help us."

"Set to it, *cara*. Find Jamie, and let us journey to *Firenze* as soon as we may. For now let us impart the news to Zio Filippo, who I am sure will bless our match." At which she spun around, pulling a nervous Cristoforo by the hand, leading him to the adjoining chamber, where her uncle awaited them.

Chapter Two

Dunkerque: 24th January

The freezing fog enveloped the countryside around the port, reducing visibility to a few yards. Brands flared in spectral halos, held aloft by townsmen seeking their way about in the early evening, as the failing light added to the chaos. The Watch had yet to be called out, and everyone abroad was keen to return home to the shuttered safety of their homes and a warm hearth.

The sound of footsteps were muffled by the conditions, making them appear more distant than they were, and softer to the human ear. A gentle, guttural rasp sounded through the passage of humanity in the street, but that was muffled too, and few heard it.

"Easy girl...wait." A man's soft voice soothed the dog, and a gauntleted fist dropped down to smooth its large shaggy head. At the sound, the group that had been making its way cautiously through the half deserted streets halted as one.

A voice whispered from behind the man's shoulder: "They

are there ahead of us. They will kill us all. We are now so few and we have just you two to guard us. We will be taken and tortured, we –"

"Silence!" the man hissed. "Have faith, we shall prevail. Now, follow me into the centre of the street, with your swords ready."

"There are more behind, Jamie, I count maybe five, by their steps," another voice floated from the rear of their party.

"Good, it worked," Jamie whispered in reply, moving from the cover of the alleyway within which they had been hiding.

The footfall now came from in front of them. Flaming brands appeared from the mist as a party of men fanned out in front of Jamie's group, forming a loose semi-circle that effectively blocked their path. Their leader, slightly ahead of the group, called out: "Halt! Come forward and be recognised, for we suspect you of treason to the crown of France." He spoke French with a Parisian dialect.

"Oh *Messieurs*, you surprised me, and I know not of what you speak. We are just sely merchants returning to our lodgings ere we become benighted by this foul weather," Jamie responded in a pleading tone, using the native Flemish dialect.

For a vital moment the Parisian hesitated, as Jamie closed the distance, his right hand hidden from view. He materialised fully out of the mist, his darker form finally outlined. Forest was almost invisible, her silvered grey fur a perfect camouflage for the prevailing conditions. Her spectral appearance at her master's side further distracted and confused the other man. What group of emissaries would bring a dog on a mission abroad?

Jamie's words and placid response lulled the group of Frenchmen; their hands relaxed on the sword hilts, blades dipping, shoulders losing their tension. It was now that Jamie struck. He unsheathed his sword beneath his cloak and swung upwards, elbow leading, rotating as he went, scouring from groin to jaw in a swift upward movement. He knew not if the man was mailled, but suspected not. Either way, he took no chances, as the blade scythed up through the jaw. The Parisian cried out in anguish, releasing his sword, and dropped mewling to the cobbles. At this Forest launched herself at the next unsuspecting victim, before he could raise his sword in defence, her jaws instinctively clamping upon the Frenchman's throat.

From the upward slash Jamie continued his forward motion, driving the angled sword down into the next man in line, straight through his gambeson to the chest beneath. The man gurgled blood, sighing in surprise and dying as he fell. Jamie was through now, the dagger in his left hand pinning the next opponent's newly raised sword against him, trapping the blade between the slightly bow-shaped hilted guard of the Rondel dagger. He rotated the newly released sword at the wrist in an outward arc, slashing laterally into his opponent's exposed neck. The blade made contact too close to the hilt to decapitate, but severed the carotid artery and released a spray of crimson, as the edge drove home.

Four of the eight-man party were now dead or dying, Jamie counted, mentally approving the odds as a dagger sighed through the misted air, barely catching the torchlight before thudding home into an exposed neck. Cristoforo ducked down into a forward roll, neatly avoiding the lateral slash where his neck and head had been, half a second before. Continuing the momentum, he came forward at the feet of his attacker, driving a second dagger upwards into his exposed groin before his opponent could correct the attack and aim his sword downwards. The man's pain drove all thoughts of aggression from his mind as he grabbed his ruined groin in horror, hoping to stem the tide of pain and the life blood that seeped from him.

New sounds of fighting came from behind as the hunters

became the hunted. The three Armagnac envoys had formed a triangle between the two warring parties, their swords drawn to battle two of the advance group who had broken through to engage them. Meanwhile, the last Frenchman took to his heels and melted into the mists of the coming night.

Satisfied that the threat was gone, the two men whirled around, with Cristoforo stabbing one of the emissaries' assailants as the other emissary gave a good account of himself, finishing the final man with a straight sword thrust. The sounds of the fracas behind halted, with cries for mercy being called into the street. Finally, men appeared from within the curtain of mist, Englishmen by their dress and attitude, pushing before them two Frenchmen who were cut and battered from the fray.

"Jamie, well met! Stay your blade, for I've no wish to be mistaken for one of these *crapauds*," called out the tall figure of Sir Richard, Lord Grey of Codnor. "Is all well?"

"It is, Sir Richard. They are all dead bar these two here, and one more who fled into the night."

"So your plan worked, and the trap was well-baited. And here we have two caught right well and ready to tell all they know, I'm bound."

The Englishman had met the three emissaries in a local tavern earlier by prior arrangement, with only Jamie and Cristoforo declaring themselves to the Frenchmen. A fourth emissary remained safely at their lodgings in case this was yet another plot to capture and kill them. They had lost three of their number in an ambush earlier in the week, and barely escaped with their lives to Dunkerque, seeking sanctuary first within a church and then secretly at an inn. When they left the inn, Sir Richard and his party had betrayed no sign of recognition, but had trailed them at a distance, hoping to catch the would-be ambushers in a trap. The plan had worked perfectly.

The two sorry looking captives were half dragged and

forced into a side alleyway, no doubt thinking that their time had come. There was no one around, and the hue and cry had caused no one to summon the Watch, as the sounds of swords clashing had been brief and muffled by the fog that blew in from the sea beyond the harbour. The two men were forced to their knees, one insolent, the other clearly frightened as to his fate. One of the men-at-arms cuffed the insolent captive with a gauntleted fist, drawing more blood with the harsh blow.

Cristoforo retrieved his dagger from the neck of the man he had killed and held it in front of the kneeling pair. Despite the fog and the darkness, it still somehow managed to glitter menacingly. Sir Richard came forward before them. "I need answers to questions. Time is pressing and the weight of your lives is light against my quest for the truth and my devoir. Answer my questions and you will be released to slink back to your master like the curs you are. Stay silent and you will answer first with your eyes, then I'll have you gelded like a pig. Who sent you and whom do you serve?"

The two men looked at each other, the stronger man still insolent, the other cowering in fright, believing all of the punishment that awaited them. Cristoforo moved forward, grabbing the hair of the weaker man, resting the tip of the blade just below the eye, piercing the skin and raising a trickle of blood.

"No! No!" the man cried at which the surly one lunged forward with an oath to silence him. Cristoforo expertly turned his knife and slit the throat of the other captive, blood spraying the first man, as his companion's insolence turned to a series of gurgles and then silence. Cristoforo had been expecting such a move, and had the knife point back at the first man's eye before his companion's blood had finished washing the rough cobbles of the alley. He didn't have to say anything. He just raised an eyebrow.

"'Twas the Duke of Burgundy whom we serve. He gave the orders."

"How did you come by them? Were they betrayed?" Sir Richard demanded.

"Yes, I know not by whom. We were given instructions of their route and told to waylay them and take all papers."

"Waylay? Why, that is a fine euphemism. Kill and silence them, more like. And what of the papers?"

The leading emissary interjected. "They took them, sire, and broke the seals to ensure what they had was genuine. We have duplicates safely hidden, but they will be of no avail to our cause and that of England if Burgundy hears of our plans."

Sir Richard raised a hand, silencing him from further disclosure, and turned back to the hapless prisoner. "Where now are the papers?"

"They are carried by another of our number who returns to Paris directly to my lor...to Burgundy." Sir Richard cursed at the news. They were too late to prevent the interception of the papers. He waved his hand in dismissal at the cowering figure.

"Shall I kill him, my lord?" Cristoforo asked, as though asking permission to swat a fly. Life was cheap in his work, and these Frenchmen were the enemy.

"No, I gave my word. But take his boots and leave him thus," he answered. "Come, let us away to safety and out of this cursed fog. Jamie, go with Monsieur Allard to their inn, retrieve their belongings, collect the final member of their party and return to our lodgings."

Cristoforo nodded, and turned with Jamie and Forest, to follow the emissary into the fog.

Jamie's party returned to the lodgings that Sir Richard had rented for their time in Dunkerque just as the night closed in. They settled around a fire that kept the night and the cold, damp air at bay, until they were joined by the rest of the group.

"So, Jamie," Lord Grey said, "now that you have returned, we can understand what was contained within those documents that is of such import that so many men's lives were made forfeit. Monsieur Allard?"

The man sighed, sipping at his hot spiced wine, and embracing the goblet as though it would take away all the ills that had befallen them.

"There have been talks between their graces the Dukes of Berry and Charles, the head of the Armagnac cause in France. We are aware that in parallel with our discussions, that whoreson Duke of Burgundy has been suckling at the teat of Prince Henry." The disdain in his voice matched the crudity of his words. The Englishmen present frowned, not knowing if he was insulting their prince or just the duke. "I am sorry, Sir Richard, my nerves are raw and my manners rubbed thin at what has come to pass. My lords have reached the end of their resistance, and Burgundy has the ears of the king and the court. Yet still he cannot triumph. If the English were to come out on our side too, we would prevail and offer the return of the Duchy of Guyenne to English rule, as a gesture of our appreciation."

"This is encouraging," Lord Grey offered. "Yet hardly catastrophic to the Armagnac cause both in and beyond France, I would surmise."

"There is more," continued Allard. "My lords have finally conceded in writing that in return for England's support for the overthrow of Burgundy and thereby the crown of France, they will recognise King Henry as rightful king of England...and of France." The final words were almost whispered, yet lost none of their import for all of that. The company were aghast. Sir Richard let out a low whistle.

"Ye Gods, they would admit fealty and submission to King Henry as their liege lord of France? And this news has been delivered to the French Court? Christ on the Cross, 'tis no wonder you were waylaid. They will consider this proof certainty of treason to King Charles and the French Crown. There will be anarchy and full civil war."

Allard looked balefully at Lord Grey and he nodded his head, suddenly looking much older than his forty-two years.

Chapter Three

Westminster, London

Monsieur Allard stood before the dais and the members of the Council. All eyes moved to watch the small procession as the king was carried forward by two strong pages bearing his ornate, gilded chair on two palls. There were barely stifled gasps at his altered condition. His skin had a grey pallor, and the hair beneath the crown was lank and shorter than it had been, to hide its thinning condition. Yet his eyes showed that he was not defeated in spirit even if his body was failing him. They burned with a fire of determination. He had succeeded in retaining his crown only a few weeks before, despite threats to the throne and fears of assassination, but on his bad days he needed to be carried into the chamber upon this gilded chair. It was his iron will that kept driving him forward, a strength of mind that even his enemies had to admire, convinced as he was that he would see death only in Jerusalem, as a seer had once foretold.

As Chamberlain of the King's Household, Sir Richard,

Lord Grey of Codnor, read out the letters of intent addressed to the king. There were cries of surprise around the court as the terms were recorded for all present to hear. None were less surprised than Prince Henry, who looked across at Jamie in disgust that he should have personally aided the officers of the crown by providing safe passage to those whose appeals he vehemently opposed. Jamie caught the look, but kept his eyes focused upon the proceedings before him.

It was now officially recorded by the royal clerks: the Armagnacs, in return for martial aid, would offer fealty and obeisance, and acknowledge King Henry as king of England and of France, if they could gain the level of power and influence over King Charles VI and the French Court that the Duke of Burgundy now possessed.

A hubbub of noise emerged from the court before the king at the reading of the letter. Henry gave a wan smile to signify that he had finally achieved what he had wanted all along: the return of the Duchy of Guyenne and acknowledgement by the French that he was the rightful king of England. His life and his work, he felt, was now complete. He shook himself as though from a reverie, and spoke in a voice that shook with emotion. From his appearance, it would have been easy to surmise that his voice would be reedy and spent, yet his words were uttered with force and determination.

"My lords of France, we thank you for your efforts to deliver and submit such a letter acknowledging our rightful status, and would ask that you return our heartfelt thanks to our cousins of Armagnac and assure them of our best wishes at all times.

"On the matter of aid, which we take most seriously, we shall need to consult with our Council. Yet we would assure you that your cause is most dear to our heart."

This last comment caused an exchange of looks between the

gathered lords and nobles before the king, with Prince Henry looking aghast at his father. At his side, the Beaufort brothers, uncles to the prince and half-brothers to the king, passed a look between them that needed no explanation – they were furious.

Thomas, Earl of Arundel, who had only months before led a war party to successfully aid the Burgundians and defeat the Armagnacs, ground his teeth, clasping a balled fist with the palm of his other hand. "What," he muttered to himself, "what treachery is this? By my honour this cannot be."

At his side the Earl of Warwick was similarly taken aback, having fought at Arundel's side at the head of the expedition to free Paris from the Armagnac yoke. Now the king seemed ready to endorse an opposite course of action.

Those who did appear pleased stood to the left of the king. Archbishop Arundel and the king's second son, Prince Thomas, could barely suppress their smiles at the news, knowing that it would bode well for their individual causes.

The emissary, dismissed at the king's promise of consideration to his master's offer, bowed and moved backwards with his fellow Frenchmen. Once they had left, the murmurs throughout the court continued at the revelations contained within the letter. Courtiers bowed deeply to the king as he was transported from the room in his gilded chair, before breaking off into different groups. Prince Henry and his omnipresent companion Richard Courtney stood apart from any group as thoughts seared through Prince Hal's head, until they were disturbed by his uncles, who moved quietly to his side in a reassuring manner. They were swiftly joined by the Dukes of Warwick and Arundel to form a tightly knit group of mutual trust and potential conspiracy.

"My prince, what devilment is this? Is it true, do we now have to bow to the whims of the Armagnacs who seek to side with us and render account to your father the king?" Bishop

Beaufort uttered in tones as acerbic as he dared, given that he was referring to the king in less than glowing terms to his own son. "Does not your father know that he will be backing the wrong horse? The Armagnacs do not have the power or the ear of King Charles. They are but men of straw."

Prince Henry turned to face his party: "Our father is aware of all matters concerning the state of politics in France. Of that we are sure. We are equally sure that he is swayed by the acknowledgement of his status – a status, we might add, upon which we agree, for he is the true king of England and has as much right to that title in France.

"What gives us the greatest cause for concern is the matter of honour. We pledged our support to the Burgundians' cause, and my lords of Arundel and Warwick –" he gestured at the two earls next to him,"– fought valiantly at their side not months past, against the very party whom our father now seeks to support. We know not in conscience where this leaves us, yet by God's grace the die is not yet cast, and we may still persuade our father to alter his course. For on this road lies madness and a stain upon our honour. Hell's teeth, but we wish it were not so," he swore. "Come, let us away from here. We are but a vessel for rumours and gossip and we would be misread in our cause."

At which the small party left the hall and retired to the prince's private chambers at Eastcheap.

×♟×

The White Horse Tavern, Westminster

. . .

Jamie and Cristoforo were enjoying a goblet of spiced wine at a small table close to the fire. A high-backed settle protected their backs from draughts as well as unwanted listeners to their hushed conversation. A cold wave of air blew through the snug atmosphere as the door to the tap room was pushed open. What light there was from a wintry sun was briefly blocked by a huge figure appearing in the opening, ducking his blond head under a low-slung lintel that was made for lesser men. When he straightened, he dwarfed all present in the room. His eyes roved the gloom and a large smile creased his gentle face. The clean features were smooth and ruddy of complexion and bespoke a genial temper. The blond hair was close cropped to the giant's head, against the current fashion, and his blue eyes twinkled in delight at seeing his two friends again. As he approached their table, Jamie spoke in exaggerated tones.

"What say you, Cristo? Does he look different? Is he much altered, do we think?"

"Indeed, Jamie. There is a look of the brow-beaten about him. The taming, mayhap, of a man who is a man no more." Cristoforo joined in the mocking of their friend.

"And yet no shackles bind his legs, nor do I see a ring through his nose."

"This I will say," came the deep voice, the burr of Cornwall stronger as its owner had recently departed those lands. "Your sight may soon be altered when I crack your heads together, and then we shall see who remains a man."

"Here is Mark of Cornwall. No sooner back than wishing to wrestle again," Jamie continued. "How does Mistress Emma, for there was wrestling to be had there, I'm bound?" he chided, at which Mark blushed, even in the dim light of the fire and the candles.

"I know not what you mean. Anyway, 'tis about time you two looked to your laurels, for I am but nine and ten years, and

Emma at six and ten bethought herself an old maid ready for a nunnery. You, Cristo, at three and twenty shall be losing your hair and ready for your dotage soon, leaving the poor contessa to search for a younger man with a bit more sap in his branch, if you get my meaning. And for you, Master Jamie, respect for my seniors bids me say no more."

Jamie laughed. "Ah, it seems marriage has sharpened our friend's wit."

"Aye, and thickened his accent with it, for I understand but two words in four 'pon his return from this foreign land of Cornwall." Cristoforo mocked. Then his attitude became gentler as he knew what was about to befall him, and sought to soften the blow from the comments that were sure to follow. "Were your family pleased to meet with Emma?" he asked.

"Aye they were right glad, yet sorry too that they could not attend the wedding. But to leave the farm in mid-winter and travel to London, why it could not be done with animals and such. Emma liked it down there, or so it seemed, but she found the country down there frightening after London and feared bears and wolves and all sorts." He laughed, shaking his great shoulders in mirth at the antics of his new wife who had not entirely taken to country life after living all her days in London.

"And what do you do now? Move into your new home?"

"Aye. Mistress Cecily gave us a house right next to hers as a dowry. Yet 'twill be right strange to leave my cottage in Chikenelane. But they would have it no other way, and Emma needs must continue working with her mother to further their business. Now, enough of my situation. What news here and of court, pray tell?"

At which Jamie could not help himself: "As to that, Cristo has some news of his own I am sure he is desperate to tell."

"What? Is all well?" Mark asked, concerned. At which Jamie grinned, unable to control himself.

"I do believe he suffers from the same terrible malady as do you!" Jamie said. Cristoforo shot him a withering look, which in itself should have been lethal. Gradually, the meaning of the barbed comment dawned on Mark.

"What? You are to be wed? By all that's holy, and the contessa agreed? Is she ill? Does she suffer from a fever? Or have you been giving her some of those strange draughts of yours that she is no longer in her right mind? By the rood I'll set her straight," he pledged, enjoying every moment of his friend's discomfort. Tears of laughter rolled down his cheeks the more he ribbed Cristoforo at the irony of the situation. At length a truce was called and he asked his first serious question. "How will you marry with no permission of her father, the count? Will her uncle's blessing suffice?" And then a terrible thought occurred. "Has her uncle agreed to the match?"

Cristoforo grimaced. "He said that he would give his blessing, but only on the agreement of Alessandria's father. For that we must return to *Firenze* and Bologna." At which he shrugged in his inimitable way. "As you know, the Duke of Burgundy is pledged to capture the contessa if she is found on his lands or upon French soil. Pirates plague the southern shores of France on the Mediterranean and a sea voyage is not safe without a powerful escort. There is a bounty upon our heads too, if we are not under political protection. As a foreigner, I am certain no such formalities would extend to me. So we must choose the timing of our travel, yet it is still fraught with danger, to which I would not wish to expose Alessandria."

"Must she travel with you? Can you not go to Italy disguised as another?"

"To face a certain refusal? Alessandria must come. Her smile will turn her father's head, her tears will turn his heart. Without her my chances are those of the last rat in a room full of terriers."

"You are in a cleft stick, for certes. Spies will report all who travel, and word is bound to reach the duke if you so much as show your head in Flemish territory. If you go and need a strong right arm, then just call and I shall be there. For it was with the aid of the contessa that I was freed from a dark cell and a terrible fate, and for that I am always in her debt."

Cristoforo clapped a hand upon his friend's solid shoulder: "*Amico mio*, I am most grateful, but I see no way to organise such a journey at this moment. We need something to distract France, and more particularly the Duke of Burgundy – may God rot his soul."

Jamie lowered his voice. "You may yet get your wish, Cristo, for war looms in France and mayhap England shall again change sides, as loyalty pays hostage to fortune."

Both of his two friends looked at him sharply. "How so?" Cristo asked, at which Jamie repeated all that had occurred in the court that morning.

"And do 'ee think it likely that the king will land on the side of the Armagnacs?" Mark asked.

"I am sure of it, as they offer him what he has always desired: the acknowledgement of his kingship and rule over France."

"When do you think that a decision will come to pass?" Cristoforo said, his face carrying a shrewd expression.

"I know little, for I am not a seer, yet I'll wager that the wind will blow in a different direction ere two months are past, and Mars will rally us all to his banner once more. I for one will welcome it; a chance to fight the French instead of this false truce that we are now forced to endure," Jamie finished, a martial gleam in his eye.

"How do you think the prince will fare? For he supported the Burgundians behind his father's back, and still does now, from the rumours about the court."

"I agree with you, yet he must come about and concede to his father's wishes. For he no longer wields the power he once did in the realm, and all his Council members are sacked. They have no power, save that which the king offers as crumbs from his table."

Mark considered these words with a frown upon his face, as his livelihood depended upon the prince's benevolence as his patron.

"Fear not," Jamie assured him. "Prince Hal will not be gone for long and will ever turn back to the martial sport that he loves so well."

"If I were not wed and tied here, I think I may return to the farm where all is safe and regular."

"Yet now you may not, for here you must stay and right glad we are to have you," Jamie replied.

Chapter Four

The French Court, Paris: February

The long, narrow face of the Duke of Burgundy scowled in anger, his skin puce with rage.

"They have declared for Henry of England! I'd not believe it, yet here it is writ bold and clear. Dear God above, this is treason! They acknowledge and accede to King Henry as rightful king of England and agree to his claim upon the French Crown! This is beyond the pale. Wait 'til his majesty hears of this. There will be hell to pay."

The two men before him flinched at his angry outburst. As the duke's proctor and envoy, they were used to his temper, but this level of vehemence and vitriol they had not seen since he learnt of the death of his friend, Sir Jean de Grisson, in Saint Omar cathedral, two years past. The taller and more imposing figure of Sir Galliard de Durfort was a knight of renown, and enjoyed his position as Proctor and Ambassador to the Duke of

Burgundy. His aquiline features were always difficult to read, so well did he school his emotions. He feared no man and had fought at the duke's side in many a battle across Europe.

"Your Grace, if I may?" The cloud of combustible rage shifted from the duke's eyes as the calming voice of his proctor soothed his consciousness.

"Speak man, and offer me solace, please God," he said.

With a slight, almost imperceptible nod of his head to acknowledge the permission granted, Sir Galliard continued. "It occurs to me that this may play to our advantage."

"How so?" the duke snapped.

"We still enjoy an open dialogue with his Royal Highness Prince Henry, through which there is influence to be garnered and nurtured."

"Yes, yes, but that will not serve. Prince Hal is out of favour and all of his coteries have been removed from office in the Council. If the Armagnac embassy aims well at the king, all will be lost, I fear."

"If it please you, my duke, I see another way," Sir Galliard said diplomatically. "I foresee that we can use the prince as a lever to persuade the king. We have more to offer: a bride of the blood royal, a genuine sway with King Charles and the martial might to smash the Armagnacs as we did last autumn. For their part, the Armagnacs offer faint hopes and empty promises, with nothing of substance to give, save words in a letter.

"If the Armagnacs break the good faith of the formal truce called between our countries, why then all of Europe will rise against them. There would be a Papal See brought before them, charged with bringing unnecessary war to France and within Christendom. So I advise you to let us continue negotiations with Prince Hal and with all haste."

"What say you, Sir Jean?"

The other man present was completely different from Sir

Galliard and the duke. He was almost innocuous. He was not particularly tall or broad, yet there was a hint of supple strength beneath the rich fabric of his cotehardie. But even this, though well-made, seemed to blend in, and were it to be cast in a more striking colour it would still not distinguish its wearer. His features were regular, unremarkable, and his brown hair and dark eyes held no marks or characteristics. In short, Sir Jean Kernezen had the perfect accoutrements for a spy, and in addition to being the duke's envoy, he also served well in that capacity.

"My lord duke, I would agree with Sir Galliard. We are still in a strong position, and I will seek to find weaknesses in the relationship between father and son when next I visit England on your behalf. As to the Papal See, there are two popes, thanks to the schism. We can change allegiance as we wish, as I hear rumours that all is not well in Italy, and that Pope Urban suffers financial hardship brought on by the war between the factions of government in Florence. Mayhap we should pay court to His Grace Pope Clement as well.

"The Alberti bankers support His Holiness Pope Urban VI, and have always done so, bringing him to power with the help of the Medici family. Now there is a financial war, with the Albizzi family among others on one side and the Albertis on the other. As always, it is about wealth and power. In Florence at least, the Albizzis are winning, as they control the ruling council of the *Parte Guelfa*. If this were to change and either Pope Urban was unseated or pressure was brought to bear to ostracise, or even excommunicate the Alberti families, the English and King Henry would have no choice but to expel the Albertis and choose new bankers. If not, then mayhap the Avignon pope could be persuaded to fall in our favour against the Armagnacs and the English Crown." He finished, shrugging as though it were a fait accompli, his shrewd eyes boring into the duke, despite their difference in station.

The duke raised an eyebrow, clearly intrigued by what he had just heard. "You are as ever well-informed, Sir Jean. Pray keep me abreast of all that progresses concerning the Papal schism."

Chapter Five

Westminster Palace, London

The king wheezed in his private chamber, free from the prying eyes of even his most loyal courtiers. The only person present in the bedchamber was his wife, Queen Joan of England. In her forty-fourth year she was still a handsome woman, her black hair offering evidence of her Spanish lineage. Her heart-shaped face was full and her cheeks had a natural bloom that shone through her olive skin. The council session had just finished and the final proposals had been heard from the Armagnac envoys.

"My husband, do you think it wise to entertain the overtures of the Armagnacs? What can they offer us in good faith? The Burgundians control Paris and Guyenne through the marriage of Duke John's daughter. How can they cede control to you? I urge you, dear heart, not to countenance such an agreement," she pleaded, grasping his hand between hers.

"Is this something new that you have just informed us of?

For if not we wish that you advise us less and heed us more." The king snapped in a manner that she was not used to hearing from him. Theirs had been a second marriage for them both, based upon a political arrangement cementing the courts of England and Spain. The marriage had later blossomed into a love match, marvelled at by all, and it hurt her all the more to hear the king speak to her so. She released his hand, realising that she would be unable to influence him, let alone change his mind. She returned to the formal speech of court, warning him that he had crossed an invisible line she would not tolerate.

"As your majesty wishes," she replied, nodding her head.

"Oh, come now," Henry responded, realising his error. His lack of manners had been brought on by the pain that constantly racked his decaying body. "Let us not quarrel, Joan, not when my work is nearly complete. We have the acknowledgement of a leading French dynasty confirming our position as king of England and as rightful heir to the French Crown."

Mollified, she continued. "Dear heart of mine, this will not serve, and no good shall come of it. Hear me on this if nothing else. To achieve this end, no written offers are made that will not be authorised save by force of arms, and the Burgundians are the stronger faction. Yet as you say, you are already cognisant of this."

"We are indeed. Yet the Burgundians ask all and cede nothing. The Armagnacs' bid is higher in its tally, by a chain." Here he sighed, keen to have peace at his own hearth. "Very well, we will give further consideration to the matter before any decision is made."

This brought a smile to Queen Joan's face, and she once more clasped her husband's hand in hers. She knew that even now envoys of Burgundy would be seeking to meet with her stepson Prince Henry in secret, and that the existing truce might be continued. She wanted her ailing husband here in

England, safe for the last years of his life and not warring in France. The time was wrong, and Prince Hal could take up the sword when it was right and he was king. May God aid those talks, she silently prayed.

✕✞✕

Whittington's quarters, Westminster

Sir Richard was pleased. His messaging system had beaten the ducal envoys of Burgundy by a day, using good intelligence and a fast skiff across the Channel. Sir William Stokes had been on alert, with his spies at all ports watching for the ship to arrive.

"James, I need not tell you how important this reconnaissance is. An embassy is en route from the Duke of Burgundy, or so my spies in France inform me. They are due to land on the evening tide and will make for the port of London under cover of darkness, holding down the river near the estuary. We know not their destination, nor whom they will meet, yet I believe they will be on a mission to talk in secret with Prince Henry. To this end, I wish you to ride with all urgency for the prince's house at Coldharbour Mansion in Upper Tamisestrete, just up river from London Bridge. Do you know of it?"

"I do, Sir Richard. There was much made of this when the king, God bless him, gave it to Prince Hal as a reward for all his endeavours, and the mansion house was inherited when the old king died."

"And you are also one of the few who know by sight both Sir Galliard de Durfort and Sir Jean Kernezen?" At which Jamie nodded. "'Tis well, for we suspect that those double dealing knaves will enter England in secret, and I would wish to know with whom they meet. I suspect that Kernezen will not stay confined, but will move secretly abroad. Hide yourself somewhere carefully and observe – but no more. I would rather they remain unaware of us. There are three hours of the clock afore Vespers, which will offer you sufficient time to find a vantage point."

"As you wish, Sir Richard. I shall return home, leave my horse and make my way on foot. Yet if I may, it sits ill with me to spy upon the prince." Jamie finished quietly, only too well aware that the prince was his patron and that he served in his household retinue of knights.

The steel rose in Whittington's visage. He had no time for morality; his role was to protect the kingdom and see that all who mattered were kept safe from any personal folly. His often kindly eyes became hard and implacable. Raising his head slightly, he pulled at his ear, a sure sign that he was about to impart wisdom or to seek to sway another to his will.

"I seek not to spy upon the prince, but to save the prince from himself. It is not he upon whom we spy but the company that he keeps. And from that –" he paused, raising a hand with one finger extended, "– we shall learn what our enemies are about. The prince, like all who are loyal to the king – and I doubt not that he is so bound – is as able to be led in a different direction as the next man. Yet I would not wish to aid those who would do harm to him, his father or the realm by presenting an opportunity to clandestinely lever him into an unenviable position. The relationship between king and prince is already at breaking point. One slip and we would have civil war as they now do in France. This would be disastrous for us all, except those who seek the crown and power for themselves. Go to, James, and see your mission not as a betrayal of your prince, but as a thwarting of his enemies."

Jamie remained entirely unconvinced by those honeyed words of explanation, yet the prospect of some excitement and spying on Frenchmen while ostensibly aiding the crown, in whatever form, won him over.

He rode home to find Cristoforo lounging and restless. His father was at home, but had no need of the Italian for any chores of his own. Cristoforo was delighted to be pressed into service to aid Jamie, especially at the promise of some action against the French in whatever form. They made their way on foot from St Laurence Lane in Jewry directly south on a familiar path onto Westchep, along to Poultry and then south to the river. They soon ended up on Tamisestrete, and were faced with the familiar rows of wharfs, warehouses and docks of the bustling London port. The mighty London Bridge was still easily visible in the approaching dusk, already well-lit by lamps alerting shipping to its presence. Carts and waggons were finishing their day's work, and the area around the wharfs was filled with piles of horseshit from the day's labours of the horses, vying for space in the narrow streets with human detritus. The central soil gulley was already overflowing in places, and would be worse by the morning. Both men wore wooden pattens beneath their boots, protecting them from the excrement strewn across the street. They clunked along, with no need as yet for silence, as they were with many others on the byways.

They approached the riverside on Tamisestrete and made their way slightly downstream to a huge, imposing building that stood before them. Directly beside the Thames, which was not too malodourous at this time of year, the building stood out from the adjacent structures for a number of reasons: It was constructed of stone, not half timbered or of wattle and daub, like its rivals. It was, they saw, extraordinarily high, rising from the river bank like a huge monolith to fully four stories above street level, with proud buttresses gracing its length and a smaller castellated turret at the western end. It was a true manor house, with hipped and gabled roofs and all its many windows fully glazed. It had been built some hundred years earlier by a merchant, Jamie's father had told him, to show off his wealth in the most ostentatious manner.

The two men exchanged glances and proceeded down Tamisestrete to the next building, a wooden wharf-side warehouse that was constructed on wooden piles and extended at the upper levels out into the river, via an overhanging jetty. Here they found a night watchman, and plied him with a couple of pennies to let them settle down in the upper gantry that afforded a good view of the river and the adjacent building. From this vantage point, they could just see the large arched stone steps that afforded direct access to the building from the river. Cloaked against the cold, Jamie and Cristoforo took it in turns to look out upon the river near the open shutters. They had an excellent view of all the craft that passed the buildings, now lit with nightlights to avoid collision on the busy waterway.

"*Porca miseria*, this Godforsaken country is always cold and foggy!" Cristoforo cursed as he pulled his cloak tighter about him. His instincts and training as an assassin reigned true, as he masked his face against any possible detection of his escaping breath showing against the backdrop of the building.

As the evening drew onwards a frothy, ethereal mist lifted from the murky waters of the Thames in curls and waves, making it hard to define shapes, muffling the sound of passing craft and distorting voices.

They did not have long to wait, for as soon as darkness settled and the city became a huge dark grey morass punctured by spluttering pinpricks of light, a dark beast, lit with port and starboard navigation lights, made its way slowly upriver, the hulk of its superstructure dwarfing the smaller craft around it. The ship dropped anchor in the current with a forward cable that held it steady against the current of the Thames, shifting in and out of view as the mist ebbed and flowed.

"Jamie, our prey approaches," Cristoforo warned. Jamie levered himself up from a wool sack and made his way quietly out onto the platform.

Hushed voices of command could be heard from the large cog below, and with a creak of cables and pulleys, a low boat was being let down under the torch light. There was a perceptible slap as a rowing boat was launched and made contact with the murky waters of the Thames. Figures thrown into shadow appeared, cloaked and hatted against the cold, and all bar one with the hoods thrown back. Jamie stared hard, invisible against the dark awning of their hiding place, realising that he recognised the leading figure, Sir Galliard de Durfort, whose face was cast into relief by the flaming brands secured in sconces around the archway and along the front of the mansion house. The rowing boat made the short journey to the steps of the arched entrance, and then as his hood fell back, the face of the final figure was revealed. Jamie had seen him once in passing, but he was almost certain that the bland features now exposed were those of the Frenchman whom he sought.

"So, the fox has come to England," Jamie muttered to himself.

"You know this man?" Cristoforo whispered, knowing how easily sound could carry across water.

"I know of him, and I am near certain he is the ducal envoy and Burgundian spy, Sir Jean Kernezen. He is to be watched, though there are many ways out of that fox's lair should he choose to go abroad."

✕✦✕

With the bitterness that had followed his ejection from the Council by his father, Prince Henry had set up his own court at his private mansion in Eastcheap, away from the prying eyes and gossip of the court. It was to here that he had invited the Burgundian contingent. As the law of the land prohibited any foreigner from staying unaccompanied on English soil, his visitors needed to be in the household of an English citizen. Prince Henry had ample room in his own capacious dwelling, and here they were lodged, within the west wing in separate quarters. Certain levels had access across the majority of the floors, but the Burgundian party were not afforded this degree of freedom. They were summoned to Henry's private quarters, and when all were seated and all introductions made, the Burgundians began to ply their trade in earnest. Sir Galliard, sleek in his winter garb, his dark hair pulled back from his face in a Latin manner that offered his swarthy countenance an air of sincerity, addressed Prince Henry.

"My lord prince," he began. "We are here to entreat you to continue in support of our cause after my lords of Arundel and Warwick fought so gallantly at our master's side suppressing the Armagnac forces last autumn." He nodded graciously at the two lords he had named, who were seated at the table. "We are most surprised at the turn of events, for we understand that his majesty is erring towards the Armagnac faction, despite our truce and our own pledges of allegiance and fealty to the English Crown.

"We would stress that our lord Duke John is most keen to

see a matrimonial alliance between our two houses. He repeats his offer of the beautiful Lady Anne's hand in marriage to you, along with lands and a substantial dowry of property held in France."

The English contingent around the table were only too aware of how much hung in the balance at this moment. Sir Galliard continued. "Mayhap you should be aware that his gracious majesty King Charles VI has formally signed a writ declaring all the so-called Armagnac lords to be accused of treason to the French Crown. There is a strong feeling not only within France but throughout Europe. His Imperial Majesty Sigismund, the Holy Roman Emperor, has condemned their actions and has offered his backing, both fiscal and physical, to any venture that may bring about their defeat and capture. There is believed to be a papal decree abroad to that effect, and the potential threat of excommunication that comes with it."

The prince frowned, and Sir Galliard worried that he may have overplayed his hand. No warlike prince responded well to threats, and that is exactly what the knight had insinuated with his last words. Prince Henry's voice when he spoke, was clipped and unfriendly.

"My Lord Galliard, we thank you for your concern at the state of our imperilled souls. Howsoever, we support the Italian pope and not some anti-pope in Avignon. That said, we have sympathy for your cause, whether we are threatened by an Emperor or not.

"We are unable to sway the Council in its entirety, but we still seek to persuade our father to act in an honourable manner towards you and my lord of Burgundy. Yet we adjure you do not press us, for we will move forward as best we can, rest assured, with your best interests at heart."

Here his voice softened. "Please assure Duke John that we welcome the proposal of marriage to the Lady Anne, and would embrace such a connection between our two houses. We will study in detail the missives that you have brought from Duke John and continue our discussions on the morrow, once we are apprised of the full scope of your gracious offer.

"We feel for certes that you must be fatigued after your voyage and we adjure you to benefit from our hospitality. We shall reconvene on the morrow and would ask that you excuse us, as we have pressing matters to consider ere our meeting with his majesty. Please enjoy the comforts of your accommodation." At this the prince rose, extending his arms widely in an expansive gesture.

Sir Galliard and his party knew that they were being dismissed. Bowing to the prince and his factors they left the room, to be escorted to their quarters.

Chapter Six

"What say you, my lords?" The prince asked once they had all read the letters from the Burgundians.

The Earl of Arundel was vociferous as ever in his defence of Burgundy after his battles alongside the duke the previous year. As with all who fought together and faced death from a common enemy, a strong bond of honour had been forged between them, in addition to the formal pledge of support. The earl had also been invited to the court of King Charles VI, where he had been royally entertained by the king.

"My lord prince, you know my thoughts and feelings on this matter. We have been pledged by his majesty to fight for the Burgundian cause, and to change sides now would be against our honour. We vowed to give support in arms and conduct to the court of Burgundy and indeed to the French king. The rest of Europe would pour scorn upon us if we changed our allegiance. It would seem a *volte face* and a breach of faith."

The prince made no immediate response, but raised an inquiring eyebrow at the Earl of Warwick at Arundel's side. "I too stand with Arundel in this, my prince," the earl responded to the prince's unasked question. "We cannot be seen to shift with the wind."

Richard Courtney, the prince's favourite, interjected. "Yet my prince, the tally from the Armagnacs will tempt your father. Its strength lies not just in promises of gold and land, but they too offer ladies from the blood royal of France to marry English earls and princes. The scales will weigh heavily in their favour in your father's eyes, I fear."

"You give wise counsel as always, Richard, and we are with you all in our feelings for our honour, my lords. What say you, my lord bishop?" he asked of Bishop Chichele.

"My prince, I am concerned with all matters raised, but there is an ecclesiastical issue that must also be aired. If the Italian pope enters this conflict and falls on the side of the French, for whatever reason, we will have to change sides and seek the solace from the Avignon pope. This would not be a good position, for he as you know has been cast as the anti-pope, and matters arising from this course may not bode well for England."

"It is a point well made, my lord bishop, yet we support that pope through the finances of the Albertis, who are our bankers and staunch supporters of the true pope in Naples."

"In that you are correct, my prince, at least at this juncture. However, rumours abound of financial problems within the church and the need for renewed coin, to aid Pope Urban."

"Hell's teeth, can this coil get any tighter? We are assaulted from all sides, and things are made worse by our father's obduracy in not seeing the true path to clear our rights back into France." Prince Henry sighed and pinched the bridge of his nose between finger and thumb, the scar on his cheek throbbing, as it always did when he was anxious. He rubbed his palm gently over the puckered tissue there.

"By God, we can think no more of this tonight. Arrange for

guards to watch carefully over our guests," he adjured his squire, then turned to the others in his company. "My lords, let us away to lighter company and forget for a night, at least, the labours that beset us. We are in need of ale and a wench's smile to put us right, and lighten our load of office."

With this, the company set off for their rooms to prepare for a night of revelry. As they made to leave, having changed into less fine gear, Thomas Earl of Arundel clapped his forehand to his head, stopping dead in the street. "My lord prince, I am but a common mutton-head, I have neither my purse nor my sword. One to guard the other, I fear. Where do you make for, the Dancing Bear?"

The others laughed at his expense, and with many a ribald comment at Arundel's stupidity, promised to see him at the inn, where they expected him to buy drinks for them all.

Once he turned and left their company, Thomas re-entered the mansion house and made for his rooms, where he had secured both the purse and sword. Then he diverted to the western wing of the building on the second floor, and passed along the corridor watched over by two armed guards. He commanded them to let him pass, his stern features brooking no argument, and moved to the main door at the end of the corridor. Here he knocked at the entrance offering access to the French contingent's apartments. A servant answered his knock, at which he whispered a command. Within moments Kernezen appeared, and a low-voiced conversation took place out of earshot of the guards. The earl finally raised his tone to normal levels.

"I am delighted that you are safely ensconced and comfortable, and I shall pass on your best wishes to Prince Hal. I bid you good evening and trust that you may sleep well."

Thomas offered the Frenchman a respectful bow and strode

arrogantly back along the corridor, to join the royal party at the tavern.

On the gantry, Jamie and Cristoforo had given up hope of seeing anything more of importance from their vantage point, and had gone inside. Jamie moved to another window on the streetside, through which he'd seen the prince's party leave for the tavern. He also saw one of the group turn back, but he wasn't able to see who it was.

"Now what to do?" he muttered. "I feel that the French will not venture forth to the river for that way is guarded – yet something is afoot. Who returned to the prince's mansion and why?"

"I believe they might try for a secret meeting whilst the prince is at play," Cristoforo said.

"I agree. We must watch the street from all sides. Stay here in comfort and watch from this side, whilst I suffer in the freezing cold of the street and find a doorway to watch to the west and the turret," he mocked his friend, his white teeth flashing in the gloom, since Cristoforo had moaned all evening about how cold and damp England was.

"Ha, I swear it is colder in this room than it is outside, for it holds the damp, and the cold seeps into my very bones. I shall never be warm until I return to *Firenze*. *I* shall go down. I am more skilled at concealment, for the darkness is my friend."

"As you wish, but fetch me if you see aught. And Cristo?"

"*Si?*" came the innocent response.

"Don't go killing anyone. We need them alive and able to move, and we need them not to be suspicious," Jamie commanded. In answer he received a mocking salute, as the assassin faded off silently down the wooden steps and into the night, merging with the gloom. Cristoforo found an archway offering both a view of the river at quay level and the street to the west. Around half an hour passed and his vigilance was rewarded. A shuttered window opened and a figure appeared from the second floor of the turret, briefly silhouetted against the flickering candlelight from within. The figure silently and carefully uncoiled a knotted rope that fell just short of the ground, before making a downward descent with practised ease, landing lightly on the ground. He backed against the wall and remained completely still for a few seconds, before moving off towards a lighter staging pontoon some hundred yards upriver. He passed directly in front of Cristoforo's hiding place, unaware of the figure lurking in the shadows. Once it was safe for him to move, Cristoforo slid from his lair, waiting patiently to ensure that the mysterious figure had taken a night-lighter wherry downriver, and sprinted back to alert Jamie, who was watching vigilantly for any movement on the street below. Motioning with his hand and calling softly to him, Cristoforo beckoned Jamie down, and within seconds Jamie appeared at the door of the warehouse.

"Quickly! A man escaped the turret and hired a lighter, heading down river towards..."

There was no need for further explanation, as the two men sprinted the short distance to the pontoon and secured a boat for their own journey, telling the ferryman to head for London Bridge. There was little traffic at this time of night, with most boats heading south to the Southwark stews. Only two lighters could be seen in the distance on the north bank, illuminated by the lamps that gave them their name.

Jamie was cautious and spoke in Italian. "*Quanti?*"

"Just one, and careful he was too, for he moves well," Cristoforo replied in the same language. "Where do you think he will land?"

"There are many in that nest of vipers who lurk at court and who would entertain such a meeting." Jamie fell silent, watching the two lighters twinkling ahead of them as they bobbed on the river's currents, until one of them suddenly changed course before London Bridge and headed south across the Thames.

"By the rood, I think I know where you go, Master Kernezen, if it is indeed you who skulks at this ungodly hour." Jamie muttered almost half to himself.

"*Dove stanno adando?*" Cristoforo asked.

"They are making for the Palace of the Bishop of Winchester," Jamie muttered a reply, before calling to the wherryman. "Boatman, cross here to the south bank and the Palace of Winchester."

"Aye sir," the man answered, changing course and crossing the perilous Thames, losing the full momentum of the current as the wherry rocked a little at the change of course. Jamie watched Cristoforo's hands tense as the little boat moved away from the shore into the main body of the river, its hull slapping against the waves as it headed out across the current. He heard the Italian mutter a low curse. Water was one of the few things the assassin feared. But they arrived safely at the south bank near the landing stage of the palace.

Jamie turned to the ferry man. "Thank you, boatman. Some added coin for your trouble."

"Thank 'ee sir." The man nodded tugging at his forelock, showing gaps in his teeth as he spoke. "Will 'ee need me again t'night?"

"Mayhap, stay presently, and if we are not back within the half of the hour, depart. Here are two more pennies for your wait." The wherryman was delighted with his fee and promised to await his charges for the agreed time.

Once on dry land and out of earshot Cristoforo asked, "Do you know of this place?"

"I do. Sir Richard has me watch it from time to time. This

is the residence of the Bishop of Winchester, one Henry Beaufort, uncle to the prince."

Despite the boatman's skill, they were not in time to see who it was that had entered the palace.

"What shall we do now?" Cristo asked.

"We wait. I wish to see who it was who entered the palace. Whoever it was cannot afford to be away from Coldharbour for long, lest his absence of the rope he left be discovered."

Jamie was correct. Within minutes the guarded gates opened again to permit the dark figure to exit, and in the brief flash of light before he raised his hooded cloak, Jamie saw that it was indeed the face of Jean Kernezen.

"By God it is the scheming *crapaud* himself." He turned to Cristoforo. "Come, let us offer him time to leave, and then we can go back to our beds, for there is naught we can do tonight and Whittington can wait until the morrow."

Chapter Seven

"So the spy Kernezen conspires with Henry Beaufort and mayhap the Earl of Arundel as well. Think you that the prince was cognisant of this meeting?"

"I think not, Sir Richard, for as their party left for the stews, unless good actors all, their reactions were that of comradeship, not conspiracy," Jamie answered honestly.

"What I would give to hear the conversation that ensued between Bishop Henry and the accursed French spy. You have done well, James, yet it bodes ill for us all, and now I have a terrible cross to bear as to whether to inform his majesty, through conduit or not," Whittington mused, half to himself. "No word of this to anyone. I shall inform Sir William and he will have a watch kept upon all the ports. I suspect that the Burgundians will not tarry here long ere they are discovered.

"The prince meets with his majesty this morning, and I fear the meeting will not go well. I caution you most strongly if you are called by the prince, to serve him well, and give no hint of what you have seen. Your life may depend upon it."

The prince stormed out of the private chamber where he had met with his father. His private clerk, Bishop Chichele and the Earl of Arundel scurried in his wake. No others from the prince's contingent had been allowed to attend the secret meeting with the king. Prince Henry's face was suffused with anger. He did not flush as most men but went sheet-white, so much in apoplexy was he at his father's addresses. The others of his party, who had awaited him outside the chamber, did not need to ask how the discussions with the king had ended.

"Highness?"

"Not now, Richard, lest we be overheard. Come with me to my chambers and there you shall hear the answers to your questions." He stormed along the palace corridors, his long legs exceeding the pace of all others – even the Earls of Arundel and Warwick, who were normally able to match him – so consumed by rage was he. Bishop Chichele huffed as he sought to keep up.

Only when the door to his chamber had been securely closed and a guard posted at its entrance was he able to vent his spleen. His head was pounding from the previous evening's revelries and the audience with his father had exacerbated his ill humour. He found Bishop Beaufort waiting for him, as he had directed.

"By all that's holy, our father seems as possessed as a young squire in courtly love. He moons for battle, and dreams of taking a force to France again – this time in league with the Armagnacs! Hell's teeth, does he not see the folly and dishonour in such an alliance?" His question was rhetorical. "His heart is ruling his head or his purse, for they offer much in finance, and would persuade him with fiscal pressure and promises we very much doubt they can keep."

"His majesty still feels bound to this new course, my lord prince?" asked Bishop Beaufort.

"He does, and we can no longer stand to be around such musings. We shall see the Burgundians this evening, and on the morrow we leave court. We shall instruct Edward Lord Charlton of this and of all that should be done. Our steward will attend to the rest of our affairs here."

Everyone bar his steward, clerks and Richard Courtney left the chambers, leaving the prince in peace after the turmoil of the morning. Ever a man of action, he paced the chamber, his mind roiling at all that had occurred.

"Richard, you are as dear to us as ever any friend could be. Now, we bid you go and summon Whittington to attend us with Lord Charlton, for there is much that we would put in place ere we depart."

"As you wish, my prince."

When Lord Charlton and Sir Richard Whittington arrived at the prince's chambers, they were both dismayed to hear his news.

"I depart upon the morrow and leave court for my estates in Coventry," the prince said.

"My lord prince," Whittington protested, "is this wise? Consider that in your absence those who wish to do so will seek to drive a wedge twixt his majesty and yourself, furthering the discord that has arisen between you both. I adjure you to reconsider."

"We care not, for those that would do such things seek to fill a void they created, and would surely as soon steal the crown were we here or away from court. We shall retire and build support for our cause away from prying eyes, for it seems whichever way we look some knave seeks to turn our actions against us, and our very presence appears to cause ire in our father's eyes. The irony –" here he laughed humourlessly, "– is that we both seek the same ends: a strong and united England and our lands in France." He shook his head sadly at this thought. "It is the means by which we achieve these goals that sets us at each other's throats."

Whittington knew when to press and when to retreat from a course of persuasion, and remained silent.

"We are ever grateful to you for your loyalty," the prince continued. "And we doubt not that you serve best the interest of England. As such, we would ask that you be our ever faithful eyes and ears, and report regularly all that is of import."

"For certes, my prince, without fail," Whittington assured him.

"Good. We are ever blessed with such loyalty. Now in this regard, we intend upon sending an envoy to Paris with Bishop Chichele as its head, in a final effort to see if there is a way forward with the Burgundians, and if, mayhap, they can embrace my father's wishes and turn him from his current course." A frown creased Whittington's brow at this, knowing the inherent dangers of such an action, yet he held his peace.

"Now," Prince Henry continued, unabashed, "if we do so it must be a small contingent of clerks, with men-at-arms under a strong captain to lead them in safety. Any more and it will provoke suspicion that we send an envoy or arms to aid Burgundy, and this is not our intent. Who would you advise for such an escort? They must be loyal and steady and able to protect the bishop, for these are treacherous times."

"My prince, I have someone in mind who would do well in your cause, and would ask that you hear me in full before pronouncing judgement. Any contingent sent to Paris at this sensitive time will incur comment derogatory to your cause. To wit you should, I believe, embrace those neutral, or indeed seen as standing against the Burgundian's suit. To this end, his grace Bishop Chichele is an excellent choice, as he is looked upon favourably by his majesty, and he could, may I suggest, visit Pope Clement and others whilst in France. This would assuage any fear of showing direct support for Duke John. The king may eventually receive intelligence of this mission, yet it would seem a sely cause if Chichele led the talks.

"Similarly, should you send as his escort a leading lord it would seem more a deputation – particularly if you chose my lords of Arundel or Warwick, who are known to sympathise with the Burgundians. No, I feel the way lies in protection alone and not status, for Bishop Chichele is sufficient unto that role."

Here the prince took up the line that Whittington was taking and his lips formed a thin, tight-lipped smile. "Someone perhaps, who is also accepted by my father and has his trust, yet does not tread the steps of diplomacy nor has ambition beyond his status, mayhap?"

"Your highness is as prescient as ever." Whittington inclined his head in deference to the prince's words, although the idea had been his own. "To which I would add that should such a guardian already be seen as an enemy of Duke John, it should hardly appear even to the most cynical observer that you were colluding to conspire against your father."

"Sir Richard, would you venture to suggest such a paragon, willing to step into the lion's den?"

Whittington hesitated, realising what it would mean for the man that he was about to commit to such a task. "Sir James de Grispere. He is not politically ambitious, is hated by Duke John for allegedly burning the cathedral at St. Omer and for killing his dear friend in combat. There is, I hear, an unofficial bounty upon his head should he step foot in France again. You knighted him for his loyalty to the crown and he serves you well."

"De Grispere? He also saved our father's life, for which we are eternally grateful. Who better to appease our father, who has already commanded Sir James not to conflict with his needs and ours? He must tread a difficult line, for it is never easy to serve a king and a prince in conflict. But you have the right of it, he will do well in such a mission."

Whittington watched the prince's reaction carefully, for neither Jamie nor he had been entirely convinced that Prince Hal had been as pleased as he professed upon hearing that Jamie had thwarted the attempt upon his father's life the month before.

Prince Henry massaged the puckered scar upon his cheek absentmindedly before turning to Lord Edward. "Have him so instructed and ready to sail as soon as his grace has made his final preparations. He shall command a company of men-at-arms – with no archers, for that will provoke and antagonise both the French and my father. They will see it as an act of war. I will sign letters of safe passage offering him royal protection as a servant of the crown, for as much good as that will do him in the cutthroat court of Paris, and pray for his safe return with my lord bishop."

The following day, Jamie was summoned to meet with Whittington at his chambers in the Palace.

"You have now met with Lord Edward?" Whittington asked. Jamie nodded. "And what think you of the mission for the prince?"

"I think it a fool's errand," Jamie replied emphatically. "For certes the king will not be turned from his purpose. And why should he? He has been betrayed by the duplicitous *crapauds* so many times. They claim honour and cry that we defile all agreements, yet have they not done the same to us in times past? The king will take a bastard's silver and the promise of Guyenne returned, of that I am certain sure. Then, when his back is turned, they will renege, mayhap when we are committed and in France. For that is their way, Burgundian or Armagnac, and I trust them not. It is the same with the Scots and the Welsh, whoresons all. The only ally that England can depend upon is England herself.

"As to Chichele and the prince's orders, I shall serve them well and sleep with one eye open."

Whittington nodded, a smile upon his face: "And so you come to realise the ways of the world and your naivete flies to the four winds. All you say is true and I commend you on your sagacity. Yet think on't, for now we have a spy in the emissary's camp who can report with impunity on who speaks to whom and all that is said. This will be invaluable, and whilst I look not to undo a prince or indeed a king, I seek to know the French intent, be they Burgundian or Armagnac, even before they do themselves. I also have a contact with whom you should meet, to pass on any information that you should deem important. He has courier pigeons that can fly across the Channel and be with me in a matter of hours. His name is Franceis L'Amaury, and he has a house near the palace on the Rue Dviardin. You will know it by the blue weaver's sign without and his name above the door.

"As to Henry Chichele, he is a good choice of emissary. For he negotiated the peace and the Anglo-Flemish Treaty and brought the Burgundians to the table last year, as you know. The king finds him acceptable and even pardoned him for seeking a papal bull to gain income and position. Yet for all that, he is a trained lawyer, old and with no martial traits to be perceived as a threat. In all you will make a fine company that should offend no one.

"Yet I adjure you have great care, less for the health of the bishop than your own. The court of Paris is full of discontent, even more so than here, and if Burgundy can kill the king's cousin and be absolved, a lowly English knight may also disappear."

"I shall keep my sword sharp and ready," Jamie answered.

"All that is harmful may not be clothed in maille." Whittington warned. Jamie looked at him quizzically, but said nothing.

"You will have a company of ten men-at-arms as guards and protection for you and the bishop's party. It is intended that you leave from the port of London in two days' time on the evening tide, launching directly from the prince's mansion at Coldharbour where the bishop is currently residing. There will be little ceremony, and at this moment I doubt that even the men-at-arms will be aware of their destination.

"Now I wish you Godspeed, and I prithee, not a word to anyone at court of where you are bound or your mission."

"As you wish, Sir Richard." Jamie nodded and made to leave. Once the door had closed behind him, he permitted himself a small smile. *A chance to go to France and cause havoc amongst the French? So be it. I am blessed, and by God's grace this may spark a war in which I can fight for the crown!*

He left court in high order, pleased at the prospect of some impending excitement and keen to meet with Lady Alice before he departed. The negotiations could take weeks, and she would travel with her family in the early Spring to visit their estates in the north.

Sir Andrew Bloor, Baron Macclesfield, kept a house on the La Straunde, an imposing building set slightly back from the wide street. Upon Jamie's knock at the studded door, the baron's steward answered. He was now slightly less frosty than he had been in previous months, as Sir Andrew had begrudgingly permitted Jamie to call upon his daughter.

He was asked to wait at the door, and after some moments was ushered inside to the grand entrance hall to await the appearance of Lady Alice. He swore that he caught a faint trace of her perfume upon the air, and surmised that she had been within the parlour and had made a hasty retreat before he was permitted to enter the house. It brought a smile to his lips. A few minutes elapsed, and he warmed his hands in front of the fire that blazed in the large hearth, while it crackled and spat forth sparks. Light steps alerted him to Lady Alice's presence; she was followed closely by Nesta, her maid.

She appeared with a rustle of silk and curtseyed. "Why Sir Jamie, this is a pleasant surprise and most unlooked for, or is there an errand to furnish you with a cause?" she asked, a faint smile on her lips. She knew him well and read his face as an open book, her head fetchingly tilted to one side as she questioned him. Her kohl-lined eyes danced in the firelight as she teased him.

"My lady, I need no errand to be entranced, but if that were the case I would seek one at every opportunity." He responded chivalrously, offering her a bow from his waist.

"Fie, my lord, for you soothe my ears even as you seek to steal my heart. Now join with us in the solar, for it is cosier within, and I have arranged for wine to be brought." They moved through the adjoining doorway and to a comfortably lit and warmed solar, at a slightly raised level above the street and away from prying eyes. As always, the scents of sandalwood, lavender and sweeter fragrances were in the air. A servant knocked and entered, bearing spiced wine and sweetmeats. When he had departed, Nesta took an embroidery pad to a far corner near the window and busied herself in her needlework. As Jamie explained his presence, she deliberately ignored her mistress and her companion, turning her back on the room.

"Now you are correct in one regard, for I wished to see you ere I depart," Jamie said.

"Depart? For where? Jamie, to what peril do they send you into now? Are we to war with France again? No, for you to be involved, it must be some secret matter at Whittington's behest, I'll wager."

"My dear Alice, you see through my guard and have the right of it. Yet –" Here, he looked about to see if Nesta was listening.

Alice caught the look to her maid. "Nesta, would you fetch us some more wine? This has become as cold as the night." The maid rose and bobbed a curtsey, departing at her mistress's beckoning.

"I must be quick, and this must be for your ears only. I am to travel to France as protection for a royal emissary on behalf of the prince, to entreat further with Duke John of the Burgundians."

Alice cut short his speech: "What? By the Lord God, have you taken leave of your senses? You travel into the heart of your most powerful enemy and lay yourself bare before him? He has pledged, has he not, to take you dead or alive for what he believes you actioned at St. Omer? Yet you would enter his lair exposing yourself to his power and influence. Jamie, what have you done?" she exclaimed.

"Hush, my heart, and fear not, for all is not as bad as it might seem, though I dare say I earned the rebuke." At which he caught her hand in his calloused palm, squeezing it gently. "I travel as part of Bishop Chichele's party upon an embassy to bring us about ostensibly to aid the talks."

"Then I have every right to be afraid for you, as I know without word from you that you shall spy for Whittington and report such intelligence as you see, under the guise of an embassy. Fie, do you take me for a fool?" she retorted crossly.

"No my love, never a fool, and the more so should I be complacent if I thought you in that mould. I prithee, hear me out afore you pass judgement upon my ideals." He related all that had happened at court and why he had been chosen to protect the embassy to the Burgundians.

She sighed and proclaimed, "I would rather you in a battle, for I've seen you fight, and yet to have traitors and assassins at your back..." At which she shuddered.

"Fear not, my love, I shall return and shall remain within the confines of the palace. Now, no more of this," he muttered gently, lifting her chin between finger and thumb and brushing her lips with his. "I hear Nesta returns. When do you depart for the north?"

"We are delayed this year as father now hates to travel when the weather is inclement, as his leg wound pains him in the damp. Yet praise be that he still lives, thanks to you. Now, will you sup with us? For the evening draws on, and I would lief as not steal as much of your time as I am at liberty so to do ere you depart."

"I shall be delighted to accept, yet I fear your father and I still make ill bedfellows and that he suffers me, despite himself."

"I care not a fig, for he comes about and my mother is ever persuasive."

Chapter Eight

St Laurence Lane, Jewry

The safest place for Jamie to meet with his two friends and apprise them of all that had occurred was his father's house. Two days after his meeting with Alice, he invited his friends to supper at St Laurence Lane.

Lady Alice was present, chaperoned by her groom and Nesta, together with Mark, Emma and Cristoforo. Lent had commenced, so the diet was restricted to fish, but for all that Thomas de Grispere's table was well provisioned and his cook offered wonderful piquant sauces to accompany the restricted fare. Thomas de Grispere was in his element, sitting at the head of the table and enjoying this convivial company, as well as the banter and good humour it produced. Even John, his factor and bodyguard, became less garrulous under such conditions.

"So, when do 'ee leave?" Mark asked.

"Early on the morning tide," Jamie replied. "Directly from

Coldharbour, and we can slip away quietly, as the prince is not in residence."

"I know the prince left in ill humour after meeting with his father, and the Devil to pay. We are all on reduced stipend, as there be little enough wrasslin', though that means little to me – sorry, I should say *us*." At which the giant grasped his wife's small hand in his huge paw and squeezed it gently. He was rewarded with an adoring smile. "Takes some gettin' used to, though *our* needs are few," he corrected. "I keep in training though, humping bales of wool for Emma. Yet Cristo and I were talking, and we wondered if we could accompany you on your mission. Anything to frustrate the Frenchmen." Mark grinned, eager for a fight. He had clearly discussed it with Emma as well. Cristoforo looked keen from across the table as well.

Jamie laughed: "Nothing would please me more, and I am honoured that you should wish to aid me so, for I would dearly value your company. Yet I fear that it would not be wise, for I am protected by Royal Warrant directly from the prince. You would not be safe, being at the mercy of Burgundy's power – which is far reaching at the French Court, for he holds sway over all there, including King Charles. No, it will not do, much as it ill pleases me to say so.

"Not so glum, Cristo, for your nuptials must be planned. Where is the contessa this evening, for she was invited?"

A frown passed across the Italian's face: "She has had news from Florence. Trouble is afoot there, and it involves her uncle and all the Albertis. I know not the full implications, yet it does not augur well, for it will concern finance and that will affect the prince and the king." Cristoforo was clearly disturbed and unsettled by the news.

"I hope that it is happily resolved and you may soon return

to Italy to settle matters with the contessa's family," Jamie declared.

Jeanette looked on in concern, for she had talked at length with Alessandria, who had spoken of her worst fears concerning the state of politics in Florence, and the impediment that it may course to her impending marriage.

×✠×

Coldharbour Mansion.

The following morning before the light of dawn had broken, torches from the river archway flickered and flared in the chill rising off the river. A huge cog rocked and creaked gently in the swell as the tide changed, to return its course back to the sea. The final preparations were underway for the voyage. The ship's crew stowed away the personal belongings of the bishop and his entourage.

Jamie had arrived just before the ship was due to sail, entering on foot and having ridden there from his father's house. He gave Killarney back to his father's groom and made to knock upon the main street door. He found it strange to return to this house so soon after his night-time vigil with Cristoforo. How he would have liked to have been within its walls a week ago to hear the conversation contained therein, he mused. The prince's household steward answered the door, illuminated by torchlight, and bade him enter the inner room. He was shown to the steps that led down to the rear river level, where the company had gathered around a flaming brazier set in the centre of the stone flagged floor. Assorted groups stood about, gaining comfort from the blaze.

He immediately recognised Bishop Chichele, who was in deep conversation with Nicholas Ryssheton, the eminent lawyer of the King's Council. The elderly prelate must, Jamie surmised, be approaching his fiftieth year and was showing his age in the unflattering torchlight. His grey hair was close cropped and he had forgone his mitre, choosing instead a woollen hat trimmed with fur lining. A warm cloak enveloped his portly body and he finished his hushed conversation as Jamie approached. Jamie's cloak was thrown back on its clasp and he carried a simple but well-made leather war bag. He bowed to both, kissing the bishop's ring as it was proffered, worn on the outside of his gloved hand.

"Your grace, Sir Nicholas, I bid you both a good morrow," he offered.

"To you too, Sir James, though 'tis an early hour to be abroad I'll warrant. Still the tide waits for no man," Sir Nicholas replied in his rasping voice. It would be a rough crossing for both knight and bishop, who were no longer young or in their prime.

"Indeed. Sirs, if you will excuse me, I should like to meet with the captain of the guard and see to the men." Jamie nodded a brief bow and turned to the steps below that led to the waterway. He wanted to avoid associating too freely with the leading members of the embassy and becoming too involved in their politics. His value lay, he knew, in being as inconspicuous as possible and seemingly uninterested in the reason for their journey. His job was nothing more than to provide a strong sword arm leading a small, protective force.

At the river level, he dropped nimbly into the waiting tilt boat and was transported to the side of the cog. When he climbed aboard he immediately saw the captain of the guard, a shorter man with broad shoulders built up from long use of arms. He was gnarled and battle hard. Jamie had seen him in the prince's party from time to time, and the two men had a nodding acquaintance.

"Sam, so you're to be captain of the guard on this folly," he joked, soldier to soldier, with the mutual respect of men of the sword.

"Aye, and folly is the word I use. And you in command? Well now, who is the fool, Sir James, I beg you?" he said with a chuckle.

"Indeed, yet we must not be heard by those who would plead on the prince's behalf, or we shall be put to shent as traitors to the cause. And talking of such matters, I hear the pirate cur Prendergast is free again to plunder?"

"Aye, yet we will not see hide nor hair of him on this dark night. He'll be safely warm in his cot, like any sensible dog," he mocked.

"You have the right of it, I'm bound. Now, let me see the men." Jamie went forward to inspect them and they formed a loose semi-circle about him. They were, he was pleased to see, well picked and battle hardened, not mere courtly fops in armour. All were well-armed, with good quality gambesons in the royal livery, and each had a crossbow, as war bows had been banned on the prince's orders. He addressed them quietly, seeking each man with his eyes in the torchlight and making a bond, as his life may depend upon them following his orders with impunity. Sir Robert de Umfraville had taught him this lesson, and he remembered it well.

At length the final preparations were finished, and all were ferried aboard. It was to be a long, cold crossing. Jamie wrapped his cloak well about him and settled down in a corner against the rear bulkhead on some canvas, in the lee of the prevailing wind, seeking to gain some sleep while he could.

×✠×

Bishop Henry Beaufort paced his chambers within the episcopal palace, and at this moment his demeanour mirrored that of his brother, more warlike than clerical. He had risen steadily in power and rank during his thirty-seven years but now, demoted by his half-brother from the position of Lord Chancellor, he was biding his time until the king died.

"They departed these two days past it seems, slipping out in the night to *paroli* in France on behalf of the prince. I knew nought of it, and the prince has deserted the court to retreat to Coventry, leaving us with no access to our half-brother, thus reducing our chances of forcing an abdication.

"The king is a dying fool who would render our nation emasculated by his new choice of allies. And built upon what? A false dream of reclaiming French lands and gaining dominance over France? Why, I'd as soon wager on a dove against a hawk. By all that's holy I am frustrated at every turn, and still the old fool will neither abdicate nor have the good grace to die," he ranted.

"Yet consider, brother," Thomas Beaufort began, "for with the prince absent there is no one to deny rumours or dissention against the king. If instead of supporting the prince we pitch prince against king, the outcome may be more to our advantage. Think how easily rumours are spread abroad, and there is Prince Hal in Coventry, away from court and prying eyes and fomenting rebellion no doubt, whilst at this very moment an emissary is in France suing for terms the king's new enemies? Why I should lief as not believe it myself. The king loses his grip, yet with strong Lancastrian knights and Prince Thomas around him the civil war may not just be in France, and in a weakened kingdom, a strong leader can step up.

"For what is the worst that could occur as we are safely distanced by events? Why, a prince may rise early to his throne and we shall, with civility, support him to his rightful place if he is not killed in the action that may follow. And should the prince's support for Burgundy fail, to whom will the king turn to lead an army to France? Not Prince Hal for certes, a usurper to his father's throne. I think not. Meantime I shall play the fool, appeasing the king, supporting Thomas, and making ready to strike when all is made ready."

"We must take care, brother. Should the trail lead back to us neither king nor prince would have mercy, as we are too close to the crown. We were so nearly exposed with Stanhope, Arundel and others, and 'twould not do to go to the well once too often. Yet that is what pawns are for, is it not? We should unloose our tame Armagnac to France and seek a way to dishonour the prince. For by God's grace, I fear the king will have his way and we shall fight for Armagnac, not Burgundy. Therefore what better way to anoint such a war than by ridding ourselves of an emissary and one of Whittington's meddlesome pawns in one fell swoop?"

"Amen to that. We must give careful thought to all that you adjure. Rumours are easily spread and I will seek, in the prince's absence, to ingratiate myself further with our brother the king," Thomas Beaufort declared.

Chapter Nine

Hotel des Tournelles, Paris.

It took seven long days and six nights before the royal embassy finally arrived within sight of Paris and the French Court. The going had been hard, on wet and muddy roads that were, at times, little more than rutted tracks. Passing under the north-western gate of Paris, they made their way through the streets until they saw the many towers and fluttering flags of the palace. It brought back unpleasant memories for Jamie, who had barely escaped from its confines with his life.

The party paused at the turreted entrance to hand over their papers for examination by the captain of the guard, and were eventually allowed through into an open courtyard. The palace was almost as Jamie remembered it – like a town within a town, much larger than the English Court. Within the confines of its walls were gardens, a friary, houses, places of work and a tangle of streets.

Not for the first time, Jamie considered that the many

turrets and flags gave it a feel of Camelot brought to life, as described by Chrétien de Troyes in his poem of King Arthur and the Knights of the Round Table. A royal park led off towards the city walls of Paris, which included a permanent tourney theatre that was part of the royal estate. A thin, wintry sun appeared to garnish the walls and towers, while the March winds buffeted the grey clouds that slid apart for a brief moment, offering the vista of a magical castle. As quickly as it appeared the sun was banished again, and the harsh realities of life came to the fore. There was noise and bustle, with everyone seemingly in a hurry, clacking through the dirty streets on pattens, keeping their courtly footwear above the detritus.

The English contingent rode onwards to the array of stables set on the western side of the enceinte, where they were met by grooms who took their tired and muddy horses. Once the full complement was assembled Jamie saw to the soldiers, while the ambassadors were escorted by a squire to the inner chambers of their allocated accommodation. All was, on first impression, more sumptuous than the English Court, and being farther away from the Seine, the pervading smell of the river was not as noticeable within the boundaries of the palace.

Having made sure the men were settled and comfortable, Jamie was led through a maze of corridors and steps to his own quarters. He had been allocated a room adjacent to the others from the English contingent, and after washing off the dirt of the roads, he heard a soft knock at the door. One of Chichele's servants stood there: "My master begs an audience with you, my lord."

"I shall be there directly," Jamie responded, and minutes later found himself in Chichele's more sumptuous rooms together with scribes and Nicholas Ryssheton, where he was offered refreshment.

The bishop spoke in his slightly pompous voice: "We are to

attend an audience with his majesty in half of the hour. I shall lead and introduce the company. You are to remain no more than an observer adding status to our embassy, as we discussed upon the road, my Sir de Grispere. Is that understood?"

The relationship between the two men had been a little strained, with no degree of favour offered from the bishop's side. In contrast, Sir Nicholas Ryssheton had been affable and engaging. Jamie wondered if Chichele had been deliberately aloof or was following some kind of direction or unseen command. Either way, he had seemed suspicious of Jamie from the commencement of the journey.

"For certes, your grace, as my lord pleases." Jamie nodded his head in compliance. Inside, he was not sure of the bishop or his motives, yet he presented a bland and obedient exterior. Finishing their repast, they left the apartments and were directed to the intimate chamber and court of Charles VI.

They were announced as the doors to the large chamber were opened, presenting them with a vista of the scions of French nobility. The immediate impression of the assembled company was luxury. Reds, blues and vivid greens fought for the eye's attention. Velvet hats with feathers in the latest fashion sat upon the heads of the male members of the court, while the ladies' heads were netted with gold and dusted with jewels and pearls, or wimpled in cones of dove grey and white.

The vaulted ceiling was curved and lined with blue velvet and studded with golden bosses; deeply piled light green carpet patterned with offset squares covered the floor leading to the dais. The walls, Jamie noticed, were covered with huge Arras tapestries, each depicting a hunting scene or flowers and birds. The whole panoply, while intoxicating of itself, was further enhanced by the heavy scents of exotic perfumes and colognes that pervaded the air. Conversation stopped as they were announced by the herald and made their way along the carpet towards the raised dais and the regal figures of the king and queen of France.

The canopy above their majesties' heads caused gentle shadows to form, slightly masking their countenances and throwing their features into relief. The gentle hubbub of conversation began again as the English group's progress continued. They stopped some feet before the throne, where all bowed thrice as protocol demanded.

"Your most gracious majesty, we humbly beg an audience with you and the queen in the name of His Royal Highness, Prince Henry of England. With his most heartfelt felicitations, we pray that you are in good health, may God be praised," Bishop Chichele declaimed.

The king nodded and in a lisping voice responded: "My lords, we bid you welcome to our court, and it is our honour to receive you in good faith. Yet we are bound to enquire and we are curious to the fact that your addresses do not include the salutations of our cousin, Henry of England." The waspish comment was uncalled for, but Chichele recovered quickly, realising that the madness of the French king often gave way to lapses in manners.

"Majesty, a thousand pardons for the omission. Of course your cousin the king is, as always, most interested to hear of your health, which is always at the forefront of his thoughts. He too sends his felicitations."

The Duke of Burgundy sought to ease the awkward passage of the discourse.

"Majesty, e'er it please you, I beg that you recall 'twas in good faith that we summoned his grace here to abide with us in finding a solution to the impasse between our countries, and that we may join again for the best interests of our kingdoms."

"Mmm, what? Yes, quite so, quite so." And at a loss to how to continue, his wife Queen Isabeau filled the breach. She was as ever exquisitely dressed, with her golden hair twisted up into elaborate tortoiseshells and covered with double hennin. Her golden brocade dress and train were trimmed with ermine and jewels matching those draped around her exposed neck and decolletage.

"Majesty, perhaps we should invite his grace to our private chambers later after supper, there better to discuss matters of state for all concerned." The court proceeded with other matters, but all the time Jamie felt the burning eyes of his old enemy the Duke of Burgundy upon him. At length, the duke approached the English party.

"Bishop Chichele, would you do me the honour of presenting me to your companions?" The voice was strong and the accent courtly Parisian. It was the first time that Jamie had been introduced, or had indeed been within speaking distance of the duke, and the malevolence emanating from him was palpable.

"Of course, your grace. May I have the honour to introduce my Lord Nicholas Ryssheton, our legal representative, and Sir James de Grispere in His Royal Highness's service."

"My Lord Ryssheton, your reputation precedes you – as does yours, Sir James." The duke let the remark hang in the air cryptically.

Jamie could not resist the challenge flung down by his enemy. "Your grace is most kind, and I pray to be able to remain your most obedient servant, sir."

The duke ran his finger down the side of his long nose, malice glittering in his eyes. "We shall see with the outcome of your visit just how such service may be rendered. Now, *messires*, I would ask your forbearance, for I have official duties to which I must attend. I look forward to speaking with you at length later this evening." All bowed and the duke strode arrogantly towards another man.

Once out of earshot he declared to one of the courtiers, "That d'Anquetonville is James de Grispere. Have him watched, and if he moves without the protection of the palace, bring him down however you may wish."

"May it please your grace."

Following the passage of the duke with his eyes, Jamie saw the man with whom Burgundy spoke and was put in mind of someone else. *But whom?* he mused. Then he had it: the same dark looks, the lithe frame and a feeling of deadly nonchalance about him – Cristoforo. He reminded him of Cristoforo. *Now why should that be?* Jamie wondered.

Jamie turned his back on them both and was faced immediately with a beautiful vision. The perfect teeth, hints of the mane of tawny hair beneath a single hennin that did little to restrain the thick strands of honeyed gold. Then the eyes locked with his: amber with flecks of gold. It had been many months, yet he was again put in mind of a prowling lioness.

"Why 'tis James de Grispere. Prithee, do not break my frail heart and say that you remember me not? For I should feel the more foolish or ill met."

He recovered quickly to respond. "My Lady Nemours, how could I forget such beauty, and perish me for a goky fool should I be so remiss."

"Oh, monsieur, I support not the rumour that the English are a barbarian race with no charm, for by your honeyed words you prove them quite wrong." At which she curtsied and Jamie bowed deeply, taking her offered hand to kiss it lightly.

It would be nearly two years since he had first met Monique, he calculated, yet her beauty had not waned one iota, and if anything her allure had grown. He remembered the contessa's words well. Widowed at an early age, the Lady Nemours was wealthy and devastatingly beautiful, rumoured to be a spy for the duke and a skilled seductress. She was, Jamie knew, both dangerous and potentially useful, for if anyone would know the inner workings of the French Court it would be she. He proceeded in a moment of caprice to enter into the web of deceit spun before him.

"My lady, I shall do all in my power to dissuade you of such notions if you would afford me the opportunity. For I am here only for a few days occupied in matters of duty, and should very much enjoy the opportunity to disavow you of any such inclinations towards my race and its barbarity."

"Ah you sojourn here in the palace? Why that is perfect." At which she gave a delicate clap of her hands in delight. Turning, she addressed her lady-in-waiting: "Claudine, attend us, for I intend to show monsieur the delights of the French Court."

"Yes, my lady," the maid replied, and Jamie remembered the pretty but scornful servant who had attended Lady Nemours when last he had met her. He looked down into the leonine eyes of the lady in question and was met with the full coquettish charm of a woman who knew well the value that charm held to cast a glamour on any man, and began to apply her artifice with full measure. Without so much as a touch, she gently led him away from the hubbub of the court, seeming to beguile him. All the while the Duke of Burgundy looked on, his lips compressed into a thin smile.

"Lead on, my lady, I am your most obedient servant," Jamie said.

"Oh, I do so hope that is true," she replied archly.

He ended up passing a pleasant day with Lady Monique, who flirted outrageously with Jamie; he responded in kind. There was an unspoken promise there, which was ever present between the constant fishing for information and the testing of each other's mental armour. Without her realising it, he had gained valuable information on the way the court was moving and who was powering which faction. She had not yet realised that he was now a household knight, and bethought him merely part of the guard as a lowly esquire risen from his father's trade. He managed to skirt and circumvent his direct employment, and he hoped that he gave less away than he received.

That evening, he met with Chichele and Ryssheton for a private meeting after the day's talks at the negotiating table. The two looked tired and spent, for it had been a thankless task with limited room for manoeuvre.

"How went the day?" Jamie asked.

"The elements are there for the taking," Sir Nicholas replied, "and we can surmount all impasse on most excellent and favourable terms. Yet to move forward, we must achieve the impossible and make the agreement sound so attractive that it sways his majesty. That is a feat of legerdemain that may ultimately elude us. We have secured better terms than originally proposed, and these alone in the normal course of events would sway any sane man, yet we fear that all will not account against the excessive proposals put up by the Armagnacs."

Chichele gave Ryssheton a stern, forbidding look that spoke volumes and declared that in his mind, at least, that Ryssheton had revealed too much to Jamie.

"Perhaps they will at length concede a little more, sufficient unto persuading his majesty against his folly," Jamie offered, taking the line that he hoped fell easily upon Chichele's ears.

"And pigs might fly," quipped the bishop in response. "Yet 'tis our devoir to press onwards to see what we may make of the case, and by God's grace that we may be assoiled of all that we offer, should it be greater largesse than authorised."

Chapter Ten

For three more days the negotiations proceeded, as did the amorous inclinations of Lady Monique. Jamie felt trapped within the web of politics and the wiles of courtly love, constricted wherever he turned by a python whose devious coils he strove to resist. Lady Monique had entertained him well, and they had toured the palace and the delights of Paris. As they returned on the Rue des Celestins, she had pointed out her private apartments with a raised eyebrow of invitation. He deftly avoided the trap with a commitment to work.

He spoke with many at court and listened constantly, gleaning snippets of information from any and all on the state of the Armagnacs and the real disposition between the king and queen. The Duke of Burgundy's name came up again and again as the real power behind the throne – with hints of more where the queen was concerned. The Council ruled as had Prince Hal in England, driving policy forward with the king, who was at times too mentally unstable to be free to provide royal assent.

In a moment of frustration at the inactivity and tired of courtly life with no respite, Jamie sought out the captain of the guard, Sam, who he found was largely redundant and had been enjoying the fruits of Paris. Jamie realised that he could turn this to his advantage as a legitimate excuse to leave the confines of the palace. He found Sam by the stables and asked for sword practice, to which Sam gladly acceded.

"Your mind is as blunt as my sword, aye?" Sam said. "For I swear the novelty quickly wears off, and I shall rot of inaction soon in this gilded cage. Come then, let us practice." He produced two hefty, lead-weighted wooden practice swords.

"By the rood, who weighted these? They are clubs, not swords," Jamie exclaimed.

"Aye, and well enough. I use them to better train these scurrilous fools," he joked, jerking his thumb at the watching men-at-arms, from whom he received jeers of derision in response.

Jamie hefted the sword and strove to find the balance, which was all wrong for him. He was glad of his gauntlets when Sam crossed him twice, striking for the hands and forearms rather than going for killing blows. It was a salutary lesson, and it took Jamie a while to get the measure of the ungainly weapon and the style of his opponent. Aiming at the hands could be effective, he knew, and he lured Sam into a false sense of security, making him think he was safe and out of range before taking advantage of a dropped guard to feint and strike to cut a hand or wrist. It was dirty fighting for the street or poor duels, and Jamie enjoyed it. His gauntlets were not of articulated armour, but thick leather protected by flexible maille across the backs and lower knuckles. Without them he would have felt the blows, and possibly suffered broken fingers or wrists from the strikes that were dealt sharply by the captain, who knew his trade. It was a good lesson in feint and strike, finding the distance deceptive and aiming to maim rather than kill, as no one's life was at stake and each fighter could afford to experiment.

Once he had got the balance of the practice sword, Jamie upped the ante and tried the tactics of the captain. The pace increased and drew the attention of the captain's men and some passers-by, as the wooden swords clacked and jarred. Jamie now pressed forward, pressurising Sam into retreat. Yet each time there was an opening he chose not to take it, retreating to look for distance and exercising patience. He had not had so much fun since learning with John in the yard at home years ago. If he made an error, John would rap his knuckles as a punishment. In the end Sam called a halt. Puffing and battered, he grinned at his opponent.

"Hell's teeth, man, you set a pace and chose my game, which you mastered me well in the end."

"Aye, a lesson well re-learnt for me as well, for which I thank you. Take back this bastard club ere it breaks my wrist." Jamie offered the notched wooden sword back to the captain. "Now as the day draws to a close, ale is called for. Let us retire to a tavern and quench our thirst. I shall wash and return forthwith, for I've worked up a sweat."

As the two men moved off, laughing at their bruises, one of those who had been watching the display moved back into the shadows. His curiosity was piqued and he was now more the wary, having seen the sword play. *Others may be persuaded to take the risks*, he thought.

A few minutes later Jamie reappeared washed, refreshed and wearing a different gambeson, a little stiffer, which enhanced the bulk of his physique and was almost black in colour upon the torso, while the arms were crimson.

Sam eyed it with a professional appraisal. "Is that black armour, pitched with glue? I have heard of such things but never seen it myself," he commented. "Are you expecting trouble?"

"I trust to providence, the good Lord and my own common

70

sense. I am in a foreign city with known enemies about me and about to leave the confines of my sanctuary. It is my experience that God above aids those who aid themselves," Jamie responded with a smile.

"Yet the arms are not so treated?"

"No, just the torso, for a full jacket would be an impediment to my arms, and that I cannot abide."

Sam said nothing but gave Jamie a telling look that bespoke volumes. "Come, enough of arms, let us to the tavern," he said.

The evening wore on with Jamie, Sam and members of the guard enjoying ale at a local tavern, all the time bemoaning the fact that the refreshment was not good English ale. Jamie left early, offering official duties as an excuse and wanting to keep a clear head, his sense of duty gnawing at his conscience. He had another motive for being abroad on the streets of Paris, and there was now far less pedestrian traffic. A few horses bore their riders home in the gloaming with a clatter of hooves upon cobbles, amplified by a light drizzle that was now falling upon the city. Shops were shuttered, and there was little opportunity on offer for Jamie to pause and check to see if he were being followed. Outside the walls of the palace he was now fair game for any assassin, royal warrant or not.

He paused to make reference to a street name, looking upwards against torchlight and appearing lost. Then, apparently puzzled, he span quickly around, as though to verify his position with an opposite street. He saw nothing untoward – two townsmen going about their business or heading for home; a couple of men-at-arms seeking a tavern no doubt, and a lady escorted by her groom and hurrying home in the drizzle. Everything was as it should be, yet the hairs on Jamie's neck were raised, and there was a nagging feeling that all was not well. He was being followed, of that he was certain. He took a few more steps, moving down an alley in an apparently aimless fashion. Finding a concave entrance, he waited.

He was about to relinquish his hiding place and move on, seemingly satisfied, when he sensed rather than saw a deeper shadow of grey against the darkness of the grimy walls. The figure was light upon its feet and cloaked, making silent passage along the alleyway, keeping to the walls and hugging the shadows.

Jamie sought the advantage of surprise, ready to apologise if he was wrong and the man was a simple Parisian on his way home.

"Halt!" he called out in French. "Why do you follow me?"

The figure jumped at the sudden apparition before him. "What, by God's grace, a wight? No, a chicken for the plucking, and I have waited long for this moment, de Grispere." The figure hissed, emerging from the shadows as the dying light of the day fell upon his face.

"Jacques de Berry!" Jamie exclaimed. "By what black arts do you arrive here?"

There was no time to hear a response before he saw the flash of steel. De Berry's sword was already drawn and flying upwards in a vertical slash from a low guard beneath his cloak. Jamie realised his mistake. In seeking surprise he had not drawn his sword, for fear that even the slightest whisper of steel against wood might reveal his action and purpose. Now it was too late. He leapt backwards, the sword point barely missing his legs and groin. The stroke had been fast. At his next backward step he sought the throat catch of his cloak, and with another step he avoided the next slashing stroke and released the clasp, wrenching the garment forward, whipping it through the air into de Berry's eyes. The move bought him enough time to draw his own sword, and thus armed, the two knights met each other on an equal footing.

Distance in the darkness was hard to judge and their efforts were further hampered by the narrow confines of the alley and the cobbles, slippery with rain. De Berry took a high guard, while Jamie remained at half guard, his sword tip forward ready to block the downward stroke. He sensed the movement from the change in de Berry's shoulders as the sword sliced downwards, and caught to parry, but instead of feeling the full force of the blow, he heard and felt the rasp as the blade was withdrawn. The move was fast and well-practised, and Jamie knew instinctively that the next thrust from de Berry's point would cut past his guard. It struck the gambeson hard but failed to pierce the thickened threads and layers of cotton. The strike was enough to warn him that he had met his match in speed and guile.

Jamie redoubled his attack, changing the angle as best he could, rotating his wrist overhand as de Berry quickly withdrew his sword to guard. He slashed across the open guard to create distance, causing de Berry to flinch backwards as the tip of the sword sliced across the space where his neck had been. From this move Jamie gained clarity, and all motion seemed to slow now that he had the distance and the measure of his opponent. Without allowing his full sweep to finish, he drove the point forward again. It was de Berry's turn to parry, and Jamie realised he had found the Frenchman's weakness in distance.

He slashed again, deliberately falling short of a strike to the torso, allowing de Berry to gain confidence and to try to dominate the rhythm of attack. Twice de Berry returned to the high guard, building attacks on long strikes, and twice Jamie permitted it, retreating. The second time Jamie moved away, he moved sideways rather than backwards, giving de Berry the apparent upper hand as he realised that Jamie could not strike the torso or legs from that position. But Jamie chose not to, and instead struck at the hand of the extended sword arm. The feinted slash hit home, whistling through the air into the exposed hand. He knew not whether he broke the hand or cut in through the gauntlet to the flesh below, but he heard a cry of pain erupt from de Berry's lips as he reflexively pulled back his damaged limb, somehow still managing to retain his grip on the hilt of his sword.

Jamie did not hesitate. De Berry was too dangerous to leave armed. The battle lust was upon him as he reacted with instinct, driving the point of his sword home through the dropped guard, closing with his opponent, whose face writhed in a rictus of pain. In that closing moment, de Berry pulled his dagger with his left hand, and sought to drive it up and through Jamie's guard. The dagger struck, but with little force, and failed to cleave through the stout gambeson. Jamie pulled back, bruised by the blow. Removing his sword point, he watched as gouts of blood pumped from de Berry's wound and the Frenchman fell to the wet cobbles.

Pushing the dagger away, he knelt at de Berry's side. "Who sent you? Tell me and save your soul, as I will forgive you," he adjured.

De Berry coughed and croaked weakly: "Go...and...rot in hell, de Grispere."

And then he was dead. Jamie rocked back on his heels and crossed himself. De Berry had been fast and skilled, a worthy opponent who, on another day in different circumstances, may have beaten him. The luck of timing had allowed him to triumph over his old enemy.

He had no time to consider the victory, as he heard soft footfalls approaching from behind. Someone sought to close the distance quickly between them. There'd been two of them! His actions were instinctive. Jamie sought not to rise from his squatting position, but rolled to his left. The blade sliced downwards where he had been but a moment before, accompanied by a grunt of aggression from his assailant. Jamie watched as the sword slashed into the fallen de Berry, who, had he not been dead before, would certainly have been rendered so. The weapon cut into his exposed breastbone, cracking home through the cartilage, such was the force of the strike.

The commitment to the strike meant that Jamie's new opponent was exposed to counter attack, yet his torso was still too far from Jamie's position to ensure a killing thrust. He sought an easier target, slashing laterally as high as he could to reach the man's legs. The forward leg was beyond the sword's arc and the blade missed, but the back leg was closer and Jamie's stroke cut home, slicing through bone and nearly severing the leg half way down the shin. All thoughts of retaliation were forgotten as the man screamed in agony, reaching down instinctively to his leg, which appeared to have grown a new joint between knee and ankle, and now bent outwards at a strange angle. In so doing, he brought his torso within range for a thrust, and the tip of Jamie's sword plunged into his heart, cutting off the man's cries as he collapsed to the street in a heap. Jamie sprang to his feet in case there were more of them, but all was silent; he tried to control his heavy breathing and listened hard. Adrenalin still coursed through his veins, but his arms became heavy as the drug of action began to wear off.

Now he stifled panic. He had killed a member of the Armagnac faction – albeit a traitor – and he would be held accountable if caught, sent back in disgrace for breaking the proposed truce and killing one of the scions of that noble family in a street brawl. He thought quickly. It had only been minutes since he'd left the tavern, and he could return and claim that the weather made him think better of returning to his quarters so soon. With his companions he would have an alibi.

He wiped the blood from his sword on the cloak of one of his victims and sheathed it. Clasping his own cloak around him again, he ran lightly back to the tavern. It took but a few minutes to return, and he entered from the rear and the direction of the latrines with his cloak over his arm. He made to appear casual and slipped quietly back to the table of Englishmen, smiling at a ribald comment from Sam about the richness of the French food and its effect upon the English constitution. Taking a seat next to Sam, he surreptitiously whispered in his ear against the sound of the raised voices of the men, who were deep in their cups.

"Sam, I need an escort, and I would be indebted to you as a boon to me if we could leave now, together. I wouldst not give leave to explain in great detail, but suffice to say I was attacked and I have killed my assailant, a man who may be of the blood royal."

The captain caught on quickly, and not by so much as a flicker of expression did he express surprise or question the order.

"Right lads," he called. "We may be leavin' on the morrow, so I'll 'ave no sleepy 'eads or bleary eyes when we do. Drink up and we'll be on our way. We don't want to miss curfew at the palace."

There were moans from the disgruntled soldiers, but they were seasoned men, and when the captain spoke they obeyed. With a scraping of chairs they rose as one, flinging back the dregs of their pots of ale and making ready to go out into the cold, wet night. Jamie made a point of thanking the landlord as he rose to put on his cloak. They briefly discussed the quality of French ale against British, and Jamie gave the man two extra coins for his service. He would now be remembered, of that he was sure.

Chapter Eleven

The following day, the bodies of Jacques de Berry and his accomplice were discovered lying cold and stiff in the side alley. The constable of the commune was informed and reported the news directly to the Duke of Burgundy. The bodies were brought discreetly to the palace and identified by Raoulet d'Anquetonville. When he arrived at the small private chapel, he was shocked and surprised to see the body of de Berry, expecting that of de Grispere. He cursed inwardly, letting no one see his true feelings, and hurried away to find the duke.

Knocking and entering his private chambers, he found the duke in conference with his two of his household knights, together with Sir Galliard de Durfort and Sir Jean Kernezen. All looked up expectantly as he entered.

"I trust that you come with good tidings," the duke said. "I hear that bodies have been found on the streets outside the palace. 'Twas well done and timely, for the bishop leaves on the morrow for Avignon." The duke paused, seeing the visage of his servant. "What has passed?" he demanded, scowling.

"My lord duke, it is not as you would wish for. 'Tis de Berry who lies dead in the chapel, along with his squire," he finished, waiting for the storm that he knew would erupt as soon as the duke took in the news.

"What?" The duke raged. "Christ on the Cross, de Berry was a deadly blade, and de Grispere took them both from ambush? First Jean, now de Berry. Who is this devil? Must I kill him myself? Is there evidence that de Grispere was party to the affair?"

"None, my lord duke. He left with a party of English men-at-arms and their captain and returned with them from the tavern. I shall make enquiries in that regard, your grace."

"Do so – and more than that, rid me of him."

"I have plans made and shall attend to the matter myself."

The duke gritted his teeth and nodded, waving his servant away in a black rage. D'Anquetonville clenched his fist in anger to be so summarily dismissed, bowed briefly and left the chamber.

×✟×

Jamie had explained to Sam in full what had occurred and that he needed to be exonerated. Anyone who was asked would swear that he had stayed at the tavern with the men all evening until they left together. Next, he reported to Chichele and Ryssheton.

"You were attacked?"

"I was followed and waylaid from ambush. The worst of it is that one of my assailants was late of the English Court, one Jacques de Berry –"

"De Berry?" interjected Bishop Chichele. "What have you

done, man? For he was a stalwart of the Armagnac faction. If we are seen to have caused his death we shall lose all credence with the Armagnacs and fall foul of the king. Our mission here could be ruined."

"Think on't," Jamie retorted. "He was the perfect pawn to send against me. He was known outwardly to be of Armagnac persuasion, yet secretly he was in Burgundy's employ. If I am accused, they will say that I was set upon by one of the Armagnac faction who sought to disrupt the peace talks through my death. If I had been slain in his stead, it would remove another barrier that Burgundy hates, and would be providential to his cause."

The bishop was appalled, but Ryssheton was more sanguine: "How many were there in the ambush?"

"There were just two," Jamie answered curtly.

"And what of the other?"

"They both lie dead in the alley, mayhap seeming to have set upon each other and died in the ensuing quarrel."

Ryssheton looked strangely at Jamie with a mixture of awe and respect. *He speaks as lightly as if he had just strolled around the palace grounds, not fought for his life in deadly ambush,* he mused.

The bishop, as ever, was worried about appearances: "Did anyone see you? Can anything be tied to you from the debacle?"

"Not that I could ascertain. All was quiet and I quickly made my way back to the tavern. I had been absent for but a few minutes, and entered from the rear as though I been to the pissyngholes, though the room was mightily crowded and I would not have been missed. It was a wet night, and all were seeking warmth within. I spoke with the landlord and ensured that he noticed me ere we left, and I will be remembered on that account."

"This is not good, and it is well that we depart on the morrow for Avignon," Chichele muttered.

"Your grace, in that regard I would adjure great caution and advise against such a journey. Once on the road with the threat of *routiers* and mayhap other more focused aggressors, we could easily find ourselves prey to forces stronger than ours. I was always against such a journey and would now put my case more forcefully."

The bishop eyed Jamie and then looked at his legal colleague. "What say you, Sir Nicholas?"

"I am inclined to agree with Sir James. It would be an unnecessary and a redeless action to travel many leagues to the south with no guaranteed purpose at this juncture, and with us exposed to all manner of dangers. I would lief as not return to the safety of England 'til there is peace following de Berry's death.

"We have much to report and discuss with both Prince Hal and the king. Reports abound that all may not be well with Pope Urban in Italy, and it would be cautious at this juncture to avoid favouring one side or the other with a visit from a prelate of your standing, Bishop Chichele," Sir Nicholas concluded smoothly.

"Mmm... Mayhap you have the right of it. I shall seek my answer in prayers and discourse with my counterparts of the ecclesiastical See in Paris."

"As you wish, your grace." At which Jamie bowed and departed.

He was wary now, expecting at any moment a summons to demand an explanation as to his involvement and his where-abouts the night before. Yet no summons had arrived when he returned to his quarters save a missive, sealed with red wax and seemingly anonymous. Prising open the seal, Jamie caught the traces of a familiar perfume and then read the lines contained therein.

We are watched. I have information for you dear to your heart and safety.
Have great care and come this evening after Vespers to my home.
Ever yours,
M

A trap? Most certainly, or maybe a lure to see what might be caught. He mused to himself. *Very well.* He needed to visit Monsieur L'Amaury and send information back to Sir Richard Whittington. He would take precautions, and knew well how to escape unseen over the palace walls, for he had done so two years past with Cristoforo and knew where the weaknesses lay in the security of the palace.

Jamie would attend supper and then, with his excuses made, he would slip out under the cover of darkness. He gave thought to all he must achieve and went to his warbag. Within it was a piece of gleaming mail which he retrieved. He took it by the neck and shook it loose from the grease-lined sack, to reveal a short habergeon. When on, it would reach no more than his belted waist, but in the dark a torso was always where a quarrel or sword would strike first, being the most obvious target. He was ready, and strolled out into the grounds to refresh his memory of the route he would take, under cover of darkness.

Chapter Twelve

Jamie closed the door to his chambers gently and padded along the corridor to one of the stairwells that served all the floors. He descended to the next level, eased himself through an open window and dropped three feet to the ground below. Crouching, he listened for any sound of pursuit or discovery. Satisfied, he moved across to the low wall, no more than twelve feet high, that formed part of the inner enceinte. Stone steps led to a rampart that ran around the whole compound. Few guards patrolled the long running wall, with most of them concentrated at the various gatehouses around the confining walls.

Once on the rampart, he slipped the rope from around his waist and threw both ends over, leaving a looped end around a raised crenulation. He pulled himself up and over the rampart and overhanded himself down to the orchard below, pulling one end of the rope down behind him so that it dropped at his feet. He looped it around his waist again and moved off to the cloisters that he remembered so well.

He passed the friary and the herb gardens beyond and then slid through the wicket gate. All was quiet, and he eased back the single bolt smoothly in its runners. He pulled the heavy door to and prayed that no one would bolt it in his absence. Then he crept through parkland and orchards before climbing over a low wall to the streets beyond. The whole process had taken mere minutes, and he was free and undetected.

Pleased with himself, he now had to avoid the Watch who prowled the streets periodically. He knew where he was and moved onwards, keeping to the shadows and hugging buildings wherever possible, to arrive at the door of Monsieur L'Amaury's shop on Rue Dviardin, only a few streets from the main entrance to the palace. The blue sign swayed gently in the night's breeze; the merchant's name was embossed above the door. Giving one final look around and sniffing the breeze, Jamie smelled only the night-time stench of human effluent. He moved to the side alley that gave access to the rear, for deliveries of cloth. The gate was barred shut, but he saw a large embrasure. Bending, he picked up a handful of stones and threw them up one at a time to the shuttered window. In his mind the sound was magnified to that of thunder, and at any moment he expected to be discovered as the whole street woke to the noise he made. As the fourth stone struck, the shutter opened carefully and a voice called softly down in French.

"Whittington," Jamie whispered back as loud as he dared. In answer the head disappeared and the shutter closed. Moments later Jamie heard the door whisper open, and saw a flicker of light from a candle lamp as a figure appeared. He did not speak, but beckoned Jamie forward into the courtyard and in through the back door of the house. The room was a rear parlour with a table that the merchant used as an accounting room. As the door closed he lit another candle, and Jamie saw a man of middle years, corpulent and well-padded against the night. His eyes squinted at Jamie, liking not what he saw.

"Sir, you have the advantage of me," he proclaimed curtly.

"Monsieur L'Amaury, I must offer my apologies for the lateness of the hour, but needs must when the Devil drives. I am Sir James de Grispere and I come in Sir Richard Whittington's name."

At which L'Amaury crossed himself: "Monsieur, there are devils abroad, yet I bid you welcome and will aid you if I may."

"I shall take brevity as my guide and must away in haste. I have news and listen well. Do you need to write any of that which I am about to impart?"

"Only numbers and dates. Proceed."

Jamie told him all that had occurred and the state of the talks with the duke's proctors. In addition, he added the latest rumours from Rome and recounted the death of de Berry.

"Was it you who killed him and his squire?"

"'Tis better you do not know. Now, is everything clear, for I would not daddle longer than I should?"

"Indeed. Have a care leaving, for the Watch may be about."

"I shall. Give my regards to Sir Richard, and inform him that we leave for England in two days' time and no longer intend to journey to Avignon."

"I have it all clearly. Now, I bid you good night and begone ere we are caught."

Jamie nodded, pulled up his hood and left the room, disappearing carefully into the night. L'Amaury crossed himself, cursed Whittington and began writing beneath the lamp light, using the code that he had been given to construct the message. Once coded he would then reduce the size, re-writing the script using a magnifying glass, and attach it to one of the homing pigeons for its cross-channel flight to London.

Outside, Jamie hesitated at the entrance to the side alley of L'Amaury's residence. Satisfied all was quiet, he made his way north to the Rue St Pol before turning east down a side street that took him at last to the Rue des Celestins, which was divided by a staggered crossroads. Jamie waited at the corner, all instincts alert. He could see nothing untoward, yet that could be of little consequence; the street was wide, with many tall buildings overshadowing the junction, and any or all could offer cover for an assassin. Patches of light from a pale half-moon flitted in and out of the cloud cover, streaking the night with light and dark. He knew how easily Cristoforo could manage an ambush, and this would be a perfect spot if he was lying in wait. Jamie shuddered at the thought of someone in the mould of his friend waiting out there, against him. Finally, he stifled caution for the sake of expediency and moved softly to cross the street, aiming for Lady Monique's house, expecting an attack at any moment. He looked up to see dim candle light in the first floor window, and turning slightly, the hairs upon his neck rising, he rapped lightly upon her door.

Jamie turned to his left, looking up the street in the direction from which he had walked. He heard a muffled sound from within, then a high pitch trilling. He started to move in closer to the house, but he was too late. The crossbow quarrel hit home directly over his heart. He was driven backwards, crying in pain, thudding into the door, smashing his head, hearing ribs break with the force of the impact, as he collapsed into a sitting position against the doorway. The simple act of breathing was now an exercise in pain, and half bent at the waist he could manage only shallow breaths, panting in agony. He slipped between consciousness and unconsciousness, drifting in a sea of pain, his heart pounding with every beat as if a sharp knife was cutting him there.

He was vaguely aware that the door opened and he flopped backwards, just as another quarrel slammed into the door post where his head had been a second before.

There was a cry from inside the house and Jamie rolled inwards: "Shut the door!" he cried.

He heard the door slam into the frame and felt a sense of relief, then rolled to his knees, survival instincts making him reach for his dagger with his right hand and pull it upwards. Seeing the action, Lady Monique sprang back, her hands spread in front of her.

"No!" she cried. "I was not responsible. Please, before God I beg you, I had no knowledge of this." Her face was a mask of horror. She then did the unexpected, and it saved her life. She moved forward, her hand extended in a show of gentle concern. "Keep your dagger yet let me aid you, for I am innocent."

Jamie eased himself upright, one hand upon his broken ribs, the sharp pain around his heart lessening a little. *Only my ribs now. Only!* They were on fire, and it still hurt to breathe. Exploring with his fingers, he realised that the light habergeon and his black gambeson had saved him. Something fell to the floor and he saw before pain-hazed eyes that it was the first quarrel, a flesh cutter with a barbed head. Of all the arrow heads, that would have been the worst if it had pierced his gambeson. No one would have had the skill to remove it and he would have died a painful death within days. Thank Christ for providence and for having the foresight to wear his mail. He had seen those heads pierce gambesons where bodkins and plate crackers had failed, the resulting wound was evil and always festered without specialist skill and great good fortune.

"Christ on the Cross, I am blessed and that the evil bastard chose a flesh cutter, for a bodkin may have pierced both."

"Jamie, dear God, please let me aid you. Come to the bed." At which Monique pointed at a day bed, close to a dying fire of glowing embers that twinkled behind a gauze guard. He walked painfully to the bed and eased himself down. Not wishing to raise the servants, she removed the fireguard and threw more wood upon the embers, which revived almost instantly to healthy flames. She thrust a poker into the heat, then turned back to Jamie.

"You must let me aid you, for I fear that your ribs are broken. I know this feeling well, for my husband used to beat me, wishing to leave no visible marks for the outside world to see." He made to speak but she moved forward, pressing a finger to his lips. "Later," she whispered.

Monique undid the throat catch of his cloak and unbuckled the sword belt, lifting the heavy weapon away, letting him retain his dagger, which he still gripped firmly. Jamie slowly lifted his arms, causing a sharp intake of breath as she lifted the sleeveless maille from his torso. Once it was off, she attended to undoing the frogging tabs from the front of his gambeson. She gently eased back the shoulders and slid the heavy garment backwards, leaving Jamie in just his linen shirt. This too she removed, and moved away on silent feet to return with a bowl of rose water, a sponge and a soft cloth. She gently bathed his exposed skin, moving methodically and carefully with actions that spoke of experience.

"By some miracle you have avoided being punctured through the skin and do not bleed. Please either kill me now or put your dagger down, for I cannot stand the threat of death and do my work at the same time." She gave him a baleful stare, completely composed as she exposed her throat, offering him the perfect target. Jamie sighed, relented and placed the weapon at his side.

"Now this will hurt, yet I shall be gentler with your ribs than you are with my conscience," she chided him. With a soft pad in place over the swelling and bruising she bound the ribs as tightly as she could, tying off the bandage. "There now, all is done. How do they feel?"

"They feel much better, though I fear I shall not be entering a tourney for a few days," he attempted to jest. She responded with a wan smile, rose and retrieved the poker from the fire, for one second Jamie was alarmed and his hand dropped to the dagger.

"Dost thou think so little of me that I would bandage you and then seek to take your life?" she hissed. "I am not of that mould, and would wish to prove this to you." Monique thrust the glowing steel into a flagon of spiced wine and as it sizzled, she dropped some dark seeds into the brew. "Poppy seeds. They will aid your pain, and lest you beshrew me to poison you I shall drink from your cup first," she offered with her eyebrows raised. The firelight sparkled in her eyes, and her cheek bones, enhanced and framed by a mane of wild, blonde hair, made Jamie feel that he was more in danger here than from the point of any quarrel.

She drank first from the goblet then passed it to him. He hesitated until he saw her swallow. She looked at him in frustration, a tight smile upon her mouth. She closed the distance and knelt before him, her eyes molten amber, lips red with wine in the firelight, her perfume enveloping him in its aura. She took another mouthful of wine and sealed her mouth against his lips. Jamie was shocked and seduced in one fell moment, as his mouth opened to receive both the wine and her lips and she twined her tongue with his.

Chapter Thirteen

"Where the devil is de Grispere?" roared Bishop Chichele. "He embarks upon adventures of his own, imperils our mission with his divers endeavours and unseemly manners, forswearing the rules of God and church to cause havoc and devastation. And now he is absent without a by your leave. We are to travel this day or on the morrow, and we need our guards, by the good Lord."

"I know not, your grace," Sam answered. "I have searched Sir James's room and there is naught to evidence his position, for his cot is unslept in. I shall search further for him."

"Do not. The man has crossed authority yet again, and must resolve the issue on his own recognizance. We shall make plans and leave early on the morrow. Better yet today, for if he brings ill repute down upon us, we shall all suffer the consequences. I would be safe in England ere such a calamity befalls us. Have the men made ready, and I will inform the clerks and Sir Nicholas."

"Aye, your grace." The captain agreed and left his presence, cursing Jamie inwardly, for he would be left behind and beyond the protection offered to him by the company, and that would do no man any good. *Well, I shall fetch his belongings and his horse, in case he should have plans to meet us on the road.*

The embassy made ready to move in very short order and was seen off by an affable Duke of Burgundy. At his side was Raoulet d'Anquetonville. As the party was mounting, the duke stood on the steps above the courtyard and quietly spoke to his servant: "I see no evidence of de Grispere. You were obviously successful."

"I believe so, your grace. It was a smaller crossbow, and not quite full strength, but the shaft caught him at the heart. If he is not dead already the wound will fester, for there was poison on the tip. There were two of us, and Albert missed as he fell."

"You're sure?"

"My lord, we used flesh-cutter barbs, they will breach any gambeson at that distance. We were but across the street, less than a hundred feet from him."

"And what of my Lady Monique?"

"She has wisely stayed from view until the English depart. She will appear to side with him, if he still lives."

"'Twas well done, for we may have use of her abroad ere the year is out."

In the courtyard the party was now mounted, and the duke walked down the steps to bid them a safe journey.

"I feel we have made all our thoughts clear and reached an understanding which is sympathetic to both our houses," the duke said. "I pray to God, my lord bishop, that you will find some way to imprint this upon his majesty's mind. With that I wish you Godspeed, and may the Lord watch over you."

"Amen to that, your grace. Mayhap we shall return with better tidings in due course. May the Lord have you in his keeping." At which Bishop Chichele crossed himself and urged his horse forward.

The party moved out from the enceinte and set off down the road for the north-western gate of Paris.

Splinters of light pierced the gaps in the drapes around the bed, one of which landed squarely upon Jamie's face. He rubbed his eyes and moaned, his ribs throbbing in protest as he made to roll over. *Ah, so it had not been a dream*, he thought. *So where am I?* He sensed another presence, assailed by a wonderful familiar perfume and cinctured by warmth, and there by the side of him, draped elegantly even in sleep, was the curvaceous form of the Lady Monique. Her golden mane was tangled around her head and at his movement she stirred, raised her hand and gave him a beguiling smile through eyes that were immediately open wide.

"Ah, he wakes. How do you do, my lord?" She mocked him gently as her hand sneaked across to his recumbent form.

"In truth my lady I know not, for my head aches and my side is breached most foul whene'er I move."

"Your condition did not impede you yester eve," she answered, her eyes meeting his and holding his gaze.

Jamie coloured under his pale countenance. "Ah...well, mayhap that was the poppy seed." He grinned sheepishly.

"Why then, I had best find some more," she responded.

"I must offer you my thanks for your kindness in aiding me in my time of need. I am eternally grateful and I shall always be at your service, my lady. For without your intervention I would now be lying dead in your doorway."

She smiled again at his gallantry. "And now I shall aid you

further," she continued, amused by his discomfiture, "and break your fast whilst you lie and rest."

Then the worry dawned upon him.

"By the rood, what is the hour?"

"The bells ring now for terze. I would adjure caution, Jamie, for they think you dead or dying, and should you appear magically conjured before them seemingly in good health, I cannot answer for your life."

"I trust not the bishop, who will be gone should I not return within the day, and mayhap has already seen a chance to save his own skin. I would ask one more favour." At which she raised an inquisitive eyebrow. "Would you aid me to dress, for I am severely discomposed?"

She laughed outright at this and maintained a lively banter, as she helped him into his clothes. Finally, a thought occurred. He had forgotten what had caused him to be at her door the previous evening.

"My lady, I have a question that needs must be answered. I received a missive from you yester eve, asking that I attend you here at your lodgings, as you had information to impart of great import. What was the nature of that information?"

Her visage undertook a dramatic change. "I sent no such note to entice you here. I was more surprised as you when I answered the door. Beshrew your heart should you think I would entice you here to be the subject of an assassination. Yet, I see in your eyes that you believe this to be true. I do not give a fig for your politics and intrigue." At which she snapped her fingers. "Yet you would be intemperate to such a cause, and judge the quality of our intimacy by such a measure. Fie on you, knave, and leave this instant if you offer such a verdict upon me," she finished crossly.

"I would not vex you so, my lady, and apologise if I should give offence. Yet it was I who lay wounded and set upon at the guidance of a note that, to all appearances, was in your hand and perfumed just so," he offered.

She stamped her foot. "Where is this incriminating note, that I may be the judge of its *véracité*?" Her anger was rising. "Your actions would seemingly decry those thoughts of amour that we shared the past evening. Dost thou not trust me yet still prick me thus, that I would trade in matters of the heart as you would in commerce? So be it. Yet I will entrust to you information that may aid you and those whom you serve." She let the ambiguity hang in the air. "I have heard that the Scots are to aid Burgundy upon his request. A force of some four thousand of their men is to be supplied to fortify his ranks here in France."

"By God's grace, is this true? Who is to lead them and where do they land?"

"Ah, so it is commerce, not love, in which you seek to trade," she mocked him. "Very well; the noble I believe is named Douglas. He was at court and pledged his troth to my Lord Burgundy. As to when and where they land, I know not. Are you now satisfied?"

Jamie steeled himself not to take the bait and expose himself to further interrogation and ridicule. "My lady, I adjure you, I would not part with you on such terms. I owe you much." He finished lamely, shamed by her vehemence, her eyes burning with anger, her whole being a furnace of ire.

At his words the tension left her, and she seemed to capitulate to his plea. "Very well, I will accede to your request. Now come here and let us part as lovers should, not in quarrel, but in love."

Lady Monique reached up as he approached and pulled his head down to hers, gripping him fiercely in a passionate kiss. Jamie was stunned and unbalanced, unsure what to think. Once they broke apart, he grabbed his cloak and sword belt with its weapons and made to leave. She kissed him one last time and bade him adieu, not looking back as the door shut upon him.

The distance to the castle was short, and he passed along but two streets before coming to the gate, where he asked if the English embassy had departed. Upon being told that they had left an hour past he cursed and went in search of a livery stable that would furnish him with a horse. It was not until he was safely outside the gates that he gave serious thought to all that had occurred, recalling Whittington's words: *"All that is harmful may not be clothed in maille."* The words echoed within his head and he questioned again the role that Lady Monique had played. Could he trust her? He wasn't sure. She was in all probability a very skilled actress and he laughed to himself. She was very talented in other areas as well, and the night had been memorable in many ways!

Jamie soon arrived at the northwest gateway, and he slipped through uneventfully. Knowing that he followed Chichele and his party, he calculated that even with a head start of an hour or so, he would overtake them before nightfall. He caught up with the English embassy towards the end of the afternoon just outside Montsoult. They had made good time as the roads nearer to the city were in better order.

He came upon them as they were approaching the town and hailed them from down the road. As he pulled up he was met by Sam, who grinned warmly.

"By all that's holy, we had given you up for dead, Sir James. What has ailed you to be so tardy?"

"A crossbow and a lady – and I'm not sure which was the more deadly," he answered, making light of the situation, and having no desire to offer further explanation. "I shall return shortly, but for now I must speak with his grace and Sir Nicholas." At which he nodded to Sam and nudged his tired horse to the front of the column.

"Your grace, Sir Nicholas. I see you made an early start."

"Sir James, how do you do and where were you? We would have waited," Sir Nicholas continued, "but my lord bishop was keen to be on the road and away, as he feared you had been taken or were lying dead somewhere." Sir Nicholas placed the blame firmly at the cowardly bishop's door, exonerating himself of any faint-heartedness. Jamie saw all and ignored the barb, realising that he had been left to fend for himself. He was after all, he knew, merely a pawn.

"I apologise for my dilatory arrival. I was delayed by force of arms. But more can wait until we are alone, for I would not impart all in public."

"I am of course glad that you are safely returned to the fold. What travails have you endured, and will they reflect poorly upon our cause? I have no wish to anger the duke when all hangs in the balance as it now does."

"Your grace, I give you my pledge that naught has occurred to place either you or the circumstances of the embassy in danger. Yet I may safely say 'twould be a great wonder if the duke expressed displeasure at my disappearance," he answered ambiguously.

PART II

SPRING

The Journey South

Chapter Fourteen

London: early April

It was six days before the English embassy set foot once more upon English soil.

"By God it has been nearly three weeks since we last saw England's shores, and it feels like a lifetime. And London never looks so fair as when I return from France," Jamie commented.

"Amen to that," Sam echoed.

"Thank you for your aid, captain, and mayhap I shall buy you some ale once I have reported back to those at court who would hear my report."

"Sir James, I shall hold you to that pledge, but now I must see to my men and alert Lord Grey that we are returned."

The two men nodded to each other, and Jamie set off northwards through the maze of streets and the familiar smells of London. He was glad to be back on dry land, where he could walk off his sea legs, as he strode to his father's home in Jewry. The smells of London were more familiar to him than France. Even Calais, he mused, was not the same, though it was as much English soil as the streets of the capital. Even the dank smell of the Thames that had invaded his nostrils since entering the estuary was perversely comforting.

He was tired and his ribs still ached, but Jamie knew that he had much to report to Whittington, and wished to be received by him and make his report, before Bishop Chichele gave a biased account that might besmirch his name.

Jamie hurried north, then, with a tired sense of regret, decided he would see Whittington before reaching the comforts of home. He changed direction, travelling back towards the river, but further upstream and out of sight of the quay at Coldharbour. A wherry was always a faster way to travel in daylight hours when the streets were so crowded with pedestrian traffic. He summoned a boat to take him across to Westminster Palace.

Half an hour later he found himself in Whittington's quarters, explaining all that had occurred.

"Now, you report the passage of talks with Burgundy and Chichele, yet what else brings you here on so urgent an errand? For you look ill and weary."

"I have other news that near cost me my life – and by the rood I should heed your warnings more." Whittington's face creased into a frown, not understanding the reasoning behind Jamie's words, at which Jamie explained all that had occurred on the night of the ambush.

"A clever ruse, and one to which you cannot bear all the blame. Dost thou think Lady Nemours was the catalyst behind the attack?"

"For certes I know not, and would not wish to live on the knife edge twixt her word and the truth." Jamie answered honestly, as he still could not deduce the lie of her loyalties.

Whittington looked at him keenly in his habitually piercing manner, tugging on an earlobe.

"Yet by your account it was she who saved you, by her precipitous actions?"

"She did, and rendered me great service when I was struck by the quarrel. Yet still I know not if she expected to see a dying man at her door or one to whom she wished to render aid. I kept my dagger close and remained able to defend myself. I will never know full well her motives." He shrugged, as though to temporarily banish the thoughts from his mind. Whittington took the hint and moved on.

"So the young Earl of Douglas proposes to fight for the Burgundians. I had no intelligence of this. They will doubtless slip away quietly and proceed down through Flemish lands held by Burgundy. The king will want to know, and so will Prince Hal if he has not already been made aware of the circumstance," Whittington opined.

"If our enemies side with Burgundy," continued Jamie, catching on to the theme, "it sets another obstacle for the prince siding with the Burgundians. Scots and English forces make uneasy bedfellows, and it has ever been thus. That whoreson Douglas breaks the peace with Scotland with the ink just dry upon the treaty. 'Tis a shame that he was not killed at Harlaw and be done with it."

"Ha! To his eyes we have his king, and the treaty specifies 'from the river Spey to the Mount of St. Michael' and nothing to do with France. His family have ever hated the English and he will find every way he can to frustrate our cause. I will send word to Sir Robert to watch his actions well," Whittington responded. "In the meantime your return is timely, for much has occurred in your absence. The prince, as you are aware, has retired to Coventry to lick his wounds, and ostensibly seek support for his father away from the coils of the court where he has little support from his majesty. Worrying reports have been heard abroad of the prince fomenting rebellion against his father; clandestinely assembling an army with which to steal the crown."

Jamie interrupted, aghast. "The prince? By God's grace, he would dare seek to tread so treacherous a line? I'll ne'er give credence to such rumours."

"That may be so, but you are not a king who seeks to cling to his crown whilst his very life seeps from his body with each day that passes. He is encircled by all who seek to deliver him of the crown, like jackals held at bay by a dying lion. Yet I blame him not, for he is as weak to rumour as a young man is to a maid's coquetry." Here he paused as the barb hit home. Jamie had the good grace to cast his eyes to the floor. "There is irony here, for we have news supported by Signor Filippo Alberti that may unify their majesties, if they can be brought to book."

"How so?"

"The Western Schism has been wedged apart to cede power to those who would wield it. As you are probably aware, mayhap from Cristoforo or the contessa herself, the Alberti and the Medici families support the true pope in Rome and Naples."

"The contessa made mention of this afore we left, and could not attend our house for just such pressing matters," Jamie confirmed.

"Just so. Well the case has now been magnified beyond the pale. The duties paid to Pope Urban are due and he needs must have coin, not promissory notes. The warring families of Florence have polluted the issue by collusion, we believe, with Burgundy. The Medici have contained and supported the pope in all ways financial and physical, throwing their considerable influence upon his Conclave.

"The Albizzi family of Florence seek to supplant the

Albertis and Medicis as the benefactors of Pope Urban. They now rule Florence with an iron fist, being the most influential family and therefore the strongest province in the whole of Italy. If this should happen and the Albertis fail to support the pope financially, the Albizzis would step in and fill the void or turn one against the other. They would then be the chief accountants with papal support and would wield the threat of excommunication over the Albertis, among others. Our banking system would collapse and we would be forced to go cap in hand to the Avignon pope, or seek to claim support from the Albizzi and Stozzi families, who are, in turn, swayed by the Burgundians. This could unify the whole of Europe against us. The Holy Roman Emperor Sigismund has already officially condemned our potential support of the Armagnacs, and my spies tell me that the Anglo-Breton Truce is about to be broken.

"Burgundian rule in Flanders and elsewhere could spell disaster for the financial state of England, with no means to send safely accounts and money abroad to pay our dues, save in coin." Whittington finished, raising his hands in exasperation at what it would mean to England, should the worst come to pass.

"So how may I aid you, Sir Richard? For I do not see what part I may play. Am I to return to France and seek influence there?" he questioned.

"No, James, a more perilous route than that, I fear." Here, he sighed. "Signor Filippo has funds available for direct trans-portation to Florence. For this is what causes so much ire from the Albizzis. As they banished the Albertis from Florence, the *Parte Guelfa*, of whom the leading family are the Albizzis, sought to secure their downfall, both financially and physically. The opposite happened. The Albertis were merchants, and diversified from just trade into banking on a scale unheard of across the whole of Europe. They now flourish, as you know, and they underpin the fiscal security of England.

"There is only one way to transport this coin: overland to Florence. The Duke of Burgundy is now conflicted, with his focus upon the talks with England and the upcoming war with the Armagnacs. There is no better time to travel abroad, as all is chaos. For this, a timely arrival to Dunkerque and across the Flemish lands – avoiding France at all costs – will serve well."

"As you wish, Sir Richard," Jamie replied. "For if it serves and aids the crown, I shall go where I am bid as is my devoir."

"Just so, just so. I have considered a stratagem that will serve. The gold will need to be protected by a substantial force, which would by its very nature attract attention. Needs must a mesnie of sufficient force could be overcome with an army, and for five hundred marks, the temptation would be extreme. Therefore, stealth and guile are our friends in this endeavour.

"To wit, I should like you to lead a small party, unnoticed, and seemingly sely in its intent under cover of trade. I envisage a meiny, travelling *incognitus* under cover as your father's representative. Perhaps with an Italian as guide? For I hear that Cristoforo may have need of a journey to his homeland for pressing reasons of his own." Whittington's grin showed his teeth, but the smile failed to reach his eyes.

The wily old fox, Jamie thought. *He plays me as a fiddle and reaps the benefit. Yet it will serve on many accounts, from saving a kingdom to aiding a friend.*

"I would adjure you to travel to the north or east on some pretext and then sail from Southend, Lynn or some lesser east coast port. I will leave it to you to devise the means and the date of departure. For all that, the sooner the better, as the payment is due by the last day of June. It is just shy of seven hundred leagues to Florence. If the roads are good and you encounter no problems, two months should suffice."

"As you say, Sir Richard. It has been many years since I ventured to Italy, and then as a young boy at my father's side learning his tradecraft. I must confess to barely remembering the land or its people. As you advise, I shall take Cristo as a guide, and mayhap we will make good time."

"Choose whomsoever you will. I shall advance funds for such a journey, to be accounted for by the royal purse, and provide papers signed by his majesty to secure your ease of passage. I prithee, have a care to whom you should disclose this knowledge or your intent, for they may at times be more impediment than aid."

"I shall, Sir Richard. Now if you will permit me, I wish to return home and begin planning the journey. When will the coin be available? And from where shall I secure the sum?"

"The most propitious course here is for me to remove myself from the organisation, lest my involvement be noted by others opposed to our cause. I shall leave you to correspond directly with Signor Alberti and mayhap the contessa, who would serve well as an intermediary, by expediting the advent and bearing part of the reason for your journey."

Chapter Fifteen

It was sometime later that Jamie stepped from the wherry clutching his war bag, and made the journey to his father's house on foot. Once home, he felt a sense of relief flood over him and sought to ease his aching ribs. Ascending to the upper floors and his bedchamber, he flopped down fully dressed save his boots, and fell into the kind of deep and dreamless sleep that had eluded him for many days.

When he awoke, he realised his face was wet and someone was annoying him, added to which was the foul taint of rancid breath. He batted away the irritant, only to be met with a low howl and a huge paw landing upon his chest. He reluctantly opened his eyes to see a large, shaggy head and panting, pink tongue facing him.

"Forest, can a man find no sleep? Good morrow to you, my girl," he offered, scratching her behind the ear. "What is the hour, eh? Have I missed my supper or is it morning, for I have no idea?" Looking across, he saw that the day had passed and it was now early evening. "By the rood, I have slept the sleep of the dead," he muttered, pushing the grey head away and attempting to sit up, causing his ribs and his bruised intercostal muscles to protest.

He winced in pain and pushed himself upright, as his muscles continued to twinge with agony with every new use. Finding a servant, he ordered a hot bath, and went down to a small room below where a wooden bathtub was permanently situated. Kettles steamed over a roaring fire ready for pouring into the sheet-lined tub. He slipped into the comforting heat, letting his muscles relax as the heat from the water seeped into his bones. When the water finally cooled, he dried himself, dressed and made his way down to the ground floor, where already the smells of cooking were drifting from the kitchens below.

In the main hall, a gathering of those he held dear had already assembled. Jeanette came forward: "Will alerted us that you had returned, and with Forest's absence, we knew you would be asleep and let you be." She went to crush him in an embrace and he gently held her back from the full strength of her arms.

"Have a care, my sister. I am tender there, courtesy of a bolt." He smiled at her.

A look of concern crossed her face: "You were pierced?"

"No, praise God. I was saved by my short habergeon and black gambeson. If I had not worn them I should be dead, for the archer was a good marksman, and his poisoned and barbed tip caught me over the heart."

Cristoforo rose and came forward, concerned at his friend's injury. "I needs must look at you, *amico*, for bad humours can rise from such a wound and cause a poisoning of the blood. When did you sustain the blow?"

"A full seven days past, in Paris. It involved a lady, one with whom we are both acquainted."

"The lady I would learn about, but first let me attend to your condition. Forego your modesty and remove your *abiti*."

Cristoforo urged him to remove his doublet and linen shirt. The skin over his exposed ribs was a rainbow of yellows, blues and purples, spreading out from the impact of the quarrel. "*Porca miseria*, you are lucky to be alive," he declared. "I will be careful, but I must ascertain the damage." His fingers gently probed the ribs, causing a sharp intake of breath from Jamie. "Broken?" he asked.

"I believe so, for the quarrel knocked me off my feet and I heard the crack as it struck."

"*Aspetta*, I shall fetch my herbs." With that he strode off to his rooms above. He turned sharply mid-stride, looking over his shoulder. "No more of your story 'til I return!" he warned him.

Upon returning, he began mixing a solution, using a pestle and mortar to form a thick paste. With care, using a spatula, he applied the paste to the bruised areas. Despite the care, Jamie still emitted a sharp hiss at the application. Then Cristoforo gently but firmly bound up his torso with clean bandages.

"That is arnica. It will help ease the bruising, and this is another solution. Drink it quickly, for it will taste foul, yet like all things that taste bad it will aid you well. Next these tablets. I found that *Consolida Maggiore* grows well in your Godforsaken climate."

"What?" Jamie asked, looking suspiciously at the pale-green tablets from the Comfrey plant.

"'Tis knitbone in our tongue," Jeanette explained.

"Ah, and this is efficacious?"

"It is. It will greatly aid the healing of your bones. Now drink it with water and tell us of your story."

When Jamie had finished, after answering questions from all present, especially John, there was silence for a brief moment, as they all considered the effects Jamie's news would have upon them.

"So this was the lady who was sent to waylay you when first we ventured to Paris, *no*?"

"Indeed it was. You have a good memory, Cristo," he declared.

The Italian shrugged as though it were perfectly normal.

"She is a beautiful woman. Lethal and full of artifice, *pero*. Most appealing." He smiled, displaying a row of even, white teeth.

Jamie broke the silence again.

"I am now charged by Whittington to take the payment to aid the pope overland to Italy." At which Cristoforo crossed himself. "Cristo, this will suit you well, for we can journey together. Think on't, the Duke of Burgundy's mind will be turned to Paris and the upcoming war betwixt Armagnac and Burgundy. 'Tis the perfect time to be abroad, to flit through Flemish lands to Luxembourg and beyond to Italy. If we travel together posing as a caravan and baggage train, all will be well. What matter should a sely band of merchants be to the forces of Burgundy at such a time?

"And by the grace of the good, Lord Signor Alberti will agree, for we bear his coin to the Florentines and the pope. The count will be grateful to you for aiding Alessandria safely across Europe to his door, and for furnishing the means to pay the papal dues. He will cast his eye more favourably on your request for his daughter's hand."

"*Dio mio,* you are right. I will inform the contessa. When do we leave?" He was suddenly very Latin and excited. Then he stopped abruptly: "Signor Thomas, forgive me, for I am bound to you by a debt of honour, and would ask your permission to depart for such an extended time."

"Fie on you, Cristoforo, for you have it arsey-versey, having twice now saved my life. The debt is fully paid by any account. There is no bond between us now save that of friendship, and whilst I should be loath to lose your company for I greatly value your presence here, you must see to your own life. I would of course welcome your return, for there is ever a place for you within my household." He finished, slightly embarrassed at the display of emotion that he had been forced to show. To hide this he finished gruffly. "Be off with you back to your heathen land, and pray God that the contessa shall return you better formed."

Cristoforo, realising the compliment and the warmth of friendship that had been offered to him, smiled graciously, rose and swept a deep bow to Thomas de Grispere. "*Molto grazie,* Signor Thomas."

Jamie was pleased at the result, and continued: "We must speak with Signor Alberti. We shall need a subterfuge, to cover our absence from London and leave quietly by sea from Lynn. Jeanette, has my Lady Alice yet departed for the north?"

"No Jamie, she resides here still, awaiting her father's readiness to travel. Why?"

Jamie had started to formulate a plan on his return journey to his father's house, and even as he spoke, it evolved more fully.

"Because it would be the perfect cover for us to travel with the contessa. She could be one of the earl's party, accompanying Lady Alice as her companion." His mind was racing with possibilities. "We shall follow by separate company and meet upon the road at Harpenden or thereabouts, and once away from prying eyes, we shall divert for Lynn. 'Twill be further by sea, but better to conceal our true endeavours. Father, I could travel as your deputy in trade, for it would be seemly."

Thomas de Grispere agreed with a nod of his head, yet he feared for his son and his safety.

"I have need to advance a shipment of wool to Flanders and

'twould suit well. It could be ready in days, and with a meiny to accompany you, all would be in accord."

"Very well. I needs must see Lady Alice and speak with her urgently." Jeanette looked at him, trying to fathom his thoughts. She knew her brother well, and she was sure there were parts of the story he had left out. He mentally changed direction upon seeing her piercing gaze. "How does Mark? Dost thou think he may be persuaded to attend with us?"

"I do believe that he would welcome the adventure," Jeanette answered. "He misses the courtly engagement from what I hear from Emma, more so now the prince is absent. Lief as not Emma too has cloth to be fetched from Flanders, and trade to be accomplished. I too would dearly love to travel to Florence and visit the Holy See. Would there be room for one more to your party? Mayhap I could travel as the contessa's maid?" she asked. "It would add credence to the story that you concoct."

Her father looked concerned, and was about to declare that he would not have Jeanette imperilled on such a journey, but Jamie spoke first.

"My dear sister, I would not wish to endanger you on such a journey. Besides, we shall move at a pace that leaves little to offer in terms of comfort."

Jeanette pouted at him, tightening her eyes in anger. "Think you that I am not up to the task?"

Jamie ignored her, not wishing to argue over something that, to his mind, would not come to pass. He then foresaw another issue, that of waggons and the obvious presence of ladies, with all the notice that would bring. Somehow, he was sure word would be passed along of their progress. The ladies would attract attention, particularly one as regal and beautiful as the contessa. It was a predicament for which he would have to find a solution.

×🕊×

Later that evening Jamie found himself at Signor Alberti's house on Langburnestrate, to the south of Laurence Lane.

"So, my Lord Whittington has apprised you of our predicament?" Signor Alberti said. "All is not well. We have more than adequate funds to supply the pope with his annual feasance, yet it must be carried as coin, not a promissory note. It is this that tests our resources.

"We are as ever at war with the whoreson Albizzi and the Stozzi families," Alberti continued. "Indeed, members of the Stozzi reside here in London not far from my house, and we watch them closely. They would relish the opportunity to force us to secede our position as bankers to the crown. Their *amici*, the Peruzzi, still bear a grudge against your old King Edward, who reneged upon their debt when war broke out with France. There is no love lost there, and if they could once more control the finances of the papal state and under that auspice the fiscal wellbeing of England –" here he sighed, in a particularly expansive Italian way, spreading his hands palms outwards, "– it would not go well for all concerned. Therefore, I must stress that much is riding upon the success of your fiat." He stroked his pointed beard thoughtfully.

"And you, my dear Alessandria, you would brave the perils of such a journey? Despite the threats from Burgundy, would you travel through his very lands?"

"I would indeed, uncle," she declared bravely, and with spirit. "I shall be with Cristoforo." At which she clasped his hand at her side. "There will be Jamie and a small meiny to protect me. With a clandestine approach and a false trip to the north as Jamie has outlined, it will be weeks before my absence is commented upon, and her majesty will agree the suit, for it rides well with the king's purpose. It is a most perfect time upon which to embark for Italy, as the Duke of Burgundy will have his focus elsewhere on the coming conflict twixt his forces and the Armagnacs."

"Mmm. Very well, as you wish. I will send a message overland by our contacts, informing your father of your proposed return – yet rest assured," he said, holding up a hand, "no word have I mentioned of your proposed alliance with Cristoforo, may God assoil me." Here, he permitted himself a brief smile and comforted Alessandria with a stroke of her cheek, before turning to Jamie. "With this in mind, when do you propose to leave for the north?"

"Signor, Whittington tells me that there is soon to be ratification between the king and the Armagnacs. At that time all eyes will be on France, and little else will concern the court or any spies still abroad. That would be the propitious moment to leave London."

"Very well. I will have a carriage and the coin prepared in readiness for your word. You will use the Earl of Macclesfield as a cover for your journey?"

"We shall, sir. His habit to stay away from London in his estates to the north for a full month or more is well-known, and therefore our move shall draw no adverse comment. We intend to divert from their party at Luton and bear north east for Lynn, and thence by cog to Flanders," Jamie explained.

"Let it be so, then. And may God protect us all," Signor Alberti concluded.

Chapter Sixteen

Canterbury

Whittington watched the reconciliation between father and son with pleasure. He had been in no small way an influence upon the king, and together with Archbishop Arundel, he had managed to persuade King Henry to bestow honours not only upon the prince but also on the Duke of York, Henry Beaufort and the Earls of Arundel and Warwick.

"The reconciliation twixt father and son is timely, my lord archbishop," he said. "For with such scurrilous rumours abroad we were as like to cede a second front of civil war in England had not his majesty seen the right of it."

"Indeed, yet I fear we have snuffed out the result not the cause, and should be ever vigilant to prevent such a chasm opening again," the archbishop replied. "The land and privileges bestowed by his majesty, although small, will appease the Earl of Warwick and my nephew Arundel. Though, whether this accord will hold when they learn that the formal agreement to an alliance with the Armagnacs has now been ratified, I know not."

Whittington made a wry face. "As you say, your grace, yet here they stand cinctured within the king's blessing, they who have sought to conspire against his intent by seeking the agreement of those who would war against him – and indeed if my intelligence is correct, are shortly to invade Gascony."

"Can this be true?" the archbishop hissed, concerned at the implications.

"Indeed, my lord. Decidedly the only good that seems to have been forged by this debacle is that we now have all eyes diverted to France, and not the impending transport of funds to aid the Holy Father to prevent further schism within the house of God."

"Had you some hand in this, Sir Richard? For if so, by the good Lord I bless you, as I could not see a way to resolve the issue safely."

"I do, archbishop, yet I would keep all arrangements to myself lest any slip still more imperil those upon whom I am reliant."

"Amen to that, and may God have them in his keeping." At which Arundel crossed himself. "On the morrow we all travel to Windsor, I believe, for the Garter celebrations."

"Indeed so, and it shall further cement the accord that exists, with eyes facing inwards towards the king and the court virtually empty." A thin smile played across Whittington's lips, but his eyes remained steely with resolve. *And so the pieces are moved around the chessboard, allowing my knight to make his move, undetected.*

$\times$ ⚜ $\times$

Launceston Lane, Jewry

"Father has given you permission to accompany us?" Jamie said, aghast at the implications. "I will not give credence to this stupidity. Do you wind him thus around your little finger? For you have been ever able so to do."

"Think on't, brother mine. You say – and rightly so – that all is to be clandestine, with no obvious account of women, let alone of higher birth, yet who is to pay this account I ask? For the contessa needs must have a maid, especially with no comfortable carriage or waggon should you forge ahead with mules and horses alone to make better time and draw no attention to your cause. Who will accede to such a fiat? My lady's maid or the contessa? I think not!" Jeanette protested. "For she and many others will not bear the pace or the arduous nature of the journey. I was ever able to play the lad, and learnt from John how to wield a dagger and a sword, aye, and ride a horse right well, until our father forbade it.

"With such skills as these I can look to the contessa and aid her, though she is far from a wilting maid, made of steel wrapped within a glove of velvet. For who saw you through in the Paris Court and aided Mark in his escape? Yes, the contessa, and she will fortify herself again I'm bound, and rise well to the occasion."

Jamie breathed in deeply, rolled his eyes and ran his hand through his dark-red hair, turning away in frustration. "May the saints preserve us, I wouldst rather fight a Conroy than war with strong women, for they are ever my bane. And what doth Kit say to you jaunting off to Italy, eh?"

"He is not my keeper, and pays court to me rightly enough,

but at the whistle of the call to arms and glory, his hand leaves mine and grasps the sword hilt right readily. Even now he looks to France and deeds of valour in the king's name. Ha, and to speak of war, how ran the talk with Alice yester eve? For as I am your sister and know you right well, I perceive there is more to your tale of evasion in Paris than you tell."

Jamie blushed at this and Jeanette, sensing her advantage, continued.

"I shall say no more but this; I love you dearly, as do I Alice. Yet mayhap at times it is more prudent not to expose the whole, for women wish to hear what they wish to hear, and see alive those whom they would cherish, whilst fully cognisant of the world about them."

At which Jeanette made a mock curtsey and placed a light kiss upon her brother's cheek before departing, swaying her skirts as she went.

"What? By all that's holy, sister dear, I'll not bear the rump of your discourse." But all he saw was her back disappearing down the upper corridor to her bedroom. *Male company is what I need, and I shall seek solace in such. I shall find our friendly giant and see if he should be able to aid me.*

Jamie left his father's house, annoyed with Jeanette and himself at being so easily outmanoeuvred and out-thought by her. What had made it worse, he mused, was that she had the right of it. Alessandria's maid had refused to go across the Channel and travel the length of Europe to Italy, especially when she had learnt that it would necessitate riding a horse rather than travelling in a comfortable waggon. *So be it,* Jamie thought. *If father agrees then it may be for the best.*

It took him little time to cover the short distance to Mark and Emma's house that was but a few streets distant from Launceston Lane. As traders in cloth and weavers, their businesses were by their very nature close by, and the two guilds often met together and traded between themselves. He rapped upon the door and was met by Mark himself.

"Jamie! By the good Lord. Come in man, come in." He beckoned, standing to one side, and clapped his friend upon the shoulder as he entered. "Do you come to sup with us, for the hour is nigh?"

"I was pledged to return home, but by the rood, is that the wonderful aroma of a beef pie? As such 'twould cause me to change my mind."

"Why you have the right of it, and dumplings too, such as me mam would make in Cornwall. Emma has got right good at 'em, and praise God that Lent has passed.

"Now have a seat by the fire and I shall fetch some wine that we might speak in comfort."

Jamie removed his cloak and sat, easing himself straight upon the chair for the sake of his ribs, and stretching his legs forward before a steady fire that glowed in the grate. Mark, he admitted, was ever convivial company, and even more so in his own home, which was given over to a woman's touch – and the more comforting for that. It had concessions to masculinity, with some paintings about the walls of rustic scenes in oils that bespoke an amateur, but were clearly of rural settings in their nature that were undoubtedly Cornwall. Arras tapestries were hung upon the plastered walls, offering shade and colour to the pale limewash.

Mark returned with a flagon of wine and two goblets, still not accustomed to having a servant wait upon him. "I have told the cook, and Emma will join us soon. She was delighted that you would sup with us. Now, not to beat about the bush, there be sommat on your mind, so tell us all."

Jamie smiled, knowing that he could conceal little from his

dear friend, who many perceived as slow until they encountered him on a wrestling mat or saw beneath the artifice of his exterior.

"You have the right of it," Jamie admitted, taking a large gulp of the wine. "Burgundy?"

"Aye and there's an irony." Mark laughed. "Still, I have Armagnac brandy too!" At which he smiled at his friend, and encouraged him to divulge all that had occurred. At length Jamie paused for breath, and Mark looked at him evenly.

"Well, the matter seems set, and I have but one question: when do we leave for the north and Flanders?"

"Mark, why you are a priceless gem, for there is naught else save one whom I would have at my side on such a fiat."

"Aye, and may God be pleased that Cristo too is in our company?"

"He does, and awaits the day he can return to Florence to ask the contessa's father for her hand. Yet what of Emma, shall she not demand that you stay here and aid her?"

"I shall not, for whatever you have planned I will agree. A man must fight with his friends," Emma decreed, entering the room on silent, slippered feet. Jamie rose in deference to her. "I caught but the last words of your discussion and forgive me for eavesdropping, but I'd lief as not Mark go to aid you and me in the same direction. For I spoke with Jeanette yester eve, and we have cloth and yarn to collect from Flanders, and Mark would be useful in such a cause. He can see it safely procured and stowed for shipment from Dunkerque. I, too, should like to see what manner of place is Flanders, and how trade is conducted there." Her strength of purpose and character had grown since her marriage, Jamie noticed.

"Why, Mistress Emma, that is most kind and I thank you, for I'd rather have Mark at my back than any other."

"Hush now, he gets under my feet here, and with the prince away and on a lowered stipend, why he eats more than he earns. Just ensure that you bring him back all whole," she chided, wagging her finger and smiling, to take the sting from her words.

Chapter Seventeen

Two days later, just as the city gates were opened, the Earl of Macclesfield's party left on the Great North Road out of London through Aldersgate, heading first for St Albans.

Jamie and all in his meiny – together with Will, some servants, the contessa and the ladies' maids – would add to the earl's numbers some hours later when they met upon the road. The ladies were to travel in a brightly coloured carriage and had resolved to bear the bumpy ride without complaint, insulated against the road by comfortable cushions within set on padded benches. Emma and her maid had departed with Macclesfield's party in her own covered carriage, for she would be protected on the return journey by John and others of Thomas de Grispere's company. She had not yet been abroad and wished to learn more, now that she was taking a greater hand in her mother's trade.

A similar carriage had been prepared by Signor Alberti to carry his niece and her maid as far as Harpenden. It had been provisioned with a false bottom in which were stored the coins bound for Florence. All looked perfectly normal to an outsider.

The horses stood patiently in the cold dawn light in the rear courtyard of the Alberti household as Filippo Alberti and his niece bade each other farewell.

"Think I shall see you again outside of *Firenze, cara*?"

"*Certo. Perche no?*"

"When you see our beloved land again with, mayhap, a husband at your side who too belongs of that fair city where all our hearts lie, why it would be a great wonder should you choose to return to this damp and chilly land."

Alessandria said nothing but looked deeply into her uncle's eyes, for he had voiced the fears that had plagued her own heart since the journey to Florence had been mooted. England to her mind had many virtues, and she had made many friends here, but she was a child of Florence and the city was in her blood. She banished the thought to the back of her mind, knowing that she could make no decision until she arrived back in the city of her childhood. Knowing also that she would go where her husband led, if her father acquiesced to their union.

"Fear not, uncle, for I shall return with gifts from our fair city," she told him, yet Alberti detected a lack of conviction in her voice, and he was not reassured.

"May God have you in his keeping, my child, and give my dearest wishes to your *babo*."

"I will, *caro zio*." And with a final embrace and a kiss on both cheeks, she swept up into the carriage. One of the two outriding servants closed the door and mounted his horse, and the two grooms on the front seat gave the order for the horses to move off.

As the carriage left the Alberti residence on Langburnes-trate, its passage was observed by one who spied for the Peruzzi family of bankers, who noted its passing and made to follow on foot, virtually invisible in the early morning pedestrian traffic. He watched the meeting with the earl's party just north of

Aldersgate and returned to his master to report all that he had detected.

Jamie, Cristoforo and Mark left separately by Bishopsgate, journeying across country unhampered by waggons, travelling much faster to intercept the earl's party outside St Albans, before heading north eastwards to the sea.

They met up at Harpenden, where Jamie prepared to travel to Lynn, taking Signor Alberti's waggon for Jeanette, Alessandria, and Emma and her maid. The Earl of Macclesfield's company would proceed north in their usual manner. Jamie found time before their departure to meet with Alice, and left alone in the ante room of a small inn, they stole a few moments of privacy.

"My lady, it does not sit well to leave you once again on so short a return. I would wish that we had more time to engage again and to seal what has bonded between us."

"And what is that, dear heart? For since your return you have been distant. There is a wall built around you. Have I wronged you or lost you to another?" At which she grasped his hand tightly in hers.

"No my dove, you are ever mine, and I durst not consider my life without you. I have fought thus far for your affections and shall not retreat from this battle now, lest I be shent and considered a scullion of the lowest order. I have much to consider that weighs heavily upon my mind, and am pulled abroad once more as a seed upon the wind.

"But I shall return hence, by my troth, and break down these walls around me to secure your heart once more."

"Jamie, you have my heart already secure, and it is your own that causes me concern. But go now, and return to me, I prithee." With this she pressed his lips tightly to hers in a deep kiss, and turned away quickly before he could respond, walking out to the company of the others with tears in her eyes. Jamie was left adrift in a sea of emotion. He could lie and scheme in all matters of men, and deal with the wiles of women such as Lady Nemours in the same way, yet here he stood, half shamed, half glad to be alone once more, unsure how to proceed. He shook his head and strode out, angry at his own inadequacies.

"I bid you God's speed, Jamie, and may he have you in his keeping," Alice said with a sigh as he passed her.

"And to you, my lady," he replied, as her father looked on with a scowl upon his face. The two parties now split, with the mules and waggons heading north east to Hitchin and beyond.

The three-day journey to Lynn passed uneventfully and they stayed overnight there to await the morning tide. The waggons would be left for their return, with the mules and horses shipped aboard the waiting cog.

At the quayside Cristoforo looked on with trepidation. There was a moderate swell, and froths of white surf broke gently against the quay as the large vessel seesawed in the water, alternately tugging at its fore and aft mooring lines.

"Oh *Dio,* the acts I do for love, may God preserve me." At which he crossed himself. Alessandria was surprised, for she had not seen this side of him, faced with an open, infinite sea. He had never spoken to her of his fear of open water.

"Yet you travel quite freely on the wherries of the Thames?" she queried.

"That is different, there I am near the shore and low down. Here –" he gestured expansively, "– all is beyond me and below me, and I am under its power." He shuddered.

John always found Cristoforo's aversion to sea travel amusing, and baited him a little.

"Well, Contessa Alessandria, if I may be so bold, mayhap you wouldst take an old soldier in his stead, for I've a deep regard to see Italy again and a fondness for the sun to warm my old bones." His words brought volleys of laughter from all present.

Cristoforo hung his head. "Fie, I'll travel, but not without complaint," he said, stepping back from the quay's edge, muttering.

He was not the only passenger to be wary. Jamie's horse Richard had seen the sea in the north, but he had never been asked to board a boat, and Jamie knew how difficult he could be.

"I know not what to do. Whether to try him with a sling or a boarding bridge."

The distance was but a few feet, and in the end Jamie opted for a gangplank with railed sides. The other horses and mules were already aboard. Jamie began to gently lead Richard forward, but the horse locked his front legs and in a rare show of defiance, rolled his eyes and pulled back. Jamie ended the resistance on the lead rope and stepped towards him, speaking soothingly, allowing him to calm down and stop snorting at the water. With his ears rubbed and some gentle persuasion, Richard tentatively put one foot upon the gang plank. He stamped down hard with his foreleg, testing the wood before him and not liking what he found.

The gangplank was built of two long timbers, cross planked, braced and some four feet wide with wooden rails and supports. Yet Richard was wary, even with his master in front of him. He pulled back again, dragging at the lead rope and ignoring the two pallets that were set up as a form of funnel to encourage him on board.

"Christ on the Cross, is that red hellion going to let us depart or shall we be here 'til doomsday?" The captain cursed.

Jamie soothed Richard once more, nudging up under his huge neck.

"Easy boy, easy. I know," he said, patting his broad back. At which an idea occurred. It was fraught with danger and could kill them both, but it might work. Jamie directed his head away from the boat towards the quay, patting the horse. He unbuckled his sword belt, unslung his cloak and removed his gambeson, while Richard stood happy and patient for his master, curious but trusting.

John looked on. Of all the puzzled audience, he alone knew what Jamie was going to do. "Hell's teeth, lad, leave him. Don't do what I believe you attempt," he adjured him.

Jamie did not respond, but turned to the others aboard: "Give me space on deck and yourselves room to move." At which he grabbed a handful of mane and vaulted onto Richard's bare back. The lead rope and his lower leg pressure was all that he needed to guide him. He walked Richard three strides further away and gave the command to turn. Jamie felt the haunches bunch beneath him as Richard performed a perfect, one hundred and eighty-degree pirouette, then he urged the horse straight into a canter. There were cries of alarm, but Jamie ignored them; he knew that Richard would ride through hell with Jamie upon his back, and it was this faith that Jamie was relying upon.

The mighty warhorse clipped onto the gangplank, not liking what he felt as all four legs landed. He pulled his back legs underneath him and launched himself into a cat leap, clearing the remaining four feet of planking and landing squarely upon the wooden decking, taking but two strides to check his momentum.

Mark, who loved his horses from the farm, cheered the move while Cristoforo swore, crossing himself: "*Dio mio*, you're all mad, you English. Yet 'tis the only time that we are in accord, that red *capra* and me."

"I've seen it," muttered the captain, too in awe of what he

had witnessed to protest at the treatment of his decking, "but I b'aint believin' it."

Forest protested from the quay side, letting out a long mournful half-bark, half-howl as she raised her huge, shaggy head. Having seen to Richard and calmed him down, Jamie returned to shore to fetch his clothing, weapons and the hound. With the drama over and the rest of the passengers and crew aboard, the mooring lines were slipped, and the cog drifted out into the current of its own volition, catching the tide that had just turned to move out to sea. Once safely out into the middle channel, the sails were released and the tack and clews were tightened to catch all the available breeze, and the large vessel creaked and groaned under the press of the wind, as the land began to slip away behind them. They were underway for the sea journey of some forty hours that would bring them to Bruges.

Chapter Eighteen

Two days later they took their first sight of the coast of Flanders, and made their way up the inlet towards the town of Bruges. Jamie had fretted over Richard, hoping that he would travel well at sea, and had given him only a little grain at regular intervals, checking that he was not sweating or getting colic. All was well, for the horse settled down and seemed to gain his sea legs after only a short period of time, looking out with a mix of fear and interest at the water all around him.

The cog made its way inland to the town of Sluys, following channels that had been dredged, to allow the deeper-drafted cogs to land.

"This be a pretty town," Mark commented, looking out over the flat fields and the rows of houses in the spring sunshine.

"Aye, but 'twas not so in King Edward's time, for we fought a great battle here and slaughtered the French," Jamie replied. "At that time my family were still in Flanders, for this is the seat of the Hanseatic League, and from here all great wealth flows, from cloth to grain and spices. Yet we must have care, for here the Duke of Burgundy has great influence among the townsmen – though he is ill-favoured, for he rules by the rod and not by kindness."

"Here it is said they have the best cloth in the world and yarn the like of which you have never seen," Cristoforo added.

"Aye, and all made from good English wool no doubt," Mark opined.

"You have the right of it, for we do produce the best wool in the world and no mistake. Ere we leave, I must show you the Bourse in Bruges itself, for 'tis a great place full of trade with bartering of stocks and goods. They say there is nothing like it in the world, not even in London."

The others noticed that Jamie was clearly enraptured by the town of his ancestors, and Jeanette too felt the pull of old family ties. It was not the first time she had travelled here, but it still held her in the same thrall. The tall steeples and the narrow Flemish buildings were at once foreign, yet familiar. It gave to Mark's eyes a feeling of both a coastal and inland town at first impression. He had never travelled here before, and he looked at the canals and waterways that intersected the town, and concluded that it gave the town a graceful elegance and a sense of romanticism. The cog moored in one of the deep waterways close to the quay, with barely a spar's gap between dockside and ship. The levels were almost of an even height, and seeing this Jamie vaulted atop Richard's back, walked him around the deck to remove all stiffness, and at a shout to clear a path, he set him to the gap in the rails and jumped him across to the quayside, to the horror of those standing near. Richard bucked and jounced at the feel of solid ground beneath his hooves, so pleased was he to be on dry land again.

"You goky fool. Steady boy," Jamie muttered, clenching his

legs, and finally bringing the horse to a stop when the creature had finished prancing. Richard shook his great maned head and snorted down his flared nostrils in disgust at the imposition of the journey.

"When your playacting and caprioling has quite finished," Jeanette chided, "mayhap you could aid us ashore?"

Jamie grinned and slid off Richard's back, tying him to a rail, and warning all close by to give him room and not to approach the snorting stallion if they valued their limbs.

They rode up from the port to the huge town in front of them, the sturdy walls offering security for the wealthy merchants within. Once inside, they were awed at the quality of the buildings and the beauty of the Great Market Square that dominated the town.

They managed to find a large inn that could accommodate all of their party.

"We shall spend one night here and then, on the morrow, shall depart together south," Jamie said. "We shall split up on the road to Ghent where you, my sister, and Alessandria will don the guise of youths. Are you still agreed to this action, for the church forbids a woman to dress as a man?"

"Fie upon them," the contessa exclaimed in disgust, flicking her hand as if to dislodge something that clung there. "We have discussed this at length and we agreed upon this course, for 'tis necessary to complete our disguise and render us safe. I am still of the same mind and will do penance for my sins when I am wed. We serve the church in any event. We shall ride astride as men, and shall be cloaked and hatted to the outside world. I have all my clothes to effect such a transformation, and shall wear no artifice."

"As do I, brother mine, and fear not, for we shall play our part right well and not give our nature away," Jeanette added.

"Very well." Jamie sighed, still filled with reservations about the venture and his sister's part in it. "John, are you set to go with Mistress Emma?"

"Need you ask?" John growled in response.

"Then all is settled." And with that he left for the stables, to check on Richard and the other horses and the mules that they would need for baggage, with Forest following closely at his heels. Jamie was ill at ease and needed time alone to think. The noise and companionship of the large company, normally so comforting, did not sit well with him at this moment. He knew that he was taking the weight of the mission upon his shoulders, yet more was in the balance than just the making of the payment. Friends – and indeed his own dear sister – were depending upon him to see them through, and against all odds he must do so. He had studied the maps, talked at length with his father of safe places to stay and a suitable route. As much uncertainty had been removed from the journey as possible, but still Jamie worried for all concerned. Sandwiched between his two confessors, he reached down to stroke the wolfhound's ears.

"Rather girl that it were just Mark, Cristo and me, for as such I would feel more at ease," he confided softly to the hound.

"You be bound for Dunkerque then, my lord?" a figure enquired.

As he span around at the voice, Jamie was startled and a little embarrassed to find that his first reaction was to reach for his dagger, he was that ill at ease. With it half drawn, he pushed it back into its sheath. He saw a man of roughly the same age as himself, dressed in the manner of an ostler. He had spoken in French, but Jamie replied in the native tongue of his forebears. He was minded to snub the enquiry, but wished to sow a story and decided to humour the inquisitive stranger.

"I wished not to startle you, sir. By your speech you are from Bruges. I took you for a foreigner, mayhap an Englishman, by your dress and manners."

"In some way you have the right of it," Jamie dissembled, eschewing his rank and circumstance. "I serve an English merchant who lives in London and aid him in the purchase of cloth and such goods as he requires. Tomorrow we journey to Dunkerque and thence back to England with our trade. The others in our party are of different houses and we travel together for safety. For I've heard there are *routiers* about and that no man can consider himself safe."

"Aye though more to the east and deeper to the French borderlands, where trouble was ever fomented."

Jamie encouraged the man to further discourse and learnt all he could of conditions and rumours. At length he had all he needed to know, and broke the conversation.

"'Tis wise to be aware of such matters. Now I must attend to my master's stock."

The following day the whole company left Bruges, heading southwest to Dunkerque, with Jeanette and Alessandria still dressed in female attire and riding sidesaddle in the accepted fashion. Some few miles south of the town, where there were no travellers in evidence, they pulled over. The ladies took refuge in a small copse where Jeanette and Alessandria changed their garb over to the masculine garments that they had brought with them, with the aid of Emma and her maid. They emerged sometime later, after giggles and cries of alarm had been heard from the trees and bushes as what looked to the world to be two female and two male forms reappeared.

Their hair was bound up, and upon their heads sat woollen hats in the manner of servants, low crowned and wide brimmed, with hooded gugel cowls that could be brought up to further cover their features. The men looked on, amazed at the transformation, noting that the only obvious gauge to their real form was the manner of their movement, which had not the manly mode of gesture.

"Why, look here! We have two new stable hands to aid our endeavours," Jamie mocked to ease the moment. The others laughed, while Jeanette and Alessandria gave a low bow each. "At your service, sir," Jeanette growled in a voice that was as low as she could make it, adding to the theatre.

"The saddles are changed. Now come, for you must learn to mount on your own or all will be in vain," he ordered them. At which both the ladies, with a struggle at first, managed to pull themselves into the unfamiliar saddles.

At length they were ready, and Mark embraced Emma within his huge arms, kissing her shyly in front of his friends, who turned away to limit his embarrassment. Unshed tears glistened in her eyes.

"Go now, my love, and take great care to return to me, unscathed."

"I will, my heart, I will." With a final embrace, Mark moved off to join his friends, while John and the others headed south to Dunkerque.

×✟×

London: 8th April

"The king has sealed an agreement with the Armagnacs!" Arundel declared angrily. "We look the more foolish now that he turns his back upon us and we are left to lick the wounds of our own dishonour."

The prince stood amongst them, his anger made evident by the throbbing of the scar upon his cheek that showed even whiter against his pallor.

"Do we stand in better suit?" Prince Hal challenged, surprising those around at his defence of the king. "For did we not by sending secret embassies abroad, lay with the Burgundians and open doors that should have stayed closed? For we sought an alliance with those who stood in direct contravention of our father's wishes. If we had brought about such an agreement and forced my father's hand, would we be better able to assoil our conscience and depose a king? For that is where it would have ended," Prince Henry declared.

"As you say, my lord prince, and I seek clemency that I spoke thus," Arundel declared, yet his expression did not speak of conciliation. Bishop Henry Beaufort shook his head in an almost imperceptible gesture, out of sight of the prince, and the Earl of Arundel kept his peace.

The prince sighed, releasing a long breath, as if to expunge his anger and frustration, then continued: "I blame you not, for we were bound so heavily to the Burgundian cause – and for you my lords –" he nodded at Arundel and Warwick, "– who fought most valiantly at their side, 'tis the more bitter pill to swallow. The question to be begged is who shall lead the force to aid the Armagnacs? Upon my soul, I would wager that it shall not be me."

"My lord prince," Henry Beaufort began. "If I may, it seems his majesty has put us all in an invidious position, more so now that the Anglo-Breton Truce is to be rescinded."

"What? Hell's teeth, is this true?" Prince Henry exclaimed.

The bishop enjoyed the effect this news had upon the

prince, yet did not show by a flicker of his eyes that he was being anything other than sympathetic.

"I beg your pardon, my lord prince, I have information to this effect from a most reliable source."

"By God, we shall have all Europe against us and be caught twixt and tween. I shall speak to my father and see what may be done." With that the prince moved from the group and sought out Lord Grey, whom he had seen on the other side of the Great Hall.

Once he was out of ear shot, Bishop Beaufort continued. "Dost my imagination betray me, or is Prince Hal weakening in his resolve to rid us of a debilitated king?"

"It would seem so, your grace," Arundel muttered. "Mayhap we shall need to remove the impediment should we wish to shorten our road to the crown."

"With this in mind I shall seek an opportune moment, and wouldst ask your aid in such an endeavour."

"Whom shall you use? De Berry?"

"Have you not heard? He was killed in a fight in Paris," Beaufort answered.

"What? By whom?"

"No one is certain. He was sent to deal with de Grispere, who still lives and thrives since his return, despite an ambush of another's making. The man has nine lives."

"De Grispere? One day I should like to meet him in a tourney or in an alleyway where none look on."

"Then I would adjure you caution and to take care of what you wish for. For de Berry too wished for such a meeting and he, even with his squire's aid, was no match for de Grispere's blade."

The Earl of Arundel snorted disdainfully and made no comment. "And dost he travel now, for he is not at court that I see?"

"I have heard he makes for Flanders in attendance to his father's trade. Upon his return we shall see where he should fit; with prince or king all the better to judge him in that regard. And should it not be to our liking, then perhaps a sword or dagger shall render us better service than the man himself."

Chapter Nineteen

Brussels

For three days they pressed on hard. The weather had held with no rain, and the roads were easily passable. They entered Brussels just before curfew and heard the gates close behind them. The journey had been without incident and many on the road seemed of a similar disposition, pressing on with their journeys and making the most of the clement Spring weather.

"We will not be able to keep on at this pace, and we shall stop on the seventh day to rest the horses and ourselves," Jamie pronounced over supper at their inn. "Father tells me Luxembourg is eight days' ride from here and roughly one hundred and twenty leagues."

They were accommodated in a large hostel catering for all travellers with money to spare on the road to central Europe and Italy, and had managed to bespeak a private room in which to dine away from other travellers. Here they could relax, and the ladies were able to leave off their disguise for a short time. It was difficult enough, as servants would not normally share the same table as their masters, and even more awkward to request a hot bath tub for them.

"Already my muscles do ache so from riding," groaned the contessa. "How do you men sit astride? I swear that my legs are fit to break should I ask any more of them. I know I pledged no rebuke, but by the saints 'tis arduous in the extreme. What more must we do for love?" She eased herself upon the settle in an effort to get comfortable.

Cristoforo looked from her side and gently squeezed her hand in sympathy. "*Cara mia*, 'twill soon pass. Once on Italian soil the subterfuge can end."

At which he placed another cushion at her back. She and Jeanette retained their knee-length boots cut in a masculine style, and wore long and unfashionable cotehardies that ended just above the knee. They were loose fitting, and when belted with a dagger, they disguised their female forms well enough. Being of a much fuller figure than Jeanette, Alessandria had had to swaddle her bosom with a long, silk scarf to complete the deceit.

Mark looked on smiling, glad now that Emma had gone with John and the others aboard a waggon. Yet he had been unexpectedly saddened at their parting and was missing her more than he would have supposed. He never thought that he would have been so affected, having always been happiest in male company, or alone on the farm living a life of relative solitude.

"For certes, yet it gives me much cause for concern that we are very close to the French border and the influence of Burgundy," Jamie said. "I am sure he and his spies pay well for all manner of janglery, ever to disseminate and learn of our existence and fiat.

"I know that it presses hard upon you, ladies, but consider

that in just over a sennight we shall be in Luxembourg and my fears will be all the easier. Then mayhap you shall return to your true selves," Jamie continued, suddenly serious. "History tells us that disguise is not just a manner of dress. For that was the downfall of good King Richard the Lionheart e'er he travelled through Austria upon his return from the Holy Land. 'Twas not his disguise that caused him to be recognised and taken by the Duke Leopold but his manner. For he could not adopt the humility of a base-born soul. His arrogance and royal demeanour were his undoing. You two ladies now face a coeval problem."

"I agreed to a penance for dressing as a man, 'pon my soul," Alessandria continued with a smile. "Yet never did I dream that such would be the punishment afore the act was complete!" The others laughed at this, relieving the tensions of the day.

Cristoforo, ever serious and never relaxing when on the road, was the first to break the mood: "I wish not to cause any alarm. Yet there are two abiding here whom I saw at the inn in Bruges and now in Brussels. They stay at this hostel and maybe are sely in their intent, for many travel this road in innocence. We must still have great care, as Jamie adjures."

"Tell me of what nature were these men?" Jamie was both curious and worried, knowing Cristoforo was ever aware of any potential threat.

"They were well-armed with dagger, sword and gambeson. They were not merchants, I'm bound, for their manner was of a rougher hue. They travelled light with no pack animals, carrying warbags only. I saw them pass us upon the road, hurrying by as though to catch up with another party ahead. They did so abreast, stalled, then pressed on.

"Espying them here in the tap room, they avoided my eye and made to make themselves scarce. There was a shifty look about them that I liked not, a hardness that bespoke ill. Now I am forewarned, I shall look for them again both on the road and yonder."

"If they spy for Burgundy or aught else they will leave ahead of us and wait upon the road, for they needs must ascertain that we travel south from here to Italy."

Twice more Cristoforo spotted them in the following days, on one occasion in time to warn Jamie, who noted their features. Once, he saw them in the distance, and once when they were about in one of the towns in which they stayed. They reached Luxembourg after a week of hard riding as the days held fair, and all were tired, especially Jeanette and Alessandria who would be glad of a day's rest, though they were now stronger in legs and back. The initial stiffness that went with long hours in the saddle passed, to produce iron-hard muscles and a better fortitude to bear the hardships of riding. The horses and mules all needed to crop fresh grass, for spring was upon them and the weather had turned warmer. But not all the news was to the good.

"The landlord says that the pass to Strasbourg is still not clear of winter snow and is virtually unpassable. We needs must divert south to Metz and thence onwards to Nancy and Basel."

"Must we then travel through French territory?" Alessandria asked.

"You are right to worry, but we have little choice," Jamie replied. "By God's grace, we shall be far enough away from Paris for it to matter little, but my concerns are for *routiers* and vagabonds, who ply their trade along the borderlands, the easier to slip from country to country as the need takes them. The two malaperts we see may be scouts for their rapacious raids, but we shall be well prepared."

"We needs must have care, for on more than one occasion I have seen the landlords or ostlers giving Jeanette and I strange looks in passing, despite our efforts at disguise," Alessandria commented.

"Yet 'tis passing strange," Jeanette continued, taking up the theme, "for I've noticed that we have both, whether by accident or force of clothes and manner of travel, begun to imitate the posture and manners of you men. We stand straighter and walk with a swagger most unbecoming of our true selves." Jeanette blushed a little as the three men grinned at each other, for they too had noticed the change that had occurred.

"Aye, we can give testament to that, and right well it has been taken, for we'll make a man of you yet little sister!" Jamie joked.

"Fie on you, brother, for I'll take the hardships and the badinage and give you as good in return. See if I do not," she riposted.

They stayed two nights in Luxembourg and left in the early morning mist, just as the main gates to the town were opening. It was an early start and there was little traffic upon the road at such an hour. One of their number was missing. Cristoforo had, with Jamie's blessing, offered to wait behind and see if any followed the party. A servant from the inn had been paid to accompany them, disguised as Cristoforo, making up their numbers to any watching spies. In recompense for a day's wage, the servant would return when they were a few miles from the town.

The ruse worked. Cristoforo had left the inn even earlier and waited by the south gate. It was two hours after the others had departed that he was rewarded with the sight of the two spies hurrying at a brisk trot towards the town gate, the early start having obviously thrown them into disarray. Once outside the gates they pushed up to a fast canter, eager to sight their quarry, splitting briefly as the road diverged. An hour later, they met again on the road south that Jamie and the others had taken, satisfied that their prey was before them.

Cristoforo hung back and watched out of sight. It confirmed all that he suspected. They were being watched, and somewhere they would be waylaid. The two men made good time on fresh horses hired from the inn. After two hours they broke south, which would, by Cristoforo's calculations, cut a corner and take them into French territory ahead of Jamie's party. Cristoforo hurried on, pressing his horse into a ground-eating canter that would have him back with his friends all the quicker.

He came upon them mid-morning, having passed other travellers on the road. The mare was blowing steadily as he pulled up.

"What news?" Jamie asked.

"It is as we thought. I am convinced that they will set a trap for us," Cristoforo responded.

"We shall rest early tonight and leave upon the dawn," Jamie decided. "'Tis but thirty leagues from Metz to Nancy, and we shall press hard and travel that distance within a day. We are now in deepest French territory, yet still less than two hundred leagues from Paris."

Jamie was now even more on edge, trying to out-think the unknown attackers and wondering how he could mitigate the danger to the ladies. But no more was seen of the pair of followers, and they passed unharmed to Metz.

Setting out after a good night's rest, Jamie almost began to believe that it was all his imagination, but for the familiar prickle that warned him that the threat was real.

Chapter Twenty

They were an hour into their journey, and the sun was beginning to rise higher, the day boding well for a warm and comfortable ride. It was at this point that Jamie's party was attacked.

The wooded area through which they rode was airless, protected by swathes of trees, cut back in the time-honoured fashion from the road to protect travellers from ambush. The company was strung out in the usual manner, Cristoforo leading with his crossbow now hooked around his pommel, Jamie next and Mark to the rear behind the ladies. Mark, upon Jamie's urging, now had his quarterstaff out of its bow bag and to hand. Jamie knew of old that such settings were perfect for ambush. Each man led a mule, but the coin was carried on saddle bags at the rear of each man's cantle.

No other travellers were in sight, and Jeanette and Alessandria had removed their hats against the warmth of the morning, allowing their hair free rein. It was this action that saved them. As they passed through a narrowed section of road, Jamie saw that the trees were cut even further back against ambush.

Richard's ears were flitting like seeds on the breeze as the tension flowed up through the reins to Jamie's hands. The hair on the back of Jamie's neck was rising as he looked down at Forest, and saw her ears twitch twice in the direction of the woods to their left. He needed no further warning.

"Ride hard now, for they come upon us!" he called out. They needed no further bidding and urged their horses to a gallop. Quarrels sighed through the air with a sinister hiss. With last minute changes in aim, the crossbowmen had been bidden to target the three men, surprised to see women in the party. They wanted them alive.

The sound of thundering hooves reverberated and battle cries rent the air. Jamie's group was neatly boxed in as men came onto the road at both ends and out of the trees. In all some twenty of them now charged at their party.

"Halt and rally! Circle," Jamie called out. "Jeanette, Alessandria, in the middle, and hold the mules for they'll hamper them. But by God's grace give us room to fight." With the excitement of the attack the adrenaline surged, and then Jamie settled and waited. He had faced battle charges many times before and knew that the hardest part was waiting for the wall of steel that bore down upon him. The shouts of the armed men grew closer. They were a ragtag group of mercenaries, some in pieces of armour, some in mail, armed with spears, swords and axes. None had shields, Jamie noticed, although a few were helmed. They were a dissolute bunch, disillusioned deserters from armies that were strewn all across France, left to fend for themselves and seeking easy pickings from travellers and any that they might attack. They would kill, rape and plunder for a shilling.

Mark was in his full length maille hauberk, as was Jamie, and despite the warmth of the day, Cristoforo wore his thick gambeson that would protect against a blade. The *routiers* on the road closed first with the advantage of ground and closer distance.

Richard cantered on the spot, snorting, eager for the fray, then with feet to spare Jamie shouted: "Now!" At which Cristoforo and Mark rode forward to meet the motley throng.

With his old battle cry of "an Umfraville!" Jamie spurred Richard on, and the horse leapt as though sprung from a trap and launched himself forward, teeth bared in anger to face the oncoming attackers. Forest leapt up at his side, evading the hooves of an oncoming horse, and rising to savage first the arm and then the face of an axe wielder, who screamed in agony, his face a mask of blood. Satisfied, she flew at the next man, pushing off from the saddle of her assailant's horse.

With a small buckler on his left arm, Jamie deflected an incoming spear that had been thrust as a lance, slashing overhand to cleave an unprotected head, sliding the blade down and back, swinging to attack another at his right. Another man rode in hard straight on Jamie's line, well-armed and set up, his sword raised in the upper guard to slash down to his left, standing in his stirrups for maximum force.

Richard extended his neck forward, his ugly teeth bared, biting at the eye of the oncoming horse's face. It shied away, squealing in pain, rearing up and back, giving Jamie the chance to thrust into his attacker's exposed armpit. He withdrew the sword quickly, twisting as he did so. The attacker fell forward onto his horse as it pulled away from Richard's attack, and suddenly Jamie was out in the open, the noise of battle coming from behind. He turned back to the fray.

Mark had gone forward, using his quarterstaff to his best advantage, knocking aside the first lunge of a spear, engaging just below the steel head, continuing the sliding motion as he met his opponent, then swinging the staff overhanded into the back of his opponent's neck as they passed each other. There was a sickening crack and the man was dead before he hit the ground. Mark's next attacker had an open guard as he went to slash with a cross cut. Mark utilised the extra length of his staff, striking end on straight to his chest, cracking the man's sternum, throwing him backwards from his saddle and making the following horse shy sideways. Guiding his own horse with just his lower legs, Mark slashed the staff around to be met by an upraised arm that the rider lifted in instinctive defence. The mail was no defence against the force of the blow of the staff at the end of its range, and the man's elbow shattered beneath the impact, his limp hand dropping the sword.

Cristoforo had found his own mark, taking out the leader of the charge with a well-aimed bolt to his neck, killing him instantly. With no time to reload he flung the bow at the next assailant, drew a dagger from his boot sheath and sent it spinning into the man's chest. A third man, made more wary by Cristoforo's actions, cut deftly with his sword in a cross strike from the right shoulder. There was no time for Cristoforo to throw another dagger, and the distance was too close anyway. He pulled the falchion from its sheath as if by magic, parrying the blow from the *routier*. His mount was no warhorse but responded well to the leg, half-passing and opening a gap for Cristoforo to remove the dagger at his belt and deflect the next blow. Pushing the blade away, he released the pressure, letting his arm slip over the guard so that the two men were now arm-to-arm, and he went over and under, trapping his assailant's arm and jerking upwards, hearing the bone crack. Instead of letting go, he pinned the broken limb to his torso, causing his opponent to lean forward against the pain and allowing Cristoforo room to swing his dagger up and around, driving for the man's exposed neck, where it sank home with a spray of arterial blood.

The crossbowmen on either side of the ambush had now

galloped in from their hiding places in the trees to claim their spoils. Seeing the others occupied, they went to the middle to take the mules, the goods and the women. Jeanette and Alessandria had looked on in horror at the bloody mayhem before them. They knew of battle but had never been at the forefront of such a barbaric display before, with all the associated gore, noise and smell. Jeanette had never seen her brother so suffused with battle rage as the red mist descended upon him. Yet they were not completely discomposed, and as the crossbowmen galloped upon them, they nudged and pushed the mules in their way, obstructing the predators.

"Come now missy, we'll have some fun, my beauty," one shouted in French, harsh with the accent of the region. His smile was a rictus of rotting teeth and bad breath. He grabbed Alessandria's reins and pulled her horse close to reach around her waist and pull her across to his saddle.

Fear and anger drove the contessa, and drawing her dagger with her left hand she raised her arm, high enough to drive it down into her assailant's exposed and unarmoured leg. The blade seared through the flesh to the bone, striking the sciatic nerve, and all thoughts of assault left the soldier's mind. Alessandria whirled her horse away, to see Jeanette deal with her attacker in her own way, first driving her fingers into his eyes as John had taught her, then her own dagger into his groin. His inhuman scream caused her to flinch, and as she pulled her dagger back a jet of crimson followed, with a sharp metallic tang assailing the nostrils of her horse, who reared up at the smell, dropping her from the saddle to land in a heap upon the rough ground.

Jamie was aware that his last two opponents needed to be finished so that he could protect the women. Yet he had found a knight who was skilled in arms and well mailled, with an open-faced bascinet helm. His horse was also trained for war, spinning and snapping when it could. The two men clashed, swords crossing, Jamie's buckler dented from a crushing blow as he stayed ever aware of the last man who strove to attack at his undefended side. This man was armed with a battle axe, but did not have the reach to do him harm, needing close quarters to make what would be a fatal blow should it land.

Jamie brought Richard's quarters to the right, thrusting with his sword under the knight's guard, the tip snaking out for a hand cut, using the short distance to his advantage. The knight was nearly caught and drew back just in time as the blade sawed into his leather gauntlet, finding flesh in a strike that was not deep enough to disarm him. The axe man, seeing his chance, pressed his horse forward to either slash at Richard or strike him from the right. As soon as he sensed the movement, Jamie sat deeper in the saddle, curbed and pressed with the spur. He sensed Richard bulk up beneath him, seeming to grow by several feet as the powerful body tensed then exploded upwards and outwards simultaneously in a perfect capriole.

The axeman took both hooves. One struck his horse, the other his open torso, as he raised his arm for a downward strike with the axe. His chest was crushed instantly. Richard's front legs slashed out, but the knight's horse was faster than his rider and pulled back out of range. Lunging in again to attack, the man drew his sword arm back in the half guard, ready for the thrust to Jamie's torso. The move commenced as Richard was landing and Jamie prepared to deflect with his buckler, but the action was never begun. A grey blur launched itself into the air and Forest's powerful jaws clamped upon the sword hand, snapping bones beneath the gauntlet, and with this distraction Jamie thrust to the exposed face, driving the blade into the open bascinet and through the man's eye to his brain, killing him instantly.

He called Forest off, and span Richard around to see what

had become of the others. All were dead or gone bar one, who had managed to grab the lead rope of one of the mules and was starting into a gallop some yards away towards the trees. It would be folly to pursue him into the forest and crossbows that may be lurking there. Then he saw Cristoforo standing behind one of the horses. He watched the Italian slide a quarrel into the tiller of his crossbow and take steady aim at the rider, now some fifty yards away. There was a familiar trilling sound as the bolt flew forward to appear half a second later, protruding from the back of the *routier* who cried in pain, keeping his seat but releasing the mule's lead rope and flopping forward in the saddle as his mount carried him away.

Then Jamie saw his sister lying on the grass and rushed to aid her. As he did so she coughed, sat up and looked about her upon the gore of battle. She heaved, sick at the sight before her. Although they all lived in violent times with death never far afield, to come face-to-face with the reality of it at such close quarters completely discomposed her.

"Are you harmed, Jeanette?" he queried, kneeling at her side, Forest came up to nudge her with her huge head, licking her face to comfort her, ruining the effect by smearing on Jeanette's face the blood of that last man she had attacked.

"It was horrible, Jamie, yet I am unharmed, praise God, save a bruising at my fall and to my self-esteem for being thrown so. Thank you, Forest, for you are a kind, dear hound." She praised her, stroking the rough coat. Jamie offered her his hand and aided her to stand.

Cristoforo was holding Alessandria tightly and she too was greatly upset at stabbing her assailant. He whispered words of comfort to her in Italian. She had seen Cristoforo's work of war first hand at the French Court in Paris, but nothing so bloody and visceral as the scene before her, with smell of voided bowels mingling with the tang of fresh blood and mewing of dying men.

Mark gathered the mules and now sat waiting patiently for the ladies to regain their composure. "Jamie, I like not our situation here, we needs must depart ere they return in greater numbers, for I do fear another attack."

"You have the right of it, Mark. Come, to horse, for we must leave this place. I would not wish to face another skirmish such as that. We had surprise with us as they knew not we were skilled in arms and were intemperate in their approach. We shall not be so fortunate again."

Mark looked around. "'Tis a shame we cannot take that destrier, for he looks becoming and well-bred."

Jamie looked to where the faithful steel-grey stallion stood pathetically and patiently at his dead master's side, as if waiting for him to wake from some dark and fevered dream.

"Aye, he fought right well and is a goodly warhorse, causing Richard some pain and saving his master twice to my attack. Should you be able to catch him, do so and take him. For it would serve well to plunder them as they would steal from us."

Chapter Twenty-One

They reached the safety of Nancy without further mishap and pressed on the next day, travelling towards Basel. There were more travellers on the roads, and the weather softened as they headed south into a warmer climate where Spring made its presence felt earlier, making travel easier and offering safety in numbers with less likelihood of further attack. Most of their fellow travellers were slower than Jamie's party, made up as they were of waggons, or pack trains of mules belonging to traders and merchants. Still the ladies kept their disguise. They rode for eight days and rested for one, where they camped at the edge of a forest next to a stream of clear, sweet mountain water. There was a lush spring meadow that curved away from sight of the main road where the stream meandered within a shaded oxbow, forming a gentle, green slope up to wood beyond.

They felt safer the closer they came to the Swiss border, and were all but certain that no one was following them. In their sheltered camp the two women finally felt able, with Jamie's blessing, to change back into their proper attire and end the subterfuge of their male dress. Forest was left on guard to warn of any who may be approaching and she settled down in the long grass, panting in the warm sunshine, her ears alert for any trouble.

With screams of pleasure and shock, the two women bathed in the shallows of the freezing tributary that meandered eastwards to the mighty Rhine River.

"I am like gooseflesh," Jeanette declared, shivering as they left the cold water and dried themselves in the shelter of a small clump of reeds and bushes. "By the Lord 'tis good to shed those itchy hose and braise – though I shall miss riding astride, for it was more comfortable I declare, once my muscles became used to the action."

"I could not agree more. The benefit of having a leg either side of the horse is somehow more secure, though I shudder to think what my *babo* would say of such things." Alessandria grimaced at her daring behaviour. "Yet I fear that there will be much of which my papa will not approve when we meet again. We are both older, and I suspect he is even less disposed than before to be of moderate disposition where my future is concerned. Persuading him of Cristoforo's suit may be all the harder for it."

"Surely you will prevail. Will not seeing you again after years apart soften his heart?"

"Mayhap, yet I fear he will agree upon terms most unfair to my decree. His remembrance of me is of a young girl, not of a woman grown old enough to decide upon a spouse. I suspect he will demand that I stay in Bologna or reside again in *Firenze.* Then knowing well how his mind twists and turns, having trapped me thus, he will seek a way to annul his permission and enforce upon me a marriage of loveless cordiality to a husband who appeases the politics of his ambition." Alessandria sighed.

Then she clenched her fists, fixing her face in a severe and forceful pose. "But I shall not be cowed by such demands! I will insist upon his agreement in full, or he shall pay the full price of undoing his daughter's love and will not like the intemperate creature that will be unleashed upon him."

Jeanette looked with sympathy upon her friend, to whom she had grown very close over the last weeks of their journey, and vowed silently to aid her in any way that she was able. Their mood was broken as Jamie approached, calling to alert them to his presence.

"Supper is awaiting you, and as the dusk approaches, you must come to the camp where we can all be together and protected." As they revealed themselves he was shocked at the transformation. "By the rood, have you two demoiselles seen anything of two young malapert rascals hereabouts, for we have lost our grooms?"

"Why, sir," Alessandria retorted, "have you checked your visage in yonder pool? For by the the good Lord, I'll forswear you'll fill the part right well."

Jamie laughed at the apt riposte, swearing that he would bathe after supper, and beckoned them back to the camp.

Mark had been further upstream catching fish with a makeshift rod and line, and had returned with six fat trout. Jamie lauded him for his efforts as Cristoforo scavenged for herbs and radicchio, marinading the fish with a sauce of oil and herbs before piercing them with green sticks and placing them over the glowing embers of the fire to cook gently. They had bought part-baked bread from the last village through which they passed and this now lay on the hot stones forming the makeshift hearth of the fire. A large costrel of strong, local wine had also been purchased and they shared this between them, feeling for the first time in weeks that they could truly relax.

Jamie looked across at the steel-grey stallion that Mark had taken from the dead knight. The animal was cropping the lush grass, hobbled against flight and seemingly happy – although he kept a wary distance from Richard.

"How does the new stallion, Mark? Jamie asked "He seems right happy," he continued rising from his haunches and walking over to Mark, who stood nearby with pleasure in his eye.

"Aye that he be. 'E's settled right well, but does things sometimes at the slightest movement and I'm not sure what I did. I suppose he's been trained differently from normal 'osses?"

"He will have been." Jamie agreed with a smile. "We shall have time enough on the journey, and I will show you the commands to which he will have been trained to respond. Once you are able to master them, he will be of more use to you and will, mayhap, save your life, for in battle he was perfect and as near Richard's match as ever I have met."

"That would be grand, Jamie. I should like that, for some things are a mystery in what he does and it is almost as though I confuse him at times, thinking mayhap I want this or that. 'E goes to obey and then stops, and when I shift my weight in surprise it seems to upset 'im."

"Aye that will be the way of it. He will be finely trained to a hair's breadth, for certes. What will you name him?"

"I have already done so, and he is now Breseler."

The others heard this and were puzzled, for it was neither a French nor an English word that they knew of.

"Breseler?" Jamie queried.

"It means Warrior in the Cornish tongue, and he be that for certes," Mark responded with a grin.

"A good choice, my friend, for he is built for war and will serve you well in that regard."

The following day they changed the saddles on the ladies' horses, for those had been strapped to the mule's backs, disguised as pack carriers by all the baggage attached. Now the two palfreys, ridden by Jeanette and Alessandria, were tacked with side saddles in the correct manner, marking them as ladies of rank.

Chapter Twenty-Two

Westminster, London: 16th May

"My lords, we thank you for attending us upon this auspicious day, for we have news worthy of celebration to impart." The king began, his voice and manner strong, despite the frailty that had reduced his body so until all thoughts of leading an army to France had become impossible. The Council was arrayed before him, including Prince Henry, latterly returned from Coventry. "We hereby announce two matters of great import. Firstly, we would have it recorded that our own dear and loyal son, Prince Thomas, shall lead our forces in our stead to conquer the Burgundians who threaten our lands in France. We shall anoint him as Duke of Clarence.

"In light of this, we shall formally seal the Treaty of Bourges pledged between our houses of Lancaster and Armagnac, who graciously cede castles, land and provinces, with well-nigh all the nobility of France, forsaking any confederacy or alliance with Burgundy or his kinsmen."

At which the ducal envoys of Berry, Orleans and Bourbon, together with those of Count Alençon, all gave a small bow of acceptance, a smile on each of their lips.

Here Prince Henry winced, as anger coursed through him at the epithet of *dear and loyal son* that was directed at Prince Thomas. He shared a look of contempt with Richard Courtney, who was as ever by his side. In the cheering that ensued, he muttered, "Yet who shall pay the price? For it shall be dear, and no account of shekels will mend the damage done here this day. Our father courts dissenters who promise all and shall leave the tally short, we're bound."

"I concur, my prince, and it is you who shall account the reckoning and right the scales to weigh in our favour."

The king continued when the hall quietened at his wave for silence. "We also have joy in our heart at the forthcoming marriage of our son to Lady Margaret Holland, may God bless and keep them." All called "amen", even Bishop Beaufort, who stood to the right of Prince Henry, scowling at the mention of his former sister-in-law.

"He steals first your birthright and then our inheritance, my lord prince," Beaufort muttered.

Henry compressed his lips into a thin line: "Uncle, we warrant that we have pleaded your case and sought justice in your cause, yet we'll not cross the Rubicon of our father's law whatever the cost to our dignity or your avarice. We shall not war with him on this matter."

The bishop was stung at the words, physically recoiling at the rebuke. "My prince, I meant no disloyalty, and if my words offended I do humbly recant them."

"As you say, my lord bishop, as you say," Prince Henry responded gently.

With Archbishop Arundel at his side, the king turned to his good friend and mentor declaring, "How welcome is this moment, the day that we have longed for? Let us enjoy God's bounty and go to France – where with a little negotiation the land shall be ours by right!"

The Bishop of Beaufort slipped from Prince Henry's side, to then be joined by the Earl of Arundel. "A day of deep reckoning and a testament to the direction of the wind, which has changed of late," the earl commented.

"Aptly put, perhaps more so than you may realise," Beaufort replied. "For I had a short discourse with him this moment past and it seems that the prince's sojourn in Coventry has turned his heart in support of his father, despite all that is laid against him. He acquiesces to the Treaty and will sign it with no thought of seeking retribution of any kind. Steps must be taken, and we shall meet in private to consider them. Away from me now, for we must not be seen to collude."

"I shall come to your palace tonight, after I sup with the prince, and a conspiracy we shall form that will alter events in our favour."

Sir Richard Whittington had been invited, along with other influential courtiers to attend the announcements. He noticed the aside between Beaufort and Arundel, together with the furtive way in which they conversed, and was immediately concerned.

Prince Henry returned to Coldharbour, and after dining with his coterie he left to visit the stews nearby. Arundel feigned a sore head and stayed within the mansion. Once all had left, he slipped out to catch a wherry to the south bank and Bishop Beaufort's palace. The guards were expecting him and he was ushered through familiar corridors to the bishop's personal solar. Incense and scented candlewax permeated the air against the ill humours of the river, and a small fire gave off a gentle heat, rendering the room cosy yet not stifling.

"Good evening, your grace," Arundel offered.

"And to you, my Lord Arundel."

"Brevity shall be the order of the night for I would return ere midnight arrives, lest my absence be noted."

"As you wish. The prince is the crux of the matter for now he sways, albeit reluctantly to his father's cause, wounded as he is by the precedence shown to his younger brother."

"'Twould have presented an awkward position for Prince Hal should he have been chosen to lead the king's forces, for but moments ago he was promulgating the Burgundian suit. Now he must bite his tongue and obey his father's whims. I shall in my turn write a letter to Burgundy, for I was of a similar persuasion and indeed fought at the man's side. I shall explain that I have been whipped into line and have no recourse but to obey."

The bishop nodded sagely. "Indeed it would be a wise course of action, for who knows when they may be friends again. Mayhap it might be sooner than we think."

"With friends in mind, how does your brother within the king's meiny? For he looked right close and entwined within his majesty's company at court today."

The bishop closed his hands about his stomach, appearing at his most benign, as a beatific smile crossed his face: "He has worked most assiduously to foster such sympathy from the king, and 'twould not surprise me to learn that he too will join the party of war to France. For he is ever happiest when he has a sword within his grasp."

"'Twould do well. For if he can control Prince Thomas and a weak king at death's door here, there is but one impediment to our plans. To wit, what shall you do with Prince Hal?"

"I have put in motion plans to deal with him when next he returns to London. For, as you say, many of the king's loyal subjects – including the Duke of York – will be in France, dividing his strength of arms. With you here and other powerful barons appearing loyal to the monarch, we should easily avail ourselves of the crown."

"Who shall be the scapegoat for the murder?" Arundel asked. "There will be many who will demand a villain to blame."

"Indeed they will – and those closest to the throne, if not in direct line to it, shall make the loudest protests. Who better to take the blame than one whose actions could benefit both a king and the younger prince?" Beaufort left the thought hanging in the air.

It took a few seconds for the earl to understand what he intended. "Hell's teeth, you mean to set my uncle the archbishop as the scapegoat, with him so close to the king and Prince Thomas and for certes no favourite of Prince Hal, whom he has thwarted on many occasions? By the rood, that is a most perfidious stratagem. The old goat shall suffer and we shall gain absolute power."

"Just so. All I shall need is you to oblige me when the time is nigh."

"Consider it done. Now I must away afore midnight is chimed."

Chapter Twenty-Three

Lugano, Italy: 16th May

They had been on the road for thirty days, stopping every seventh as Jamie had planned, and were within a day's ride of the Italian border.

"We have covered some five hundred leagues by my reckoning, and should be within the land of your father on the morrow, Cristo," Jamie said as an aside, as they were riding slightly ahead. "How does it feel to be returned to your homeland?"

"Very strange, *amico mio.* I am of course delighted to be back after so long away, and the sun that warms my back is most welcome. *Pero*, there is another, darker aspect to my country. Italy, she is a dark mistress, and *Firenze* most of all. I would adjure caution. Not from Burgundy or his ilk, for we are far from his influence now, but from other factions seeking dominance in the poisoned well of politics and ambition. Not all will be as it seems, I warn you, and those who appear friends may not be. A smile will oft hide a dagger in the dark."

"Like the English Court," Jamie quipped.

"Only much worse, *amico*, much worse. It will be harder for you to dissemble than usual, for the language will hide many emotions that you cannot fathom. I know on this journey you have been *un buon studente*, but as you know, there is more to a language than words," Cristoforo continued, alluding to the fact that Jamie had been learning Italian from him at every opportunity along the way and had found the process easy, given his fluency in Latin and French.

"In that accord, I have a proposal," Jamie said. "Mayhap, until we are safely ensconced in Florence and the gold handed up to His Holiness, we declare you to be a Welshman who speaks no Italian and has only the heathen tongue beloved of that race, and a little English. That way, people will be more careless with their tongues when we are in company. Think on't, so many Welshmen whom we met were dark-skinned Celts with hair as dark as yours. It would not be unseemly to find one such as you in our company as a servant."

Cristoforo's initial reaction of horror changed as he thought upon the idea.

"Especially those whom we might meet upon the road. *Bravo! Una buona idea*. For although I have no evidence yet, still I feel we are being watched. I look around and scout the road, yet nothing appears."

"I have the same feeling. My neck itches so from twisting and I cannot scratch the cause. Mayhap we have become preoccupied with such matters since the attack."

Cristoforo merely shrugged and looked around again at the woods, quickly rotating his head.

Two days later they set forth from Lugano on the main route to Milan, with a planned stop at Como. Mark remarked to the others how the smells of the woodland and the look of the buildings had changed as they progressed south, further into this strange land.

"To think, only two years past I had never left Cornwall, let alone England. By the good Lord, my family will not believe me when I tell them of this. How far from here to the Holy Land, Cristo, where our good Lord did walk?"

"Oh *Dio*, my friend, it is maybe twice the distance again of how far we have travelled. For you must travel to the very bottom of Italy then go by ship to Acre. Or across land to Byzantium and thence overland down to Jerusalem. Many, many leagues."

"They say it gets hotter still than here."

"Hot? This is not hot. Await the summer and the months of June and July, then you will truly know heat. Yet you are correct, for Jerusalem is hotter still, a brutal, dry heat with no respite."

Mark had more questions about Italy and the Holy Land, for Cristoforo had ventured there, and from what he had said he had been lucky to return alive.

They saw a few commercial caravans upon the roads as well as other travellers, for this was the main route south into Italy. They all moved at different paces, yet the caravans were easily overtaken. Despite the mountainous nature of the changing countryside, Jamie's party moved steadily at a pace with which he was happy.

At length, they crested a rise over a low pass to see a panoply of chaos before them. Mules and horses milled around, while a covered carriage was at the roadside, cast in a lopsided manner with one wheel off its axle. Three men stood on guard, two with swords unsheathed and a third with a crossbow strung and ready, protecting two servants who were struggling to raise the carriage up sufficiently high to reinstate the wheel. Two grooms had unharnessed the horses and were holding them calmly in front of the carriage.

Two veiled ladies, one seemingly of quality and the other her maid, stood back off the road, and by their manner in a state of apparent agitation. They were tall and difficult to define, cloaked as they were against the cooler mountain air.

Jamie's party halted some hundred feet away to take in the sight, alert for any sign of trouble.

"By their manner I would surmise that they have been attacked, and were chased. Two or three seem wounded." Jamie noted. At this point two further men appeared from behind the carriage. These were men of a different stamp. One was a wealthy merchant by his dress and manner, wearing a fine doublet of deep-blue velvet. About his neck he wore a gold chain, while a deep-set hat with a long feather pointing backwards crowned his head. A jewel-encrusted belt at his waist balanced a sword and a dagger at either hip. The man by his side was also well-dressed, and looked to be the merchant's steward, for he came forward to protect his master against Jamie's party, which he obviously viewed as fresh trouble.

"They seem well accoutred and ready for battle," Cristoforo remarked. "Mayhap we should tread warily or they will sell their honour dearly." Mark too had come forward to stand by his friends, leaving the ladies to the rear in safety.

The man they had marked as the steward came forward of the others, pushing through their cordon. He spoke in French with a strong Italian accent.

"Well? Do you too come to attack us? You will find that we shall not commit easily to the grave." He eyed Forest warily as her hackles rose.

"Do we look of that stamp, sir? With ladies in our mesnie? No, for we too have suffered the ignominy of attack from *routiers* as we left France and we have sympathy for your position. May we be of aid to you and your company?"

The gleam of suspicion on the steward's face softened, and he looked back towards his master for instruction, who duly nodded in assent.

"No sirs, you do not, and I apologise for my discourtesy, for the base-born churls who attacked us seem to have robbed me of my manners. I am Luca Barzzachi, at your service." At which the Italian bowed. "And this is my master, Signor Donato Bardi." The merchant bowed and came forward to address them and introduce himself properly, bowing gracefully to the ladies, sweeping back his cloak as he did so. Jamie noted the movement well.

The three men slipped down from their horses, with Mark and Jamie stepping forward as he handed the reins to Cristoforo. "Cris...Chris, take these horses whilst we aid these fellows." Jamie changed to English, remembering their agreement. "Stay Forest, stay girl."

Alessandria and Jeanette looked on with a slight frown, then too remembered what had been agreed. Jamie was trusting no one in this foreign land until they proved themselves worthy, and he strode forward with Mark at his side to examine the carriage, noting both its position and the faces of the two men-at arms holding guard, both of whom had what appeared to be fresh cuts that had bled a little. The position of the carriage was such that the rocks that had apparently detached the wheel from the axle were preventing more than one or two men at most from gaining access to a position where they could replace the wheel.

"We galloped off at the attack, running for our lives as we were badly outnumbered, and only stopped here when the carriage swayed and hit the rocks. We have no pole to act as a lever or pivot point," Luca explained, first out of habit in Italian, then switching to French, as Jamie feigned incomprehension of the first language. He nodded in understanding at Luca's explanation in French. "You speak no Italian?"

"No, but one of the ladies yonder is of your country and we escort her to Bologna from the French Court. I am Flemish and Mark is from England, my groom there is Welsh, so he speaks little English, let alone Italian."

"Ah, then I shall speak only in French." Luca agreed smiling, speaking quickly as an aside to Signor Bardi, too fast for Jamie to understand more than a few words. "Can you aid us?"

"I think I can, be there much aboard that weighs heavily?" Mark asked.

"I believe not, for we have removed most of the goods from inside, including Signorina Bardi and her maid, as you see." He gestured to the two women. Mark grunted in acknowledgement and unstrapped his sword belt and gambeson, handing both to Jamie. The footing was good for just one man to get at the carriage. He turned around, putting his back to the padded wooden side, obtaining a good grip upon the base. One of the servants, who had been attempting to replace the wheel, looked on as the men-at-arms fanned out to observe what was to happen. The *signorina* and her maid too had walked around the carriage, closer to Cristoforo, Jeanette and Alessandria, curious as to how such a feat might be achieved.

Satisfied, Mark looked at one of the grooms and spoke in English, "Be ready with that wheel, for when I lift this I'll not wish to be cursed with the weight forever."

The two men were clearly puzzled, and as Jamie translated from English to French, one muttered in Italian with incredulity in his voice: "*Non e possibile*, no one man can lift that by himself."

Jamie repeated the instruction in French, to make sure everyone understood and was ready, thrusting the wheel at the recalcitrant servant. His actions were followed by a volley of fast Italian from Luca. The man shrugged in an ill-mannered fashion that surprised Jamie, for no servant would dare answer so to his father or to Will, his steward. The servant, however, now stood ready and nodded. Mark returned the nod, braced his knees, and with his back straight, began to exert all his strength through his thews of massive shoulders. All eyes were upon him as he tried to attempt the impossible.

For moments nothing seemed to happen and one of the servants looked to the other with a wicked smile upon his face. But inexorably, as sweat poured down Mark's face, the carriage began to rise, inch by inch. Mark shook with the strain and exertion. Jamie cuffed the servant holding the wheel and motioned for him to place the hub, ready to push onto the axle. The man jumped in surprise, knocked out of his trance at Mark's show of strength. "Now!" he cried and both men positioned the wheel, manhandling it onto the axle and pushing the hub home.

"*Va bene, va bene. Basta,*" Luca said to Mark.

Mark let go and the wheel dropped an inch to the ground; he fell forward onto his knees at the release of effort. Jamie went to offer his hand.

"*Dio mio,*" Luca declared. "I would never have thought it possible."

"He is mightily blessed with strength by the good Lord." Jamie smiled down at his friend, but as he turned to face the Italians his smile faded, for he found two sword points mere inches from his face, held by the two men-at-arms. The two *signorinas* turned out to be lithe, young men who now held loaded small crossbows not dissimilar to Cristoforo's, their veils removed and cloaks dropped, quarrels pointed at Jeanette and Alessandria.

Luca smiled wickedly. "Ah, so easy. Do not try to fight, for you and I suspect the Contessa Alessandria de Felicini will be killed immediately."

Mark looked up to find a dagger at his throat. "By God's grace, I shall rip your head from your body." He growled.

"Mark, no, for we must bide our time." Jamie adjured in English. He cursed inwardly for being so easily taken in by what appeared to be a perfect ploy. *For if I could dress women as men, so too could losengers such as these dress men as women*. He smarted.

Forest gave a deep rumble in her chest from her place by the horses where Jamie had bidden her stay. She was confused. The men seemed threatening, yet her master stood motionless, not drawing his sword or responding aggressively towards them. Her head tilted to one side in puzzlement, whimpering as she awaited a command.

On hearing the sound, Jeanette bade her be silent, and Luca turned to the man-at-arms holding the crossbow by his side, saying: "*Uccidi il cane, prima che ci attacchi.*"

Even without the Italian Jamie had already learnt, the men's movements were enough for him to understand their intent. As a war dog there were times – such as when a knight was in full armour and impervious to a canine assault – in which a dog must be trained to run away and not face archers and fully armed knights. Jamie shouted as the man started to raise his crossbow, "Away Forest, away!"

She hesitated for a split second, not willing to leave her master, then turned sharply on her haunches, bounding left then right, unknowingly using the horses as cover. Jamie lurched sideways, barging into the crossbow man just as he was about to loose, spoiling his aim. The man cursed and smashed the weapon sideways into Jamie's stomach, causing him to double over in pain, then for good measure struck him on the side of the head with the butt of the crossbow, felling Jamie to the ground. Jamie rolled, groggy from the strike, pulling at his dagger to stab the man's foot. Two sword tips appeared as if from nowhere, held steady mere inches from his eyes and throat.

"Do not move," Luca ordered, "or you lose an eye and then your life. Now, tell the Welshman to drop his dagger to the ground, and unbuckle your own sword and dagger. Giuseppe, take the daggers from the women." The man who had posed as the Bardi's daughter sprung to obey. Cristoforo dropped his belt dagger to the ground upon Jamie's command, and said nothing.

Chapter Twenty-Four

Jamie, Cristoforo and Mark had their hands tied behind their backs, while Jeanette and Alessandria were pushed into the carriage. The three of them were then attached to the back board of the waggon by ropes around their necks.

"The man in there has orders to kill the women if there is any garboil outside, do you understand?" Bardi explained in French. They nodded after Jamie translated. "Good. You will walk behind, tied thus. We have what we were paid for, which was to collect the fee due to the Holy Father. It is done. No more was said as to your fate. The women, especially *la contessa*, will fetch a goodly ransom from her father, who will pay dearly for her safe return and mayhap that of her maid. As to you three, I have not yet decided if you are worth anything, but I would advise you to walk carefully and not stumble, as we shall not stop if you fall."

Jamie made a quick decision. It meant exposing himself, but it could keep them alive until the right moment arrived. "I am a knight. My name is Sir James de Grispere, and I have lands and property in England," he declared. "My family will pay well for my return, and I vouchsafe the same for my servants here."

Bardi looked at the quality of Jamie's sword and his build, seeing the truth in Jamie's story. No man trained in weapons could hide the features that came with it; the build-up of muscles in that strange and lopsided way of a man trained in arms.

"So be it. We will stop at Lomazzo at a quiet inn there and we can make arrangements for ransoms to be sent. This will take time, as you know, so I would advise you to cooperate, or your wait with me will not be an agreeable time for you."

They were forced to walk behind the carriage at a slower pace, and other travellers were told that they were brigands whom they had captured. All the time the threat of death hung over Jeanette and Alessandria inside the carriage if they made any attempt to tell the true story or escape, and they were forced to endure the laughter and ridicule of travellers who rode in fear of such men.

Between them, Jamie, Cristoforo and Mark managed to concoct a plan of sorts, muttering ideas to each other whenever the opportunity presented itself. Each time they were heard to speak they were ordered to be silent, and struck on the head or clubbed upon the shoulder. Mark swore that he would tear their heads off when the opportunity arose and cursed them roundly in English. Eventually, he realised that their captors were simply laughing at his threats, so he fell silent, keeping his face a mask of hatred, looking and seemingly speaking at them, but in fact helping to plan with Jamie and Cristoforo in a language the guards could not understand. The ploy worked, and the others used it as well. Soon they knew how they would escape. Jamie was comforted by the fact that twice, during their forced march, he saw Forest skulking in the boundary of the woods by the roadside. She would be ready for his call, he knew.

As the evening fell they arrived at Lomazzo, a small town with two inns, the largest of which was on the outskirts of the curtilage, some way to the south. The inn was appropriately named *La Casa del Viaggiatore* – The House of the Traveller.

The stables were set at the rear of the building in an enclosed courtyard, where travellers' horses were well provided for with a barn and stabling divided into stalls, with more capacity than would be expected for such an inn. Jamie began to suspect that this was more than just a lucky find on the road, and that Donato Bardi was well-known here and had the sympathies of patrons and the landlord. This was confirmed as two scruffy ostlers walked forward, smiled a greeting and took charge of some of the company's horses, wary of the two captured stallions. A door opened and a huge fat man appeared from the rear entrance, rubbing his hands upon a greasy apron. He was nearly as tall as Mark and his Slavic eyes had an evil slant that showed no hint of mercy.

"Ah Donato, *buona sera*. What do we have here? Some fat *piccioni* for the pot?" He laughed humourlessly. To Cristoforo's ears, he spoke Italian with a strange accent.

"*Buona sera*. Indeed, these are the pickings of the road. Three English men, amongst them a knight, together with the contessa and her maid for ransom. And we also have the tithe for the Alberti to *Il Papi*." He nodded at the three sets of saddlebags that Signor Bardi and his two lieutenants carried over their shoulders, having removed them from the saddles of the English horses. "A good day's work, but by the good Lord I am hungry." At these words Cristoforo realised that it would not be so easy to escape, as fellow travellers and the inn's workers would be sympathetic to the cause of the Bardi contingent.

"Well, come in, I have an *ottimo stuffato* of veal." The landlord offered, sweeping with his slab-like hand.

"In a moment. First I must see to the ladies and these heretics." With that he motioned to Luca. "See that they are secured, and that two of your best men remain with them, one to watch them at all times, no matter what." Bardi ordered. Luca nodded and Bardi went to the carriage, handing down both Alessandria and Jeanette. As they stepped out, Jeanette looked at Jamie.

"Soon Jeanette. Be ready," he spoke quickly. The two women were herded into the inn and away from the Englishmen.

"*Silencio, idiota,*" Luca shouted at him, raising his fist, at which Jamie, Mark and Cristoforo were herded into the capacious stables, each allotted a stall and tied by a rope to the wall ring above, with just enough slack to be able to sit on their haunches. It was deliberately uncomfortable and debilitating. Satisfied, Luca left two men in charge and joined the others in the inn. An hour later another two men arrived to relieve them, and brought stale bread and a cup of brackish, watered-down wine. As they swapped places, the new guards took it in turns to release the rope of each man, starting with Mark, first untying his legs. They were very wary, having seen his massive strength on the road. One had a dagger and the other a sword drawn, standing back, ready for any sign of resistance as an ostler untied one hand from Mark's bonds.

Mark said nothing and ate, knowing what was to come. At the changeover in the third stall along, Cristoforo had rolled onto his back, easily slipping his tied hands down and forward so that they were in front of him. He reached down and took one of the undiscovered daggers from his boot sheath. In a matter of seconds his hands were free and an evil look came upon his face. He rubbed his wrists to restore full circulation, pulled his second dagger from his left boot and waited, while holding the rope in his hands, making it appear to all intents and purposes that he was still bound. Finally, once Jamie had eaten, the two guards and the ostler approached his stall. They saw Cristoforo as the least dangerous of the three, not even having a sword and being a mere servant, alive only because his master had pledged a sum for his safety.

The two guards were much more relaxed now, having seen no trouble from Jamie and Mark; the one with the dagger came forward at forty-five degrees to the ostler who was bending forward, motioning with his hands at the rope. Cristoforo, pretending to understand, moved one pace forward. But the second foot never reached the ground. Cristoforo brought his foot up with all his force between the man's legs; the man's mouth fell open as he expelled a gasp of agony. At this, a high-pitched whistle sounded from the next stall.

The next move was so fast the guard with the dagger was barely able to comprehend it. Cristoforo slashed straight across the guard's windpipe with his left hand and a whoosh of hot air exploded from him as his final breath was expelled, blood gushing to replace it. The man dropped to the floor, writhing in the agony of his death throes as his life blood flooded the straw.

Cristoforo ignored him, throwing the second dagger at the other guard, who made to attack him with his sword. The guard was in the middle of an upward sweep with his arm when the hilt of the dagger protruded from his throat. He died instantly, dropping his sword into the straw. A door opened to the side of the stable block as the second ostler walked down the open corridor to the stables, calling out: "*Vito? Che cosa?*"

He got no further. Forest ran into the stable on silent paws and launched herself straight for his throat, crushing his windpipe. The fallen ostler began to plead for his life, but Cristoforo stared down at him without mercy, his teeth clenched in a sneer as he pulled the hidden falchion from the sheath on his back, and slashed the man's throat almost hard enough to decapitate him. The struggle in the stable yard ended and Forest appeared as Cristoforo entered Jamie's stall, her jaws dripping with blood. In a matter of moments he and Mark were released. All was silent save for the occasional stamp of horses' hooves, the munching of hay, the sound of cicadas and the croak of frogs in a discordant chorus – typical sounds of the night in a Mediterranean country.

"Thank 'ee, Cristo," Mark said. "Now what, for they have the ladies?"

"Now we kill them all." Jamie spat, picking up one of the dead man's weapons. "They took my sword and treated me like a common-born pig. No man does that. Bardi is mine." The other two nodded in agreement. He patted Forest. "Well done, my beauty," he said in praise. "First we saddle the horses and the mules, and tie them in the woods behind after we secure all our gear from the carriage."

The three made short work of saddling the animals, finding their equipment and saddles easily to hand, including their war bags. Cristoforo opened his, taking out the greased leather bag and removing his crossbow and quarrels. He clicked the crossbar into place and strung the weapon, looping it by a strap across his back.

"They took the saddle bags," Jamie said. "They will have them securely inside. So be it. Now what to do? We must ensure the safety of Jeanette and Alessandria first," he said, looking from the veranda across the courtyard to the inn beyond.

"They will be held out of sight on the upper level," Cristoforo said, looking to the inn. The sound of drinking and carousing was coming from the main tap room, through the shutters of the lower casements. He hoped everyone would soon be in their cups after their successful capture. A sloping loggia in the Italian style ran along one side of the inn, offering shade to the windows beneath in the heat of the day.

"Marco?" Cristoforo whispered, motioning with his hands. The blond giant nodded in comprehension, flexing his huge shoulders, and stood with his back to one of the supporting posts. He cupped his hands down low and nodded to Cristoforo beneath the flickering light of two brands that burned in sconces set into the wall. With a skip and three quick steps, Cristoforo leapt up to land in Mark's linked hands. As soon as he made contact the giant heaved him upwards, causing Cristoforo to fly and land with a slight grating noise on the tiled roof above. For the first time in many hours, a smile creased his face, as he marvelled yet again at the strength of his friend.

There were six sets of shutters along the wall, closed against the chill night air. He watched patiently, drawing a dagger from his boot, knowing that the noise of his landing would attract attention and curiosity in the quiet of the night. He heard the knock and scrape, as chair legs hit the floor and were pushed back. As he watched a shutter was pushed open, exposing a face within. A man peered outwards, looking to his left, then got no further as a dagger appeared to grow from his chest. In the darkness and from his precarious position, Cristoforo could not afford to miss, so he aimed for the larger target, hoping that the man would not make too much noise. But the man cried out loudly as the dagger lodged home, before slumping forward. Cristoforo did not hesitate, scrambling up to the window. Pushing the man backwards as he did so, he rolled forward into the room across the casement sill. He saw two figures and pulled his falchion ready for use. A female voice met his fighting stance.

"Cristo! By the Lord and all his saints you are well met," Alessandria cried, and went to rush forward, then halted suddenly as a voice called from the stairs below.

"*Pino. Tutto posto?*"

"*Si, non ti preoccuparti,*" Cristoforo responded.

"*Eh, va bene.*"

"*Amori!*" he called to Alessandria, as she flew into his arms asking if he was all right. "Now we must hurry, for there is little time. Jamie and Mark are below and the horses are in the trees to the rear." He helped both women over the sill, and with the aid of a rope thrown up by Mark, belayed them to the edge of the loggia, from which they let themselves down and were caught below. With little time for long explanations, Jamie directed them quickly to the horses and mules, bidding them to await their return.

Cristoforo returned to the window, having carefully seen how the inside of the inn was laid out from his higher vantage point. He whispered from the window. "Nine of the Bardi's men, plus another ten or so. A balcony runs around the rooms and stairs down here." He indicated to just beside the rear door of the inn.

It would provide good cover, Jamie decided. "Target Bardi as soon as you get to the stairs, on a count of ten," he said.

"*Va bene.*" And Cristoforo was gone, moving silently into the room, his crossbow at the ready. Jamie and Mark approached the rear door, pushed it open and slipped in under cover of the stairs, their borrowed swords drawn and at the ready, Forest by their side, now with her war collar on, spikes glinting in the dull torchlight. Jamie finished counting off the numbers, and at the top of the stairs above him he heard a familiar voice cut through the hubbub of talk in the tap room.

"Signor Bardi!" Cristoforo called, and as he did so Jamie, Mark and Forest appeared, striding forward and fanning out to command the room with Forest growling. Silence prevailed and Donato Bardi looked up, as did Luca, making to reach for his sword. "One move, Signor Bardi, and you get the bolt through the heart. Tell your men to leave their swords."

A puzzled look came upon Bardi's face, white with a mixture of anger and fear. "You are Italian? Who are you?"

"Bravo! *Sì*, I am Italian, *cretino*. I am Cristoforo Corio of *Firenze.*" He responded with a flourish, knowing that the Bardi family would too be of Florence and that the Corio name would be known to all of the town.

"Corio? *Assassino? Dio mio!*" he exclaimed.

"Ah, then you were not informed of our names. Who told you we were coming on the road?"

"*I Peruzzi*. A messenger came from England directly through France days ago," he explained. "We were told to look for an English party upon the road with *la contessa*. We were ordered to waylay you and prevent the money from reaching *Il Papi.*"

Jamie did not like the delay. The longer they were exposed to such odds, the greater was the chance of attack. He closed the distance towards Signor Bardi, moving within sword strike while keeping out of line from the crossbow above.

"The coin, Bardi. Where is it?" Jamie demanded, cutting across the man's explanation, knowing he was playing for time.

"Here at my feet, under the table." He nodded at the rough wooden floor.

"Kick it here. All of it," Jamie demanded, aware that this was the moment of greatest risk.

"Why can we not talk?" Bardi stalled, at which point Forest growled low and deep, looking behind Mark. The huge landlord had a club raised from behind the bar ready to strike downwards. Mark span around, sweeping the sword and deflecting the club, then smashed a mighty fist into the side of the man's head, breaking his jaw and dropping him where he stood. But the distraction was enough. Others in the company saw their chance, grabbing stools to throw and drawing weapons. It was just as Jamie had feared. Cristoforo changed his aim and a quarrel soughed through the air, striking Luca dead and throwing him backwards just as he was about to slide a dagger between Jamie's ribs.

Another man struck forward, throwing a stool and drawing his sword. Jamie ducked and lunged up from a crouch, skewering the man through the groin before turning to slash at another's legs.

Mark lashed out at two men close by before they had a chance to draw their daggers, while Forest savaged one and leapt to the next, who tried to stab her throat. The spiked collar saved her and the dog's huge jaws crushed his arm, with the sound of cracking bone.

Cristoforo vaulted over the banister rail and landed lightly below, bringing his bow down onto the head of one man before rushing to the open fireplace, kicking up burning rushes and pulling them back on the tinder-dry floor. Flames licked hungrily at the dry wood and he pulled a brand out of the wall sconce, waving it into one assailant's face before stabbing him with his falchion. The flames caught and all feared fire. The building would become a death trap within seconds. Old rushes spat and took flame with ease, running the fire across the floor to the air currents of the doors and casement openings. Mark reached behind the bar, grabbed a brandy flask and smashed it on the floor. A river of flame flared as the brandy caught alight, dividing the room in half.

Jamie had pierced Bardi in the shoulder and killed two of his remaining men. There were just three of his original meiny left, he calculated, and two were running for their lives towards the door of the inn. All was chaos, as Cristoforo had intended, but the village would be roused as the fire became apparent, and all would be intent upon saving the inn. Then another thought occurred to Jamie. "Mark," he shouted, "to the ladies, take Forest."

To the dog, "Go girl, seek Mark." At which the obedient hound loped off in Mark's wake.

Cristoforo ran to his side, beads of sweat appearing on his forehead, as the flames pushed a wave of heat forward, threatening to engulf them.

"Come, let us take the saddlebags and depart, but kill this *bastardo* before we leave." Cristoforo urged.

Jamie turned to look at Bardi, as the treacherous man stood before him. "You stole holy money, threatened my sister with death, or worse, and took both my sword and my honour. You are a scullion of the worst order."

"No don't kill me please, I beg you for mercy." Bardi wailed.

"Stand and unbuckle my belt and scabbard that you wear." Bardi did so, handing it to Jamie, but with the action he tried to slip the dagger free, letting the belt drop to the floor and lunging with the blade. Jamie saw the move and without a conscious thought deflected it on a vertical guard, then rotated his wrist, to cut down at the arm with all his strength. Bardi screamed as Jamie's dagger fell to the floor, along with the hand that was holding it.

"Crawl on your knees like the dog you are, you duplicitous whoreson." Jamie slashed at Bardi's hamstrings, leaving him crippled as the flames advanced. "For my sister and my honour." He dropped his borrowed sword, picked up his own sword belt and turned with no more thought for the man who had sought to ransom him and his family. As the pair ran out of the mounting inferno, carrying the three saddle bags with them, Jamie heard Bardi scream as the flames engulfed him.

Chapter Twenty-Five

Jamie and Cristoforo ran to the woods behind the stables to find the ladies already mounted, with Mark guarding them, armed again with his faithful quarterstaff. Forest had dealt with the last two brigands who sought to have vengeance wherever they may have found it.

With little ado they re-attached the saddle bags, mounted and led the mules away from the raging inn. The fire had now caught hold of part of the first floor and roof. The village had been roused, and all were intent on saving the inn rather than chasing any strangers.

They walked off into the dark to join the main road south, leading the additional horses from the stables. When they were half a mile out they let them go free, to slow any attempt at following their escape.

"Come, let us put as much distance as we are able between this place of malaperts, should they attempt to seek us out and gain retribution," Jamie advised, at which they broke into a steady lope that would not endanger them or the horses.

They rode on through the night and into the next day,

arriving eventually at the small village of Arese to the north of Milan.

"We shall stay for as long as it takes to arrange for the horses to be re-shod. Richard clanks so, I believe I am followed by an ill-bred minstrel, such is the music he makes when he walks." The others smiled at his jest, for the shoes of all the horses were loose after so many miles of travel and rang tinny and loud upon the cobbles of the street.

"I will go to and source a *maniscalco*." Cristoforo offered when they were settled at an inn. Alessandria offered to attend him, with Jeanette accompanying a few steps behind, keeping up the pretence of propriety. She wished to prepare him as the time drew near to attend upon her father.

"Do you still fear his reaction to my proposal?" Cristoforo asked.

"I do, *amori*, and as the distance shortens my concerns grow. But for all my father may say, I needs must reassure you that I shall remain faithful to my heart, which is safely ensconced with you."

He twisted, looking deeply into the dark pools of her eyes, seeing the wetness of unshed tears there. He took her hand and pressed it to his lips. "Fear not, *cara mia*, we shall prevail," he answered bravely, wanting desperately to believe his words. Alessandria did not respond to his assurance but looked off into the distance, more uncertain than she had been for all of the journey.

They stayed at the small village for two days and left on the 22nd of May with all the horses and mules fully shod. Nine days later, just before the beginning of June, they reached the outskirts of Bologna. It had been hard going over rocky roads and they were relieved to crest the last hill to see below them a natural bowl and the convergence of three rivers, the largest of which was the River Reno, giving life to the valley in which the town was situated. Mark had become a seasoned traveller, inured to the strange sights he had seen on his journey, but as they approached the walled town that formed an almost perfect hexagon, he was in awe. Coming from a slightly elevated position he saw a forest, but not of trees.

"By the good Lord, I see it but yet do not believe what I am seeing, for 'tis a forest of towers. How many? For they be beyond my counting, contessa," he declared, astounded at the sight of so many thin, pointed towers soaring many hundreds of feet up into the sky. Dark javelins of ochre and terracotta pierced the heavens, all vying for dominance. Alessandria smiled at the sight of her adopted city, the image of which was emblazoned upon her mind.

"Once, as a child, I went around with my mother counting them, and we noted one hundred and eighty or so. I know not if there are now more or less. Some lean, you see, at impossible angles." She pointed.

"I do. Why do they build them so?" Mark wanted to know. "For there seems to be plenty of land beneath to build and make new houses."

"Bologna is said to have more citizens than any other city in Italy. It is a seat of great learning, and its rich citizens are all vying for prominence and position. Some build simply because they can afford to, others for reasons of defence. The towers make great defensive positions, like your English castles."

Jamie was interested from a soldier's perspective, seeing the obvious advantages and some disadvantages from such a custom. They moved on, with Mark asking questions, beguiled by what he saw. The sun was starting to sink low into the sky, casting a mellow veil of light over the rooftops, towers and walls. They entered across one of the many bridges over the moat, circumventing the town through the north-eastern gate and riding along the wide streets. All the houses and buildings were edged by long porticos and loggias. The warmth of the day had begun to dissipate, but it left behind hard-baked walls, reflecting the stored heat back upon the travellers. After the fresh air of the mountains, the stuffy, dusty and noisome smells of civilisation invaded their senses, causing them to wrinkle their noses in distaste.

Jamie shook his head. "By the rood, the smells of the town; scitte smells like scitte wherever you go," he declared, pulling up his cloak against the unpleasant odours.

Alessandria was now their guide, moving directly to the centre and the famous Piazza Maggiore that was set as the crown jewel of the city. Upon entering the piazza, the English travellers stopped to better take in what they were seeing, for it was breathtaking.

"Why, look at the white marble and the buildings! It must be all of four-hundred-feet long. This sight will be emblazoned upon my mind forever," Mark whispered in awe.

"Wait until you see *Firenze, amico mio*. For if Bologna is a *principessa*, then *Firenze*, she is a *Regina*," Cristoforo replied.

They pushed forward on horseback out of the square towards the southwestern quarter of the town, winding their way through the pedestrian traffic of the streets. It was busy, and Mark was to learn that this was the time when Italian cities came alive. They came at last to the Piazza Santo Stefano, and here Alessandria hesitated for the first time since returning to Italy. Before her lay the entrance to the building she had once called home after her family were banished from Florence. It was exactly as she remembered it in her mind's eye.

The building fronted the cobbled piazza, rising three stories above them, with a huge archway giving access to the property within. Either side of the main arch a series of lesser arches curved away, supported upon ornate Ionic columns of marble, delicately carved with flying cherubs at the top collar. The walls above were of faded ochre, covered with a patina of age by the blast of the hot Italian sun. Not for her father the ostentation of a tower; here was a building of palatial proportions and elegance.

She looked across at her companions; Jeanette gave her a nod of encouragement, while the glib tongue of Cristoforo was for once silenced. His destiny lay within those walls and he liked it not one iota. "My dear, come, for it shall not be as terrible an ordeal as you suppose," Jeanette said with a smile. "Let us beard the dragon in his lair."

"*Va bene*. Fortitude," Alessandria declared, pushing her tired horse forward.

To the side of the studded oak doors was an ornate iron rod connected to an arm above. Alessandria leant forward and pulled the ring at the bottom. The arm moved up and down, causing a bell to sound within. After a few moments footsteps were heard upon stone flags, and a small portal opened in one of the doors.

"*Si?*" came a voice from within. Alessandria rattled off a fast response in Italian, haughtiness in her voice apparent to the others, even though she spoke in a foreign language. The portal was shut and a lock turned within. A sentry appeared as the massive doors were opened, he bowing low to Alessandria and addressing her formally. She bade the others to follow her into the courtyard within. As soon as they entered they were struck by how cool it was, compared to the heat of the street.

The whole yard was paved in brick set in a herringbone pattern, and a large fountain and trough dominated the centre of the quadrangle. Four palm trees had been planted in the ground, throwing out a generous patch of shade. A loggia of arches surrounded the piazza, with a cool shady veranda set invitingly behind each.

Servants materialised, running forward to take the horses

and mules, with Jamie and Mark holding onto their stallions and following them to the stables in a separate smaller courtyard behind. As Forest padded behind, the grooms were wary. Cristoforo explained that dogs in Italy were for guarding and hunting or both, never as a companion or pet. Most Italians were by and large wary of dogs, particularly one as large as Forest.

Alessandria breathed in the scents and sounds of her childhood that were at once familiar to her. In the noise and frenetic activity, a door opened at the far end of the square, and a figure emerged from the shade.

Count Rafaello di Felicini stepped into the sunlight, poised, elegant and refined. Alessandria saw that he had aged since she had left, five years ago. He still had the same upright posture, but there was a slight stoop to his shoulders, and lines had appeared around his eyes, with small pouches of flesh beneath them. Where once his hair had been jet black now it was heavily flecked with grey, and silvered wings graced his temples. The others could see a strong family resemblance between the two faces. The count squinted: "Alessandria? Is it really you? You have returned, may God be praised, yet why so abruptly and unannounced?"

"*Sí, babo.* Upon that score I shall explain later in full account." At which he opened his arms and Alessandria ran forward into her father's embrace, revelling in the familiar smell of him and the strength of his arms around her. He finally pushed her back to arm's length, so better to see her in more detail.

"My dear, you look more like your mother with every passing year, bless her memory. England is treating you well, I trust? Now come, I prithee, be kind enough to introduce me to your companions." The count walked forward hand-in-hand with his daughter, clearly delighted to see her returned to him.

Alessandria came towards the others with some trepidation, her heart beating. This was the moment she dreaded – the moment when Cristoforo met her father.

"I have the honour to introduce Sir James de Grispere, household knight to his Royal Highness Prince Henry of England." She hesitated, not quite knowing with whom to follow in the introductions. "And these are his two companions in arms, Cristoforo Corio and Mark of Cornwall." She turned to Jeanette, smiling. "This is Jeanette de Grispere, Sir James's sister, who has aided me greatly both as a companion and chaperone, upon what has been a long and perilous journey. May I present my father, il Conte Rafaello degli Felicini?"

The men bowed while Jeanette curtsied in deference to Alessandria's father's rank. The count could not help but glance slightly longer at Cristoforo, more out of suspicion than anything else. There was clearly much that he did not understand. The Corio name was familiar to him, but the count was far too well-mannered to raise any questions of his guest upon such a short acquaintance. He smiled and bade them welcome.

"Sirs, my lady, you are most welcome to my home and I thank you with all my heart for delivering my daughter safely back to me. Please follow me, for you will wish to wash away the stain of travel and refresh yourselves."

The men and the ladies were shown by a servant up a set of stone steps to a garderobe on the first floor, where they washed themselves and changed their clothes. When they were ready, a solicitous servant ushered them through to a large, airy *sala* of dual aspect. The shutters on one side were pulled closed against the sounds and smells of the city, while the opposite wall was open to the fresher air rising from the shaded courtyard below, in which the delicate music of the fountain trickle lifted upwards, like a calming melody. The walls were painted a delicate shade of ochre, and the floor was covered with cool marble tiles. Mark was amazed at the opulence, and as he looked up, he caught his breath. The ceiling was barrel-vaulted and decorated with hand-painted frescos of religious scenes in vibrant blues, reds and golds. The count appeared and beckoned them to a long table situated at one end of the room that bore gold flagons of wine and trays of sweetmeats, with brass finger bowls and white linen napkins.

"Please, I beg of you be seated, avail yourselves of food and drink. Once you are replete, I should love to hear news of England, my brother and your travails upon the road."

Mark helped himself to the plates of food with little encouragement needed, and the others smiled indulgently. Alessandria turned to her father and spoke in French, so that the others could understand, explaining that he was a wrestler to the court and was forever hungry.

"A veritable Hercules, by the rood, for my doorways are barely able to accommodate his shoulders," the count joked, his manners immediately putting Mark at ease. They all sat and the conversation progressed, as they explained all that had happened since leaving England. Jamie pointed to the saddlebags, which had only briefly left his sight during their capture. The three men had hefted them up from the horses personally, not trusting anyone else to handle the riches contained therein. The reason for their presence was now becoming apparent to the count.

"Ah, and you sought to accompany them, knowing you would be safe in their company, *cara*?"

"Just so, father, for there is a price upon my head – indeed all our heads – from the Duke of Burgundy. It was a most propitious moment upon which to travel."

"And yet so few of you. Did Filippo not think to provide you with an escort of greater numbers?" he asked.

"To do so would have attracted attention, and we felt that

stealth, disguise and speed were better allies to our cause. A large meiny would have attracted the duke's spies, and no force short of a full three conrois of knights would have been sufficient unto our needs, to vouchsafe our wellbeing." She defended their perilous journey, cursing herself inwardly for her mention of disguise.

Jamie, seeing the flaw in her argument, interjected.

"We were advised to that course, my lord, and only once upon Italian soil were we given away – and then to the papal levy, not by virtue of the Duke of Burgundy. Afore they died the malaperts confessed all, and it was the Peruzzi in London who suspected our transportation of gold and sought to intercept us. I suspect at the Albizzi's behest. For if I am given to understand correctly, it is they who would foil your family's right to pay the full dues."

"You have the right of it, Sir James, and I am most grateful for both my daughter's safety and that of the levy that you have transported so diligently. You must forgive an old man his manners, as concern causes me to slide towards a curmudgeonly disposition."

The count then turned to Cristoforo, who had said very little the whole time, speaking now in Italian. He took in all of his appearance, noting especially the leather vambraces upon his lower arms that were scarred, scuffed and polished by long use. "And you, sir, whom do you serve? For the name of Corio is familiar to me, and from your accent I believe you to be a citizen of *Firenze*, no?"

"*Si*, count, I am a son of *Firenze*. As to my status, I reside with Thomas de Grispere." Here he winced almost outwardly as Jamie had offered to let him use that position, to increase his status in the eyes of the count. He continued: "I am a king's messenger serving his majesty and the English Court."

Jamie stepped in here to offer his friend further aid,

reaching within his doublet: "I have here our bona fides, naming us as envoys of the crown, and sealed by royal warrant with orders to ensure that the levies reach their destination and a full account be made."

"Ah, just so. I am sure that your papers are in full order and I meant no disrespect in that regard," the count responded, but somehow to Cristoforo's ears, the apology sounded more like a dismissal, and he was only too aware that Alessandria's father was far from satisfied with the explanation of their circumstances.

The meal continued, with the conversation turning to the different topics of London, Alessandra's uncle and the way in which Florence had changed in her absence.

"Do you have any letters for me from Filippo?"

"I do, *babo*, and I will fetch them from my *valigia* once our repast is complete."

The others took Alessandria's hint and excused themselves under various pretexts of rest and needing to check the horses, leaving father and daughter alone.

With the others gone, the count took his daughter's hand and looked into her eyes searchingly. "Now, *cara mia*, tell me the parts that you are missing from this story, for I fear that there is more to tell," he said, the gentle manner presaging a change of mood. Alessandria broke his grasp and rose to better compose herself, the very action forewarning her father that he should expect revelations not to his liking, for he knew his daughter and all her wiles too well.

"Father, when mama died you bade me break free and allowed me leave to find myself at the French Court, *e justo?*"

Her father nodded, saying nothing.

"There, I followed my dreams and met the love of my life, whom I now wish to marry, for he has asked me to be his wife." She let the revelation hang in the air.

"Well, that is providential. *Tante auguri!* Who is this gentle-man? A French noble, mayhap, or one of the royal princes? Is that why you left the French Court under a cloud cast by the Duke of Burgundy?"

"No father, I left because I aided the man who fought for the English Crown and thwarted the siege of Calais alongside Sir James. We were separated, and upon my arrival in England, we formed an attachment that is strong. I love him dearly, for he is everything to me."

"So why does he not arrive with you and ask for your hand in a respectful manner? Surely if he is at least *arte maggiori* that would be most temperate?"

"Father he has arrived, yet I fear he is not *arte maggiori* –"

He cut her off mid-sentence. "Corio? Him? *Mio Dio*, is it he who seeks your hand and your heart? Tell me I am wrong."

"It is indeed, and I would be proud for him to stand beside me as my husband," she replied without a sign of fear, head high and chin jutting forward.

"Is he really a king's messenger, or is that some puff of your imagination? Whom else does he serve? For I know of the family Corio of *Firenze*, and they are not even *arte minori.* They are *contidini,* vagabonds, hired *assassinos* with not a loyal bone in their bodies! Have you forgotten your status or lost your senses? You are a contessa, well-bred and of aristocratic blood. And this...this person...where does he reside when he does not serve the king, eh, eh?"

"*Signor* Corio," she began calmly and icily, eyes wide with anger and glaring at her father, "is indeed a messenger for the king, and has served both his majesty and his son, Prince Henry, on many missions of great import. He was rewarded for saving the realm and for thwarting a rebellion by the Welsh, recognised and honoured by the prince himself in private audience. He also serves Sir Richard Whittington, financier and adviser to the crown – Hah! So here you pause and at last recognise the name? Yes, for you too have heard of him. He who aids Uncle Filippo. Seek reference from him as to Signor Corio's value and deeds if you will." She glowered at him. "Cristoforo also saved the life of Jamie's father and serves him still as a.... steward." She hesitated.

"A steward?" The count's eyes narrowed in disbelief. "In what office or capacity, that of *insidiore*? For he has the mark upon him. I see it, he is dangerous."

"He is, as are Jamie and Mark, for they too carry the marks of such a man. Cristoforo is loyal to me beyond measure, and as such, would give his life in my stead. He is not some courtly fop who would flaunt and praise to little sincerity. He loves me papa, and I him." She pleaded and rose to leave, then swept away on unsteady legs. In a rustle of silk, she hesitated and turned back to her father, full of defiance. "I mean to have him, father, and claim my dowry before the *Parte Guelfa* in *Firenze*, and as such I crave your blessing. Upon the table there are two letters from my uncle. By your leave, father." She curtsied formally, and left him with tears in his eyes and anger in his body, unable to utter a word.

Chapter Twenty-Six

Alessandria came down to supper late, supported by Jeanette. A stilted conversation prevailed throughout the meal, with everyone aware of the undercurrents of tension. Neither Alessandria nor the count knew how to break the impasse. Cristoforo had been apprised by Alessandria of her father's reaction and was afforded no opportunity by the count for a private audience in which to press his suit. The following day all was change.

In the early morning, just after they had broken their fast, Alessandria cursed her father's obduracy to Jeanette. "He will not listen to the reason of my heart. He thinks only of rank and status. He cannot see past a name, disbelieving all I have said as to Cristoforo's standing in the English Court and his employment within your father's household," she stormed.

Her monologue was interrupted by a messenger clattering into the courtyard below on a tired horse, the third that he had worn out on his fast ride from Florence. Alessandria watched as he slid from the horse to land stiff-legged, walking off with a peculiar horseman's gait with which she had become so familiar, having ridden astride for many days on the outward journey. The man was met by her father's steward who, upon seeing the seal enclosing the parchment that he produced, beckoned him forward into the inner sanctum of the palazzo and up to the first floor.

Watching this rare honour bestowed upon a mere messenger, Alessandria was puzzled. "Jeanette, let us return to the *sala*, for there appears to be a messenger lately arrived of sufficient import that he was invited to meet with my father. This is unusual and I suspect presages ill tidings."

Jeanette was bemused, following in her friend's wake with no argument and more than a little curiosity. They rushed down to the *sala*, and only at the last moment steadied their approach to a sedate walk, entering quietly through the western doors. The count was engrossed in reading the document that had been presented to him and did not even look up upon their entry, his brow creased in a deep frown as he re-read part of the missive, not believing his own eyes. He muttered a few half-heard oaths under his breath as he cursed the letter and all who had caused it to be written. "*Dio mio!* How can they do this? Whoreson *contidini!*" He raged, crumpling the letter in his fist.

"Papa, what vexes you so? News from *Firenze*?"

"*Si*, of the most heinous nature. The *Parte Guelfa*, they..." So emotional was he that he could not bring himself to speak the words until after he had taken a few calming breaths. "They have now banished all Alberti from Firenze, including the women and children, even those boys under six and ten years of age. Everyone is banished and their property and assets seized." He sighed, emotionally spent at the news. Alessandria went white with shock and then flew into a rage. It was minutes before she could bring herself to translate the words into English for Jeanette to understand.

"Alessandria, I prithee, would you be kind enough to ask

your companions to attend us here," the count said. "For it is most important that they be apprised of all that has occurred. No, that would be unseemly." At which he turned to his steward. "Be good enough to present my compliments to Sir James and his companions and ask that they attend us here in the *sala* at their earliest convenience."

"Yes, count," the man answered, nodding a brief bow and striding from the room in earnest.

A few moments later, Jamie, Mark and Cristoforo appeared. They were a little mystified at the summons and were invited to sit at the large table.

"I thank you for indulging my request," the count said. "I wish to impart news that I have received from *Firenze*. There are matters of which you should be aware and which may affect your mission to deliver the papal levy.

"This morning I received a missive directly from *Firenze* informing me that by the 12th day of this month of June, all family with the Alberti name, or any connexions thereto, whatever may be their age, be they man, woman or child, will no longer be permitted to abide in the town. All property shall be sequestered and their status mandated. This is the most outrageous circumstance that I could conceive. It is already known that the levy from Filippo in London is en route, and the powers that be would do anything to prevent the arrival of the coin that you carry."

"I prithee why, *babo*? We have done nothing wrong. What charges prescribe such a terrible response?"

"There is much to tell, my child." The count hesitated for the first time, suddenly unsure of himself, smoothing his hand down his chest and exhaling. "I kept this from you, adjuring *Zio* Filippo not to impart the news. In August of last year, your uncle, Bindaccio di Pietro degli Alberti, was beheaded and several other Alberti men condemned to death in absentia for treason to the oligarchy that is the *Parte Guelfa*."

"No! *Zio* Bindaccio? He was the patriarch of my mother's family," Alessandria cried, raising a hand to her mouth in horror at what she had heard.

"There is more. No Alberti can live within two hundred miles of *Firenze*. All this for allegedly conspiring with rebels from Bologna and seeking to bring down the *Signoria*. It is all lies built upon jealousy and to punish us for our friendship with the Medici, who control the pope. They are frightened of your mother's family, and this is a tacit recognition that they prosper still in exile, growing stronger and wealthier with each passing year. Apparently, speakers vied with each other to denounce the Alberti, prescribing terrible penalties, but praise God none were actioned upon."

Anger rose again to the fore in Alessandria's mind. She spoke out loud in front of Cristoforo and her father for the first time, in recognition of her status. "And what of me, father? I am to be married and will not be denied my inheritance, my dowry!"

Her father sighed again. "So be it, my child. I bless your union and you must go and claim what is rightfully yours." Turning to Cristoforo he said, "Signor Corio, I grant my blessing upon your marriage to my daughter, but with fair warning. Should you harm her or cause her hurt may God have mercy upon your soul, for I shall not. *Va bene*?"

Cristoforo rose, his face solemn and unreadable. "Count, I most dearly thank you for your blessing, and upon my honour I swear that I shall cherish her as no other woman has been cherished before. To me she is a pearl beyond measure, a set piece in my heart like no other. I pledge her safety and her happiness upon my honour, which is sacrosanct." At which he bowed slightly to the count and smiled at Alessandria. The whole room was silent, for none dared to break the spell that had been cast upon all assembled at the table.

Jamie was the first to speak. "Then by your leave, my lord count, I would ask your permission to depart immediately and venture forth to the lion's den of Florence, for there our destiny lies and that of your daughter, together with the salvation of the English realm."

"By all means, Sir James, yet I would have some final moments with my daughter ere you depart." Once the others had left the *sala* to pack their belongings, the count turned back to face Alessandria, taking her hand: "My dear, I truly give you my blessing. For I would not divide our house still further and compound the actions of the whoreson Albizzi and whatever devilry they are now seeking. Yet I have two further matters that require answers from you: Are you truly certain of Cristoforo's love and commitment to you, and are you sure that he does not seek to enhance himself and his house by virtue of an alliance with you?"

"Father, you must believe me. He has proved himself time and again, and his word is greater in honour than many of a more noble cast. His devotion to me and his friends is without parallel and surmounts all opposition. I feel safe with him, for he will guard me well as he does his master in London."

"I am of a perfervid disposition towards your safety and happiness and pray that you are sapient in this regard. To wit shall you be safe with them alone? Should I not order more of my mesnie to attend you, for they are but three?"

"Father, have no fear on that account. For with those three, we could storm *Firenze* and take it. They are fierce in battle and without equal."

"So be it."

"Your second matter? For you declared two subjects upon which you required an answer."

"Shall you stay in Italy, and where will you wed?"

"I have no answer to this question and I know not where we shall live. My soul belongs in Florence, but that is not possible whilst the *Parte Guelfa* rule on such harsh terms. Cristoforo can live there, but can I? Must I watch our property, our family, everything, torn from us? It is beyond anything imaginable. I know not." She sighed, opening her arms wide and shrugging.

"Will you then see me before you leave, or wed here in our home if you may?" he pleaded.

"I will father, that I promise you." At this, the door to the *sala* opened revealing Jeanette; she beckoned to Alessandria. The count released his daughter who ran from the room to change into travelling clothes.

An hour later they stood in the courtyard with the others, mounted and ready. She embraced her father one last time and moved to her horse, to be aided by a groom in mounting.

"May you go with God and do His work to save His Holiness from the lure of the Albizzi."

Once mounted they made their farewells; both Richard and Breseler pranced and shied, jockeying for position after two days with no exercise. With their legs clamped to the horses' flanks, Jamie and Mark controlled their mounts, pushing them forward to the arched gateway, the shoes echoing around the courtyard. Alessandria turned one last time with tears in her eyes, and blew a kiss back to her father.

PART III

SUMMER

Florence and the Way Home

Chapter Twenty-Seven

Florence

The party of five made the journey easily in two days, arriving on the outskirts of Florence to find the city baking in the heat of early June as the full summer sun was beginning to bathe the countryside in a curious lemon veil, making the small lakes surrounding the city gleam and shimmer.

A natural basin was before them, with the outlying marshes playing host to mosquitos and birds, many of which were unknown to the Englishmen. Swallows and swifts swooped on the insect feast laid out before them in a never-ending dance of greed, recharging themselves after their long return from Africa. The whole panoply was verdant with rich colour, furnished by the plentiful supply of water.

Forest did not like the heat and sought shade wherever she could, her long tongue lolling sideways from her mouth as she panted feverishly. Flies buzzed at the horses, irritating them. Cristoforo had made a foul-smelling vinegar-based concoction which kept most at bay, but the horses' tails swished and their heads nodded in discomfort as they fought a never-ending battle with the annoying insects.

"Alright girl, we shall soon be in the shade of the town walls," Jamie said, looking down at Forest.

They carried on, keeping the horses to a walk, passing between two knolls, and there before them lay the great city. Approaching from the north, they did not need to cross the mighty River Arno that wended its way over the plain and bisected the town as it met with the River Mugnone. The city was completely enclosed by walls, broken by dozens of castellated watch towers along its length, and by large gates and bridges that crossed the many waterways that protected the citizens within.

It was unreal to the Englishmen's eyes; a jewel-encrusted diadem sparkling with reds, ochres, greys and faded yellows blinking in the fierce unremitting sunlight. As with Bologna, towers vied for prominence, but there were not so many here, and they were shorter. Domes of various churches were far more prevalent, effulgent orbs of bright terracotta.

As they approached the main northern gate, they saw that small hamlets had been spawned by the great town's presence outside the walls where the city had been unable to meet the need for more space and more homes for the burgeoning population. Already, the evidence of human existence assaulted their olfactory senses, causing the men to pull their cowls about their mouths and the women their veils.

"It will get worse once we enter the town. I had forgotten how bad it is," Cristoforo remarked with distaste. Unlike London, the only city in Europe to have proper sewers and piped water, Florence was a nightmare of disease and noxious effluence, all of which was exacerbated by the heat.

"By the rood 'tis a fair town, Cristo," Jamie said, "and seems most engaged in trade. Did the Black Death not reach here?"

"That she did, with terrible results, for the town is ill disposed towards cleanliness and the hazards of disease are great, as you will soon observe. Yet, *Firenze*, she is a resilient mistress and suffers not for long any downturn in her fortunes. She now holds her place as the capital of Italy," Cristoforo replied, wincing as the smell became stronger. "All the *arte maggiori* will be leaving the town soon during the summer months for the mountains and its cleaner, sweeter air. They will leave the poor to struggle with the heat and the odours."

They pressed on through swampy areas and clusters of outlying buildings towards the main gates, where they were stopped by the guard, who eyed the manner of foreign dress upon the English contingent. With Cristoforo as his translator, Jamie offered his bona fides signed by the king of England and passed through the gates, but their arrival was duly noted by the guards.

"News of our arrival will be with the Albizzi within the hour. My dear friends, you must beware, for as perilous as London can sometimes be, this is much worse," Cristoforo observed. "Here, they will smile and rob you of your life for reasons that you will never live to fathom. I adjure you most strongly to be on your guard, for this is the world of the dagger and the covert assassin. Few will face you openly and each alley may hold peril. You are marked as friends of the Alberti and the Medici by virtue of your mission, and any way that may be employed to prevent you from delivering the papal levy will be used.

"For this is a war, a war for power as great as any that you have encountered before. Within these walls lies the crux of all Christianity and the power to wield great influence across the leading courts of Europe, for whomsoever controls the papacy controls the Christian world."

Rarely had Jamie and Mark seen Cristoforo so serious. Having returned to his native land he seemed a different person, more watchful and suspicious, sensing threat at every juncture and around every corner. The other two men sensed it as well, for it was not all their imagination that, despite the cosmopolitan nature of the capital, they felt very foreign and were marked as such. The mood was palpably darker, despite the light of the sun. It felt to Jamie somehow conspiratorial and cabbalistic. The streets were awash with citizens and many beggars lined the pavements, which he commented upon to Cristoforo.

"*Si*, it is known by many as the city of beggars, survivors of the plague with nothing left but to call upon the mercy of those better off. We have many thousands of them here in *Firenze*. The *Commune* does what it can to help, but..." He shrugged, as though it were perfectly natural and there was little he could do.

As they pushed forward towards the centre, the streets on either side crowded together to form dark passages that never saw the light of day, so densely packed was the town. Apart from the darkened alleys it was a mass of colours, contrasts, noise and stench. Continual building work was being carried out, with seemingly new storeys and cantilevered levels being constructed and balanced as if on thin air, as everyone strove for a place in this cosmopolitan centre. They finally arrived at an open L-shaped piazza huge in its expanse, where a bustling market was in progress.

Alessandria smiled, for here the light of the sun prevailed and it was an amazing sight. "This," she began, the emotion heavy in her voice as she almost broke into a sob, "is the heart of my city, the *del Signoria.*" Alessandria cast her arm expansively in front of her body, as though showing off a private salon in her own home. The huge square lay before them with a mix of architecture, from Roman to Renaissance. It was a sight to behold of loggias, porticos and varying colours, with every shade of pastel in evidence.

Mark, ever observant to new sights and images, looked across to a magnificent church that culminated in a dominant tower. "That tower is open to the elements. Why is it not finished, for it would be magnificent by its size? By God's grace, I've never seen the like. Are there not funds to finish such a building?" he asked of Cristoforo.

"Ha, the *duomo*? *Si*, it is the Cattedrale di Santa Maria del Fiore, and there are indeed funds, yet no one can agree on how to finish it. For it is a puzzle, and in its sheer size lies the problem. Such is the span across that no mathematician, architect or mason can agree on how it may be completed. For over 30 years, since 1382, the *cattedrale* has been finished in all but the *duomo*, yet still she lies without a roof. It is a shame that lies upon the town. One day, *magari*, it will be done."

Mark shook his head in disbelief and asked more questions as they moved out of the square, heading through more streets directly south towards the River Arno on the Via Flesolana, before reaching the Via de Benci and the wealthy quadrant of the city. There was a huge drainage ditch to one side and here, at the junction with the Borgo Santa Croce, stood a lovely church with an imposing tower on the opposite side of the street. Unusually, it had been built as a perfect polygon, with the rest of the building extending back into a vee that fronted both streets. It was a huge building that dwarfed all around it. An extended loggia shaded the entrance doors, with a double guard in evidence. Both men looked suspiciously at the mounted party, hands reaching for weapons.

Alessandria hailed them in a haughty manner that befitted a contessa declaring her identity, at which they snapped to attention and one came forward to aid her, calling for grooms and servants from within.

Chapter Twenty-Eight

Westminster, England: 11th June

King Henry was in a ruminative mood. All was proceeding as planned so far, and the last remaining piece of the puzzle lay with Brittany. The king was surrounded by his close advisers, and his eldest son, Prince Henry, had lately returned from Coventry to appear before his father and sign the latest treaty with the Flemish.

"Sire, you appear in good humour," Prince Hal said. "What has provisioned you with such solace?"

"The Flemish have agreed to our terms, with an extension of the truce in our favour for a further five years. We now have secure and safe trade routes to Flanders and beyond. It is a wonder that they acceded, given that their overlord is the cursed Duke of Burgundy."

"Amen to that, sire. What news of Brittany? For if we are to assail France, Brittany or nearby would provide the most vantageous aspect for such a landing of troops, and I would not wish my brother to be attacked on two fronts and imperilled once on French soil," Prince Hal offered, looking towards his brother, who had the grace to nod his head in agreement at what the prince was suggesting.

The others looked on, delighted with the accord that finally seemed to be developing between the king and his sons. "We believe that the agreement reached in April will be upheld by John of Brittany, and recent embassies would seem to suggest that all will be well for our invasion in July."

"As you say, majesty." The prince agreed and came forward to place his signature on the treaty beside that of his father, followed by Thomas and others. Once Prince Hal's signature had been witnessed, he bowed to his father.

"By your leave, sire, we needs must attend to matters at Coldharbour and would beg your forbearance."

"As you wish, my son. We should like to have an audience with you ere you depart for the north."

For certes, my lord king." Prince Henry acquiesced. With his meiny of Courtney, Arundel, Bishop Beaufort and others, he bowed again and backed away from the throne.

Once he had left the chamber, Archbishop Arundel commented to the king: "Sire, 'tis with God's blessing that I am joyed to see you reconciled with His Royal Highness, for all comes into alignment for the future of the realm."

"We wish that we shared your optimism in that accord, for still we hear of discord being sown abroad, and upon the tale is ever pinned the name of Prince Hal. We worry to wake one day and find on the horizon a new impediment to our crown riding forth from the north, led by a wayward prince determined on an early ascension to the throne," King Henry said, a sad look etched upon his lined and sagging features.

"My lord, I do not fear such an event, and would advise as well, if I may, that should you seek anyone covetous of the crown 'twould serve well to look further afield, yet still of the blood royal."

"Enough, my lord archbishop, we shall countenance no more in that regard, but count our blessings that the day of our conquest of France and the return of our due lands draws ever nearer." Archbishop Arundel remained silent and bowed in compliance to the king's wishes.

Prince Henry strode along the corridor, not trusting himself to speak out loud, and ordered a royal barge be made ready for the trip downriver to his manor at Coldharbour, where he would feel safe to discourse openly without fear of being overheard.

Boarding the vessel, he retained a steely demeanour as two men-at-arms stood guard, with just the Earl of Arundel and Richard Courtney in attendance. Bishop Beaufort had made his excuses and retired to his chambers within the palace. The sawing of the barge, the gentle sloshing of oars and a warm and gentle breeze that drifted across the river did much to lift the prince's mood. He let his mind and vision drift, staring into the middle distance and focusing upon nothing in particular as all around him left him undisturbed, understanding his need for silence and contemplation.

Once the royal barge had docked at the quayside of Cold-harbour, the prince jumped ashore and strode purposefully into the building, calling for his clerks to attend him. He went up to his private quarters and began dictating letters to the Earl of Warwick, amongst others, who was now stationed as the garrison commander of Calais.

The prince spent a good deal of time setting his affairs in order, and upon signing and sealing the last letter, he heard the bell toll, signifying the beginning of Vespers.

"By the rood, I have a splitting pain behind my eyes," he complained, rubbing his temples and flexing his powerful neck muscles. "Come, enough for today." At which he bade his clerks farewell and trotted down the stairs to the large general hall below. There he found his companions, including the Earl of Arundel and Richard Courtney, at their leisure with a goblet of wine in hand, awaiting the prince's arrival.

"Gentlemen, the evening awaits. Enough of this pageant, for we have need of drollery, a good wench and wine," he declared. All returned to their rooms in readiness for the night's festivities and the earl removed a red silk scarf from his window that overlooked the river. Thus roused, they rallied and left a few minutes afterwards for the stews of London.

An hour or so later, a well-dressed courtier appeared by wherry upon the dock of the mansion, and with his bona fides produced, begged admittance. The sole guard answered him gruffly.

"No, sir. For none may enter with merit or no in my lord of Arundel's absence. Should you wish a private audience with his lordship I would venture the Ragged Staff would better suit your needs," the guard joked.

"Hah! 'Twas ever thus with his grace." The courtier rolled his eyes in sympathy. "Yet you would serve me well by delivering this missive within and placing it where his lordship shall find it."

"As you wish, sir," the guard offered. "The trestle contains all correspondence and your missive will be found by his lordship on his return. I shall ensure that it is received."

With that the lone guard entered the building, shutting the door to the quay and going within. In that moment, the courtier slipped westwards along the dock towards the large turret that fronted the river and curved around to the wall that faced the street, where a stout wicket of oak, reinforced with studs and bars, was set into the turret wall. The gate was normally locked from the inside, but the courtier found that it gave inward upon a hard shove, permitting him access. He slipped in and closed the gate, barring it from the inside.

The courtier had been advised of the layout of the manor. With the prince abroad no guards were in evidence, and he found his way with little effort to the prince's quarters. Once inside the chambers he lit a small candle and familiarised himself with the room, before making his way to the garderobe, which was linked to a chute that dropped to the river below. A separate door sealed this from the dressing area, and beyond that the sleeping chamber of the prince. Large, linen cupboards lined the walls of the dressing area and it was here that the intruder concealed himself to wait for the prince's return. Three hours later, he heard carousing from the corridor outside. The song was a well-known bawdy verse, and out-of-tune voices joined with the chorus.

"We bid thee goodnight, my companions. This lady shall keep me warm whilst you serve elsewhere," the prince joked, as the shrill laughter of a woman pierced the air.

Another sober voice questioned, "Shall you need me further tonight, sire?"

"We may be in our cups, Claud, yet we doubt that your efforts will aid our cause in any further way," the prince answered. The woman who clung to him pushed back her yellow hood and offered a throaty chuckle. "For we have another servant here who will, we are persuaded, be seemlier when she disrobes than your good self."

The servant bade the prince goodnight, and as the drunken voices disappeared into other rooms, the prince's chamber fell silent but for the rustle of silk and some female laughter, as the unknown woman began to live up to the prince's confidence. Candles had been lit since the visitor had hidden himself, and as he stealthily left his hiding place, their flickering light outlined two figures outlined upon the bed. He had heard the passionate cries of the woman in the throes of ecstasy and waited until all movement had subsided.

The scene before him was one of chaos. Clothes were strewn about the bedchamber including, he noted, a yellow hood and cloak lying in a heap, made plain enough by the dim light thrown by the two candles. *So the woman is a whore,* he thought. *So be it, for I shall have no scruple in that regard and both lives shall be forfeit.*

On silent feet, he slipped across the floor of the chamber to the bedside, his unsheathed dagger raised to strike. Two forms were visible between the half-drawn hangings of the bed. He moved to thrust, then saw to his horror an arm snake across the prince's supine form, delving beneath the rumpled sheets that covered Prince Hal, as a new moan emitted from his mouth. The assassin hesitated for a few seconds and then chose to strike the woman first, as her body slid over that of the prince, protecting him from the knife.

The dagger caught her at the kidneys, stopping all possibility of her crying out. Only a faint yelp was emitted, such was the extreme pain; her back arched, thrusting her hips involuntarily against the semi-conscious prince. The assassin pulled back the dagger for the next strike, but all was now amiss as the prince's eyes flashed open, aware that not all was well. He raged in anger at the assault, pushing the dying woman at the attacker and rolling off the bed, dragging a bolster with him.

Prince Hal continued the roll and came upright on his feet, the bed between him and the assassin. He swept downward with the bolster as if it were a mace, causing a reflex action in the man, who brought up his arm and flinched, only to find hot wax landing on his face as the prince threw a candle at him. It was all the time that Prince Hal needed.

Unheeding of his nakedness, he dived forward for the dagger hand, seizing the wrist in a grip of iron. The assassin's instinct was to pull back his knife hand. The prince went with him, driving the arm backwards, rolling with the man across the mattress. In a perfect wrestling move the prince continued the movement, wrapping his left arm around the man's neck, and pinning the right arm holding the dagger to his side. The prince applied pressure across his assailant's neck with the headlock and squeezed hard, linking his left hand with his right arm, cutting off the assassin's blood as well as his breath. The man grunted in pain, as black spots swam before his eyes from lack of oxygen. The prince, with great experience gained from the wrestling ring, knew what would happen next. His opponent began to thrash around in one final, futile attempt to free himself.

The odds were stacked against the attacker. The prince was immensely strong, with corded muscle built from long use of weapons. He pressed harder into his assailant's neck with the bony part of his forearm, cutting deeper into the larynx. Within seconds the man's movements became weaker, until he lay limply in the prince's locked arms as his consciousness left him.

The prince called out: "Ho, guards! Guards, come to, we are attacked!"

Within a few seconds a sergeant-at-arms burst in, followed by another soldier, their swords drawn. "See to this man. Keep him alive, mind, alive – do you hear?"

"Yes, sire." The sergeant acknowledged, rushing forward to bind the prisoner who was beginning to moan as consciousness returned.

The Earl of Arundel appeared, sword in hand, in a state of undress. He looked aghast at the scene before him, not giving credence to what his eyes were telling him.

"Christ on the Cross, sire, are you harmed? I will kill the cur," he pronounced striding forward, sword raised to end the assassin's life.

"Stay your sword, Arundel!" the prince commanded, fully composed. "We would know who ordered this attack. Keep him alive, do you hear us? Have him bound and locked securely for the night. In the morning we shall attend his majesty, with no news of this to be spoken. Mark the faces around him, for I wish to see who appears surprised at my presence. In the meantime, we ask that none of this be spread abroad. For if this attack were to come to light, it would throw dissent and rumour upon an already uncertain tide of turmoil. We are not safe here, and we shall depart for the north before the morrow's eve.

"Have the house searched and make sure no more malaperts are lying in wait for us. Arundel, that duty lies with you. Find for us who schemed for our death, but keep them alive to give witness, do you hear us?"

"My lord prince, as you bid. To the cellars with him, sergeant. My prince, I would know this night who was responsible, and I could not sleep with this unknown. The truth will out for certes. Not dead, nor crippled, my prince, but answerable as you decree, and by your leave I shall set to."

The prince turned back, to look upon the lifeless form of the woman who had moments earlier been warming his bed, and who was now lying dead before him, tainting the room with the sickly, coppery tang of blood rather than passion. "Hell's teeth, what a coil," he said, "and she an innocent caught in our intrigue, despoiled and soon forgotten as many on the field of battle. For at this moment it feels thus, a battle for the crown.

"To whom should we turn for safety? For we like not this viper's nest in which we now reside. I fear the court will be as tangled as these sodden sheets, and just as cursed with blood." Then he had it. "Michael," he called his steward who was awaiting his orders in silence. "Order a carriage, no hue and cry mind, quietly, and no outriders, for we must slip away in silence."

"Where do you go, my prince, at such a perilous moment?" Arundel asked. "Do you leave for the north this moment?"

A mirthless smile broke out on the prince's lips as he shook his head, to remove the last traces of his earlier drinking from his mind. "Why no, I depart for Milton Street and Sir Richard Whittington's residence. For he is true to our cause, and none will seek us there."

Arundel nodded and turned, to follow the guard escorting the prisoner down to the cellars below. The solid wooden door was pushed back, and the prisoner thrust inside, where he tripped and fell hard upon his bound arms. The cellar smelled badly of damp and mildew, lying as it did at the level of the river outside. Rank puddles, bordered by green slime, covered the floor and mildew appeared upon the thick walls, despite being covered by pitch without. The sergeant-at-arms pulled the victim roughly upright and sat him upon a tall stool, tying his legs to the front feet. The would-be assassin's head lolled, his eyes still glazed.

"Now scullion dog, talk," Arundel demanded. "Who sent you on this treasonous task? Tell me and your life shall be spared, and your sentence shall be but banishment from the realm."

The man before him spoke in well-bred tones of the court. "My Lord Arundel, you know whom I serve. I –"

The earl's fist crashed into his jaw, preventing any further speech. "Don't lie to me, losenger. Get a barrel here of poor wine, for only such is good enough for this whoreson," he ordered the guard. "And bring an axe."

The sergeant moved to comply, rolling a full barrel of wine from the corner of the room, bouncing it down a wooden pallet that prevented the barrels from being contaminated by river water. He manhandled it upright near the victim and proceeded to break the end of the barrel with a small axe.

"Now messire, we invite you to join us in a celebration of your iniquity." The earl growled, grabbing the man's hair and forcing his face into the red liquid. The man spluttered, and bubbles of air left his mouth as he shook his head in protest. He came up gasping for air, half drowned.

"Well? Is your tongue loose now? Who sent you on the murderous trade?"

"I...I told you." He coughed. "My lord, have mercy, for you know whom it was that paid me to do his service." The man spluttered again.

"Still you lie. So we go again, for *in vino veritas*." The earl laughed at his own joke. "Sergeant, fetch me more rope that I might bind his head tightly. The prince said he was to be unmarked and visibly unbroken, and so be it, but there are many ways to break a man unmarked."

The sergeant looked on warily but did as he had been bidden, for no one disobeyed the Earl of Arundel. As the soldier made to leave, he looked once more through the bars of the door to see the earl readying himself to plunge the victim's head once more into the barrel.

When the luckless sergeant returned, he looked once more through the gridded door and saw the earl trying to slap the limp figure before him into life. "By the rood his heart gave out, or mayhap his lungs. For he is, as you see, dead and useless to our cause."

"Will not the prince be angry at such a turn of events?" the sergeant asked, worry evident in his voice.

"I will bear the prince's ire. Deal with the body quietly in the river. Cut his bonds and he will appear to have died a natural death by drowning."

The earl went out whistling to himself, leaving the soldier

to deal with the body. As the sergeant cut the victim's bonds, the victim fell to the floor sideways, wine seeping from his mouth. The sergeant was experienced in such matters, having fought at sea and abroad, and was curious. He had saved companions in arms from drowning and knew what to do. This body was beyond redemption however, and the man beyond saving. He pushed upon the man's chest, and was rewarded with a jet of red liquid that shot from his mouth. He continued the exercise for a few minutes, and still more fluid left the prisoner's body. "Lungs and heart my arse," the old soldier grumbled. "He drowned him as sure as Saracens be heathens."

Chapter Twenty-Nine

Florence

The Alberti Tower on Borgo Santa Croce acted as the headquarters of the Alberti family. It was now in turmoil, added to by the unexpected appearance of Alessandria and her company. The day after their arrival in the city, they took supper at a table that was full of food and surrounded by noise. Even Mark, who had grown up amongst a large family, was surprised at the informality, the constant flow of conversation and the lively company. Cristoforo and Alessandria found it tiring to continually translate and even Jamie, who thought he had picked up a good grasp of Italian on his long journey, found it difficult to follow the conversation, such was the speed of the dialogue and the thick local dialect, although he was tuning in very quickly and learning fast.

"Wait, what did she say? That there were to be more petitions for dowries? Did I understand correctly?"

"You did, Jamie, bravo," Alessandria replied. "There will be four petitions including mine, which will aid our suit, and all shall be laid before the *Parte Guelfa* simultaneously. My cousin, Margherita di Nerozzo, who sits her with us, is to marry Rosso di Strozza Strozzi, and Catrina d'Albertaccio and Maria Antonio will make applications of their own."

"And you say," Mark interrupted, ever curious, "that even when married the lady keeps her maiden name, but the children take their father's? Does that not lead to confusion?"

"No, we all understand, for this is Italy!" Alessandria declared with a grin.

"Why, the names alone are enough to twist my tongue without the need for further confusion." Mark joked, shaking his head.

The banter continued with much laughter until the tables were finally cleared at midnight, the diners keeping much later hours than England in deference to the heat. Jamie, Mark and Cristoforo left to walk in the small, internal courtyard that formed the centre of the palazzo.

"Can we visit the papal palace and deliver the florins on the morrow?" Jamie asked.

"*Si*, we have an appointment for mid-morning to attend His Holiness and there we shall be able to fulfil our duty," Cristoforo replied.

"By the rood, I shall be right glad of it, for the weight of responsibility weighs heavier upon me than any coin, I'll warrant. Once done we can then aid you in any way ere we depart for England's shores again."

"Aye, and I give thanks for helping me to arrive back home."

"Thanks? Why no, for the boot is upon the other foot. Without your aid we should still be locked in some cell to the north of Milan awaiting ransom," Jamie said.

"Still I have concerns that we may be attacked, so be upon your especial guard, for the morrow may bring new dangers." Cristoforo warned. "Our mission will then be known to all, and the Alberti have many enemies here."

The following day, the three men strode through the streets as the town began to come alive. It was but a short distance to the palazzo that housed the pope when he was in residence in Florence and they had decided to walk. The sun was not yet at its zenith, and slanted in from the southeast, casting long shadows among the towers and domes of the medieval cityscape. The heat was at least bearable.

Cristoforo knew from long memory where to go, for it was on these streets that he had grown up, despite his family owning a farm outside the city walls close to the town. "'Twas here that I learnt the art of deception to see if I could creep up unsuspectingly upon my victim, watched by my father to gauge my success. Sometimes he would plant a knowing victim to test me or my brother further." He smiled at the memory.

Mark, as the strongest of them, had been given the duty of carrying the saddlebags and was sandwiched between the two men, with Cristoforo at the front and Jamie at the rear. Cristoforo continued his recollections, pointing out churches and famous landmarks from his youth on the way, as they walked along the main throughfare heading towards the palazzo. Carts were being brought to fill up trade stands that offered everything one could imagine. Fruits, spices, leather goods, cloth, silks – the list was seemingly endless. The way was often blocked as throngs of people came up against carts that were lodged in the street.

Before them there were cries of anguish and anger, as a fight broke out between two carters. A hand cart containing apples was overturned, with the bright, shiny fruit rolling across the cobbles of the street. Keen to seek any advantage, the locals surged forward, grabbing at the fruit before the luckless trader or his apprentice could scold them and retrieve their wares.

The pitch of the noise rose, bringing with it chaos. All foot traffic was halted, and Cristoforo looked back to make sure he had not been separated from his friends in the confusion. He was immediately suspicious, fearing another ambush like the one that had occurred upon the road. Yet all was well. Jamie was only too well aware of their disadvantaged state, and thanks to Cristoforo's many warnings, he had backed up to Mark so both men faced outwards, daggers drawn, with no prospect of them being caught unawares.

The local militia were called, the fight broken up and order restored. In another two hundred yards they turned into the Piazza Santa Maria Novella, where the spectacular papal palace lay in the centre of green lawns that were cast about a graceful fountain, gushing life-giving water into an arid desert of marble, arches and porticos. This was the leading church in Florence; home to the pope when he was in residence. The frontage was of white-and-green inlaid marble, and a huge edifice rose to a dramatic bell tower above that dominated the square.

"Magnificent," Jamie whispered. "Upon every new street we seem to discover another marvel as the curtains of stone fold back to reveal more grandeur."

"*Si*, and here is the greatest irony, for the Albertis were among the leading patrons who funded the building and the marbling. And now they are banished. Ha, the irony." Cristoforo shook his head in disgust.

They moved off towards the extravagant buildings to the left of the church, where the formal entrance was guarded by two elegantly clad soldiers armed with halberds in the traditional manner. Cristoforo made the announcements, and a sergeant-at-arms arrived to check Jamie's bona fides, clearly impressed by the Royal Seal of England. They were ushered through to a large, cool vestibule decorated with elaborate frescos. More guards were present and at the rear to one side of a spectacular marble staircase was a large desk, where sat two clerks to the court of the papal administration. The royal warrant was presented by the sergeant, at which the clerks, with a certain amount of interest, stamped the document, and asked that Jamie alone ascend the staircase and await an audience with the pope or one of his senior cardinals.

"The meaning is clear, *amico mio*, the *cardinale* will speak English. Yet I adjure you, have a care and ensure all is documented, for not everything is as it seems, even here in the papal *palazzo*," said Cristoforo.

Jamie nodded and lifted the three heavy saddlebags off Mark's shoulders. He was ordered to leave his sword belt and dagger below in the care of his friends, as no weapons were allowed in the presence of His Holiness.

Jamie climbed the steps to the first level and turned to the left, as he had been directed. Here a single guard showed him through to an ante chamber, opening the double doors to permit him entrance. From within came a babble of voices in Italian; it seemed he was not the only one to have an audience with the pope this day. The room was long and barrel-vaulted, echoing all sounds and magnifying them disproportionately. Along one wall was a line of windows, unusually glazed, and shaded by shutters that were thrown back to reveal the late morning sun, adding to the temperature of the room which was already becoming very warm. There were seats set about the floor and proceeding to one of these, Jamie unshouldered the bags of coin and looked about, to assess his fellow papal attendees.

There were three groups, two clearly of churchmen, one of whom nodded to Jamie in greeting and continued a conversation with his elderly companion who bore the robes and hat of a cardinal's office. Two other churchmen were deep in conversation and a third party comprised a single man – a wealthy merchant by his dress – who paced the floor in impatience, clearly put out at having to wait for his audience. A table bore light refreshments of bread and watered wine, together with ornate goblets. Jamie moved towards it, keeping a wary eye on the saddlebags, and poured a draught of white wine. He noticed that the chamber had five doors – the set through which he had entered and two doors at either end, placed equidistantly apart. One of these now opened to emit another party of churchmen, while the other also opened to show a deacon, who read from a list, calling the episcopal party forward for their audience. The lone figure pacing the floor paused to raise his hands in frustration and swore under his breath.

Time passed slowly after the episcopal group exited the inner sanctum. The second group of churchmen entered, leaving Jamie and the lone merchant. At this point, another of the doors opened from the far end of the chamber and two figures entered, well-dressed and clearly natives of Florence by their accents. As a merchant's son who had travelled around England and Europe with his father before the age of ten, Jamie was always interested in cloth and clothes. These men wore silk sendalls of an excellent quality and carried light cloaks over their arms, more for fashion and status than of necessity, he reasoned. Both nodded to Jamie and the impatient merchant, who gave them a curt nod, apparently of recognition. They went to the table and helped themselves to wine, and as Jamie watched them sip from the goblets he saw something odd at their wrists – leather vambraces like Cristoforo wore. Jamie wondered if this was the fashion in Florence, or whether it might be something more sinister. He was not given time to consider their apparel further, for at this point the end door opened; the previous party left, and the roving merchant threw up his hands as his name was called. He muttered a frustrated "*finalmente!*" and strode for the door, leaving Jamie alone with the two newcomers.

Their thirst quenched, the two men sauntered over, seemingly keen to engage Jamie in conversation, one hanging slightly back and appearing nonthreatening. They smiled and spoke in Italian, yet something felt wrong, here alone with these men, although they were seemingly unarmed, as was he. Maybe it had been their unheralded entrance or their over-friendly manner.

Jamie responded, "Slower please, for I am new to the language and you speak very quickly."

"Ah you are a foreigner? English perhaps?" the man continued, slowing down his speech. "Or French? Do you know any French, Iacopo?" he asked, turning back to address his companion with a smile, arms harmlessly tucked within his cloak as muff. The companion shrugged and shook his head, and as the speaker turned back to face Jamie he increased his speed, flicking out the cloak, aiming at Jamie's eyes in distraction and producing a dagger from within the folds of velvet with a blur of his right hand.

The move was fast and well-practised, the cloak floating out as rete of a retiarius of old, the weights stitched into the seams lending ballast to the throw, as the man flung it at Jamie's face. Jamie knew that distance was everything in a dagger fight and controlled the centre line of attack. He had realised an attack was coming as soon as he saw the Italian accelerate, and that he would need distance. He took a step back on his right leg, giving himself a fighting stance that ensured his attacker had to advance to within striking distance.

Jamie was aware that he was unarmed against one, potentially two, armed opponents, and he knew that he would not emerge unscathed. It was just a question of how badly, and if he could gain the upper hand. The dagger thrust came close upon the heel of the cloak, preceded by a step to close the distance to just beyond his reach. Jamie kept his hands low. He knew that Italian rondel daggers, although they possessed three tines down the length of the blade, were not sharpened, and the point was the main offensive element. The point of this dagger licked out in a thrust for his stomach, deadly and fast and inside the middle line, but the action was committed and that was what Jamie needed.

He brought his left arm down straight to intercept, feeling as much as seeing his forearm meet that of his attacker. With that he sawed down and over, bringing his hand around and trapping his assailant's arm as Jamie's hand touched his chest. The dagger arm was trapped in a lock and he could now control his opponent. Yet the man was not done, he dropped down into the lock, kicking backwards at Jamie's groin. The kick was off target but it still hurt, driving into his upper leg. Jamie slashed his right arm down onto the man's already stressed joint, snapping the elbow, throwing his opponent off and causing him to drop the dagger with a howl of pain.

The second opponent, now with free space, lunged in with a weapon of his own. Jamie threw himself forward in a rolling dive, picking the first man's dagger up from the floor as he went. Now he had distance and a weapon. On his feet once more, he faced his new opponent dagger to dagger. This time the man did not start low but came with a lethal overhand strike to the chest, as Cristoforo had shown him in practice on their journey.

Jamie blocked it with the blade of his own weapon, catching the tines on the leather vambrace of his opponent, who was fast and well-practised. With the thrust blocked, the assassin threw a wild punch at Jamie's head from the inside gate with his left hand. It landed straight on his face and he saw stars, as tears of pain welled in his eyes. Jamie carried on as if by instinct, rolling the wrist over and trapping the arm. This time he did not continue the move but raked downwards with the point of his dagger, cutting his opponent open across his ribs and thrusting inwards at the last moment.

It was a crude response, but at least partially successful, eliciting a cry of pain and a spray of scarlet upon the man's sendall. The first assailant now rose, holding his broken arm, and the two faced him, but staggered backwards away towards the rear, blood dripping from their clothes. They pulled back to the far door and Jamie did not follow. His eyes were filled with tears and his crushed nose was bleeding profusely as he tasted the familiar metallic tang in his throat. It would be foolish to follow, and who knew what might happen to the bags of coin he would be forced to abandon if he did so.

"Ho guard! Guard!" Jamie shouted. The door was flung open from the side as he stood there, dagger raised in defence. Behind another door the deacon and a guard entered, astonished at the scene that met them. Jamie heard shouts below and the sound of a disturbance, then hard footsteps upon marble. Within seconds two figures appeared, puffing.

"Jamie, do you fare well?" Cristoforo asked, as two dishevelled guards came into the room at their heels and Mark turned to dissuade them of any further action.

"I am bloodied but not bowed. Two scullions sought to kill me and rob me of the levy, and I dissuaded them of their intent. They departed through the end door." He pointed. Cristoforo translated his comments in a fast barrage of Italian, at which the two guards ran towards the far end of the salon and disappeared from sight.

"*Porca miseria!* How can this happen, here in this holy

place?" Cristoforo demanded, looking heavenwards and shaking his head, yet in his heart of hearts he was not surprised, for corruption was the order of the day in Florence. "Shocked as I am I should not be so," he continued, "for power is the chief currency of corruption here and it was ever thus, and with it goes hand-in-hand that other thief: money. Jamie, I must apologise for my countrymen and the church that allows such villains to be present here." He scowled at the silent deacon, who was wringing his hands in distaste and holding his rosary beads between them, clearly discomfited by the attack.

"Sir, I must echo the *signor's* sentiments," the deacon finally spoke, "for we are very embarrassed that such an incident should occur here on sacred ground and would humbly ask that you forgive the assault upon your person."

Jamie waved away the man's concern, but decried the possibility of attack in such a place. "For myself I care little. 'Tis but a day's work. Though by the good Lord how can this come to pass with guards upon all entrances and within such sacrosanct precincts? Are there ways to enter and remain concealed through yonder doors?" he demanded.

"They lead to private chambers and corridors, and from there, down to a garth within the palazzo. It should be impossible to gain entry without wings from that quarter, as the garth is guarded from without."

"It seems the intent was to prevent our delivery of the due levy to His Holiness, and that avarice or politics were a greater aid to entry than magical powers." Jamie deliberately baited the churchman, who crossed himself at mention of magic or occult powers in the pope's inner sanctum.

"I praise God that no such powers be present and that your attack was merely man's avaricious desire to thwart the Holy Father." He declared piously.

"Then father, with your permission, I should like to deliver myself of my labours and like Hercules rest, now that I have cleaned the dirt from your stables," Jamie said, smiling a little at the deacon's piety. Cristoforo had to cast down his face, so as not to reveal a smile of his own at Jamie's image and the discomfited padre.

The cleric gave an unctuous smile and beckoned Jamie forward, with Mark and Cristoforo in the rear, carrying the saddle bags safely between them. This time there was no argument from the guards, who only bade them to remove their obvious armament, missing of course all the weapons that Cristoforo had secreted around his person.

The three of them were led through to a smaller salon, much cooler than the antechamber. It was naturally lit by ornate grisaille windows set in the ceiling and upper walls, throwing a gentle light upon the marble floor. The cool air was like a balm after the heat of the antechamber. In the centre was a large desk, behind which sat a scribe whose hand was rushing across the vellum before him, producing bird-like scratching sounds as he dipped the quill into the ink bottle and wrote at a prodigious rate.

Next to the table was a raised and ornately carved chair in which the papal representative sat. By the robes of his office, he was a high-ranking cardinal. The deacon spoke in swift Italian that only Cristoforo could follow, briefly explaining what had occurred and the nature of their business. The cardinal registered the nature of what he had been informed without so much as a flicker of emotion.

The three men bowed to him and Jamie spoke in Latin: "Your eminence, we are glad of an audience with you and by proxy that of His Grace the Holy Father Pope Urban, may God bless and keep him."

The beady eyes of the cardinal searched Jamie with keen regard for his dress and demeanour, staring at his bloodied nose. He was younger than Jamie had imagined, and maintained an upright posture despite being seated. His voice when he spoke was well modulated and rich in tone, as if used to speaking in public. "Thank you, my son, your manners do you credit and I shall pass on your addresses to His Holiness. Pray be good enough to inform me of your names."

"Your eminence, I am Sir James de Grispere, household knight to his grace Prince Henry of England. My two companions are also in the prince's employ, Cristoforo Corio and Mark of Cornwall at your service. We come to bring the levy due to your master from the Alberti family in coin, as was demanded."

With this, he turned to Mark and beckoned him forward. Mark placed the saddlebags upon the table in front of the scribe, who looked at them distastefully, but was bidden to assess their contents with an almost imperceptible nod from the cardinal.

The three men waited, content to watch the scribe and his assistant count all the coin, trusting no one. The total was recorded as five hundred marks. The cardinal was informed and gave his tacit agreement.

"All is well, and the due sum has been recorded in the tally. You may assure the Alberti that their share is now fully paid." The parchment was passed to Jamie, who read the figures and the Latin to confirm all was in order.

"Your eminence, if you would please oblige us and seal the document, we will present it upon our return to Signor Alberti. Would you be so kind as to seal it with your ring? I am sure you understand that there is nothing so suspicious as an honest man."

A wintry smile passed over the cardinal's countenance and he waved to the scribe, who brought forward a small pot of hot wax and dripped it liberally on the seam of the now folded document. The cardinal pulled back his sleeve and pressed down hard upon a small table extending from the arm of his chair, sealing the document indelibly with the mark of his ring in the hot wax. All present knew that there was no possibility of dispute: the dues had been delivered and the acknowledgement sealed.

Chapter Thirty

Later, in the Alberti Tower, they discussed at length the events of the morning in front of Alessandria and the rest of her relatives.

"Did you see the crooked smile on the cardinal's face when I asked for his personal seal?" Jamie opined with a wry smile. "Why I'd lief as not see him suck on a lemon as pull such a face."

"I should seek to know how those scullions entered the palace and who permitted them so to do," Mark said. "For there had to be collusion to achieve such a feat. They were not spirits as you teased the good deacon, although that in itself was worth the baiting."

"Ha! It was indeed, and he was most put out – unlike the cardinal, who was not disturbed at all. It was almost as though he expected such an action. I wonder how far upward the putrefaction has spread. To the very top, think you, Cristo?"

Cristoforo snorted in disgust. "I know not, Jamie, yet I would suspect the malady is stemmed not by any thought of ecclesiastical piety, but more by fear of position. *Il papa* needs the support of the Medici, who in turn are great friends of the Albertis, and only if their plans were thwarted would he leap aboard another vessel to save his position. I suspect more the cardinal, who appeared ambitious and wily beyond measure. I warned you thus. The politics of *Firenze* are as a pit of vipers, each feeding, wriggling and biting the other to obtain advantage.

"In that accord, *cara*, what news of your petition to the *Parte Guelfa?*" he asked Alessandria.

"Ah, we petition today before the twelfth, and there will be five names upon the document, all to be heard simultaneously. The numbers add gravitas to our cause and make it all the more likely to be given credence by the oligarchy. We visit on the morrow to plead our case before the *Guelfa*."

"Then I shall accompany you, for I am permitted as a citizen of *Firenze* to take my place even though I am not of the *arte maggiori,*" Cristoforo declared. His words were met with nods from his two friends, who, whilst not being permitted to attend within the inner council chamber, would at least accompany them to that point and attend upon the safety of the ladies.

The following day the Alberti women, with an entourage of armed servants, together with Jamie, Mark and Cristoforo, made their way to the grand Piazza della Signoria where stood the Palazzo Vecchio, the seat of government for Florence and the surrounding area. From this seat emanated the power of the region, casting sway in one form or another over the whole of Italy, excluding Milan. The palace was an imposing building that dominated the vast square – a rusticated stone cube with a dominant clock tower off centre rising over three hundred feet above them. It looked to the four as much a castle for military defence as a building of government, and Cristoforo confirmed this.

"*Si*, it was made for defence as much as government and as a last resort, should the heart of *Firenze* need defending. For now, it is a bastion of life and government," he said, clearly proud of his home city and the control that it gave over its dominions. Two guards made a show of checking everyone into the palace and making sure that Jamie, Mark, Jeanette and more particularly Forest, were not allowed any further than the inner courtyard.

Once inside they saw courtiers, clerks and servants moving about in and around the cloistered garth. The foreigners, especially Forest, drew glances of alarm, veiled comments and curiosity as though they were gods come to life. The women of the party were getting impatient, and at length Margherita di Nerozzo saw a clerk whom she knew and waylaid him. She spoke so quickly that Jamie could understand very little, but the meaning was clear. The ladies had waited long enough to stand before the *Guelfa* as their case was being deliberately delayed.

Alessandria looked up at the clock above as it struck the hour. "It is now ten of the clock, and we have been waiting for nearly an hour," she exclaimed, stamping her foot. At last their names were called and the four women, along with their servants and Cristoforo, moved inward to the *Salone dei Cinquecento* – The Hall of the Five Hundred.

It was magnificent, and as they entered, the murmured conversations were all quelled. Cristoforo had never before been inside, and even Alessandria had not seen it with the ruling council in attendance. It was oblong in shape, deep and dark, with windows at the far end highlighting only a marble statue and a few small fanlights at the upper levels beneath a gilded ornate ceiling, which was divided into three lines of gilded squares, formed like huge picture frames, each with its own oil masterpiece depicting battle scenes and glory for Florence.

Along the walls were further oil paintings showing victories over Siena, Milan and other historical enemies of the city. Each was some twenty feet squared, and there were significant gaps where they all assumed new masterpieces would be revealed in due course. At the far end, on a raised dais, sat the senior members of the ruling council, including the hated Albizzi and Stozzi family members, together with some of the Medici, who were outnumbered yet still held sway. All had dark countenances and were attired in black gowns and hats, despite the morning heat that was growing outside in the palazzo. Cristoforo was minded of a row of dried, crusty hawked crows, ready to scavenge on carrion, but here the squeaking quills were the order of the day. A clerk beckoned them forward, and the leading petitioner, Margherita Nerozzo, was nominated as their leader to voice the formal demands.

The petition was read out by Margherita herself, who made reference to the members of her family present behind her. No emotion was seen upon the faces of the *Guelfa*, but there were sighs and gasps from the audience within the chamber at the audacity and the scope of the demands read out before the assembled *Signoria*.

The *Signoria* were already annoyed that Alessandria and others had assembled at the headquarters of the Alberti family home, as none were permitted to stay in Alberti houses without express permission. Giovanni di Bicci de Medici silenced them by informing them that petitioners could assemble for the right to be heard without express permission. More grumbles ensued about coin rather than dowry for the women, but these complaints went unheeded.

Two Albizzi were heard, who demanded a delay, but this was voted down by a small margin, and all present knew very well that such tactics had been tried before for political gain. Having pleaded their case, the women were compelled to remain silent, and stood with dignity and hauteur in front of the all-male council. Cristoforo looked on with anger and pride, silently vowing death upon certain members of the Council. Two or three caught his dark looks, and knowing of his family's reputation, fell silent and looked sheepishly away under his piercing glare. Then the doors opened and two more Alberti women appeared. There were gasps of recognition, for these were widows of two Alberti men that had been executed for supposed treason. They were exercising their right to be heard, although none had petitioned for deceased spouses before.

The sequence of events went on, and after two hours of debate, one of the petitioners declared that any Florentine property inherited by exiled Alberti men could not be subject to sequestration or confiscation. It was a landmark decision, carried by the ever faithful Medici, who still bore immense sway while aided by the papal support.

It was several hours before the petitioners were dismissed. With much shouting and remonstrating, the Alberti women exited the chamber as one, talking at an incomprehensible rate that neither Jamie nor Mark could follow when they met them in the ante chamber.

"Cristoforo, I comprehend not one word of all that is spoken at such celerity. Prithee explain, is the news for the better? Were they successful?"

"Ah, I must apologise, for we are very excited. Yes, to save many words it is so. We have laid the petitions and we believe that they will be accepted, praise God." At which he crossed himself. "There is still much to be considered, but all was argued most strenuously, and we are hopeful that they will find in our favour. *Pero*, this is *Firenze*, where politics, spite, ambition and avarice rule mightier than justice." He shrugged. "Come, let us away, for I wish to take you to meet my family."

Jamie and Mark looked at each other, for Cristoforo had over their time together gradually revealed small pieces of information about his family. They knew of the death of his sister and the circumstances that had led Cristoforo into the service of Jamie's father, and had heard little of his younger brother and a surviving sister. Of his father little was also known, and they recalled that his mother had died in childbirth, as so many women did.

With the ladies back at the Alberti Tower, Alessandria was adamant that she wanted to go with Cristoforo and his friends to meet her future father-in-law.

"We have not seen each other in over two years, and I was forced away. I know not how he would view the killing of my sister's rapist. It was unsanctioned by him and I left of my own *volitio*. He is a proud man, and I know not how he will view me marrying *la contessa*."

"I am not good enough for you now! Are you so embarrassed by me that you hide me away?" she stormed.

The others barely hid their smiles, for they had noticed that since her return to Italy, and particularly Florence, Alessandria's attitude and mercurial temper had become worse and very Latin in its outbursts. Cristoforo raised his hands in frustration, rolled his eyes in exasperation and fired back in fast Italian.

"No, no, no, *porca miseria*. You deliberately misrepresent me…" And so it continued, too fast for Mark, Jeanette and Jamie to follow.

"I will say this," Mark whispered *sotto voce*, "their marriage will never be dull, I'll wager, for she is a spark to his kindling if ever there was one, and he the more combustible once lit!"

"Amen to that," Jamie rejoined.

"I am persuaded that they will treat tolerably well with each other," Jeanette added with a smile, gently pulling on Forest's ears, as the hound was clearly upset at the outburst and knew not what to make of it all, looking first from one then to the other, her head to one side as she tried to discern whether or not they needed protection.

Once the eruptions had subsided, the two lovers reconciled and proceeded peacefully to the stables, where thus mounted, the party made for the south gate and out into the countryside, leaving the smell and bustle of the city behind. The small settlements became sparse, and within two miles they came to a verdant plain fed by a tributary of the Arno. Cattle grazed listlessly in the heat or took shade beneath the rustling willows bordering the tributary, gently chewing the cud and brushing away flies. The ground sloped gently upwards to a point nestled between two low hills, and here there was a crop of buildings and a main house of weathered pink limewash, shaded by huge pine trees and garnished with bougainvillea in riotous colours.

The others looked at each other, the same thought running through their heads. From Cristoforo's brief descriptions, they had imagined a rustic rundown training ground or a barricaded fort holding a court of assassins, not the seemingly idyllic existence that lay before them. The air was clean and smelled of cows and summer grass, with a hint of pine upon the breeze. Cristoforo sat with his eyes misted, completely still, breathing the scents of his life deeply. Alessandria left him alone, but finally she broke the spell.

"Cristo, *questo e Bellissima*!"

Cristoforo gave a wan smile of pride and muttered, "Come, let us move forward, for we are watched."

As they rode closer to the house and buildings they saw that it was well laid out, but trenches had been dug into the ground at various angles that were unseen from far away. Their presence meant that anybody seeking to gain access would be funnelled in a certain direction, moving in a zig zag line, or would be forced to brave the deep trenches that were studded with sharpened wooden spikes. Two guard dogs were chained beneath the shade of a deep loggia that ran along the front of the property to the arched portico, and they barked aggressively at the party's approach. Forest raised her hackles and showed her teeth, but kept obediently by her master's side. It was in any event too hot for fighting, she decided.

Cristoforo called two names, and at the sound of his voice the two animals stopped barking and began to whine. Cristoforo, his eyes as sharp as ever, saw movement in the shadows of the portico and called out.

"Tommaso, *smetilla di nasconderti,* like a chained dog and come greet me," he commanded the figure by the house to stop skulking, a gentle teasing tone in his voice.

"Cristoforo? Is that you? By the Lord, you are returned. Simona! Babo! Cristoforo is come!" At which a lithe figure emerged from the shade and ran forward. Cristoforo, in turn, vaulted from his horse and ran to embrace his brother, kissing him on both cheeks. The reunion between the two brothers was emotional, and they were then joined by a young woman who ran up screaming at Cristoforo, berating him for leaving without a word and barely a letter in two years, beating his chest with a small fist.

"Contessa, I beg thee, are all Italian women thus?" Mark asked. "That they beat their men and scold them so, when seemingly they have great regard and care for them? 'Twould seem a most contrary disposition."

Alessandria shook her head, laughing. "Marco, praise God that you married an Englishwoman, for you would be lost to all if you ventured your heart in Italy."

"Amen to that," Mark responded.

Then they saw another man appear. In appearance he was an older version of Cristoforo, slightly stockier and with grizzled grey hair, but the family resemblance was there for all to see. There was a deep-seated and latent deadly intent to the older man, a sense of coiled energy that bespoke strength of purpose. For now he was benign, as his deep-brown eyes sought out his son, his arms wide, with emotion written large upon his face. The two men, father and son embraced and hugged each other for what seemed like an eternity, reluctant to break the hold for fear that it might be an illusion. Finally, Cristoforo's father pushed him to arm's length to better see his son, speaking in fast Italian to welcome him home. The welcome over, he kept his arm around Cristoforo and turned to the others, extending his hand in greeting. They dismounted and came forward to be introduced. When Cristoforo's father was introduced to Alessandria, his eyes widened and he bowed graciously, his calloused palm bringing the back of her gloved hand up to his lips.

"*Molto piacere di conocerti, la contessa.*"

Alessandria bobbed a curtsey as graciously as any she had placed at court and was immediately taken with this older version of her Cristoforo – whose eyes, she noticed, twinkled in the same manner. The conversation flowed and there seemed to be a quality of ease about the meeting, as they were invited inside to enjoy cool wine and a cold table. Simona, Cristoforo's fiery sister, watched him carefully like a hawk, her slate-grey eyes a mirror of his. She alone had known of his lone mission to avenge his dead sister, nearly three years earlier. In a lull in the conversation she asked the one question he had been avoiding: "Did you avenge Caterina?" she asked coldly.

Cristoforo looked from his sister to his father and brother and he saw a shadow fall across his father's face.

"*Si*, it is done."

"Good. I hope he squealed like stuck pig." She spat vehemently.

"Simona!" Their remonstrated, gesticulating with his hand

turned upwards, his fingers steepled in that peculiarly Italian fashion.

"What?" she demanded.

Alessandria saved his face, declaring that she would love to walk around and see the farm. The spell was broken and Cristoforo smiled gratefully in her direction. All the men rose as Jeanette and Alessandria made to move, with Tommaso seemingly unable to keep his eyes from Jeanette, whose blonde hair and blue eyes were a source of great interest to him. The party moved outside and the cook was ordered to prepare a feast for the evening meal in honour of the guests.

As they came to one of the barns, Tommaso beckoned them inside. Cristoforo grinned, knowing what was coming. For inside were not cattle or stalls, but a collection of platforms at different heights, some well-lit, others in shade. Ropes hung from the ceiling and dummies stuffed with straw were set at various angles and positions. Various posts were also set at different heights. One in particular about thirty feet away had a wooden board secured to it, marked with a series of circles.

"Have you grown slow, older brother? I wonder if the time in England has slowed you down, has perhaps made you an old man." He teased Cristoforo, waving his hand at the board. It was then Jamie noticed that Tommaso wore the leather vambraces similar to Cristoforo's upon his arms. Cristoforo disengaged himself from a puzzled Alessandria and the two brothers stood feet apart, while Jeanette looked on askance.

"Jeanette, would you be so kind as to raise your arm?" he asked in French, "and drop this cloth when you are ready."

The two men faced her away from the board, upright, relaxed, but with a frisson of excitement apparent in both of them.

Jeanette smiled, still puzzled, and did as she'd been asked. As soon as she released the cloth the brothers, moving seemingly as one, dropped into a spin, their hands flying to their boots. Light glinted on steel as four daggers flew almost as one, thudding home into the wooden target thirty feet away. One was off centre, the other three vibrated within the inner circle, inches from each other. There was scant difference to tell, but Jamie had been sure that Cristoforo's dagger had thudded home slightly ahead of his brother's first lethal onslaught.

"No! *Dio mio*! You beat me again!" Tommaso cried. "I was sure that you would have slowed. Where do you practise?"

"I practice upon the bodies of my enemies," Cristoforo replied. He motioned to Jamie and Mark, explaining who they were, that Mark and he practised locks and holds while Jamie was faster with a blade than anyone he knew.

"I must try you before you leave, with your permission, of course." Tommaso begged with all the enthusiasm of youth. Jamie smiled and bowed acquiescence, suddenly feeling old in front of the callow youth before him.

As night fell, they settled down to a supper of many courses including quail, chicken and a wild boar stew, with piquant sauces and strange vegetables that none of the English party could recognise, all washed down with strong Tuscan Sangiovese wine.

Cristoforo and his father left the table after the meal and strolled off into the early dusk. They were gone a long time, the others noticed, although the hubbub of conversation continued unabated in their absence. The evening drew in and they decided to stay for the night. Simona directed the servants to prepare rooms.

The following morning was an emotional departure for Cristoforo, yet he felt more at peace with himself and his family than he had for a long time. His father gave his blessing after some persuading that his son was perhaps not reaching for the stars in marrying the contessa. He could see that the couple were clearly besotted with each other and he vowed to attend the wedding, wherever it may be held.

On the journey back to Florence, with all goodbyes said, Jamie sought out his friend: "Cristo, I have learnt much of your vocabulary thus far and one word comes to mind – a *forbo*. For indeed you are a fox, to waylay a man so with a vision of your home as some spartan refuge with little comfort perched upon a precipice, as those of Persia. Yet we were made welcome in a wonderous setting by your family and there was no fierce dragon lying in wait for us to slay."

"I thank you my friend, for you are very kind. Yet you see my father now in his older years. In his day, he was a fierce task master who beat us if we were dilatory as he moulded us to the profession of our family. Now...well, he has mellowed, *va bene.*"

Jamie smiled at his friend and they rode on in companionable silence, content to let matters rest.

Chapter Thirty-One

Westminster

Four men loyal to the king had gathered in the private council chamber: Richard, Lord Grey of Codnor; Sir John Pelham, the Chancellor of the Exchequer; Sir John Prophet, Keeper of the Privy Seal; and Sir William Stokes, financial spy for the king. They were awaiting one final member before their secret meeting could begin. The latch on the door to the chamber lifted and Sir Richard Whittington entered, closing the door firmly behind him. He bowed to the assembled company and moved smoothly across to the meeting table, although to their eyes he looked less composed than usual.

"My lords, I must apologise for my tardy arrival. It was unforeseen yet timely, as I have received this day a message lately arrived from France with ill tidings that concern us all," he declared. "I was latterly with Prince Henry, who sought sanctuary within my house some nights past. He had, may God preserve him, been subject to an attempt upon his life." The other four present spoke at once and Sir Richard answered their questions in detail. "But my lords, no word of this must leave this room, for it links too closely with the intelligence I have learnt this day."

The other four sat in silence, unsure what new calamity to expect. "The news I have is grave indeed," Whittington continued, "yet not wholly unexpected." He paused, whether for effect or because he was considering how to deliver the tidings none present could tell. "The Duke of Burgundy and his forces have laid siege to Bourges, the capital of the Duchy of Berry in the heart of Armagnac territory. Within the town are the Duke of Berry himself and his uncle, Duke John, who have taken refuge there to withstand the assault."

There were worried looks around the table. "Dost thou think that the Armagnacs will hold fast?" It was Sir William Stokes who spoke.

"I know not. Better to ask Sir Richard, for he has soldiered there and knows better than most how it may be provisioned." Whittington raised an enquiring eyebrow at Lord Grey.

"It is a well-supplied town with stout walls and upon the rivers of Yèvre and Auron, and will not easily succumb to siege or starvation," Lord Grey opined. "However, it is some hundred leagues south of Paris, and Burgundy is close to his own homelands to the south where he can re-provision and gain reinforcements. The tally will be high and the loss great on both sides before any victory is gained.

"My fear is that Duke Charles will surrender upon negotiation of a truce to save his forces and his life, despite the loss to his honour. Burgundy is strong, and seeks a united France under his dominion. If such terms were achieved and France presented a united front against us, it would be grievous to our cause, and Prince Thomas would face a terrible foe upon his landing there."

"A curse upon Burgundy." Whittington swore. "For he will spoil it all – not just in France but here – and his majesty's balance of power will turn, making him more fool than fooled. I would have more knowledge of what occurs, how matters fall and who prevails. A soldier's view, mayhap." At which he tugged on his ear in deep thought, somewhat distanced from the company.

William Stokes cut into his thoughts: "We must set insidiores to work within France and have them report to us. We should at all costs hurry the effort or all may be lost. I will make arrangements and have messengers sent abroad. What of his majesty? Should he be told, think you?"

Sir John Prophet answered: "He must be informed before he sends his son into a deadly trap, especially if the French forces align – and worse, should the Scots side with them as your intelligence advised and pour into battle against us. They pledged four thousand men, did they not?"

"They did," Whittington replied. "We shall keep his majesty apprised and mayhap Prince Hal, for I hear rumours that he is to return to court, so aggrieved is he with the discord that is being put abroad at his expense."

"I durst not consider the consequences should we have civil war here while they fight in France. Henry's reign has not been easy since he fought the old king, may God assoil him, for it was a great day when he won the crown. And now the jackals that once supported him so strongly seek to wrench it from his grasp, all in the name of power and riches to further their own cautelous ends." Sir John concluded, shaking his head in disgust.

"Sir Richard, is there a date yet set for Prince Thomas's sailing?"

"His majesty palters by the day, sawing both this way and that, seeking still, I'll warrant, a way in his own mind to lead the charge. 'Tis a vain hope, for his body ails so, yet not his mind, which is ever strong. The time now set to sail is the middle of July, God willing, and the weather being in their majesties' favour."

"Time enough then for the French to unite against us and play foul with their own honour should expediency demand that they so do," Whittington commented cynically. "I needs must move in haste and seek knowledge of their campaigns with all at my disposal. Come Messires, let us to other subjects of importance for I must return thence to matters of intelligence abroad."

"Have a care, Sir Richard, for I needs must not tell you what perils any who land in France will now face. The French shall seek to tighten their grip upon all who travel abroad, as would I in their position, especially those leaving Calais, Flanders or landing upon French soil. They will be watched and arrested upon the merest hint of suspicion. I would not wish to be a spy entering France at this time from any of those directions, for it would be perilous in the extreme." Sir William Stokes warned.

"For certes, Sir William, you have the right of it and I concur. Therefore I have a different stratagem in mind which, God willing, the French and in particular Jean Kernezen will not foresee."

Chapter Thirty-Two

Florence

The *Signoria* pontificated for another week, considering all deputations placed before them, prevaricating upon the outcome as the Alberti had suspected they would.

"I am told that a decision will be made today, and we are summoned to the *Signoria* this evening," Alessandria told her English friends with a smile, as they received the news from a page, dressed in the livery of a civic official. There was a tempered expectancy in the atmosphere as the whole family, in all its extended forms, became cautiously optimistic and slightly nervous at the same time. Alessandria began to pace the *sala*, unable to contain her impatience. The time of reckoning had arrived, and all depended upon the ultimate decision of the *Guelfa*.

They set off for the Palazzo Vecchio when the time came, knowing that the fate of the Albertis hung in the balance. Upon seeing their friends and family depart into the building's dark interior, Jamie, Mark and Jeanette were equally nervous as to their fate. It seemed to the three that they had waited for many hours, although in reality it was a matter of just thirty minutes, and the look on the faces of Alessandria and Cristoforo after their return from the chamber told the whole story. They had been triumphant and the awards equitable.

"My full fortune has been awarded!" Alessandria cried between hugs and embraces from her fellow family members. The others were delighted, and only Cristoforo looked on in a rather diffident way.

"Why so downcast, Cristo? Should you not be overjoyed?" Jamie asked.

"For Alessandria *si*. *Pero,* for me, I have been put in an invidious position. For just one of her properties – think on't, just one of her settlements on a single property – was for three thousand florins!" He stated this in awe, clearly aghast at the sum and what it meant.

"Cristo, mayhap you have forgotten the balance of the scales of love, for they reckon right well and do not consider the weight of avarice. Alessandria knew well your station and position, yet wished for nothing more than your affection in return. Think on, be you fair, as Tamar or rich as Croesus it matters not, for it is you she values and you alone."

"Thank you, Jamie. Your words bring me up short and I am grateful."

"That said with your visage? Why she should have eyes for me and look upon you closely only in the dim light of a candle."

Cristoforo replied with scornful words in Italian and went to cuff his friend about the head. A smile replaced his downcast expression as Alessandria approached. "Now, *amore*, now we can truly plan our wedding day in full."

The feeling of ease and anticipation lasted another week.

Alessandria and the company were set to return to Bologna when a messenger arrived at the Alberti Tower. He was part of a string of men alerted first by carrier pigeon and then by messages, passed hand-to-hand after coming overland through southern France, and finally by ship to Livorno and across to Florence. The messenger asked for Jamie, and upon meeting with him, presented a parchment bearing a wax seal with an unknown crest of some foreign design. Jamie's eyes narrowed, suspecting the worst.

"I thank you for your effort to bring this so to me. With your permission, Alessandria, I would beg of some refreshment for this man and stabling for his horse so that both may rest." Jamie turned to the messenger. "You, sir, appear to be hard pressed. I shall speak with you again should I have need of your services." Aware that Jamie wanted space and time to read the missive unobserved, Alessandria nodded her agreement.

"For certes, Jamie," she replied, instructing a servant to take the man away, to show him where he might be fed and his horse stabled.

Mark and Cristoforo stood close by as Jamie broke the seal and read the Latin, calling for a pen and parchment. Scribbling notes as he deciphered the flowing script, Jamie frowned then read it a second time to ensure that he had understood it correctly, as it was partially coded to render it senseless to anyone but Jamie. Whittington had used the time-honoured method of treating names of people they knew and places, or cloth and yarn to be reassembled using every second letter. It was a code particular to their calling and only they would understand its full meaning, as there would be no symmetry to unravel and no repetition in which to find and assemble patterns.

"Well, what are your orders?" Cristoforo asked.

"I am to leave with all haste upon royal fiat for France, travelling northwards to Vaast-la-Hougue. There I shall meet His Royal Highness Prince Thomas, now invested as the Duke of Clarence. Yet there is more. Burgundy makes war upon the Armagnacs and besieges Bourges. Whittington fears a truce between the parties who will present a united front to ambush Clarence upon his landing. All ports to the north are watched, as are forays from Calais. There is hell to pay and a fine coil has been snared around us. His majesty is caught twixt and tween, it would seem, as he is ever asotted with the lands in France that are by right his for the taking. This means the price may be the sacrifice of his son upon the alter of his ambition. What to do? For if I leave now, I shall miss your wedding," Jamie opined, distraught at the idea.

"*Amico mio*, we understand all too well the pressure of your devoir. You shall be sorely missed, yet will be there in spirit for certes," Cristoforo replied.

"I would add my thoughts upon this time," Alessandria added. "Your devoir and honour are paramount, and to lose a prince and, mayhap, a kingdom upon the price of attendance? Why, the scales do not balance and I could not countenance such an action. For even now –" at which she glanced at Cristoforo, her head tilted to one side, as she sent a mocking glance in his direction, "– with nuptials abroad and a date so close, I see my dear heart quiver with a different fervour, as his sword arm twitches and a light of battle enter his eyes.

"So begone I say with all good blessings, before he decides to accompany you, and we shall pray for you on the road and wherever it may take you." She smiled and took both his rough soldier's hands in hers, smiling up at him and removing some of his discomfiture.

Jamie was grateful for the reprieve, yet still sad that he

would not see his friends wedded. "Yet still I see an impediment. For what of Jeanette? She cannot ride with me, as I shall travel fast with a relay to ease Richard's burden and mayhap to battle. 'Tis no place for a lady. Mark, would you escort her back to England upon the end of the nuptials?" he asked.

Mark looked embarrassed, staring downward. "No, I fear I may not. For if there be danger, with crown and prince threatened, 'tis at your side I should be, that we may share the perils and see all through to the end. With your permission my lady, and you too Cristo?"

"Marco, I should have expected nothing less and salute you. You must protect this foolish English knight who travels abroad with only hauberk and no armour," Alessandria said. "We shall ensure that Jeanette is safely returned. For the count has messages to send abroad and she will be well protected upon a fleet of Genoese galleys that will be more than a match for any *pirati* that threaten the Moorish coast of Spain."

"Fear not, brother mine, for Alessandria has already advanced a coterie of ladies who journey to England, and I shall be in good company and well protected when I travel home after the wedding," Jeanette added.

"Ha, then we are of one accord and I thank you dearly, Alessandria, yet I shall rue the day that I miss your time before the altar."

"Amen to that." Mark echoed. "And when shall we see you back in England, Cristo? For surely you will return, or has all changed?"

"Ah Marco," Cristoforo began diffidently. "My return here has rekindled my love for my homeland and I find the pull most strong upon my heart. I know not if or when we shall return, *magari e questo punto.*"

"England shall be the poorer for your absence," Mark responded.

"Come," Jamie said. "We must make plans for our journey. We heed the command as bid and must not tarry, for we are not pigeons and must obey the laws of man."

At these words they all felt a sadness in the air, as if somehow the impending wedding and the victory had been annulled, despite the fact that they knew at some point they would need to depart, and it was ever likely that Cristoforo and Alessandria would stay to make their home in Italy.

After two days of preparation, Mark and Jamie made to leave the Alberti residence and Florence for the journey to Livorno. It was a sad parting for all and most confusing for Forest, who stayed tightly against her master's side, unsure of what was occurring. All the company embraced in the less formal Italian manner, which the Englishmen had slowly become used to over the period of their stay.

"Cristo, you had better look well to Alessandria, for should I hear ill reports I shall return to admonish you," Jamie warned, feigning severity, pleased that he had managed sufficiently well with the language that he had spoken these words in Italian so that the assembled company could hear and understand. He and Cristoforo embraced arm-to-arm in the Roman fashion and bade each other farewell, words unspoken between them. Mark crushed his friend's hand in a firm grip. He hoped that he would see him again soon, but in his heart of hearts doubted that he would.

Mark turned to Alessandria. "Fare thee well, contessa. I would thank you from the bottom of my heart for showing me your fair country, which I would never have dreamt could be so marvellous. Its mysteries and sights shall remain in my heart forever."

He bowed slightly over her hand and gently kissed it. Jamie bade his sister farewell and ordered her to have great care on her return journey home. Then it was time, as all knew. Jeanette rubbed Forest's ears for the last time as the hound sidled against her master. They mounted and were gone, with a final clatter of hooves.

Chapter Thirty-Three

London: 1st July

Prince Henry's mesnie had arrived in time for the assembly of
the Royal Council at Saint Martin-in-the-Fields. The assembled
host appeared incongruous to all who bore witness to it, for the
setting was a rural one, centred on a church that lay between
the cities of Westminster and London, in meadows that were
ripe with the smells of summer and the sounds of buzzing
insects. This reflected well upon the scene, for the rights to the
church had been in dispute between the Bishops of London
and Westminster, and the outcome had finally been decided by
the Archbishop of Canterbury who found in favour of Westminster. The coincidence had been noted by many, mirroring
so closely the situation between the king and the prince. Yet
here, no man of the cloth could seemingly resolve the issues
between father and son.

Prince Henry had lodgings nearby in the form of a manor
house, which, despite its size, was unable to house the whole of

his coterie as its numbers were too great. He held his own private counsel with Thomas Langley, Bishop of Durham, who was there as a peacemaker.

"My lord prince, I do so earnestly pray that my presence and that of others of ecclesiastical persuasion will dissuade your father from thoughts of your arrival here as a military offensive," he offered as they finished their evening meal. Others around the table held their breath at the comment, knowing only too well how precariously balanced matters were between father and son.

"Mark you well that my letter of open intent was deliberately sent to all corners of the realm," Prince Henry replied, "and I had Walsingham ensure it was noted so. Though by the rood, I despair to know whose side he appears to be upon, as it seemingly changes as often the direction of the wind. Yet we would not appear as a weakling before our father, for he ever respects strength over diplomacy, even now in his dotage. To this end we have sought a private audience with his majesty, and we hope in all to prevail upon him not to heed the rumours that abound of our supposed insidious intent."

The following day the prince's wish was granted when he was given a private audience with his father – at least as private as any audience could be with the king of England, who arrived with a coterie of attendants including the Bishop of Durham, the Earl of Arundel, Bishop Beaufort, and of course Richard Courtney. The prince was aware that he would have at least one ally in the chamber with Sir Richard Whittington present as chief financier to the crown, and that all would centre on the forthcoming invasion of France.

The prince stood head and shoulders above his party, dominating the company by his height alone. Despite the summer heat, he was oddly clad in a long cloak that reached to his knees adding to the drama of the panoply. Arraigned either side of the throne were Thomas Beaufort, who had succeeded in inveigling himself within the king's trust, Archbishop Arundel, Prince Thomas and surprisingly, Prince Hal saw, James, 4th Earl of Ormond, who had travelled from Ireland to join forces and fight at Guyenne. Sir Richard Whittington smiled encouragingly at the prince, and then a respectful silence fell as King Henry was ushered in on a litter, looking pale and wan, with only his eyes showing the vitality of the life force still vibrant within him. All bowed before the king, and once his majesty was settled, the proceedings began.

"So, our son, what concerns you that you should make the long journey from Coventry to attend us here?" The king's voice was still strong, if slightly reedy in delivery.

"Majesty, it ever pleases us to attend your court, yet we come upon an errand of ill report with an offer to rectify the issue. Rumours have been stirred abroad by certain children of iniquity, disciples of dissension, supporters of schism, instigators of wrath and originators of strife. These creatures have plotted with serpentine cunning to attack the proper order of succession, lying that we are longing for the crown of England with a murderous desire, and intend to raise rebellion against you, sire."

Here the prince paused, and reaching for the clasp of the cloak about his neck, he threw it off, revealing the garment beneath. At which there were indrawn breaths as all stared at Prince Hal, for he was dressed in a long, blue satin gown pierced by eyelets at multiple intervals. From each eyelet hung the needle and thread that had been used to make it. About his upper right arm, the prince wore one of the rare SS collars of the Lancastrian dynasty, all to signify his loyalty to the crown and his father.

Prince Hal knelt, protesting his undying loyalty to the crown and his father: "Father, should there be any who is an enemy to you, we shall by all power vested in us punish that person. to erase that sore from your heart.

"I have this morning taken sacrament and confession with Bishop Durham with a clear heart and conscience." At this Prince Hal pulled forth a concealed dagger, reversing the grip and offering handle first to his father, remaining on his knees before the king. "We wish you here before us all to slay us with this dagger, for our life is not so desirous to us that we would live one more day that should be to your displeasure, and we forgive you our death." The prince bowed his head in obeisance, the dagger held forward.

The king screwed up his eyes as though in pain, and wept before his son, rising to snatch the dagger. He threw it aside in a dramatic gesture and pulled Prince Henry to him, embracing his son. Having been restored by that gesture and by his father's associated words of comfort to his former grace and favour, the king promised to bring to book those who had traduced him at a parliamentary summons.

All present breathed a sigh of relief at the reconciliation they had witnessed. Whittington smiled as all cheered, yet he was silently still perturbed: *I wonder if any such summons shall come to pass or all will come to naught?* he mused.

Two days later, he was in private conference with Lord Grey and others close to the king. "Can his majesty not see that by investing Thomas as Duke of Clarence he is undermining Prince Hal's status? Prince Hal is by the good Lord effectively Duke of Guyenne and it should be he, not Thomas, who seeks to relieve and re-conquer the duchy. 'Tis ill that he promotes Beaufort to be Earl of Dorset, for I trust not that man's motives. And still we see no move to a summons from parliament as his majesty promised, to bring the slanderers to book, and here is the real thorn in the prince's side: his brother is still to lead the invading army. That above all else promotes a schism between the brothers that will not be easily reconciled."

"Aye, it bodes ill indeed." Lord Grey agreed. "Added to that we have the Earl of Warwick sent to command Calais, and he a close confederate of Arundel who fought with Burgundy against the Armagnacs, when both declared that it scourged their honour to go against the Burgundians. They scruple so, yet twist and turn to suit their own ends," he finished cynically.

"For certes you have the right of it, and I fear for both princes – one caught twixt loyalties and one in the jaws of Burgundy's trap." Sir John Pelham agreed.

"Then we must ensure that such things do not come to pass. I have put in place arrangements to countermand his moves, and please God that they may come to pass," Whittington offered.

Chapter Thirty-Four

Livorno, Italy

The sloping land led down to the fortressed town that lay before Jamie and Mark, who had taken but two days to reach Livorno. It was set against the rocky coastline protected on the landward side by angled walls, within which was a secondary moat and further fortifications. All this was commanded by a huge castellated tower that looked out over the sea.

"'Tis good to smell sea air again and be away from the stench of a large town," Mark said, breathing in deeply. He looked up at the cawing gulls that swooped and scavenged, fighting upon the wing for any scrap that they could rip from each other's mouths. The fishing boats provided them with a constant source of food as they plied their trade around the old port.

"Now we need to find a galley that's willing to take us to Narbonne. We can land safely there and avoid any risk from

Moorish pirates who are active around the coast of Spain." Jamie stated.

"The Moors only go as far as the border, you said?"

"Yes, there are too many Genoese galleys and warships to the south. The Italian ships are always loaded with troops, and the pirates prefer to plunder merchant ships that have little protection. Their galleys carry much more sail and are lower and sleeker in the water, manned by lethal crossbowmen, and much faster than cogs. Constructed differently too. Cogs are clinker-planked, but galleys are lap-planked," Jamie explained, showing Mark with his hands, "making them lighter and broader. They displace less water, but they aren't as sturdy. They are no good for rough seas, but here in the calm summer in the Mediterranean, hugging the shore, they are perfect."

"Aye, I've seen a few from a distance but never worked on them in the English yards. It's always been cogs and such like," Mark replied.

They moved through the town, Forest close by their heels, and made for the western gate opening out onto a stone palisade that sloped down to the waterfront. Here the quay was alive with seafaring craft of all sizes, dominated by the long, sleek galleys so feared by the English when they had been used to harangue and plunder the supply cogs during past sieges of Calais. They were deadly, loaded as they were with troops and pirates cooperating under the flag of Spain, despite the supposed peace agreement between the two countries.

Close to, Mark also noticed that unlike the English cogs they had many more oars, with two banks per side aiding the three sails as a means of propulsion. Lines of them bobbed in the harbour, tethered to the quay, waiting to be loaded and for men to take them to sea once more. There was the usual frenetic harbourside activity, loading and unloading, shouting and the cawing of gulls above. The rich tang of the sea was strong here, making Mark homesick for Cornwall. Two galleys were side on to the stone harbour front, riding high and almost level with the quayside.

Jamie saw a ship's master seated upon a stone stool, marking a sheet of vellum upon a makeshift table as various charges of cargo were loaded aboard by the steves. Jamie interrupted his work to ask in Italian if they sailed west to France and possibly Narbonne. The man answered in rough Italian of which Jamie understood but half, yet it was sufficient to gain the gist of the meaning.

"How many of you?" the master asked in simple terms.

"My companion and me, two horses and my hound."

"A dog on board my ship? No that is not possible – or maybe it is but will cost you," the man responded slyly, quoting an outrageous price in return for their passage. Jamie, who had learnt something of Italian ways, knew that it was a number to bargain with. He made to walk away, snorting and waving his hand. Sure enough, the master called him back and the haggling began. Minutes later they struck a deal and shook hands.

"They sail upon the high tide, which makes less difference here on the Mediterranean. Now we must see if my training of Richard has paid off, or if we needs must swim back to England," Jamie jested. For days he had been training Richard to walk upon unsecured and wobbly planks over ditches and streams. After much encouragement and bribery, he had finally become used to the idea, while Breseler had seemed completely unfazed by the exercise.

As the tide rose so did the height of the galley, until it was almost level with the quay. The rails were slid back and a short gangplank of just two feet crossed the distance.

Richard approached and rolled his eyes, straining back. As Jamie relaxed the rope the contrary stallion launched himself, eschewing the planking, to land firmly on the deck, knocking

Jamie backwards, their heads colliding upon landing. He cursed the horse for all kinds of a fool and had to placate the master, who ranted about mad Englishmen and their ill-trained animals. Breseler, in contrast, stamped his feet a few times, but plodded across easily, led by Mark who grinned in a superior way. Forest just looked on in disgust and then leapt over the gap, landing softly on the planking of the deck.

Two hours later, with all stowed aboard, the galley slipped its moorings and was rowed out into the calm blue waters of the Ligurian Sea, taking a straight line across to Nice, where they docked briefly to take on more cargo. From here, the craft hugged the coast, passing Toulon on the peninsula and then heading straight across to Narbonne on the south coast of France. The whole journey took just over two days and already Jamie felt that he was halfway home.

They landed without incident and hired two fit looking pack mules upon which they stacked their gear.

"So now where do we travel?" Mark asked, as all was new territory to him. "For by the good Lord it is hot, and I fear that once we are away from the breeze of the sea we shall be roasted."

"In that I am in accord with you, Mark. We make roughly northwest and travel first to Toulouse and thence to Bordeaux. If we steer this line and vary neither too far north nor too far south towards Spain, we shall stay within lands that are friendly to the English Crown. Once we arrive at Bordeaux I shall be mightily relieved, for from there we shall be in the duchy of Guyenne and on home soil. The Gascons are loyal to his majesty and will aid us should we need assistance.

"So come, let us not tarry. Let us speed upon our way, for we have many days' travel ahead of us and we are already at the sixth day of July. My Lord Prince Thomas shall sally forth soon, if Whittington's reports be true, and all will hang upon how long the Armagnacs can hold against Burgundy. This heat will aid the spread of plague and dysentery that always accompanies any siege.

"My fear is that the hearts of the Armagnacs will be swayed by expediency, and their resolve shall weaken like an Autumn leaf upon a tree, blown this way and that. I would not give a penny for a Frenchman's word." At which he snapped his fingers to emphasise the point, causing Forest to look up at him sensing a command. Mark nodded, agreeing with Jamie's summation of the French.

Bourges, France

The old castle walls were pounded at regular intervals by the huge cannons installed on high ground around the perimeter, on high ground to gain the best advantage of their trajectory and reach. The stench of saltpetre and sulphur was rank, poisoning the air to any who were close to the great guns that belched flame and noxious gases twice per hour. Great clouds of grey smoke rose upwards in plumes, shrouding the crews, with no breeze to dissipate it. The gunners, seemingly immune, wore no protection, but those around them wore linen scarves about their faces as their eyes watered in sympathy with the assault. It was hot, unpleasant and dangerous work. One cannon had already exploded, ripping apart the brass barrel, sending lethal shards of metal flying into the air, scything down everything and everyone in its path.

Jean de Kernezen rode to the outskirts of the assembled

army wearing a scarf about his neck and mouth, for the stench of humanity was appalling to his nose: human excrement, sweat, campfires and the foul odours of the guns were everywhere. *My God,* he thought, *should this be hell upon earth, then I fear for my eternal soul when I leave this world*. He crossed himself in hope of redemption.

Soldiers milled around in groups, some appearing half-starved, with sunken cheeks and lank hair. Their looks told their own tales and they eyed the spy warily, looking at his fine horse and clean clothes with envy and suspicion. He did not stop, moving through their serried ranks, fearing that he may be pulled from his horse and eaten. Kernezen searched, finally seeing the regal standard of the Duke of Burgundy hanging listlessly from the tall, flag pole above the duke's large command tent. He was pleased to see that it was set well apart from the melee of soldiers at the highest vantage point, offering a perfect vista of the siege below.

Pitched as it was beneath a copse of trees, the duke's camp was blissfully shaded, offering respite from the full heat of the sun as the shadows of the trees fell across the canvas. Groups of soldiers and courtiers mingled about the entrance that was guarded by two men-at-arms. The spy dismounted and tethered his horse with a free rein, allowing the beast to nibble at the remnants of the green grass beneath the trees. He eschewed the front entrance and wandered into the copse, approaching the tent from the rear. Here he found a tent flap tied with but two strings and guarded by a sergeant-at-arms. In addition there were two horses, loosely saddled, waiting ready to be mounted in urgency should the need arise. *Our brave leader considers every contingency,* Sir Jean mused to himself.

The man didn't recognise Sir Jean and began to ask his business, reaching for his sword hilt as he did so and raising a hand in resistance: "Monsieur, there is no entry here. It is solely for the duke's personal use."

"I think that his grace will attend upon me, sergeant. I am Sir Jean de Kernezen, at his service."

"Monsieur, a thousand apologies, I did not recognise you. Await here one moment, please."

A ghost of a smile played upon Kernezen's lips at this reply, for he greatly valued his ability to seem both invisible and unremarkable in his physical appearance. The sergeant reappeared moments later and beckoned him forward through the small flap. It was cooler inside the voluminous campaign tent, with large vents set into the upper canvas that allowed air to circulate. A number of guards were present, together with courtiers and nobles, one of whom was Sir Galliard de Durfort, who nodded as Kernezen entered. The spy bowed to the Duke of Burgundy, who was seated at a travelling table towards the end of the tent.

"Your grace, I trust that you are well and prosper here?"

"I bid you welcome, Sir Jean. As to prospering –" here he snorted, "– the malingerers protect themselves against our cannonade, and we have laid siege these three weeks past, yet they continue to hold fast. Please God that disease and famine will prevail soon, for we too suffer those maladies and cannot sit idly by whilst we await their capitulation. What news have you for me from England?"

Here the spy compressed his lips and sighed: "My lord, I am latterly returned from those foul shores and was able glean much that will not please your ears."

"Inform me with a brief summary and then in more detail, for I must have intelligence upon this day on how to proceed."

"Very well, your grace. The king is partly reconciled with his son Prince Hal, yet all is not well there, I perceive. Prince Thomas still sits at his father's side and is thus favoured with an army that is planned to invade our shores. He is to be formally invested as Duke of Clarence, and Beaufort made Earl of Dorset, his rank raised to command in joint esteem with the Duke of York, who too shall accompany him on this foul mission."

"When do they sail?" Burgundy snarled the question ill-humouredly, his long jaw clenched in anger.

"They plan to leave before the end of this month with some four thousand troops, including archers and knights."

"And where do they intend to land?"

"They gather at Southampton, my lord, and would contrive to land somewhere to the south of Calais. Mayhap at Cotentin, which as you know is in Guyenne and at the heart of their dispute. They will find friendly Gascons there who will join them upon their mission. If they can link and form a strong resolve, we shall be caught twixt two armies, with relief to the Armagnacs apparent. I need not tell you how perilous this would be."

The duke silenced him with an arrogant stare. He did not like being lectured by subordinates, however useful they might be, and fought to control his temper. Finally, drawing a deep breath, he spoke: "Very well, draw yourself some refreshment and tell me all in detail of what you have learnt."

The duke was soon fully apprised of all that had occurred. His shrewd mind bent itself around aspects of warfare both martial and political, at which he raised a question that had been of concern to him: "Afore, when we spoke, you promised to reckon the tally with the pope and the matter of swaying him in our favour. How goes this?"

Kernezen hesitated, for he had received unfavourable intelligence from his network of spies. "My lord, I regret to inform you that the levy due for the Albertis has been received, and was paid in full in Florence."

"What? How so? In coin?" Kernezen nodded. "How was this achieved? For we agreed with His Majesty King Ferdinand that Spain and her waters were to be impenetrable, and so too the lands of the north guarded by his Imperial Majesty Emperor Sigismund. Did the coin leave from England?"

"Apparently it did, your grace, for it was presented by an English contingent at the papal court in Florence," Kernezen said. "I am hoping for further information in due course."

"This English contingent must return to their cursed land, and I would know who they are and how they achieved this feat of legerdemain. For they must have passed through my land in Flanders and I would know who aided their passage. Now begone, for your tidings make us dependent upon winning this battle here without delay, and seeking an accord to unify us against the forces that shall surely be sent to our shores."

Chapter Thirty-Five

London

Bishop Beaufort looked on, outwardly impassive yet inwardly seething. The final decision as to the division of his late brother's estate and dowry had been decreed by his half-brother the king, with the larger portion to be distributed to Mary Holland, wife of the Duke of Clarence Prince Thomas. He clenched his crosier so tightly that his fingers turned white. *I swear by all that is holy you shall not prosper, whore, nor your japing prince who would mock me and turn the tide of finance against us. By God, I shall turn Hal against you now and stir such turmoil that shall fall upon you as a plague of Egypt*, he swore to himself.

As soon as he was able, he left the king's presence feeling bitter and vengeful, vowing to seek out Prince Henry and do all in his power to instil trouble and jealousy in the prince's heart.

Sir Richard Whittington watched him depart fearing the worst, as this new development had tipped the balance of favour once more in Prince Thomas's direction. He bade a servant attend him. "Follow carefully where the good bishop travels and report back to me on whom he meets and for how long. No more – and do not get caught, for I venture this will be easy."

"Yes, my lord." At which the young man sauntered off in pursuit of the cleric, who had left the palace to summon his carriage.

Whittington's servant found that the bishop's journey was not a long one. Prince Henry had refused to attend the ceremonies that heralded the promotion of his brother and Thomas Beaufort to the Earl of Devon, as it signalled the start of the muster to arms for the invasion of Guyenne. There was now too much ill will between the brothers, as no actions had been brought or investigations instigated to bring to book those who had spread lies and false witness to Prince Hal's character. The bishop found him in private conference with the Bishop of Durham, the Earl of Arundel and Richard Courtney.

"Your grace, you are most welcome to join our company," Prince Hal offered. "Yet we hope that you bring us news of good cheer, for we fear that we are very dull company this day."

"I fear not, my prince, for I am lately come from the investiture of your brother and my brother, now Earl of Devon, both of whom are risen in rank and made us the poorer for it, for my late brother's estate is now found in favour of Prince Thomas and the dowry settled."

"We feared such a turn of events, and despite our earnest remonstrations, we could not prevail upon our father to arrive at a more equitable resolution. So be it, for we all suffer, and naught is settled as we would wish. We pray to God that the venture to France is successful and a good wind sends my brother from Southampton – though in faith we trust not the Armagnacs to stay the course if they be sorely tried afore Prince Thomas arrives to relieve them."

"Amen to that, my lord prince. For much hangs in the balance of his success." Almost as an afterthought the bishop continued diffidently. "Where does he land to gain a foothold for the relief of Bourges? At Harfleur?"

"No, we believe that he makes for Cotentin, as did my great grandfather for his invasion in Guyenne, many years ago. We are persuaded that he will find safe haven there and a ready port from which to build his attack."

"May God have him in his keeping, my lord prince." The bishop intoned piously and continued probing further. "Do they sail soon, to benefit from the clement weather?"

"They depart upon the end of the month, should the wind prevail in their favour, though they have much do if the numbers are true at some four thousand troops and archers. We venture they will do well upon the muster to achieve such a feat in the time prescribed."

"Indeed, my lord. And what shall you do my prince? Aid your father who ails so, or return to Coventry?"

"We leave on the eleventh of this month of July, seeking to rally support in the shires for our father to spite the doubters of my loyalty at court. I shall be shown to be the true son in due course."

"It was never in doubt, sire." Bishop Beaufort reassured him. Bowing, he turned the conversation to other matters of court.

×⚜×

Nantes: End of July

. . .

In conditions that suited rapid travel, Jamie and Mark made good time and arrived in Nantes towards the end of July, riding and leading two extra horses. They had avoided many of the larger towns, preferring to sleep in woods rather than stay at inns where their presence might be noted. The weather had been hot and fine with no rain, aiding their passage along roads that were in good condition, with a gentle breeze pushing them along from the south east. Here in Guyenne territory they found a contact of Whittington's, a merchant and financier, and bespoke a bed for the night. Both men felt that they could relax, and with the horses and mules fed and watered and in good stables, they vowed to rest for a day to see what intelligence they could gain. Monsieur Adalais, a Gascon of serious disposition, welcomed them cautiously into his house with a sense of trepidation at being seen with foreign agents. He settled them down in his parlour, where Jamie began to gently interrogate him as to the current position of the latest rumours.

"Messieurs, then you have not heard the news. By the good Lord, your time on the road may be in vain, for Bourges fell to a peace accord between the Armagnacs and Burgundians on the twelfth day of July. You caught no news of this?"

Jamie and Mark shook their heads in response. "The twelfth you say, fourteen days ago?" Jamie asked, aghast. "Does Whittington have knowledge of this? For certes it will imperil any attempt to recapture Guyenne and bring it under English dominion. Does the prince's fleet yet sail?" He made to rise from the supper table and set back out upon the road.

"Calm yourself, monsieur. There was a problem with the weather, and all sailings were delayed by an unfavourable wind. Whittington has told me that they now plan to sail upon the first day of the month of August."

"Then we shall be lost, for it must be over one hundred and

fifty leagues to Cotentin from here, and they will have landed, or attempted to, afore we can arrive to warn them."

"Fear not, for Sir Richard – and I believe the court – are aware of the repudiation of the Treaty of Bourges. Yet I fear that they do not appreciate what forces may be drawn against them, and still plan to assail these shores, may God have them in his mercy."

"Hell's teeth, so the damned Armagnacs about faced and reneged upon the treaty! I swore that they would. I dare not trust them or their word, for 'tis as thin as the parchment upon which it was written." Jamie cursed.

"When do we leave, Jamie, for we cannot travel to Cotentin in time to warn the Duke of Clarence or aid him?" Mark asked.

"I know, and it grieves me, for I'll wager that there will be forces of Burgundians awaiting their arrival and a trap will be sprung."

"Not all the Armagnacs agreed to the repudiation of the treaty," Monsieur Adalais said. "I hear reports of that the Duke of Alençon is still sympathetic to your cause. He has retired to his lands near the Chateau d'Essay, and there with others, I believe he will rally to the English cause with his honour intact."

"Then we must away as soon as the horses are rested and make haste for the coast upon the morrow, praying that we find an English force still fighting with which we can join."

They slept soundly in good beds, and the horses were well fed on oats and fresh fodder. They rose with the sun and walked around the town, gaining what knowledge that they could. Everyone seemed to be sympathetic to the English cause and gave them a pleasant welcome. There was some talk of a muster to the north and rumours of troops marching to Cotentin, all with the Burgundian colours at their breast, playing fanfares of victory.

Chapter Thirty-Six

Southampton: 1st August

The fourteen war cogs had been assembled and loaded with provisions. The flagship bore the colours of the Duke of Clarence Prince Thomas, and the brightly coloured shield, quartered in *gules* and *azure,* and the *lions d'or passant guardant* seemed to roar ferociously as the pendant flapped and snapped in the stiff breeze.

Of the three commanders Prince Thomas, at just twenty-two years of age, was considerably younger than the Duke of York and the newly promoted Thomas Beaufort, Earl of Devon. Yet he had gained respect from the army that surrounded him, as well as from his two joint commanders. While not as tall as his brother Prince Henry, he was broad of shoulder and blessed with the good looks of his mother and his once handsome father. He was the victor of many campaigns in Ireland, when his father had put him in charge of his armies at just fourteen years of age, and in other sorties to France. He was no newcomer to command, with a reputation for being a fierce fighter and a desire to always be in the thick of any action.

"What say you, uncle and cousin, shall we make our crossing this day, for the wind seems rightly in our favour?"

"Please God that it stays that way, sire. We will not countenance another delay and needs must land, where we will deal harshly with the French whom we know seek to now join forces to prevent us landing upon our rightful soil," Beaufort opined.

"As you say, uncle, as you say." Then, raising his voice so that all the assembled company of men-at-arms, archers and knights could hear him, he shouted. "Come, let us to war and raise carnage with the whoreson French who dare to defy my father, the king of England and France!" All cheered at the brave words as the three commanders walked across the plank to take command of the flagship. With orders given the crew slipped the mooring lines, and the sails were unfurled to catch the capricious wind that cut across the estuary, making the fleet's progress uncertain. The cogs were pulled out by longboats to catch the outflowing current and reassembled in the English Channel in the lee of the Isle of Wight, until full sail could be engaged and they could travel as a single unit.

The strong and contrary wind forced the ships to tack against it, bobbing and constantly changing course to take advantage of what favourable wind they could find. After several hours of laborious sailing and with the far coast of France just visible on the port horizon, the captain came down from the fo'c'sle to the assembled commanders on the lower deck.

"My lord prince," he began, bowing to Clarence, "I fear that we are in vain, for the wind has blown up against our favour and we shall not make the port of Cotentin this day – nor on the morrow, I fear."

The prince was in an ill mood, for they had been ready to

sail since the end of July and the wind had not been with them. "By the rood, why cannot we achieve the crossing? For neither God nor the French will wait for us." He ranted.

"I cannot command the wind, sire, and see –" the captain gestured with his arm spread wide, "– the fleet is already broken and disparate, with some of the ships having turned back. It is an ill omen and does not bode well, my lord prince." He was a seasoned hand and had known the Channel and all its varied moods from an early age. With luck he knew they would make England's shores this night, but feared that to be blown abroad on a sea such as this was dangerous, and they could be flung hither and thither to fetch up on rocks.

Prince Thomas clenched his fists in frustration, aware of how his brother and the court would see this action to be so thwarted again. The infamous Lancastrian temper flared to little avail. He wanted battle; he wanted to show his brother how he would conquer France, and return covered in glory. Now, he would be laughed at and ridiculed, spawning more resentment and strife within the court and fuelling their sibling rivalry further. He looked out again at the sea that now roiled and chapped with white-topped waves all heading towards England's shores away from France, and all the while his destination was so close that he could see it.

"Very well, turn about afore we are cast in so many directions that we know not where we go," he muttered. At this all men present cast down their eyes, not wishing to engage with the prince at this inauspicious moment. It had been so exciting to roar to the muster in such a short period of time, then only to be delayed by onshore prevailing winds once they were at sea. It was too much for him to bear, and he cursed all that stopped him giving battle to the French.

×⚜×

Valognes, France: 8th August

Jamie and Mark had ridden along narrow country roads that led towards Cherbourg-en-Cotentin at the top of the peninsula, and when they were within a few miles from the coast, they realised it would be a perfect point to stop and gain some intelligence of what was happening. They had heard stories of soldiers moving forward, with troops heading for the coast to meet the long-expected invasion by the English. They had seen no firm evidence of troop movement, but they had observed plenty of frenetic activity among messengers travelling backwards and forwards.

"Think you they be spies?" Mark asked. "Or maybe troops? Surely they cannot have organised so soon after the surrender at Bourges?" He was puzzled. "Leastways we are not too late, for it seems no war has been declared, and all is seemingly chaos around us."

"Amen to that. For certes there has been no battle, and I durst think it only a scouting party to alert Burgundy when – and indeed if – Prince Thomas should land at this point and engage him. We needs must not tarry, for I should like to travel the few miles to the coast and see for myself what has occurred."

The two men bespoke rooms at an inn and left their tired horses and mules there, hiring a couple of mounts to ride the few leagues northwards. After the heat through which they had ridden these days past, it was good to feel the cool breeze of the Channel against their faces. The landscape had become very flat, and open fields vied for space with forests that were being cut down, to make way for cultivated land.

As they rode closer, they saw more evidence of soldiers who had camped in a loose semi-circle around the main road into the town. Many were masked by the trees, and to an observer from the sea almost nothing would have been noticeable, Jamie realised. Camp fires gave off a smoky odour and the meat cooking upon spits made both men's stomachs rumble, for they had not eaten all day apart from some dry bread and cheese.

The soldiers cast suspicious glances their way as the two men moved closer to the town. There was no large grouping as was normal with a war party, and no banners fluttering to herald a substantial force.

"I like this not, Mark," Jamie commented. "There must be hundreds of troops here, but being so disparate they are difficult to count. I have ne'er seen a gathering like this afore except as a scouting party, yet the numbers are too great." A frown creased his forehead. They cantered to within half a mile of the town, still not stopped by sentries, and rode down into a small dip shielded by a copse. Suddenly exposed, the view revealed a slightly sunken plateau; Forest's hackles rose before Jamie heard or saw anything. But before long, he too picked up the sound of Italian being spoken and the gruff shortened vowels of the Scots tongue that brought back memories of his time with Sir Robert de Umfraville. Passing through the screen of trees they saw them. A small army, camped within the hollow: legions of Genoese crossbowmen and the roughly armed Scots of Lord Douglas's army. Forest looked up at her master unsure, for she knew a war camp when she saw one.

They both pulled up short in surprise. "Christ on the Cross, it's a trap," Jamie exclaimed. "That is how they seek to achieve it. Mercenaries and whoreson Scots. The prince will be lulled ashore thinking all is well, and his forces will be slaughtered as soon as they land."

"Do we go back now and find another way?" Mark asked, disturbed at the sight before him.

"No, I would see how the coast looks down by the sea and what preparations are made there. We shall look suspicions if we turn around now, and besides, the sentries have already marked our presence."

They rode on towards the town and the familiar sight of the harbour castle that lay before Jamie. It was, he knew, regarded as one of the strongest castles in Europe. The peninsula curved around the estuary of the River Divette, creating a natural harbour, within the basin of which stood an island that had been enhanced by man. Within the confines of the almost oblong land mass lay the strongly fortified castle. Turreted and castellated, it was a daunting and forbidding symbol of dominance and power. Jamie knew it had been taken in the past by King Edward, who had ensured its surrender years earlier before he went on to win at Crecy.

"By God, that castle looks strong," Mark whispered quietly as they sat on their horses outside the town walls.

"For certes, and it has an immense enceinte securing its position, commanding all within its reach. Yet it has a fault: all the land around is flat, and the castle can be assaulted with ease by an invasion force landing beyond the range of the crossbows on the towers. This was the tactic used by good King Edward third. Victory would come easy with time and the dominance of the sea, allowing them to wait out a surrender by siege, rather than take the castle by assault.

"And if God is on our side, this time it will ease our cause, as the local populace are of a friendly disposition towards England. Aided by the Count of Alençon, all may go well for Prince Thomas," Jamie said, then continued. "Or would, were it not for that army waiting to ambush him as soon as he comes ashore, to be caught in a trapping pincer 'twixt castle and land-born troops, all ready to spring the trap." He finished, shaking his head in disgust. "Mayhap we can find a way to thwart such an action and save the prince from his fate.

"Come now, we shall take our turn here at an inn and see what more we can infer of intelligence, as well as wine."

Mark smiled at his friend's jest and the two rode on into the town, surreptitiously spying out the land and keeping their eyes and ears open. Mark spoke little. In his two years in London he had mastered the French of the court, but his accent was strong and foreign. Most men gave him a broad berth due to his size, and it was Jamie posing as a Flemish merchant who engaged with them the most, seeking information of the tide and when he might ship goods upwards to Flanders. They met with a merchant trader of his father's acquaintance whom Jamie had not seen for many years. Upon entering his place of business, the merchant was surprised to see the man grown whom he had known as a youngster at his father's side.

"Well, by all that's holy," Monsieur Alon Greaves exclaimed, throwing questions and answers in a garrulous fashion as he bustled about, welcoming them inside his private parlour. "I would not have recognised you so grown to manhood. How does your father fare? Right well I hope, and better than the tidings from England, I trust? Now come, where are my manners? For I should fetch you wine and refreshment." At which he moved again, swiftly despite his bulk, ordering a servant to attend them with wine and food.

Once settled, and with the food presented, Jamie answered the trader's questions and tentatively enquired about what might have been happening locally, mixing fact and fiction by way of explanation.

"We are lately returned from Calais, and before that Flanders, and upon our journey we see a land despoiled by strife and threats of war with armies everywhere. Rumours spread abroad that the English will land here soon. Is that true? For I should not wish to be within these walls should that be the case."

"Aye, 'tis true enough, and the army lodged here is convinced that a landing will occur very soon. They must have secure intelligence to suppose such an action. We shall suffer for it both in trade and security." Greaves bemoaned. Jamie exchanged a brief look with Mark. *So the English were betrayed by someone at court,* he thought.

They continued talking with the merchant for a while longer, enjoying his hospitality. Jamie said he would return when matters were resolved and bring his father's business back to trade with him again, upon which he and Mark returned to their inn at Valognes. "Our devoir is clear," Jamie said. "We needs must attend upon the prince, and by some means alert him to his plight afore he lands and finds himself in the jaws of a trap. We shall scout around the coast or speak with the land-lord at the inn and find the names of towns to the north east."

The following evening saw them fully equipped again and entering the fishing village of St. Vaast-la Hougue. It was little more than a small collection of fisherman's crofts and houses set along the esplanade, which was surmounted by a stone harbour wall. The natural lie of the land, with a hooked promontory and a strip of headland that calmed the waters of the Channel and the harbour, provided a safe haven for the fishing boats. A quarter of a mile out to sea, they discerned a large island in the dimming light of a setting sun that threw long, refracted shadows of gold and vermilion across the slate-grey sea.

Fishermen were still tidying their nets and some were preparing to start a new expedition, venturing out in the evening air for a night catch. Jamie called upon a couple of boats, and finally raised interest at his request to charter the boat for the next two or three nights. Explaining that they could fish to their hearts content but that he would be happy to take their money for passage to the Channel, one fisherman with a two-sailed skiff agreed, saying he would be setting off for the night in an hour's time if they were interested. Terms were agreed, and the two Englishmen hurried off to find an inn and stabling for their horses and mules.

The first night at sea was calm, with hardly any movement apart from the gentle slap of waves against the planked hull. They were anchored a league or so out to sea, level with the peninsular of land that jutted out from Cherbourg Cotentin. The night passed without incident and they thanked the fisherman, Gidie, for his time, paying him before they went ashore.

His seamed face creased in an expression that could have been a grin. "You want to try again tomorrow, messieurs? The tide and wind, she may be with you."

Jamie gave a tired smile, and agreed that they would indeed venture out again. "Where do you sleep, old man, for we may need you afore the coming hour?" he asked.

"There." Gidie pointed to a pink-limewash coloured cottage a few houses down from the inn where they had rented rooms. Jamie and Mark were exhausted after the long ride and a fitful sleep on the boat – although Mark often settled with ease into any waterborne craft – aiding the old man and his son whenever the catch was brought in.

They took it in turns to sleep or watch the sea from their bedroom window, knowing any fleet would be large enough to spot easily. Jamie took the first spell and then flopped onto his cot fully clothed. He awoke sometime later feeling cold. Rousing himself he rubbed his shoulders, warding off the feeling of stiffness of the chill from cold muscles.

Mark sensed movement behind him, and turned to look

back from the open window where he was seated. "The wind's changed direction, it now blows inland. 'Twill do well for the prince, should he be abroad."

Jamie nodded and rose, pulling on his gambeson to warm his bones in the shady room. Mark folded out the settle upon which he was seated and dropped to his cot, falling asleep within seconds. The day passed slowly. *Action is what I need, the time for waiting has gone. I want to kill some Frenchmen and Scots,* Jamie thought to himself.

The evening came, and they ate at the inn, and then met Gidie at the harbour side.

"Fare ye well, messieurs. The wind she has changed, and we shall have to work hard to be in the Channel this night."

He tacked out of the harbour, and once free of the wind-break, they could all feel the stiff breeze. Gidie tacked harshly across and back, seemingly for hours, until finally they were able to use the drift of the wind more in their favour.

The evening slipped into the dark of the night, and just before dawn broke, Jamie was shaken awake by the grizzled seaman. He rubbed his eyes to peer in the direction the man indicted. Mark spoke in hushed tones as Forest's ears pricked to the faint sound of voices carrying on the breeze.

"There, looking dark against the grey sea," Mark said. "Two...no three...no four or more. Large cogs of war by their silhouettes."

Jamie was sceptical, but then he too saw them. "Probably half a league off. Raise your nets and anchor, old man, and let us greet the prince, for certes 'tis him, praise God."

Chapter Thirty-Seven

Two torches were lit on either side of the fishing skiff as it moved onto a new course that would intercept the oncoming fleet. As they drew nearer, Jamie and Mark began shouting, hailing the flagship; they could just make out the prince's colours flapping from the mast head in the light of the torches. Sensing the excitement, Forest began to bark loudly too, as men-at-arms lined the rails of the huge cog, and crossbowmen readied themselves with quarrels loaded in the tillers of their weapons. It was a tense moment for Jamie and Mark, who did not wish to be skewered by an over-zealous archer.

"Do not loose! Stay your weapons, for we are Englishmen on the king's errand and needs must speak with the prince."

"Who are you, sir?" a commanding voice called some hundred yards away, for the skiff was fleeter by far than the lumbering war cogs.

"I am Sir James de Grispere of the court, here with my companion, Mark of Cornwall of the prince's household. We have urgent news for His Royal Highness. Throw down a line that we may heave to and board you. Do not tarry, for much depends upon the hour." Jamie ordered, becoming anxious and angry at the response and delay.

He heard orders given to furl the mainsails and commands were shouted from ship to ship to order the rest of the fleet to follow suit. The cogs used dredging anchors, slowing to but a knot, and lines were cast and tied to the skiff, enabling Jamie and Mark to make the perilous climb up the side of the huge vessel. Once at the rails, strong hands grabbed their arms and hauled them aboard.

The familiar figure of Prince Thomas appeared before them, windswept, his long, brown locks damp with sea spray and ragged with the wind. The two men bowed deeply before him. On either side of the prince was the Duke of York and the frowning face of the Earl of Devon, Thomas Beaufort.

"Sire, Sir James de Grispere at your service. I beg pardon for this rude arrival, yet I have grave news and brevity shall be my excuse."

"Why de Grispere, 'tis you indeed. We had reckoned you dead or ill abroad. This is most unlooked for. We thought ourselves mad to hear English voices in the midst of the sea," the prince said. "And when we heard a dog bark this far from land we were sure on't!"

"'Twas my own faithful hound, sire, and I beg your leave to bring her aboard, for she has mayhap helped save us all."

"For certes, de Grispere. If she will bear the indignity of a net we shall have her carried up." The prince turned and summoned servants, who hastened to obey, ordering sailors to lower a net and pass instructions to the skiff below.

"From whence did you arrive?" The prince continued as Forest was lifted aboard.

"Highness, may it please you, from Italy and beyond. But

the tale is too long for the telling at this moment, for a trap awaits you, sire, on yonder shores of Cotentin. A contingent of mercenaries, Scots and Burgundians lie in wait to slaughter you as soon as you come ashore.

"The truce is no longer, and the Armagnacs now side with the Burgundians, their word and the treaty broken as the Confessor's Sword of Mercy. Please God, I adjure you, change your course now that I may aid you to a safer haven, for the dawn approaches and all will be lost if you be seen abroad on this course by watchers at the port of Cherbourg Cotentin."

To his credit the prince absorbed the information quickly, as those listening gasped at the news, with talk bubbling up amongst those present.

"Where do you advise that we make for?" Prince Thomas asked curtly.

"To the south east. Go around the peninsula and land at the village of St Vaast-la-Hougue."

"Why then history serves us well, for my great grandfather landed there, and success was his at Crecy. Send the signals! Captain, come about and set a course for St Vaast, there to come ashore and serve these dogs as they would serve us. And whilst I speak of service, it seems that you have again served us and your king right well, de Grispere, for our father shall hear of this and mayhap our brother too, for 'tis on his errand, we venture, that you travelled forth to Italy?"

"As you say, sire. With your father's blessing and in great secrecy we carried the papal levy, now duly paid to His Holiness upon the behest of the Alberti bankers."

"By the rood, this was your doing? Then may God assoil you, for all is well we hear, and the schism is neither settled nor falls in favour of the French. A blessing upon you and your companions upon that venture.

"Now that we have time in hand, apprise us of all that you

know of the placement of troops set against us." The prince's commanders gathered around to hear what Jamie had to say concerning the arrangements of the French army. There were many questions and Jamie drew a rough map upon a piece of parchment, produced at the prince's behest.

At length Sir Thomas Beaufort asked: "How came you here so swiftly? For it seems whenever I am upon a ship or strife arises, there you be with the Devil's own luck to aid you in your cause."

"I received orders to depart Italy in all haste, carried by a messenger who was lately arrived with a missive from England. I cast all to the wind and came post haste in that regard and find myself here, supposedly too late to aid you, yet I find I am none too tardy," Jamie answered, ignoring the earl's latent aggression.

"Aye, and praise God for the foul weather and a hindering wind that impeded us, and providence that delayed our arrival here to meet with you at such an auspicious moment," the prince responded.

With that they felt the ship lurch and shift as the sails caught the wind. The tiller bit harshly into the sea, causing the huge cog to change course, as the pilots heaved upon the tiller bar at the rear deck. Mark and Jamie exchanged glances and the prince then addressed the giant wrestler. "We too have seen you at court, Mark of Cornwall. The champion wrestler who defeats all comers, we're bound."

"I know naught of that, my prince, for I too have felt the mat and been tumbled in my time, yet I have had my share of luck within the ring, of that I'm bound. I am now bound to your service and would aid you in your endeavours here, for there is war to be had and no mistake."

"Well spoken, Mark of Cornwall. We shall be glad to call you blanchemain in this affair and have you fight by our side.

Yet it will be armour, not a suit of cotton to defend you here, I'm bound. Are you well equipped thus?"

"Aye, as your highness pleases, for my hauberk lies within the inn, rusting from little use. I shall be pleased to don it in your service, sire," Mark responded.

Chapter Thirty-Eight

The fleet made St. Vaast harbour before full day dawned, blown in by a strong following wind. The cogs lined up and anchored to disembark the four thousand troops, along with their horses and equipment.

Mark, looking on in awe, commented: "Why, there must some three thousand archers here. We shall slaughter the French."

The prince and his captains set guards on the roads to prevent travel before the army moved off, and all boats were stopped from leaving the harbour. In this way they hoped to maintain the element of surprise. The prince's temper was short. He knew battle was coming and was eager to be on the road. He stood with his commanders watching order emerge from the apparent chaos.

"Sire, if I may," Beaufort began diplomatically, "knowing the setting of the assembled troops from de Grispere's map..." He was an experienced soldier and the victor of many a battle.

"Proceed," the prince responded curtly.

"As you please, sire. The entrapment of the rear ranks will

work well, but were you to send the fleet around the peninsula upon this course, with but seamen at the helm, mayhap with a company of men to complete the decoy –" Beaufort traced a route around the headland, "– the weight of the defender's view would be seaward, affording us the better chance to approach undetected at their rear. They will, I am persuaded, hold back upon seeing the ships appear collected thus, as well as our apparent arrival in strength and numbers, and will collect in the hollow near the shore to spring their trap. We shall all the easier be able to come upon them from an unexpected direction. A conroi of knights, together with a company of archers, will prevent a sally from the castle – though from what de Grispere says, there is little appetite for a local attack without the assurance of great odds in their favour."

The prince narrowed his eyes in concentration, liking little to take advice from any man. Yet he conceded to the older and more experienced soldier. "Bravo, for that is a most excellent plan. Have it made so, captains."

"I should be pleased to attend you in this matter," the Duke of York offered, "and we shall form the feint for your strike to the rear."

Jamie watched as other knights spoke up, seeing a chance for glory and looking to head an attack from the seaward side, with the promise of slaughter and valuable hostages. Among the congregation of knights, Jamie saw a figure move forward, his arms stretched wide: "By the Good Lord, Jamie, 'tis you!" Sir Christopher Urquhart cried. "We thought you dead or taken by the Italians. How came you here? Though I know for certes that wherever there is battle and glory to be had then Sir James de Grispere shall be there too."

"Kit! By the rood, I thought that my eyes deceived me, yet I am little surprised, for Jeanette wagered that you would be close to the prince if it came to war."

"How does your sister? She is not here in this chaos, I pray?"

"Nay, fear not. She was safe and well in Italy when last I saw her, pledged for a ship home guarded by Genoese galleys. There is too much of a tale to tell, and upon the finish of this battle, I will relate all over a flagon of good French wine, but now I must set to and arm myself, or a sorry cushion I should be with no maille."

The captains ran off to follow the prince's commands. The war party separated and the cogs made ready to sail about, as the prince sent scouts out and the company moved off along the road to Cotentin. The sun was rising as they marched westwards. The standards of the prince, the duke and the earl were all flying from heralds, and the armoured knights sparkled as the first shafts of sunlight etched the countryside from the east, throwing long shadows in front of the advancing army. The horses, glad to be upon firm land once more, pranced and jolted, keen to be moving into battle.

Leaving their pack mules with a groom, Jamie and Mark went ahead with the scouts to show them the lie of the land and point out where the French were positioned, with Forest ever alert for sounds that the others might miss. The company made a rapid forced march and arrived upon the plains approximately a mile outside the French encampment by late morning, to ensure that they were there in time for the cogs to be seen from the town of Cotentin. There, in hushed tones, the scouts reported back to the prince, led by Jamie and Mark.

"It is as we described, sire. The French have small companies thus at the rear –" Jamie pointed at the crude map that he had created earlier, "– with the main forces close to the town in the lee of a basin here. These are a mix of Scots mercenaries, mostly on foot, and Genoese crossbowmen in two companies.

All seem at their ease and have dug defensive positions and trenches to the seaward side of their encampment."

Beaufort was a soldier with great experience and it showed in his next question: "How does the land lie here?" He pointed to the map where the outline of trees had been sketched in.

"The encampment lies in a hollow of sorts, while the land leading to the trees slopes very gently. The angle is almost insignificant, but it offers a slight advantage to any army placed within the trees. As it is, anyone wishing to attack them would need to move uphill, my lord," Jamie replied.

"Ah, I see you take my meaning. And what of the opposite wood? Could this be infiltrated afore an attack is launched on the main body?"

"I doubt that very much, for any company of archers or foot soldiers would need to circumvent the rear body through open ground, or make such a detour that they are sure to be discovered."

"So be it," interjected the impatient prince. "We shall have to make do with an attack on two fronts, while the sea and my Lord of York's force pin them from the front."

Lord Beaufort made to argue, but wisely conceded and nodded in agreement. It was agreed that the forces of knights be held back, in readiness for the sounds of fighting between the main force of Genoese and Scots and the English archers. They had allowed five hours for the fleet to circumvent the headland and be seen by watchers from the port and castle, who would then alert the French forces of the impending invasion. The fleet was to drop anchor away from the main castle but still within the deep water of the port. Lord Ormond, Jamie and Mark, together with other household knights, foot soldiers and captains-of-arms, accompanied the companies of archers through the woods. It was hard going, with only single tracks to follow.

They all knew that secrecy and stealth were the watchwords, as timing was down to their ability to loose a lethal storm of arrows upon the unsuspecting French and the mercenaries camped in the hollow below. They assembled in the woods out of sight and the captains gave a final briefing. James, Earl of Ormond, was in overall command of the party, an Irish lord who had fought with Prince Thomas in Ireland. Jamie had taken to the man immediately. This form of clandestine warfare was the sort of fighting both men had experienced in both Ireland and Scotland. They led their horses with the other mounted knights, keeping back to prevent the noise of their bridles and tack carrying to the enemy.

Given free rein over their companies, the captains of archers ordered the bowmen to their places. It was tense, the sun was hot and the men were pleased to be in the shade of the trees that were still in full leaf, offering relief from the dry August heat. The undergrowth was like tinder, as the exceptionally hot and dry summer drew towards its end. The men took a final glug of water from their costrels, strung their bows and prepared for battle.

Jamie sensed the old feeling of anticipation, as the blood coursed through his veins in excitement and his muscles became leaden and sluggish. He knew from experience that this would dissipate as soon as the fighting began. Then he heard it, the high, mournful whine of a trumpet being blown: The fleet had been spotted!

The camp below sprang to life, with men running for crossbows, donning armour or mail as sergeants and captains called for order. Shouts of glee were heard, and the harsh tones of the Scottish tongue filled Jamie with memories of the border wars with Sir Robert de Umfraville. He reached down to buckle Forest's war collar around her neck, calling her to heed his bidding when the fighting started. The air became palpably tense. Every man wanted the fighting to start. Jamie watched as two or three of the soldiers threw up in the shade of the trees, wiping the acid bile from their mouths after it left their throats.

Like ants working inside a nest the activity below progressed, with all focused forwards or readying their war gear, as they prepared for an invasion from the sea. None looked to the woods and the noise rose to a cacophony of shouts and cries. Jamie looked across at the earl, knowing that this was the best moment to attack, hoping that the Irish lord was in accord. Too early and they would be seen, too late and the enemy would have time to ready themselves to repel and thwart the trap.

"Now captains," the earl ordered. "Bring the archers to the fore and loose upon your command."

"Move forward!" The command was whispered down the lines of expectant men. As it did so, each archer pushed a sheaf of arrows into the ground by his feet, to gain better access to them for swift retrieval.

"Nock arrows, draw..." For two brief seconds, all that could be heard was the straining of thews, the creaking of yew and deeply drawn breaths, as nearly three thousand men pulled back in unison.

"Loose!" came the command. The twang of bowstrings clipped the air, followed by the sibilant whistle as nearly three thousand shafts of ash soared, flashing in the sunlight before dropping one hundred and fifty yards away, into the massed ranks of the French soldiers and mercenaries.

Some among the enemy heard the awful flaysome whistling sound, and looked skyward in horror as the arrow storm finished its lethal trajectory, before the sickening thuds of arrow tips biting into flesh began, followed by the cries of pain from injured and dying men. Victims looked like puppets cut from their strings as they were thrown backwards, to writhe in their death throes upon the ground. The Genoese crossbowmen had not had time to string their bows and were unable to reply to the lethal hail that assailed them. Five seconds later another storm whistled home, decimating the closed ranks in the camp. There was panic and horror as men sprang ash stems like porcupine quills, running for shields, to protect themselves from the hail of steel barbs.

The full cry of battle took hold. The Scots were braver than the Genoese, who made to retreat into the woods behind, where they knew they could load their cumbersome weapons and fight from a distance, as they were used to.

Jamie saw the move and shouted to the captains of archers: "Fire the grass to the rear! Fire arrows, quickly!" he ordered, not seeking permission from the Earl of Ormond, but the earl realised Jamie's intention and added his voice to the order.

The captains, upon hearing the command, shouted, "Every third man, loose fire arrows, full distance!" Flints were struck by the soldiers, tows lit, and the flaming arrows roared across the sky to land a full three hundred and fifty yards away. The parched undergrowth flared as though it had been soaked in pitch like the arrows, fanning to a wall of flame. Thick, acrid, choking smoke began to rise amongst the running Genoese crossbowmen. Some made it through to the woods, but in disparate groups who would need to relinquish their cover to put themselves within crossbow range of the English.

The Scots were raw fighters and more used to hand-to-hand combat. Relishing the idea of facing their old enemy, they grabbed swords, spears and shields, and started to run toward the lines of archers in the woods, war cries issuing from their lips. They advanced in their tribal lines, angry and murderous, shouting as they came. The angle of the bowmen changed as they lowered their aim and winnowed the Scottish ranks like chaffed wheat. Yet the Scots were not cowards and the survivors and the uninjured ran onwards, closing the distance.

"Now, charge!" Lord Ormond called, at which the mounted knights and foot soldiers left the cover of the woods and charged down the hill towards the Scottish fighters. Jamie, now in his element, was at the van of the charge, with Forest bounding by his side and Mark on Breseler in his first mounted combat on his new warhorse. Richard pulled at the bit, fully engaged and collected, his head high, muscles tight with strain. Through the excitement Jamie heard the clang of battle to his left, indicating that Prince Thomas and his army had engaged the rear ranks. The battle madness came upon him: "An Umfraville! An Umfraville!" he called.

Hearing him shout, some of the mounted Scottish knights heard the hated war cry of the English on the Borders and changed direction to engage him. Jamie recognised a trio of knights, with Earl of Wigton as their leader – familiar from his time with Sir Robert – and intensified his pace, bearing down upon them and shouting his war cry. He lowered his borrowed shield, for without armour he had only his mail hauberk and helmet to protect him. The Scottish knights too were lightly armoured, having had no time in which to prepare for battle. The distance closed, with Mark at his side and Forest bounding just behind them.

Wigton, the leader of the Scottish knights, lowered his spear war-side, and as the distance between them closed amid thundering hooves across the dry ground, all seemed to slow down in Jamie's mind, becoming clearer right before the rush of impact. The point of Wigton's spear wavered just as the experienced knight tried for a feint, changing to tilt-side, as he sought for any weakness in Jamie's guard. Jamie lowered his shield to a seemingly suicidal level. The change in guard caused the knight to cross his line, and Jamie nudged Richard with his left leg, pushing the horse into a balletic prance to the right, setting his master up in perfect time. Jamie brought his shield upwards, deflecting Wigton's spear tip at the final second, and pressuring Richard further, they collided with the smaller mount of the Scot. Their legs briefly caught and Jamie kicked hard, prepared for the collision, then twisted sharply in the saddle and lashed back at his opponent, who tipped beyond the point of balance and fell ignominiously to the ground, one foot still caught in the stirrup.

The blow had not broken through the steel rings of the mail, but Wigton's horse had continued with its journey, wrenching its rider's knee from its joint before he could release his foot from the stirrup. He cried out in anguish, bounced on the hard ground and sought to rise from all fours, finding his right leg unable to support him.

Jamie had no time to capitalise upon the success as he crashed through the first line of knights, charging onwards. Mark at his side, with his poleaxe held two-handed, swung to his right and smashed a rider from his saddle, breaking his back. A second rider appeared from his left. Breseler snorted in anger beneath him, and needing only the slightest of bidding drifted sideways, light as a feather upon the breeze, driving into the oncoming knight's horse and biting with bared teeth. The opponent's horse shied, unbalancing its rider, and Mark drove his shield directly into his face in passing. Then he too was through and the knights wreaked havoc among the foot soldiers, slashing down, hooves trampling and lashing out. There were still many soldiers to fight, as the archers had ceased loosing arrows once the charge had begun for fear of hitting their own men. The banshee howl of battle raged, anger and death merged into one evil cacophony.

Yet all was not lost for the French side. The Genoese cross-bowmen had formed two sides of a square, linking with the now organised Scots, who had raised their shields to save themselves, first from the hail of arrows and then from the attack of the English knights. The Italians began to load and loose bolts from their slow-moving and cumbersome weapons. Some had even managed to erect wooden palisades with slots, through which to aim their deadly bolts. With the heat, flames and smoke, it became a scene from hell. Jamie slew his latest opponent and turned to find new victims, seeing that one Genoese had just pulled back the string of his weapon and was aiming for him as he fought. A flash of grey rushed through the air as Forest savaged him, first crushing his arm and then his unprotected face.

Jamie called her off, fearing that she may be targeted by his comrades: "Here girl, by."

Then there was a new thunder of hooves. The French rear guard had been vanquished, by surprising and overwhelming odds, by the knights of the prince's army who now came thundering around the bend in the road, with others emerging behind from the trail through the copse.

The sight of knights in full battle rage charging forward, banners flying and war cries sounding, drove fear into the hearts of the remaining mercenaries, who fought with no loyalty save coin. Some of the Genoese retrained their weapons, turning the willow palisades to cover the new angle of assault, but it was in vain and too late, and they were cut down. Others ran through gaps in the wall of flame to the woods, where they were slaughtered by the avenging knights. Many just threw down their weapons and raised their hands in surrender. The feeling of defeat was endemic and swept through them like the plague. Some were felled despite their surrender; others who looked like valuable knights or lords were spared for ransom. None of the English liked the mercenaries, and afforded little respect to the Scots or the Genoese, seeing them as the hired killers they were.

In the space of a minute before the charge, the bowmen had poured wave after wave of arrows into the massed ranks of the camp, dealing death in a lethal storm of bodkins. Nearly thirty thousand arrows had been loosed in that short time, upon the unprepared and barely armoured ranks of the French mercenary forces. The dying and wounded were now splayed across the field like wilted poppies, red and bleeding upon the dry ground. The sheer enormity of the archers' firepower took an inevitable toll, while the fires they had started were now sweeping up towards the woods behind, blown along by the incoming wind. The resulting smoke dislodged the crossbowmen and the Scots who pulled farther back, and began the long and arduous journey inland to link with the oncoming army of the Burgundians.

Prince Thomas pulled up his visor and looked around, with a profound feeling of satisfaction. "Why, by God's grace this was a good day's work and well done." He turned to address the leaders of the charge as the looting began among the archers, who retrieved their spent arrows for reuse, and the foot soldiers sought the spoils of war. The dead and dying were picked clean. "Well met, my Lord Ormond." The prince greeted his ally. "For what was planned as a trap by the rebels turned into death and an ignominious defeat for them. This day's work will set the tone for the campaign to come and soon all France will be ours, we'll wager."

"Amen to that, sire, for we shall rout them elsewhere as here, despite their knavery."

Jamie approached with the luckless Lord Wigton lolling in the saddle, his sword gone and *paroli* given not to defect or ride off. His face was white with pain and the foot of his right leg was twisted at an improbable angle. Once before the prince, Jamie bowed in the saddle.

"Who may this be, to be so sorely abroad?" the prince asked.

"My prince, I have the honour to introduce the Earl of Wigton, son of Lord Douglas. Bow to your betters, my lord, for this is His Royal Highness Prince Thomas of England."

The surly lord barely bowed his head in a minimal show of obeisance.

"Well, I see that your manners match your father's dishonour. He should look well afore he sends you on a man's errand again." The prince taunted the captured lord, who shot hatred in return, his darkened eyes narrowing in anger.

"Guard him well, for we durst trust him not, Sir James. Though to you goes the honour and the glory. Had you not apprised us of this trap, we should be in a sorry state with roles reversed, or at least severely discomposed."

"My lord prince, 'twas merely my devoir and honour, yet I thank you for your kind praise. Now sire, may I ask what do we do? For I see that the contingent from the ships comes hence."

"We shall march inland and take more of the French lands. There are battles to be fought in our father's name against all comers now, as it seems that the Burgundians and Armagnacs are resolved to stand as one against us."

"As you wish, sire. By your leave, I would secure my prisoner for ransom and make haste to report upon this day's deeds."

"You may indeed see to your prisoner and his ransom. Thereafter, you must not tarry, for we would have you at our side by royal command the better, to aid us in our strike for the heart of France. Together we shall rout the French from his majesty's lands and return them to their rightful ownership, and we have work of a specific nature that you may perform. I would have you attend upon us in our tent once you have settled your affairs."

Jamie was surprised, but his training forbade him to show it. Bowing, he replied, "As Your Royal Highness commands." He was greatly intrigued by his new orders, yet failing to see how he could aid the prince, but he was quietly excited at the prospect of more battle and more glory to be gained.

Chapter Thirty-Nine

Jamie and Mark gathered their two mules and made their way back into the town, weary now, as battle fatigue hit them. Their muscles were cold, despite the heat of the day, and with nothing to bring hot temper to their souls, they both felt a sense of anti-climax. Jamie was used to this feeling, and had expected its arrival like an old, familiar friend, acting as a badge of courage, showing him that he had performed well upon the field. The two men were quiet and glad of the stillness between them. With no words needing to be spoken, they felt the common bond that binds men who have lived and fought together, and had witnessed death and destruction.

Mark reflected upon how much he had changed since he had left Cornwall after the fateful wrestling match in which he had accidentally killed his opponent. In this period of stillness and introspection, he also realised how much he missed Emma, and how he longed to see her again, to lie in her arms after five months apart. To ease his own thoughts he broke the silence, marvelling once again at the ability of the war horse under him.

"Why, 'twas all over so quickly and Breseler had the most

incredible agility. He moved as soon as I bethought the action, or so it seemed to me," he commented, patting the horse's neck gently and praising him. The grey stallion jerked his head up and down, rattling his bit, whether in gratitude or irked at the petting, neither man could tell.

"He is a fine horse, and has been well trained – as you found out today," Jamie replied. "Treat him well and he will look after you. The bond will become closer as you ride him more and train with him. A good warhorse will know what to do and how to do it before you are of the same notion. Respect him, yet I adjure you, do not to allow him to obtain the upper hand, for on that road lies danger."

Mark nodded in acknowledgement and then asked, "To speak of gaining a command or upper hand, what dost thou think my lord of Clarence has in mind for us?"

"I suspect it not to be directly in battle, for he will want to find a way into the next town of note, as he strikes forth into the territory of the Armagnacs. He has taken it ill to be so betrayed by them and will strike at their heartland in the Loire, I durst say. The great town of Meung in the Loire valley will be his target, I'll wager. 'Tis a great town, fortified upon a hill with a strong castle without. No other towns along that route are as easily defended. The prince, with no canon to ravage the walls of the castle, needs must lay siege, opening himself to attack as the main French forces try to relieve the town. Therefore, he must conquer all those in his wake and quickly, leaving none behind who may strike a counter attack at his rear as we did today. For in that way lies folly.

"No. It shall be Meung that will draw him, and to be south of the Armagnac capital of Orleans will bring them to book for certes."

"How far be this town from here?" Mark asked.

"Some two hundred leagues or thereabouts, to the south

east. Why, think you of hearth and home? For we have been on the road now for nigh on five months."

Mark smiled gently. "I do indeed, and I think of Emma too. 'Tis a goodly time to endure such a separation, yet I would not desert you now, for there is much still to do."

"You have the right of it. Yet I'll wager that my time will be spent as an *insidiore* from now forward, with little to be gained by your presence." At which Jamie paused, considering his next words carefully.

"Mark," he began gently, clasping his friend upon his huge shoulder. "I adjure you, go home now and take Richard with you. For in that last charge, though still game, he showed that he was tired. Long will this journey be, and subject to much privation as we lay waste to the French soil. Richard too needs must have rest, for his road has been long and he has endured much for many a day, with little rest but in the heat of Florence." Mark made to object but Jamie raised his hand. "Nay, think on't. You draw attention by your size and accent. To be so abroad above anything other than a soldier will attract the attention of all. Whereas I may move freely as I wish, being Flemish or Scots, for I know their tongue and have their looks from my mother. This next part will take more guile than strength."

"I shall own to being glad to see England's shores again and feasting upon beef and good ale."

"'Tis settled then, and well done. For the prince did not include you in the call to return to his side, and with no royal fiat, it will be all the easier to slip away under the guise of returning intelligence to the crown on all that has occurred."

They found their way at last to the house of Monsieur Alon Greaves once more, and upon making themselves known at his door, were given a friendly welcome, especially as the town had fallen to the English after the castle had surrendered.

"Ah, Messieurs, I hope that all is well and that you thrive? Come inside, do, and let there be no need for secrecy now." But upon closer inspection, he recoiled slightly at the stench of them and their image, for both were streaked with blood and dirt, their hair plastered to their heads, smelling of death and sweaty horses. Forest too was a mess, her fur matted and streaked with red.

Jamie and Mark were relieved at the welcome, and with their horses and mules looked after and Forest bade to stay in the stables, they stepped inside the merchant's house.

A servant showed the two men a garderobe, and after they had washed away the dirt and blood of battle, they sat as food and wine was brought before them. They realised that they were tired, and at the thought of returning to England that very day, Mark was especially relaxed. The afternoon's feeling of lethargy sloughed from him as the cool wine slaked his thirst, taking away the sweet, sickly tang of blood from his throat and nostrils.

"Tell me," the merchant asked tentatively, no longer wrinkling is nose in disgust. "How do the English fare? Were the Scots and Genoese beaten soundly?"

"They were right well, for we slaughtered them, and we now march inland to better teach them a lesson."

Jamie gave a short account of the events, advising him that Mark was returning with a full report upon the next tide. They did not stay long at the merchant's house, making instead for the quayside to seek a ship that would carry Mark back to England. They found a merchant cog that was bound for home, and for a fee Mark's passage was secured. Forest looked up at her master expectantly as Richard was boarded with little bother this time. To Jamie, it was as if the horse knew he was going home.

Jamie squatted down to Forest's eye level and ruffled the fur at her neck.

"No, girl. From here I go alone, for I fear that you will be more hindrance than aid, and I should worry for your safety against armoured knights." Forest put her head to one side and let out a low whimper. When Mark beckoned her aboard Jamie looked up and said, "You will need to watch her well, for she may try to swim ashore."

"I will look after her, Jamie, be not concerned." Mark assured him. The tide was already high and the captain was ready to cast off. They clasped hands and Mark placed his other huge hand upon Jamie's shoulder, squeezing hard enough to make him wince, as he bade his friend farewell. Forest whined, but Mark held her firmly as the cog floated out to sea, catching a gentle breeze that pulled upon her single sail. At last Jamie turned landwards, walking towards the waiting mule and the saddle that he had stripped from Richard. *So once again from knight to spy I'm bound,* he mused to himself.

PART IV

AUTUMN

France; The Winds of War

Chapter Forty

When Jamie returned to the prince's camp his suspicions were confirmed. He was tasked with days of scouting ahead and seeking ways to defeat the towns before the main party arrived, assessing the strength of the enemy in each region, learning their strengths and weaknesses in each town. He rode the horse he had claimed as spoils of war from the luckless Lord Wigton. It was no Richard, but the animal was well enough trained, and Jamie found it hardy and comfortable for long hours in the saddle.

His task offered him a break from the constant scrutiny of Sir Thomas Beaufort at the prince's camp. He felt the enmity there, or at best a grudging respect from the earl, whose eyes seemed always to be upon him, seeking out his motives and questioning his actions in small ways, trying to undermine Jamie in the eyes of the prince. Sir Richard Whittington had forewarned him of Beaufort's efforts to drive a wedge between the two princes, and this had seemed apparent from the earl's action in campaign. His time at court had served Jamie well and he was now ever cynical of others' motives, particularly where the princes and the king were concerned.

Twelve days after leaving Cotentin, Jamie and one of his fellow scouts found themselves in woods outside the castle at Meung-sur-Loire, looking up at the forbidding walls that rose above them. Small villages had sprung up outside the castle walls, within the lee of the town to the north side of the mighty river Loire, where it was joined by the river Mauves. The bridge across the river was well fortified, he noticed, as were the gates to the town. The adjacent castle commanded both aspects, and it was apparent that whoever had control of the fortress would be able to defeat all comers and orchestrate a perfect assault upon the town from the shelter of the emplacement.

Jamie and the scout were some distance from the road, in a small copse of trees.

"Look –" Jamie pointed, "– the bridge is the line of defence. If it were to be taken, the town and the castle would be divided. 'Tis there that the prince must gain his first hold upon the town. Once he has secured the fortifications of the bridge-works he will be sheltered from bolts on all sides. You needs must report all we have seen."

"Aye, Sir James. Where will you be upon our return?"

"Why, in the castle, and when I can see that the bridge has been secured, then I will wave a brand from the ramparts at night, side to side thus –" He motioned with his arms, "– signalling that I have secured a way for the prince to enter safely and take the garrison by surprise, unless I devise a different stratagem and leave a message here to advise how the assault should be delivered."

"As you wish, Sir James. Yet how will you gain entrance?"

"As a Scotsman!" Jamie declared, mimicking the accent that he had heard for many years on the borders. At one time, Sir Robert had chastised him for inadvertently picking up a Scottish burr to his voice and using the dialect about the castle. The scout looked at him aghast, unbelieving at the change in his voice. "Now, I will scout the town and bridge. Mark this tree here, score it with your sword so that you may know it again." He commanded, pointing to the huge French oak at the edge of the road. "Here I shall leave a message upon the branch fork."

The scout obeyed Jamie's orders and departed. Jamie looked to the castle and then to the town.

"Come then, horse, for we shall look over the town first and mayhap make friends there, the better to secure a place within the castle and see what we can of the defences they have mustered against us." He patted the horse's neck before urging it forward, clanking down the stone causeway towards the fortified bridge, his horse's shoes loose from wear. Jamie himself was as uncurried as his horse, rough from the long road he had travelled.

His hair was now streaked with strawberry blond from the sun, and he had gained more scars across his body from fighting. He had lost all surplus fat and was honed to a being of sprung steel, stropped to within an inch of its life. Tightly drawn lines were etched at the corners of his watchful eyes, gained from living on a knife edge, ever wary of ambush or attack. Although he still had a healthy pallor from the sun of Italy and France, his cheeks were sunken from fatigue, spying and the reduced rations of an army upon the march.

The guards upon the bridge were wary, seeing a tired, yet fierce warrior approaching the gate, battle hardened and in ill humour. A sergeant and two men-at-arms stopped him, and the sergeant asked his business. Jamie responded curtly demanding entrance, claiming to be of Lord Wigton's army and in no mood to be halted by formalities. Hearing his tone and the manner of his speech they let him pass, and recommend ale houses for him to frequent where he might find more of his kinsmen within the town.

As he passed through the first gatehouse he saw a portcullis at each archway, set around the fortified towers. There were machicolations over the corbels and once within, sensing eyes upon him he looked upwards, seeing the *meurtrière*, doubtless loaded with boiling oil in preparation for attack, as everything appeared to be on a war footing. Jamie went through a second archway and another set of fortifications, the hairs upon his neck rising more as he entered this enemy town along the final stretch of the stone bridge. It would be the devil to take, he knew, and he turned his mind to the task as he sought one of the taverns within the town. There was an atmosphere of danger and wariness everywhere he looked. Everyone knew that the English were coming and some were praying that they would pass and march directly upon to Orleans, the Armagnac stronghold.

The town was huge, rising upwards from the river in a maze of streets and small alleyways, half-timbered houses merging with old stone cottages. The cobbles opened out onto a large square, where he found directions to The Bear tavern. He found the inn half full, with the sound of Scottish burr mangling the French tongue, as the soldiers ordered ale and food in the middle of the day. There were one or two knights present, judging by their demeanour and dress. Jamie stood in the doorway a moment, letting his eyes adjust to the dim light within after the harsh sunlight outside. He attracted more than a little attention; his attitude, weapons and build telling the tale for all to see – another knight lost from battle.

He ordered a flask of ale and made to sit at a table, when a voice nearby hailed him.

"I see by yon sash ye're a Douglas, laddie." The knight nodded at Jamie's borrowed plaid sash of dark-green and blue tartan that graced his torso from shoulder to hip. "Sit wi' us and take a wee dram."

Mentally preparing himself, Jamie responded in the Lowland accent of the borders, settling into their company and swapping stories of Cotentin, claiming that he had been settled in the castle, but the locals had surrendered upon seeing the fleet, and he had barely escaped with his life. The story was plausible enough and would hold water, as he had been told that none of the Scots or Genoese had escaped, apart from those involved in the direct battle in which he had taken part. Two hours later he made his excuses to leave, with a promise to return here or to the castle, where he would enlist again to fight the whoreson English. Then his luck held.

"Why we return there this night. We'll meet you here and go together once your horse is shod," one of the men said. The others grunted words of encouragement, and Jamie nodded and thanked them.

Once outside he breathed deeply, releasing the tension that he had been holding the whole time. It was, he knew, one thing to take on the accent for a short time, but to maintain it with no slip took great concentration, though it had become easier as he fell into the lilt of his companions' brogue. He found a farrier and left his horse to be shod, walking the town and seeing other Scots, who hailed him as a friend. He made for the ramparts overlooking the river and the bridge, seeking to better understand the lie of the land from the vantage of height. He spoke to a bored soldier on guard duty who paced to and fro and was more than happy to pass the time of day in conversation. Here he gained more information as to the castle's strengths and weaknesses.

That evening he returned to the tavern and met with his two new companions, Sir Dermit Ferguson and Sir Callum Cochrane. Both were knights in Douglas's army, and when enquiring why they had not seen him for the muster, he claimed to have been at the French court serving his lord there as a courtier and proctor, with hints of spying in London. The clan areas of Lord Douglas were huge, covering a large geographical area from the Borders to Angus, Lothian, Moray, as well as France and Sweden. There was, he reasoned, every chance that they would not be acquainted. It would also, he knew, explain the occasional lapse of a French twang into his Scottish accent when he spoke.

As he approached the castle, Jamie saw that it was more of a defensive chateau and one that would stand little barrage by artillery, in the unlikely event that the prince should manage to procure such weapons. It was surrounded by a moat, with some curtain walling and circular turrets and towers set around a rectangular keep that provided the main defence. However, upon closer inspection, he realised that a direct assault would open any attackers to crossfire from the cleverly positioned turrets. There were buttressed walls that led to fighting platforms on elevated positions of an unconventional nature. A bell tower abutted two turrets at one end, and it was this that interested Jamie the most, for here he perceived the weakness in the castle's defences. A small, barred cripplegate was set into the base of the tower on the castle side of the moat, and if this could be surmounted, then access could be given to a conroi of knights and soldiers to wreak havoc from within. He must explore carefully and learn the rhythms of the sentries and the order of the fortress, for he knew that was often where weaknesses could be found.

Jamie was led across a solid stone bridge through to the inner enceinte where the horses were stabled, and thence into the inner bailey before the great keep that towered upwards and was of later construction, judging by the stonework. Here he looked left and saw that the small chapel and bell tower led from this inner courtyard. *The storming of the curtain walling and moat will cause great loss of men if no diversion of a separate clandestine assault can be made,* he mused to himself. With the horses seen to, Jamie followed his newfound companions up into the fortified keep, inside which a more comfortable atmosphere prevailed, with tapestries and plastered walls befitting the home of bishops. Present were Scottish, Genoese and French knights, none of whom did Jamie recognise. He breathed a soft sigh of relief.

At the episcopal throne sat the Bishop of Orleans, Thomas Basin. The elderly prelate observed him carefully before beckoning the constable of the castle to his side. The knight was Sir Bouchard de Meung, a man of middle years, swarthy, with long hair and strong features. He faced forward to welcome Jamie, who unconsciously held his breath, praying silently that he would not be challenged, for torture and certain death awaited him if his true nature was discovered.

"Monsieur, you come with an invitation from Sir Dermit and we welcome you, for, by the Cross, we shall need all men to our gathering that we may have if the bastard English arrive at our walls."

"I am Sir James Arasgain." Jamie lied, using his mother's maiden name. "My sword is yours, sir, as I pledged it to my lord, so be it for your good." He responded gallantly with a bow. Others in the gathering heard the accents of a Scotsman speaking French and were drawn to him immediately, asking questions after his introduction.

"Where have ye been, laddie?" asked a grizzled laird with grey in his hair and lines upon his sun-browned face. Jamie gave him the same story as he had to Sir Dermit and Sir Callum, relating the story of the loss of Cotentin and how he had pushed ahead with rumours of the fall of Le Mans. From the comments, he realised that he was not the only one to escape, as other survivors had returned from Cotentin in dribs and drabs, seeing to reunite with the French and fight again in revenge.

"Are they far behind ye, Sir James?"

"No, but I tarried little, keeping away from their scouts, but wishing to see how fared the fortune of those towns upon their route. They all fell afoul of the English bowmen or succumbed to siege and rout. The English prince rides roughshod over France and is now aided by five hundred Gascons to boot."

At this, there were shouts of anger from the French present and curses raised against the ancestors and habits of the Gascon breed, for there was no love lost between the Gascons and the rest of France, which remained loyal to King Charles.

He was questioned further on the numbers and ranks of those present, at which he dissembled, before answering the final question that was upon everyman's lips: "D'ye ken how long afore the whoreson English arrive at our gates?"

"I durst not swear to it, yet would say maybe three to four days at most. For they travel fast and light with no artillery or waggons. Just horse and baggage train." And with those words, a plan emerged in Jamie's head that caused him to lurch with excitement, for he now knew how the well-defended bridge might be defeated.

Chapter Forty-One

Jamie walked the castle for two days, learning all he could. In the process he discovered that his plans were feasible. He sought as much time as he could within the church, having found the barred cripplegate behind a small chapel at the base of a turret. It was well secured and of half height, ensuring that anyone who used it would need to stoop to enter through the opening. The oaken door was bolted and barred, and lay directly beneath a machicolation, which would make any attacker vulnerable from above. A guard was posted within the church at all times. Bored with such mundane duty he was not alert, and paced around, nodding to Jamie on the frequent occasions that he entered, ostensibly to pray.

At the end of the second day, Jamie was satisfied and went to take his borrowed horse from the stables. He tacked up, mounted and walked unhurriedly out through the main gate. Two hundred yards out, another rider came into sight from the direction of the west. He was clad in a rough looking gambeson that was ripped and battle scarred. He moved slowly and was clearly tired. He frowned at Jamie as he rode closer.

"Why that's Archie's horse, I'm bound," he said. "Where did ye find it and who are ye?" The last was said with aggression as he reached for his sword.

Jamie did not answer. He pushed his horse at a swerve straight into a canter, heading for the woods. He did not wish to engage the man in full view of the castle, and needed time to silence him away from the lookouts posted upon the turrets. The Scot spun his horse around and gave chase, following Jamie and shouting obscenities at his back. The road curved towards the woods and the pair raced onwards, Jamie deliberately holding back to allow the other rider to slowly gain with each stride. As soon as they were shielded from view by the trees, he reined up and span through one hundred and eighty degrees, drawing his sword and racing back towards the Scottish horseman, blade held low to the off side.

The Scot accelerated on his tired horse, thinking Jamie scared and guilty, and that he would easily be overrun and dealt with, having only turned to fight as a last resort. He was wrong.

The knight's sword swipe was wide – whether by virtue of his being tired or thinking Jamie an easy kill, it mattered not. He wanted blood and vengeance on the man who had supposedly killed his companions and his lord. His sword came point first at the charge, then at the last moment, the attacker pulled it back to slash overhand. It was an act of pure aggression with little skill, driven by revenge. Jamie closed the distance and almost carelessly flicked aside the downward strike, coming around and under to slash downwards, cutting his opponent's thigh to the bone. Losing all control, the knight fell forward off his horse, landing badly in a heap. Jamie spun around, knowing he could not be found out, and slashed downwards, killing him instantly.

He pulled up his horse and dismounted, holding the reins until he was sure that the knight was dead. Satisfied, he tied both animals to a branch and proceeded to drag the dead man off the road into the woods and out of sight. He stripped the body and left it under a cairn of stones. If animals found the body so be it, no one would know where he came from or whom he served. He found a small scrap of parchment with scrawled notes on the body telling of the English numbers and their deployment, which he destroyed.

Jamie rode in a circle, coming out of the woods by a lesser trail that ended near the large oak tree, where he had agreed to leave a note in the fork of the branch. Standing on the saddle of his patient horse, he hoisted himself into the branches and tied the note carefully to the top of the branch. Satisfied that it was all he could do, Jamie dropped down to the ground, re-mounted and set off back to the castle.

He clipped across the stone bridge and was waved through. But once within the enceinte, he was approached by a captain of the guard and a French knight serving the castle constable. "Sir James Arasgain, you will accompany us to the keep, where your presence is required."

"As you wish, sir. I needs must attend to my horse, but I shall be there forthwith," Jamie responded.

Minutes later accompanied by a guard, and seemingly under arrest, he found himself in front of the constable, Sir Bouchard de Meung.

"Sir, you wished to see me?" Jamie asked with more confidence than he felt.

"Indeed I did. Where did you venture this day? For you were seen chased by another who was proceeding towards the castle. Where is that rider now? For some claim that he was a Scottish knight lately returning from Cotentin."

"Sir, I was exercising my horse and sought to pair this with a scouting mission. Fearing that the English may be close, I rode forward to attend upon such matters. As I left the castle, I was called out by a rider unknown to me, hailing me under strange circumstances and bearing a challenge with no badinage in his words. I wished no crossing of swords and would not oblige him in his inflamed state. I sought to avoid him and galloped off, thinking he had mistaken me for someone else."

Sir Bouchard was still puzzled at the thin explanation Jamie gave. "Then prithee, what occurred when you were lost from sight? For those watching upon the ramparts tell me of a chase, with the unknown knight following you thus. The horse was later captured running free near the wood. But what became of its rider?"

Jamie inflected some anger into his voice, no longer the misunderstood sely soldier caught abroad by mistake. "Sir," he began with asperity, "why do you seek to address me so? I have come to your assistance with my sword at your disposal, yet are seemingly accused of some malfaisance while seeking to aid your circumstance. Should you wish me to retire and leave I shall do so, and gladly, for I know where I am unwelcome."

The constable recoiled slightly at this verbal assault and sought to placate the fiery knight before him. "Hold fast now, Sir James, we seek only the truth and I shall press those who witnessed the meeting for a full account, and am sure that it will be explained satisfactorily. We would ask that you attend upon us on the morrow."

Jamie bowed and left, assuming a position of anger that had chilled to good manners, and breathed a sigh of relief, never dreaming that a horse would get him into so much trouble. Jamie walked down the corridor to his barrack room, spine tingling and a damp patch upon his shirt – not caused by exertion or the heat of the day, brought on instead by the cold spirit of fear.

Once he had left the chamber, Sir Bouchard called upon the captain of guard.

"Have him watched carefully by whomever you wish. Something is amiss here and he had blood upon his gambeson sleeve, still fresh and red. I trust him not for all his intemperate disposition and perfervid claim to our cause."

"As you wish, Sir Bouchard." The captain offered a brief bow and left to follow Jamie closely, before he put others to spy upon him.

At supper that night there was a sense of unease, with eyes cast about in Jamie's direction. No one said anything directly, yet all were aware that questions hung in the air and the focus was upon him, drawing unwanted attention. He knew that the English would not be far away, but how soon would they get to Meung, and would they find his note?

Chapter Forty-Two

When a large army travels overland, it is impossible to keep its movement a secret unless its speed outstrips word of mouth. Any marching army is held back by its slowest moving element, and in this case it was those on foot – the archers. News of the English force passed swiftly.

Now within a day's march of Meung, the scout who had accompanied Jamie returned on a tired horse, bearing the message he had found in the tree. He had already read it in case it was necessary to leave an answer, and he passed the opened letter to Prince Thomas.

"Here, my prince, a missive from Sir James." He said no more, bowed and took one step backwards, awaiting the prince's response.

Prince Thomas read the words once, smiled and read them a second time, before handing the parchment to Beaufort, who shared it with the Duke of York. Edward, Duke of York, raised his head exclaiming, "Why Sir James gives us a right good stratagem. By God's balls, he has."

Hearing the knight curse so, the earl and prince laughed.

"He does indeed, and we must make haste and not daddle, for time will be against us as news of our arrival will fly upon the wind. Captain, four waggons with hoops covered in hide. Those that we took from the farms will do well." The prince gave out rapid orders, seeing in his mind's eye how the stratagem Jamie had cleverly outlined might be fulfilled. "Have the captains of archers attend us."

"Who will lead, sire?" The Duke of York asked tentatively.

"Durst thou ask such a question? Why we shall, and be right glad to prevail upon this whoreson company set before us," the prince answered, ever keen to be at the forefront of any action and impetuous to a fault.

"Sire, I would adjure you most strongly to lead up to the walls, for it needs a stratagem of your cunning to prevail, should the way prove difficult. The bridge shall be mine, I prithee, for this boon."

The prince scowled at his cousin, not liking his decisions being challenged. Beaufort remained silent, seeing whether the wind would blow to his advantage or not, remembering his true intent, and that hatched by his brother and Warwick. The duke sought to play upon the prince's vanity and secure safety for the royal leader.

"Think, sire. The taking of the castle is where the glory and the thickest fighting shall be set. Here you should be, taking the castle in your own right, not by the proxy of a bridge secured."

The pendulum in the prince's mind swayed and finally he fell, to the relief of the Duke of York, in his favour.

"Very well. We concur, let it be so. You shall take the bridge, and here are my orders." At which the prince outlined in detail what he had seen in Jamie's letter. Thomas Beaufort looked on, showing no hint of emotion, and only by a hardening of his eyes did he betray any sign of his true feelings.

As the two senior captains approached, they bowed and

awaited instructions: "Dickon, take some of your men to the woods and cut some trunks of youngish trees, thus round." At which the prince circled his fingers to a circumference of around four to five inches.

"How many, sire?"

"Some six to eight, all trimmed of branches and lean, of a man's height."

"Now Adam, the Duke of York, shall lead the attack upon the bridge. All will be hidden within – men-at-arms, archers and some crossbows. For crossbows shall better serve in the close warfare of a tower fight. The waggons should be stuffed with ripe hay."

"Yes, my lord prince." The puzzled captain strode off to carry out the orders.

The camp was now bustling with activity, and after some two hours, all the preparations were made. The four farm waggons were loaded with men and hay, each harnessed to two strong work horses. They set off on the journey to the town, lumbering along the main road towards Meung.

Jamie was on the battlements of the castle walking along the parapet facing the woods to the west, hoping to see any advance warning sign of the English army's arrival. He was aware that he was under scrutiny. Three different servants of the castle had been following his every move, and he had been told that he was effectively under arrest and not to leave the confines of the castle, unless with express permission signed by the castle constable. A gentle breeze was starting to lift the torpid heat that hung in the air, and the listless colours of the castle flag began to flap and snap with newfound vigour. One servant now was seemingly loitering, engaged in conversation with a guard some thirty yards away, casting furtive glances in Jamie's direction at every opportunity.

Jamie decided that he'd had enough, and walked purposefully along to join the conversation and engage with the wily man. The servant looked embarrassed and was about to make his excuses and leave, when a shout from the castle's topmost tower caused all to look towards the woods. They saw four farm waggons being driven at speed, with the horses lumbering along in a canter, and the two herders on the front bench of each cart urging them on with looks of fear as they drew closer. Yet it was not to castle that they approached. Instead they took the flat road to the town. All attention was directed towards this spectacle, as cries of alarm were being shouted that the English army were coming, causing fear and excitement in equal measure.

Jamie watched, inwardly smiling that his plan seemed to be working, for as the waggons approached the gates upon the fortified bridge, they slowed but a little, the carters seemingly in abject fear and showing no signs of stopping to be inspected. The waggons entered in tandem and were only halted when the leading vehicle was through, stopped at the last of the three gates, causing chaos and shouts of anguish from within.

The horses were sweating, stamping and snorting inside the hot, guard towers and the guards were shouting for all to halt and dismount from their benches so that they could inspect the contents. The Englishmen posing as carters heard noises above from the murder holes, then smoke started to emerge from inside the waggons. The smoke began to billow in great clouds, to the taint of burning lamp oil and dry hay. Then everything happened at once: the carters jumped down, slashing the leather tresses of the horses. The soldiers, archers and Gascons within pulled back the covers, jumping out with war bows and Gascon crossbows, nocked and ready. The lighted hay, suddenly given more oxygen, billowed roofwards, blocking all sight from the murder holes. The men above, realising the truth of what they were witnessing, poured down scalding oil upon the English. It mostly missed in the confusion and added to the combustion, causing acrid smoke to fill the upper chambers of the towers.

Two men from each waggon ran to the portcullis guides, jamming the thin tree trunks into the stone slides with their archer's malles. Soldiers of the guard ran forward only to be struck down by arrows and bolts, and then retreated with cries of "lower the portcullis!"

It was too late. The tree trunks held and the portcullis stopped six feet off the ground, allowing the horses to escape from the flames, driving for the fresh air of the open stone bridge before the town. From the road outside came the thunder of hooves as mounted knights, led by the Duke of York, galloped from their hiding place in the trees. Archers ducked and sent arrows skyward to keep the crossbow men above from seeking a target. Some fell to the sheer surprise of the attack.

Then the dirty fighting began, hand-to-hand, up the stone spiral stairways, seeking command of the battlements above. With shields as their aid, the invading soldiers stabbed and thrust, as the French sold their lives dearly. Cries of battle and screams of pain filled the air as smoke-filled lungs sought oxygen within the confines of the corridors. Eventually, with crossbowmen sniping, the English took the fighting platform above. With this secured, the burning waggons were pushed out onto the open stone of the bridge between the towers, now fully alight and flaming in the sunshine, fire fanned by the breeze.

The English watched from their newly-acquired vantage as the knights' charge led them to the town gates, which had not been fully closed in time, where a vicious fight ensued. The guards on the door wore mail and helmets at most, and were ill-equipped to counter a knight in full plate armour. Crossbow bolts hummed and arrows whistled from the nearest tower, now secured by the English archers, who picked off targets only fifty feet away with easy and unerring accuracy.

The cries of the dead and dying mixed with the harsh clang of steel as the town guard fought an unequal battle with the English soldiers and knights. Dead soldiers were pushed into the gaps of the open gates, making it impossible to fully secure them. Knights poured through, attacking everything in their path, and with this panic ensued. No one was safe and the English began to sack the town, as a terrible toll was extracted for having barred them entrance. There were scenes of sick depravity, with no quarter given to soldiers or civilians alike, while the women fled to the barred doors of their homes or the sanctuary of the churches.

To the watchers on the castle parapet it soon became apparent that a trap had been sprung, upon seeing the charge of the knights across the bridge.

"The bridge is being taken. To arms, to arms!" came the cry, as heralds blew trumpets summoning the muster. Jamie ran along the rampart to the western tower, and with all eyes eastwards, ran up to the lookout post next to the church. Here a solitary guard had drawn back to the outer view, from which point he could see the English party of knights and archers crossing the narrow moat in small rowing boats they had found, moored upstream on the river. They were nearly across in all the confusion, and had only this moment been seen by the lone guard. The soldier turned to cry, but was cut short when Jamie's dagger drove upwards between his ribs, finding his heart and silencing him. The soldier fell back into his arms and Jamie propped him against the battlements, as though looking outwards.

Jamie knew that he had no time to lose. He ran down the internal spiral staircase, knowing that it would bring him out next to the church. During his visits to the church, he had found an episcopal chapel and robing room for the bishop, located on the first floor. This had a direct staircase down to the church, close to the private chapel with a small outside doorway. He pushed open the door to find the bishop within, who spun around in anger. For there, on his private bed, lay a naked young woman, her legs akimbo and in the act of being seduced by the elderly priest. Jamie growled in anger and in two strides closed the distance, driving a battle-hardened fist into the bishop's jaw, felling him unconscious onto the bed next to the frightened girl.

"My lady," he quipped, "find some raiment and begone, for the English are upon us." With that the poor wench shrieked and pulled the sheet up around her, searching around for her clothes.

Jamie went to the side door and ran down the steps, stopping at the cleverly disguised door at the bottom. He made to push it open, sliding back a neatly contrived lock that released on a spring catch. Beyond it he saw to his dismay the church guard, who was clearly protecting the bishop from unwanted visitors. The man turned reflexively when he heard the urgent steps upon the stone that were clearly not the bishop's steady gait.

His spear dropped point down upon seeing Jamie, knowing all was not well.

"What is your business here? Hold and declare yourself."

Jamie needed space and time: "It is the bishop, he lies panting with illness, his face ill of humour and of puce pallor. I need to fetch a physician." He remonstrated, looking scared. The guard was worried and confused. Jamie urged. "Hurry, fetch a physician."

The guard dropped the spear, turning to race for the church doors as bidden. As soon as he turned his back, Jamie grabbed him around the throat, sliding his arm up to the exposed neck and pulling back against his other arm he had placed behind the guard's head. It was a deadly headlock that cut off both oxygen and blood to the brain. The guard writhed a little, struggling. He flapped his arms, gasped twice through his crushed windpipe and fell unconscious. Jamie could not bring himself to kill a man in cold blood within the confines of the church. He crossed himself as the guard fell to the floor, his breath shallow and pained.

Jamie raced to bar the church doors from the inside. Only one of the two doors was open, with the other locked in place by a horizontal holding bar. Jamie looked out into the court-yard, before closing the other door fully and dropping the long, wooden bressummer into its holding bars. He saw to his satis-faction that a party of mounted knights was mustering to sally forth, in an attempt to relieve the bridge and regain it for the French. *'Tis well done*, he thought *for their forces shall be divided in strength and our assault shall be the better for it, as they will be ambushed in their turn.*

Satisfied that the bar was securely in place, he turned and ran to the small chapel which housed the cripplegate leading to the outside world. There he heard sounds of anguish as the raiding party had been spied by the watch above, upon the second tower. Bolts and rocks were being hurled down upon the attacking English. Coming upon the cripplegate, Jamie began to prise back the three long, iron door bolts, with one jamming fast. He swore and searched for something with which to hit it. He grabbed the two-foot solid-brass cross off the altar and a small bottle of anointing oil; he poured the oil over the bolt to lubricate it. Cries from outside become more urgent.

"The bolt is jammed. I will free it soonest," he called to them.

Jamie then took the cross in two hands and wielded it like a hammer, striking the head of the bolt, which did not move. In desperation he struck again, so hard that the reverberations hurt his hands. He ignored the sharp pain and struck a third time; he was sure that the bolt moved a fraction. Thrice more he hit the head of the bolt, and finally he saw movement – half an inch, no more, with a squeak of rusting metal. He heard banging upon the main church doors without and renewed his efforts, pouring the anointing oil upon the bolt and hitting it again. This time it moved a full inch. Twice more and he wrenched at it with his hands, wishing he had Mark with him, who would doubtless rip the entire door out with his bare hands. Then suddenly it came free.

He lifted the heavy latch bolt and shouted, "Push! The door is free, kick it forward." Thuds were heard, and after two hard kicks, the door squeaked open on rusted hinges. Knights rushed inwards, desperate to avoid the storm of missiles without. Jamie saw to his relief that Kit, his companion-in-arms, was one of those who had reached the safety of the interior.

Then the archers followed. Soon, some fifty men were inside the small chapel.

"To the main doors, this way." Jamie urged. The prince was there and the Earl of Devon, Thomas Beaufort, with him. They ran into the main aisle as the cross bar holding the door began to crack.

"Here, archers to me," Prince Thomas called quietly, so as not to be heard outside. "Crossbowmen to the front and low, archers to the back." He arrayed the knights in a loose semicircle on either side, ready to attack when the doors burst open. The crossbar finally gave way with a crack of splintering wood and the first wave of soldiers pushed forward through the open doors. Too late they saw the archers in the dimly lit interior.

"Loose!" called the captain and a flutter of shafts shot forward at point blank range, skewering the leading and second ranks of the castle garrison. Some were Scots, left after a force of knights had made a sally to attack to try and regain the bridge; others were of the French contingent. They were halted by the dead falling and flailing, at which the English knights rushed from the sides, slaughtering them all before charging out into the inner bailey. It was an uneven battle. Some crossbowmen sought targets from the ramparts, but two successful escalades had breached the walls above, and any last ditch efforts to defend the castle were swiftly prevented.

In the heat of the assault Jamie and Lord Ormond called a band of archers to them, together with a few knights, including Kit. "Kit! To me, for we take the gates," Jamie called above the din of battle. They ran towards the gates of the castle, using the garth as shelter from the remaining crossbowmen above.

At the main gates a group of men-at-arms from the garrison waited, and the assault began upon the barred entrance. A barrage of arrows struck the defending soldiers from the rear as they turned to face the new onslaught from within. Four men-at-arms rushed at the knights and were cut down without mercy, the English running through their guard, leaving only dead men behind. Upon reaching the barred gates, the archers formed a defensive ring while Jamie and Lord Ormond, aided by four more archers, lifted the heavy, wooden bar to open the gates. There was a cheer as more English poured inwards. The battle became a rout, to the sound of clashing weapons and the smell of metallic blood and gore. There was little mercy in the English army, who slaughtered with no clemency in their souls, and the castle became a charnel house.

More archers had poured in through the cripplegate and formed lines to pick off the last few defenders, while the knights ripped through the men-at-arms, who threw down their weapons when it was evident that the castle was lost to the English.

Only the keep now held fast, with the last of the French forces retreating to this final bastion of resistance.

"So the rats scurry back to their nest in the hope of being saved. By the good Lord we shall oust them yet." At which a crossbow bolt whistled past the prince's head, missing him by inches. The prince ducked when he heard the sound. "Fetch de Grispere," he said. "For he knows how all is held within."

Jamie arrived moments later to attend upon the prince. "Ah Sir James, we have bearded them in their lair, see them skulking thus." He motioned upwards, clearly rejoicing in another battle won.

"As you please, my prince."

"Now prithee, inform us of the nature of the keep. Can it be taken? For we would not wish to tarry here too long ere reinforcements arrive from Burgundy to relieve these devils here."

"If it please Your Royal Highness, the roof is beamed and slatted with a covering of wooden shingles." At which Jamie looked towards the bell tower of the church, pointing. "From such a vantage point, good archers could fire the roof with tows alight and burn the *crapauds* and traitorous Scots from their lair."

The company all looked skyward including Beaufort, on whose face there was a reluctant look of admiration. The prince smiled wickedly.

"A most excellent stratagem. Have kindling brought forward, for we should seek to burn the keep from below as well. The smoke shall aid us as we secure our advantage from an escalade on two sides. We shall feed upon smoked Frenchmen ere this day be done." With which he clapped Jamie upon the shoulder and called for a costrel of wine to slake his thirst. A clatter of hooves heralded the arrival of the Duke of York who had come up from the town.

"My Lord of York how goes it? Do we hold the town?"

"Indeed we do, sire, or what is left of it after we have sacked it. It will be a lesson for the Armagnacs not to betray us and resist our advance."

"Well done, sir. Let the men have their spoils, for battle is not enough. Once sated and this matter resolved we can march again, for we needs must not tarry afore we reach Blois. The campaign season will soon be ending and thus we must secure our lodgings afore winter arrives, and consolidate our position."

"Not to Orleans, sire?" Beaufort asked. "For that is the Armagnac capital."

"No. 'Tis a strong town and will not be easily taken. 'Twill require a long siege and cannon to blast the walls. We lack the artillery and time is not upon our side. Blois shall be our aim, and once ensconced in safety, we shall throw down the gauntlet to the Armagnacs and Burgundy alike, having secured all lands for our father that are rightly his by God's will," he stated, head high, brooking no argument, and for once not acting as the reckless prince of his reputation.

"As you wish, sire." Beaufort acceded.

The prince nodded in acknowledgement and called the captains of archers to take men to the top of the tower and rain down fire arrows upon the roof of the Keep, upon his command. This done, he gave orders for the bundles of kindling and faggots that had been readied to be set alight in each corner, with oily hay to aid the screen and discompose those inside.

With one last thought to aid the speed of the conquest of the castle, Jamie offered. "Sire, if I may?" The prince nodded, not wishing to be delayed from more battle.

"I found the bishop *in flagrante* with a young woman and I am having him brought to attend us. It may inspire the others to surrender if they see their vassal lord secure and safe, albeit in the pocket of hypocrisy."

Here the prince surprised Jamie, for Jamie never knew which way his humour would fall. The prince roared with laughter as the venal prelate came in procession, prodded from behind by two archers, clad only in a bedsheet and being harried by the young woman he had been seeking to seduce. His portly frame looked ridiculous in the stark sunlight as he protested and blushed with shame, trying pompously to recant all wrongdoing.

"Ah, my lord bishop, how do you do this fine day? For your grace seems lightly attired. Is this your summer robe, your worship? Perhaps it is more appropriate for your other calling," mocked the prince, nodding at the woman; the company laughed. Prince Thomas turned to a herald. "Go forth and wave a flag of truce."

The herald did as he was bidden. Then the prince looked up to the keep, while shield bearers protected him from any errant bolts.

"Ho the Keep, see you?" he shouted. "We have your vassal lord, unharmed save by the tongue of this lady here, who flays him thus. We are Prince Thomas, Duke of Clarence, and would seek paroli with your constable. Show yourself thus that we may offer terms."

There was no immediate movement. "If you do not surrender we shall assume the truce is annulled, and shall commence to burn you out. There is no aid coming to save you, for we have control of the region and all its roads. It is for you to decide: a charring or surrender? Make your peace. We give you our word as a prince of the realm that you shall not be harmed if you agree to terms."

All was silent, until the huge door was opened above the steps and a figure appeared. Everyone tensed and raised their swords and bows, trusting not a flag of truce. They all remembered how good King Richard had been killed by a bolt from the battlements of a French castle, and were wary.

"It is the constable, sire, Sir Bouchard de Meung, and those by him are the Laird Douglas, with Sir Dermit Ferguson and Sir Callum Cochrane of the Scottish court," Jamie mouthed quietly to Prince Thomas.

"My lords, what say you? We are waiting and our patience is sorely tried thus, for the day is hot and so is our blood to do battle. Speak now or hold your peace and die."

They were not placatory words, but the prince cared not, for he was of the blood royal, and the men above were traitors to his father's realm. The Scots scowled in anger, but the constable prevailed.

"My lord prince, what are your terms that we should surrender our keep?"

"We give you our word that you shall be treated according to your rank and released, upon sworn pledge not to take up arms, surrendering your swords. You will be held upon ransom to those of your families and kinsmen. These are the terms. Do you accept them?"

On the steps there were mutterings, as they all conferred. The laird spat on the floor and looked disgusted at the ignominy of defeat to an English prince, but finally nodded curtly.

"We agree to your terms," Sir Bouchard said. He came forward and bowed, withdrawing his sword and holding it hilt first as he walked down the steps.

Chapter Forty-Three

Blois: 17th September

The English had installed themselves in Blois the day before, having wreaked a bloody trail of destruction across France, looting, scavenging, burning houses and farms, destroying the land and everything that lay in their path. Their fearsome reputation went before them, and upon reaching the gates of the town of Blois, the constable had sued for peace and granted them entry without a fight. Prince Thomas, Duke of Clarence, was only too aware of how the seasons were moving towards winter and the end of the campaigning season and accepted the constable's terms with alacrity, seeking to set up his winter camp within the city's walls.

Blois had been the royal seat of the Duchess of Orleans, mother to the young duke, Charles d'Orleans, whose father had been assassinated by the Duke of Burgundy, and all within were sympathetic to any who saw the Burgundians as their enemies. The royal party were given accommodation in the main apartments of the large chateau that overlooked the town. Parts of the building were still being constructed, with two huge wings adding to the already opulent splendour of the majestic palace.

Later that day, heralds arrived bearing the crests of the Armagnacs upon their livery and banners, showing the arms of the young Duke of Orleans, with the bizarre depiction of an azure *biscione,* or dragon eating a child, in opposite quadrants – a design inherited from the Count of Milan.

The leading knight came before the royal party and dismounted, dropping to one knee and bowing. "My Lord Prince Thomas, Duke of Clarence, scion of the English royal line. We bring you greetings, Your Royal Highness, from our lord the Duc du Berry d'Orleans of the House of Valois. He bids you most graciously to accept letters, written with the intent of resolving this most unfortunate discord that has come to pass."

The knight rose and beckoned forward a page bearing scrolls sealed with the ducal crest. They were received by a squire who presented them into the royal hand of Prince Thomas. The prince looked down at the parchment, initially with interest, and then a deep frown appeared across his brow.

"What is this?" he cried out in anger. "These missives are not addressed to us! How dare you insult us with this trite response to our presence?"

"My lord, I beg you, they were written in good faith and I would appeal to your most gracious nature, highness, as a representative of His Majesty King Henry of England." The knight pleaded, embarrassed at the response from the prince.

"If that is so, the duke should attend upon us directly. For experience has shown us that good intent is no security to action, and we have been ambushed and deceived, with treaties broken as easily as the seal upon this parchment. Should he be minded to uphold such terms as may be contained within these letters addressed to our father and brother, why he should arrive to wait upon us here, to offer his faith and loyalty in person." The prince finished disdainfully.

The French knight was now angry himself, clenching his jaw at the flippant dismissal, but he knew that he was standing before a prince of the royal line who had cut his way through France, leaving a swathe of destruction as he went, arrogant in his success. He knew the prince would brook no argument.

"As you wish, sire. I shall return to my lord the duke and respond as you have asked."

At this, Prince Thomas turned and walked away, dismissing the knight as someone of no consequence.

The Duke of York remained to intercede on behalf of the prince. "Sir, we would ask that you remain here, where you shall receive courtesy and refreshment ere you return to your lord."

Two days later, the Armagnac proctor and his mesnie returned to Orleans with a letter signed by the Duke of Clarence in response to the Duke of Berry. Jamie, along with the Earl of Ormond, had been assigned to accompany them and report back all that he heard and saw. Neither man was at ease despite assurances that they travelled under a flag of truce, for all of France was in uproar at the carnage and desolation caused by the passage of the English army. They travelled with a company of ten archers, two squires, men-at-arms and a pair of armed servants. It was, they reasoned, a sufficiently strong presence for the return journey to dissuade all *routiers* and opportunist bands from attacking them.

When they entered the fair town of Orleans they were presented at the court of the Armagnacs. Jamie had been dreading the presence of the Duke of Burgundy, but he found to his surprise that the accord that existed between the two French factions was as brittle as that between them and the English. Once again he was presented to Charles, the young

Duke of Orleans, who, at just eighteen, was younger than Jamie by three years, although Jamie felt much older. Had campaigning aged him so, he wondered, with the weight of responsibility and living on a knife edge for so long, barely sleeping in the same place for months on end, haunted by the prospect of a knife in the back at every town in which he spied?

To Jamie, the duke looked frightened and ill at ease beneath the rigidly schooled mask of royalty, possibly because he and the house of Armagnac had raised the ire of not just the French but English as well, with little prospect of a reconciliation in sight.

"My lord duke, we offer you our most gracious felicitations and honour from His Royal Highness Prince Thomas," the Earl of Ormond offered, as the two knights bowed deeply before the assembled dukes of Armagnac.

"You are bid most welcome to our court, Messires." The duke addressed Jamie. "I recall that we have met before, sir. 'Twas was at Rouen last year, when you served us well in the delivery of a letter to his majesty King Henry, if my memory serves me well?"

"It does indeed my lord duke," Jamie replied. "And I thank you for the honour of remembering my presence and the small service that I was able to render at that time."

The young duke gave a small smile of acknowledgement at the response and continued. "Yet now we are reacquainted with each other again in less fortuitous circumstances, I fear. For as ever we have set sail upon a sea of uncertainty, tossed this way and that upon the whim of kings, *n'est-ce pas*?"

"Indeed, and here I defer to my lord Sir James, the Earl of Ormond, if it please your grace?"

The duke offered a wave of his hand, indicating that he was ready to hear what the earl had to say. The earl took great pains to explain in the most diplomatic language – completely unlike that used by the Duke of Clarence a few days before – that a position of compromise could be reached providing there was sufficient incentive. As was expected the Armagnac faction did not respond directly, and merely listened to the proposed terms upon which any agreement could be founded to prevent further bloodshed upon French soil, and any further devastation of the countryside.

The English party stayed in Orleans for three days, and with new terms prepared rode back to the prince's quarters at Blois, where they were met by an expectant crowd of courtiers.

"Well my lords," greeted the prince, "how does the Duke of Orleans? Is he now more minded to treat with us upon fairer terms?"

Ormond answered. "My prince, I believe that the duke is now of a more conciliatory attitude and will come to heel in the fullness of time. He begs that we inform you that he greatly regrets the breaking of the terms of the Treaty of Bourges and asks for clemency. He has returned to Paris to garner support and coin for an appeasement of that breach."

Jamie smiled inwardly at this, for those had been far from the words used during their stay in Orleans, where the Armagnac lords had argued over terms and the need for reconciliation. Finally, the elder statesman in the form of the Duke of Berry had prevailed, swaying all to his will.

"Then we shall await his response upon his return, and please God that the terms are ripe for the picking, or we shall rain war and pestilence upon this land, the like of which has never been seen before." The prince promised with a martial look in his eyes.

Jamie and the earl left the court to return to their lodgings at the Wild Boar tavern. There he found Sir Christopher Urquhart among the knights frequenting the taproom below their rooms. The local inns, Jamie knew, were the best places to find out what was really happening in any campaign. Away from the restrictions of the court, where everyone was careful about opinions they raised, one could learn more in an hour in a relaxed atmosphere where wine and ale flowed freely than in a whole week at court. He hailed Kit, ordered wine and went to sit at his table. Jamie had seen little of Kit since the fighting within the castle at Meung.

"Ho, Jamie, how does the Armagnac court?" Kit asked once he was at his friend's side.

"All is yet to be decided, but I'd wager a hare against a rabbit that the good lords of Armagnac will come to heel afore the winter sets in. Yet my lord of Clarence seems to care little either way other than to wet his sword in French blood once more ere the year be out."

Kit sighed, raising his eyebrows in sympathy. "You have the right of it for certes, but this is not war as I would have it. Since you departed the course of action has worsened, and I feel we have become *routiers* in everything but name. We make war upon the people of France as well as its armies, killing and destroying, and other shameful acts that would make the Four Horsemen of the Apocalypse weep. The prince knows right well that we can sit here cinctured by the warmth of good quarters and make war by raiding, weakening all and destroying all chance of income to the Armagnacs and others mayhap, and those we don't kill starvation and the cold of the coming winter shall.

"It does not bode well and goes against my honour. I would rather fight a good battle against my peers, testing my sword in the melee, not burning and looting farms for feed or ransoming merchants we find upon the road."

"It has come to this?" Jamie asked. Others around the table heard the words and nodded in agreement with Kit.

"Worse, we sack churches and other sacred holdings, and blameless French citizens hide their wives and daughters for good reason. No good will come of any of it, and I pray that all shall be resolved so that we may return and ready ourselves for new battle against Burgundy in the Spring."

"I pray God that the new terms be acceptable and a peace accord can be struck before winter comes," Jamie offered. "For I have no wish to wage war upon innocents."

"Amen to that – and speaking of prayers, why, they are said for you by the fair Lady Alice, for your safekeeping I'm bound. This despite many a fox circling the chicken run." He warned his friend.

Jamie's heart fluttered, for Alice had been much in his mind on the road, especially when Mark had sailed home to return to Emma. He ignored the jest and asked diffidently, "Does she do well?"

"She does, and upon some premonition, asked that I give you her favour should we meet upon the road." Kit hesitated, uncertain of how to phrase his next words. Eventually he picked up the courage to speak, even though it might harm his friendship with Jamie. "I speak now as a friend and adjure you to seek her hand upon your return, despite what you have said of her father in the past. And now I shall say no more upon you procuring more wine, for talking of thus is thirsty work."

Jamie laughed at the riposte, but the words struck home to him, and he felt the sudden need to remove himself from this dirty war and return to England.

Chapter Forty-Four

Bologna: November

"Do you believe that Jeanette has yet safely reached England's shores, Cristoforo?" Alessandria asked, her head propped up upon pillows as she looked across at her husband. Cristoforo had just washed and was stripped to the waist – his body showing the scars of past encounters – padding about the bedchamber of the palazzo. It was chilly outside, with early morning frosts, but the servants had already lit a fire in the grate, which was warming the room.

"Let me think," he said. "She departed Livorno in *Augusto...si, io penso di si*. She will, God willing, have returned to *Londra* some weeks past. In fact the galleys will be safely docked in Flanders now for the winter, and we may even receive a letter from her before Christmas."

"Your eyes changed when you mentioned *Londra*. Do you miss that city?" she asked.

He came across the room and grasped her hand, kissing it.

"Cara, if you could be there with me then *si*, a thousand times, *si*."

Alessandria and tilted her head on one side, arching an eyebrow in a manner which Cristoforo had come to know as a sign of danger, akin to Mt Vesuvius spewing smoke and rumbling. "That is no answer at all. *Dimi tutti!*" she commanded.

Cristoforo sighed acceding to Alessandria's request to tell him all. "There are aspects of England that I enjoyed and grew to love, not least my friendship with Jamie and Marco, and all the others with whom we are friends. Yet here is home, I am of *Firenze*, Bologna and Italy to my soul. That is how I truly feel. And the weather is much nicer." He ended with a smile.

"*Va bene*, now I have the truth. Yet *Firenze* is barred to us, and we may not return there except by special permission of the *Guelfa*." She declared.

"And what of you, my love? How do you feel?" Cristoforo asked, knowing that this was dangerous ground. They had both avoided the subject since their wedding, afraid of what demons they may set free from Pandora's Box.

"I am torn, for I adore the new friends I made and the freedom that England offers me. Despite the fear and danger, I found our adventures there and through France..." Here she hesitated, seeking the correct word to adequately sum up her feelings. "Liberating! Yes, that is it. I felt liberated, whereas here, with all the trappings of rank and my father upon our doorstep, it is almost stifling in comparison."

"You will adjust. It is but a short time since we were returned, and England, she will be cold and damp now. But here, why we are still in the summer compared to *Londra*." He joked. But despite the words, he was as unsettled as she was. He felt restless and had little to do. Her father had forbidden him to take out any more contracts as an assassin, although Cristoforo had done so on one occasion, using the excuse of a trip to see his father as the reason for his absence. As a result, there was one less *Guelfa* member who had opposed the Medici and voted against Alessandria's petition for her dowry. He had been an evil man with blood upon his hands, and in Cristoforo's opinion he deserved to die. Cristoforo would lose no sleep over him.

He was shaken from his thoughts when Alessandria cried, "*Oh dio*! My father, I promised him I would visit some shops to pick out cloth for a new doublet and visit a new trattoria with fine food. I shall be late." She jumped up from the bed in a flurry of bedclothes.

An hour later, the count was still pacing the salon below, in exasperation at the tardiness of his daughter. When she finally appeared he was in no mood for civility.

"My child, the sun is nearly set, so long have I waited for you." He grumbled.

"Bah! Why it is not even midday." At which she swept past him gracefully and descended to the courtyard below.

As they mounted, the count asked, "No Cristoforo?"

"No, *papa*. I wanted time with you as I promised, and he has some errands to attend to, and mayhap will arrive in time and meet us at the merchants."

Suitably mollified at the prospect of some time alone with his daughter, he relaxed, as they formed a small expedition with two servants and a groom. All were wrapped in cloaks against the early frost that was even now being melted by a wintry sun slanting through the towers, casting spear-like shadows amongst the streets and piazzas of the town. The area was bustling with commerce and the streets became more crowded, forcing them to ride slowly towards the merchant's quarter, pressed by the weight of humanity that was impeding their travel.

"Is Signor Bartolo expecting us?" Alessandria asked, looking left and right as they entered the quarter, ignoring the shouts of the apprentices as they hawked for business.

"*Si*, I made an appointment and he expects us before the hour of sext." At which he shrugged.

"*Ma* for *il Comte di Rafaello*, they will wait all day," Alessandria replied.

They turned a corner off the main street between two very tall towers, and Alessandra recognised the whistle of crossbow bolts that had become familiar to her on her journey through France that spring. The two servants were struck simultaneously, driven from their horses by the force of the strikes. The loyal groom launched himself forward, saving the count from certain death as the quarrel slapped into his own back. The count reacted fast, pushing his daughter sideways. She went with the movement, falling from the saddle and putting the horse between herself and the attackers' quarrels. One struck her saddle, where she had been a second before, and the second pierced the count's leg. He cried out in pain, sliding down onto his good leg and drawing his sword.

There were cries of alarm in the street as the owners of the shops and stalls looked on in horror, calling for the militia and the constables. They all recognised the count, and some picked up wooden staves or drew daggers in an effort to protect him. It was to little avail as four men dressed in black and red, with cowls and scarves drawn up over their faces, ran from the ambush points where they had been hiding. Two merchants were scythed down as the four assassins rushed towards the count and his daughter, daggers raised and short-arming swords drawn and ready.

Cristoforo had been to see his banker, intent upon receiving funds pledged by his father from a client. This achieved, he made his way to the merchant quarter to order a new pair of boots before heading back along the street in the direction of the count's palazzo, hoping to intercept his wife and her father.

He rode his horse casually, yet as always he was alert while in crowds. He heard the cries coming from the next street: shouts of alarm and the sound of people screaming in fear. He pushed his horse forward into a canter, knocking two pedestrians flying as he went, and turning the corner, he was faced with a scene that would be embedded upon his memory until the day he died. Half way along, before the shop fronts, he saw three figures in black-and-red gowns and cloaks, while a fourth lay supine upon the cobbles. Two were attacking the count, who stood, blood seeping from the wounds in his side and leg, fighting valiantly against two of the assassins as the third stood above Alessandria, who lay motionless, covered in blood, pinned to the ground beneath her dying horse. The assassin's sword was raised to strike her.

"No!" Cristoforo cried in horror, squeezing his horse into a gallop, crashing through all before him. His right hand dropped to his boot top to retrieve one of his daggers. He was presented with a terrible choice: one of the two men attacking the count went forward to lunge past his guard, and Alessandria, who lay dead or dying, was about to be struck again. He had no choice. The dagger flew, cartwheeling in the pale light, lodging in the throat of the assassin as he turned to face Cristoforo, upon hearing his cry and the sound of the galloping horse. The man flew backwards at the impact, barely having time to register his own death as blood spurted in an arterial spray from his neck.

Cristoforo changed hands upon the reins, finding his left dagger, and knowing that he would be too late, watched the fatal lunge of a blade cutting into the count's torso. His dagger struck a moment later, killing the second assassin. The final man turned to face Cristoforo, slashing at his horse's nose, hoping to make it rear or die, dropping the rider in the process.

But at the last moment Cristoforo threw himself from the saddle. Not for him the chivalry of mounted battle, his were the gutter tactics of an assassin. He vaulted into a somersault, pulling out his falchion even as he flew through the air, landing on his feet with his legs apart in perfect balance, the falchion ready. The assailant went to cross back with his blade, ignoring the horse as it reared away in pain and fear.

He made to strike down from the backslash, driving forward and committing to the strike. The move was fast and practiced, yet Cristoforo came off the centre line of the lunge, swatting the blade sideways and slicing back towards the shoulder, aiming to maim rather than kill. He wanted the man alive. He dropped the blade diagonally, scouring through the body in a shallow cut that would only disable, striking deeply at the end to run the sword into his opponent's left leg, severing muscle and sinews, rendering the leg useless. He then stamped forward against the other knee cap, dislocating it as the figure fell to the ground mewling in agony, no longer able to walk or fight.

Cristoforo ignored him, looking to the count whose life blood pumped out onto the cobbles. He moved to aid him, ripping a scarf from one of the dead assassins, pushing it into the mortal wound in his stomach.

"See to my daughter..." the count wheezed.

"Hold this tightly," he ordered a woman standing by and looking on in horror, hand to her mouth. Then he ran to Alessandria, her torso covered in blood as the fallen horse thrashed on top of her in its death throes, spraying blood from an arterial wound to its neck. The sickly, cloying, coppery metallic scent of blood was everywhere mixed with the smell of excrement from the assassins' voided bowels. He knelt by Alessandria's head, raising it off the cobbles; her dark hair spilled backwards.

"*Cara*, no! Don't leave me," he cried, and with his hands

upon her neck he felt it – a slight pulse. A small sigh came from her lips as her chest struggled to rise and fall beneath the weight of the horse. "Quickly, pull the horse off her, *subito!*" he ordered the gathered crowd. Four strong men pulled and pushed the luckless animal from different directions, trying to avoid the flailing hooves.

Alessandria's eyes flicked open. "Cristo..." She sighed.

"Where are you hurt? Tell me. Please tell me so that I may aid you."

There was a gash to her head where a blade or crossbow bolt had cut across her shoulder that was bleeding profusely. "Hurts to breathe," she murmured. "My ribs..."

Cristoforo felt her side gently, drawing a sharp cry of pain from her. "The ribs are broken from the horse. Be brave now and take one deep breath." She did so, but cried out in pain and coughed. To Cristoforo's intense relief there was no frothing of blood bubbling upon her lips or nostrils. "My father...does he live?" she whispered through the pain.

"*Si cara*, rest. You and he will be all right." He realised then that a good deal of the blood had come from the dead horse and little of it was human. He pulled off his cloak and placed it gently under her head.

He looked around at the stalls. "I will buy that cloak there." He pointed at a nearby stall. "Bring it and carefully wrap her in it. She must be kept warm."

Then he went back to the count, who by a miracle was still alive. His breath rasped with every heave of his chest.

Here he saw the tell-tale frothing of red bubbles that he had so dreaded in Alessandria. The count's doublet was soaked in dark arterial blood. In one last effort he looked deeply into Cristoforo's eyes, grabbing his cotehardie with surprising strength and with it the crucifix around his neck. "Does...she...live?" he asked.

"She does, my lord count. Your own actions saved her."

The count's face relaxed and a thin smile etched his lips. "*Va bene.* Look after her for me, swear it on your mother's honour..." Cristoforo nodded and promised him that he would. The count arched his back in pain, gasped and then sighed his last breath, going limp, his fist clenched in death around the crucifix at Cristoforo's throat.

Hot tears burned Cristoforo's eyes. After the prickly start to their relationship, he had grown fond of their acquaintance in the last few months and had come to know and like the count, who had done all he could to welcome him to the family. "I will avenge you, *conte*, I swear this upon the Madonna and her child."

At which Cristoforo broke the death grasp and kissed the crucifix around his neck. He went back to Alessandria who was now trying to sit upright with the aid of shopkeepers and traders. "*Piano, piano, cara,* it will hurt terribly," he warned.

"Not as much as the pain in my heart," she whispered, seeing the body of her father before her, tears streaming down her face. Then the moment was broken as cries of pain were heard from the other side of the street. Two men were kicking and beating the surviving assassin whom Cristoforo had crippled and who was now bleeding heavily

"No!" he ordered, remonstrating with them. "I need him alive, for I wish to know why this happened and on whose orders. Bring him to the side alley, away from prying eyes."

"No, take him to the yard at the rear of my shop," one of the men answered, "for they killed my apprentice in their lust for death."

Once they had moved the hapless assassin to the rear yard, Cristoforo saw a small brazier that had been lit for enamelling and soldering fine jewellery. He took a small, sharp knife for cutting leather and placed it in the heart of the flames.

"Hold him tightly," he told the two men. At which they grabbed his good arm and his neck.

Cristoforo knelt before the assassin, staring him in the eyes and withdrawing the knife from the brazier. "I am going to start using this knife upon you," he said. "You can end all the pain and suffering at any time, just by telling me what I wish to know."

"And then you will kill me," the man whispered with a dry mouth.

"No, I shall not kill you, I give you my word." He shrugged. "But this way, you will die painfully in the most horrible of ways."

The red-hot knife came close to the assassin's eye, the heat making it water. "We start here and work downwards, and when I have finished you will no longer be a man." Cristoforo's voice was slow and measured, his tone almost conversational. Somehow that made it worse.

The assassin whimpered as Cristoforo grabbed his wounded shoulder harshly, causing waves of agony to shoot through him. "All right. *Va bene*, there is a bounty upon all members of the Alberti family who live, or who are found within one hundred and fifty leagues of *Firenze*."

"You lie!"

"No, 'tis true!" the assassin cried. "Search the doublet of the man who lies dead. A secret pocket lies within, holding the papers. You will see a signed warrant certifying that there is a bounty on the head of the count and his daughter, signed by the *Parte Guelfa*. I swear it is true."

One of the shopkeepers went to search and returned with the document the man had described.

Cristoforo read the document in disgust and horror, realising what it would mean for all members of the Alberti family. It was a death warrant for all who stayed where they were.

Bologna was but sixty leagues from Florence. Only Genoa would be safe to the northwest or the mountains over the valley of the Po above Parma. Even Rome lay just within the boundary. The entire Alberti family had effectively been exiled. Cristoforo turned away, struck by the barbarity of the bounty.

Then the thought occurred. "Why here? Why the *Conte* and his family?"

"The count is not Alberti except by marriage, and his wife is dead, so..." The assassin gulped and Cristoforo knew the rest. It was Alessandria that they had been sent to kill. She was the target of this ruthless attack.

His eyes widened in fury. "So upon whose orders was she targeted, and why her?" Cristoforo asked, his voice as steady as the hand that moved the still-hot knife back to the other man's eye.

"Giovanni di Giovanni Strozzi."

"Why? What wrong has Alessandria or her family done them?"

"Strozzi married an Alberti daughter, Antonia, some four years ago, and they were awaiting the apportionment of the dowry. If Contessa Alessandria was unsuccessful, they were next in line to receive the inheritance. Yet the contessa was successful, but if she were to meet with an accident..."

Cristoforo nodded, but sensed the man had only given him a partial answer. "There is more to this. They would need help to organise this and reconcile the account," he said.

"I think that he was aided by...Antonio Albizzi."

"Then he shall die, I swear it." Cristoforo's voice had fallen to a whisper, but the look in his eye told the other man that he meant every word, and would not rest until he had carried out his threat.

Cristoforo made to leave, clasping the crushed parchment.

The assassin breathed a sigh of relief. "Now you will honour your word and not kill me?"

"I will. I gave you my word of honour, which is sacrosanct." Cristoforo turned and left him in the hands of the two merchants. From the street as he walked away, he heard the final screams of the prisoner as the two men gained their revenge for their slain apprentice.

Chapter Forty-Five

Buzancais, France: 11th November

The small village of Buzancais was playing host to the greatest assembly of lords and nobles outside Paris. Prince Thomas, Duke of Clarence, had made a swift two-day march south to arrive at the village ahead of his French counterparts. Wary of a trap, he had sent out scouts ahead to assess the land and report of any large troop movements that might indicate false play by either the Armagnacs or Burgundians, whose territory bordered to the east.

As further security, he had ordered Jamie and Lord Ormond to meet with the Armagnacs upon the pretext of further confirmation, and to be at the Armagnac Council to accompany them on their southward journey. The two knights rode side-by-side away from the main column and out of earshot.

"I know not whether to consider myself a hostage or a fool upon an errand of mercy," Lord Ormond declared.

He was of a similar age to Jamie and had a thatch of wiry, red hair and a full, trimmed beard that gave away his Irish ancestry. The two men were becoming fast friends on their adventures, learning to trust each other in all matters, thus helping them to stay alive.

"I declare I am of a similar mind, for every time I show my back, I half expect to feel a dagger between my shoulders or a quarrel through my heart. I durst not trust a word a *crapaud* utters – albeit that he is a duke. Dukes abound in this land, it would seem, and all pay lip service to one cause while being swayed by another, pulled this way and that like the strings of a mawmet."

"Amen to that," Lord Ormond replied. "Mayhap I am inured, for we have similar politics in Ireland, and there are few that I would trust. I see the Burgundy coat of arms upon the servants and fear a reprisal there more than an Armagnac's knife in my back."

"I fear more another figure whom I saw lurking within the Armagnac court, Sir Jean de Kernezen, a malign influence if ever there was one, and one to be feared. I have had dealings with him afore and was the poorer for it."

"Pray tell, for it is still another two hours ride to this Godforsaken village and 'twill pass the time to hear your tale."

"I will do so – if only to inform you of all that is arrayed against us."

Two hours later, with Jamie's tale told, the Armagnac contingent came upon the small village of Buzancais. It was no longer sleepy, and had grown to many times its normal size. It now lay at the heart of a forest of flags and tents that had sprung up to accommodate the huge English army that had travelled en masse to witness this auspicious meeting and the signing of a new treaty.

The ground was hard as an early frost was melted by a pale

and watery sun. Autumn was giving way to winter now, and Jamie shivered a little, thinking of the fireside at home and a flagon of mulled wine. The now familiar smell of resiny wood smoke filled the air, as green French oaks had been felled to make camp fires; the wood was more acrid than its English counterpart. Wild boar had been hunted, and their carcasses were roasting upon spits over the fire pits; the sweet aroma of roasting pork caused the visitors to salivate and their stomachs to growl in protest.

The two Englishmen had travelled on ahead with their servants and squires, leaving the French to make their final entrance to the village. Dismounting from their tired horses, the two knights waited upon the Duke of Clarence.

"My lord prince, we bring you a gift of Armagnacs," joked the earl when Prince Thomas arrived.

The prince was just as ebullient, sensing that he had won this long and terrible campaign and was now at the end of it. "Why then, we hope that they shall be to our liking," he quipped in response. The court was amused and laughed in good humour.

"What say you, Sir James, is all well? For you know these malaperts right well?"

"I do, my lord prince, and I believe there to be a bad apple among them in the form of Sir Jean de Kernezen, chief emissary for his grace the Duke of Burgundy." Here he paused slightly, allowing his next words full import. "He serves also as a spy and I would trust him as much as an eyasmusket off its jesses."

The prince snorted at the quip, but Jamie's comment drew a searching look from the Earl of Devon, Thomas Beaufort, who knew of his brother's connection to Kernezen, and for a moment feared that Jamie knew more than he was admitting.

"You know this man, de Grispere?" he asked, his tone ambivalent.

"Our paths have crossed in the past," Jamie answered vaguely, and then realising the depth of Beaufort's question and indeed his concern, he added, "at the French court."

"And yet you live to tell the tale?"

"As you see, my Lord Beaufort." Then Jamie deliberately and rudely dismissed himself from the earl's inquisition and turned to the prince. "Highness, ere it please you, sire, I needs must wash the stain of travel from myself. I shall return forthwith, by your leave."

"Of course, yet we would have you with us at our table of negotiation, for you know better than any how these Frenchmen's minds will bend."

"As you please, sire." At which Jamie bowed and left with the Earl of Ormond.

"Is there some friction there twixt you and my lord of Beaufort, for he ever seems at your throat?" Lord Ormond asked.

"There are matters which are better left unsaid, Sir James, and I fear this is one that should be left so," Jamie answered.

The earl looked at him askance. "Very well, I shall ask no more, yet one day I should like to know the whole."

For the rest of the day very little happened. All was settled upon the following morning when the two companies came together and a treaty was forged and signed by all present, bearing the seals of the great lords of Armagnac and Prince Thomas.

Looking on, Jamie spoke with the Earl of Ormond. "I am in disbelief: 210,000 *ecus d'or*, why that must be 40,000 English pounds if it's a shilling!" Jamie declared.

"Aye, and we have hostages to boot, including Duke Louis's brother, John. I'll wager there'll be no reneging upon this treaty. The pledge of brothers-in-arms should stand in good stead, and the prince is to be the new Lieutenant of Guyenne.

Indeed he could wish for no more, and shall return to England covered in glory."

"I'll warrant that there will be those who are green with envy at such lauding, though the king shall be pleased that his lands be restored and his favourite succeeds in his stead. And homeward now I should like to travel, for I saw mention of *sauvegardes* signed by King Charles himself. With the prince wintering at Bordeaux and safe passes guaranteed for all, my services will not be needed here, and I should like to see London again and turn my back without the worrying prickle between my shoulder blades in case some unseen assassin stalks me."

"Amen to that. I needs must return to my duties in Ireland too, if the prince will grant me leave. Where shall you sail from to reach England's shores?"

"I shall travel north to Cotentin, for all is safe now across those lands. They are held by the English and in no league with Burgundy. With hostages held, 'twill be as safe as any for a landward passage and the seas shall be calmer than the Bay of Biscay at this time of year, I'll warrant."

"A wise choice. Of the men-at-arms and archers many will remain, for here they are paid as they are not on England's shores, where they would spend a winter rotting as they awaited a new muster. Yet many a knight will wish to pass the winter at home by his own hearth, and the prince will welcome such a cause if only to lessen the strain upon his purse, I'm bound." The earl finished cynically.

For two days they waited for final arrangements to be made and to join the celebrations that followed the signing of the treaty. After the rejoicing had died down, Jamie and other knights, as the earl had predicted, arranged themselves into a party to head north, following the road to Cotentin to broker a passage home across the Channel. The journey seemed longer as the winter chills had begun to blow across France, yet the rain held off, and after the dry summer the roads were still in good order, making travel easy. The lands were untroubled by strife with little sign of *routiers* or vagabonds. Besides, no one with any sense would dare attack a party of fully armed knights and soldiers.

When they reached Cotentin, they found the wind to be against them and had to wait for three days before any ships could venture forth.

Finally, the captains of the waiting cogs prepared their ships to set sail and the choppy passage to England began. It was uncomfortable on board, as the holds were laden with cargo on what was probably one of the last regular runs across for that year, before the storms and the winter weather made sailing unpredictable and dangerous. They gained the port of Southampton three days later, delayed by adverse winds and dragging currents. All on board were relieved to see the shores of England once more, Jamie especially, for it had been nearly nine months since he had left the country. He hired a horse and mule and made his way up to London with some of the other company from the ship. Three days later, on a weary horse, he arrived outside the city of London at dusk, just before they closed the gates.

"My way lies in this direction." He motioned to the Earl of Ormond. "It has been of great cheer to have you as a companion, and if you lack for a warm hearth afore you return to Ireland, my invitation to join my father's house still stands."

"You are very kind and well met, Jamie. Yet as Lord Lieutenant of Ireland, I have matters to attend to and needs must be upon the road west to obtain passage to Ireland afore the storms close the sea for the winter. Fare thee well and, God willing, I shall see you on the field of battle soon for the glory of the king and England."

"Amen to that. I wish you happy Christmas and a safe journey, and may God have you in his keeping." The earl reciprocated and set off into the drizzle that was falling around then, coating everything in a wet sheen and rendering the cobbled surface slippery.

At last Jamie sat upon his horse outside his father's house, almost not wishing to enter, partly savouring the moment and partly fearing that his absence would have changed everything. He chided himself for his foolishness, but he knew that he himself had changed, worn down and honed by fatigue, never knowing when the next bolt or sword might end his life. He shook the maudlin thoughts from his mind. He was here, God be praised, and would live to fight again.

He went to the large gates of the rear yard, and finding them unbolted, he pushed up the latch to enter, seeing torches lit and servants in evidence, still working until the later hours. He walked forward, and as he did so the door opened from the main house and a female voice called: "What, you foolish hound? Damn you for a goky fool, there is nothing there untoward."

At which a blur of darker shadow bounded forward on silent feet, aiming for Jamie. At the last moment the quarters bunched, the back arched and huge, front paws landed upon Jamie's shoulders as a pink tongue licked his face. "Forest, you oaf, by God you've grown bigger and heavier." He grabbed her newly grown coat of winter fur around the ruff, holding her off, until she finally relented and dropped to all fours, not leaving his side.

Jeanette ran forward to embrace him. "Jamie! Why now 'tis truly Christmas, for you are returned to us, praise God." She felt the lean, hard frame beneath her hands under the cloak and gambeson. "By the rood, you are thin. Have you been unwell?"

"No, my sister, except from want of a good meal and rest,

for I declare that I could sleep for a week." Jamie's father and John appeared. Both greeted him heartily, despite John's normally taciturn disposition.

"'Tis good to see you, lad," John said. "You look stropped to a razor's edge, but campaigning will do that to a man."

"Come in my son, come in, there is a warm hearth and mulled wine. Let the servants attend to your horses and baggage," Thomas de Grispere ordered. Jamie looked around, half expecting the shadow of Cristoforo to appear from nowhere like he always used to. With a sigh of regret, he realised that it was not to be.

Later, after his tale of adventures had been told to all his family, he left the house on the excuse of seeing how Richard fared. In truth he was feeling slightly stifled; he did not know why, but he felt the strong need to be alone. He badly wished to see Alice – yet not this night, he mused. He was still unable to relax after months of tension. Thoughts tumbled through his head unbidden and he was tense, jumping at strange, sharp sounds.

John patted him upon the shoulder as he left the house, and in a rare show of emotion, grunted, "It will pass lad, 'tis always thus for a soldier returning home." He said no more, and moved on so quickly that Jamie could not respond and only look back at the old warrior, who was shaking his head sadly.

As he entered the stables, the warm familiar smells hit him. Feed, hay and the slightly sweet, musty smell of horses. A huge, chestnut head with a white blaze raised curiously above the stall, jaws rubbing from side to side and a wisp of hay protruding from one side of its mouth. A snickering whinny came from the stallion – his master was returned. Jamie walked up, unbolted the door and was butted gently by the nodding movement of Richard's head.

"Hello, old boy. By the rood you've grown a shaggy coat

and become fat, much like Forest," he muttered. "No doubt you are full of oats, and upon the morrow shall test me sorely as you try to unseat me. Ah, but all is well, for we are together once again. I just wish Cristo was here to complete the journey's end, for I miss the Italian rogue."

Chapter Forty-Six

Bologna

Three days after the attack in the street, Mass was called for the count and his funeral followed. Alessandria had wept all her tears before the service, and showed no emotion beneath her dark veil. Cristoforo by her side was inscrutable, supporting his wife gently, as her ribs were still very sore, and her strapped and bandaged shoulder would carry a scar, despite his best efforts to stitch the wound neatly.

After the ceremony was over and all the mourners had departed, they stayed together in the salon watching the embers of the fire glow and gently crackle in the hearth. Cristoforo sat at Alessandria's feet, holding the hand of her good arm, their faces lit by just two candles and the light of the dying fire.

"What do we do, my love? Where do we go, for I am lost?" she murmured.

Cristoforo had been choosing the correct moment to begin

this most difficult conversation with her, and he knew that the time was now right.

"*Cara*, there is a bounty upon your head, and men who will stop at nothing and have the law on their side will be determined to collect it. Anyone who seeks to redeem this bounty will be able to return to the sanctuary of *Firenze*, blessed by a corrupt *Parte Guelfa* against which there is nothing I can do – much as I would like to kill every last one of them. But one day, when you or I think it is safe, we shall be riding as you were with your father, or hunting, or walking to Mass and there they will be, too many for me to stop and all with the legal right of the *Signoria* to take your life. I believe we have two choices: we either stay here and become prisoners in our own home, or go far away: Genoa, *Milano*, south of *Roma*..." He left the sentence hanging.

"I want none of those places, and to stay here a prisoner with papa's ghost haunting me every day? No. Those towns, they are not *Firenze* nor Bologna, they are not home," she offered.

"So we shall go further, to England, where we have friends and where the reach of the *Signoria* will be annulled." Cristoforo decided. "There, I have said it. I have said what I really think, God forgive me." He turned to face her, looking up into her eyes.

"Oh *caro*, you too? Madonna, I wish this as well. When can we leave?"

"Immediately. Arrange everything tonight, for the longer we are here, the more dangerous it will become. We shall set out for Livorno before the gates open in the morning."

"Before the gates open? How?"

"I have a way. Trust me, all will be well." He offered her a conspiratorial smile.

Alessandria rang for her maid and the girl came forward to

attend to her mistress. The girl had dark hair and well-proportioned features that held the promise of great beauty, and reminded Alessandria a little of herself when she was her age. "How old are you, Francesca?"

"May it please you, contessa, I am ten and three years. I shall reach my fourteenth birthday in January next." She spoke well, carried herself gracefully and was very earnest in her manner.

"How would you like to accompany me upon a long journey? For we are to travel fast over the seas to England. The journey will be hard at times, yet it will be a great adventure."

"Contessa, I have little to keep me here now, for all is sadness. I would, by your leave, very much wish to accompany you."

"Do you have no family here?"

"No. My family are in *Firenze* and I was brought up by my aunt who was in service to the count. I was raised within the household, after..." Here she paused. "After your mother and brother died." She cast her eyes downwards and made to say more, yet stayed silent.

A slight frown creased Alessandria's brow as she tried to remember the child, but she would have only been young herself in 1407 upon the death of her mother and brother from the plague that year.

"Very well. You shall accompany us. Prepare all you can, for we leave this night."

They left Bologna before dawn on horseback, accompanied by two grooms and Francesca as Alessandria's personal maid.

The others within the household were loyal and would keep the secret of their leaving for some time, maybe even weeks. The count's old steward was so distraught at his master's death that he promised to ensure loyalty from all upon pain of death. They clipped quietly through the streets on horses whose shoes were muffled with rags, until they came to a small, postern gate from a private courtyard that had been left open for them, upon coin paid by Cristoforo. There were, he knew, always ways to pass quietly out of a town.

Two days later they reached his father's farm outside Florence. It was just before midday but they had been careful, skirting wide around the city to approach from the west, and had seen no one. Cristoforo's father ran out when he saw their small cavalcade and embraced his son tightly. They were beckoned quickly inside and Cristoforo spoke to his family about all that had happened, although he was surprised to learn that they too had heard the terrible news. His father was very gentle with Alessandria and held her softly, expressing his sympathy. They all ate a quiet and reserved meal at the main table.

"So the Strozzi killed your father. May they rot in hell." Simona swore.

"Oh they will, my sister, they will," Cristoforo whispered, and his words sounded more deadly than any swearing and ranting.

"No Cristoforo, no vengeance. I do not wish you to be caught and killed. Signor Strozzi will be well guarded and *Firenze* is home to him. He is surrounded by friends and family here." Alessandria pleaded, grasping his hand.

"As you wish *cara*, yet one day he and the Albizzi shall pay dearly for what they have done." His father looked on in silence, nodding gently, and across the table Tommaso's eyes were alight with the fire of vengeance. The conversation moved on, all agreeing to change the subject by silent consent.

"I am fatigued, Cristoforo. Would you please excuse me, Signor Corio? It has been a long day." Alessandria addressed them all at the end of the meal.

Rooms had been made ready for them, and she was suddenly very drowsy as she dropped onto the bed. She fell asleep in Cristoforo's arms, and it was then that he betrayed her.

As soon as he heard her breathing deeply he disengaged himself from her arms and left her, dressing and going to the main room of the farm house where his family waited.

"Did you put a draught of dwale in her wine?"

"I did, my son. It was only a light dose, but mixed with wine..." Cristoforo's father shrugged. "She will be groggy no more, and will not wake for two hours or so."

"*Va bene*. Now I go to seek vengeance," Cristoforo hissed.

"No, brother, *we* go, I will not let you go alone," said Tommaso.

Cristoforo made to argue then realised it was futile; with his brother's aid it would make life easier and quicker.

"Thought you that you would go alone?" Simona added. "No, I love Alessandria as a sister. We shall restore our family's honour together."

"Very well, let us go," Cristoforo replied and smiled.

It felt good to have his family around him. They entered the town separately through different gates, and no one who knew them would have recognised them. Simona hid beneath hides in a waggon driven by Tommaso, cowled and anonymous, whilst Cristoforo entered as a beggar stinking of horse manure.

It did not take them long to find the tower of the Strozzi, and Cristoforo sat down to beg beside the doorway. The streets were busy and no one paid any heed to another beggar claiming rights to the streets of Florence. Cristoforo's brother was opposite, tending to the firewood within his cart. The door opened just after four o'clock and Giovanni di Giovanni Strozzi emerged with two servants. He threw a coin at Cristoforo, who thanked him.

Strozzi had gone but a few paces when two cowled figures pulled back his servants' heads and slit their throats. Cristoforo and his brother pushed them sideways into an alley, and such was the speed of the attack, that hardly anyone noticed. Two men looked on aghast, not believing what they had seen, but it was too late. A hand was cupped over Strozzi's mouth as Cristoforo's dagger slid up between the eleventh and twelfth ribs from the back, driving for the kidneys, taking all sound from the victim other than a brief sigh, as the dagger was ripped sideways and Strozzi's lifeblood spewed onto the cobbles.

Cristoforo turned Strozzi to face him. "For the *conte*, and for his beloved daughter." Their eyes met and Strozzi's opened wide in horror that such a bold plan could have succeeded, literally on his very doorstep.

"I, Cristoforo Corio, take my vengeance upon you. Rot in hell, Strozzi *bastardo*," he hissed as the life fled from the eyes of his victim, whose last vision in this world was of Cristoforo's merciless grimace of hatred.

Cristoforo and Tommaso ran down an alley, using the familiar maze of streets to escape all pursuit. In the commotion the wood cart moved off, driven by a peasant girl nobody would ever remember. There was chaos and cries of fear, but no one saw or recognised the culprits. Cristoforo and his brother joined Simona near the southern gate and hid within the cart. No one challenged them, and within half an hour of killing Strozzi, they were back at the family farm.

Washed and wearing new clothes, Cristoforo shook Alessandria awake. She was dozy but none the worse for her induced sleep.

"Come, we must go," he urged in a tone that brooked no argument. "Rumours are abroad of our escape, and I have no wish to be found here."

"*Oh Dio!* How do you know?"

"My sister heard talk in the town. Come, *subito*, we go. Raise Francesca and let us be gone." He left her to dress and prepare and went to check that their mules and horses were saddled and ready.

The women prepared themselves to leave in a remarkably short space of time, sensing the urgency of the moment. Cristoforo embraced his family one last time.

"We shall return as soon as we are able to do so safely," he assured them. They mounted, and the party rode out of the courtyard in the direction of Livorno.

Two days later they stood on the dockside, where Jamie and Mark had stood some months earlier. Cristoforo returned from speaking with a captain of a Genoese galley.

"We leave on the evening tide. The captain makes his last voyage, hugging the coast to avoid the winter storms. We make for France, where I hear rumours that there has been a great war, and that the English prince has slaughtered the French. Therefore we must have care and mayhap winter in Bordeaux. From there we shall travel when the spring comes once more – to England, where our future awaits us."

Historical Notes:

WARNING: This section contains spoilers, if you are reading this ahead of the story.

Distance

There's a lot of long distance travel in this volume, so I thought that I should clarify measurements of distance. In the early fifteenth century, a statute mile was not as it is now and in fact varied considerably – especially outside England, where not only different countries but also different parts of the same country had a different idea of what a mile meant.

However, leagues were more universally accepted, and the league was the term everyone used to define distance, whether by land or sea. The general consensus from my research indicates that a league was equivalent to 1.3 miles today, and this definition is what I have used when calculating time, distance and travel.

Regarding horse travel, I have assumed that horses – especially those encumbered with baggage and mules – would travel roughly 20-25 miles in a single day. I appreciate that it is easily possible to travel farther, and some will say, "Oh that's nothing, I've done 40 miles in a day on horseback." Possibly, but did you do it every day for a month, with no stops, and without the shoes wearing out or coming loose and the horses getting tired? Even long distance riders in competitions will do no more than 75-100 miles in a day at most, with no baggage, on good tracks, using support teams and with rest stops already prepared. They also do this for one day only, and are not forced to fight battles at the end of their journey.

Language and the court

All the events I describe took place at both the English and the French courts. Jean de Kernezen was Burgundy's spy and assassin, and he made regular trips under cover to England.

Nearly all the courtly speeches made by King Henry in this novel represent the real words that he used, taken from records of the time. I kept his dialogue as close to verbatim as my editor would allow me to. He did bring me into line sometimes, mostly when he hadn't got a clue what Henry was talking about. English is a changing language, and the events described here took place nearly two hundred years before Shakespeare. I soon realised that I would need to bring the dialogue up to date every so often, or at least render it more comprehensible, so I took the occasional liberty with the words the king used.

An attempted assassination of Prince Henry took place in his own quarters at Coldharbour Mansion, and the Earl of Arundel took charge of the attacker – who mysteriously drowned while in his care before he could be properly questioned. Nobody knows why, and no one knows for certain who was behind the attempt. Many suspected Archbishop Arundel or Bishop Beaufort (as I have done), who was a close associate of the Earl of Arundel. This seems to me to be the more likely case, and certainly suits my story line.

I mention that the prostitute in Prince Henry's chambers was identified by her yellow cloak and hood. It was written into the Sumptuary Laws of the day that any prostitute who ventured north of the river must identify herself as such by wearing a yellow hood and cloak.

The relationship between Prince Henry and Prince Thomas deteriorated in reality as I have described here, and Prince Hal was furious. He had a doublet made as I describe of needles and eyelets, which he wore when he knelt before his father and offered him a dagger with which to kill him.

The Western Schism

The schism in the Catholic Church and the papacy was very real, and the politics involved were wide-ranging and affected everyone, especially the Alberti, who were asked to make payments in coin as I describe. They made their payments in record time and to everyone's surprise. The period was one of terrible upheaval, especially in Italy, although church politics had huge ramifications upon many other countries, whose rulers swiftly put the schism to use as a political lever. The schism was not resolved until many years after the events described in this book, and caused all sorts of problems in international relationships – particularly between England and France.

Italy

The terrible actions of the *Parte Guelfa* and everything I describe – including the names of the petitioners, the sums of money involved and the timing of the doctrine against the Alberti on the 12th of June – all happened. The judgements were as described, and Alessandria's case represented the first time that the courts ruled in favour of deceased members of estates, who made claims from that point on. I used a little artistic licence when describing the construction and appearance of the Hall of the Five Hundred, which was probably not as complete as I describe. It was finished over the next few years, but it is such a beautiful building that I couldn't resist depicting it in all its glory.

The bounty placed on all Alberti within a radius of 200 miles of Florence was very real, and family members were assassinated in similar ways to the attempt I describe on Alessandria and the death of the count.

The city of Florence was known as the city of beggars. Some 17,000 of them lived there, so the description of Cristoforo outside Strozzi's door reflects the historic situation. Here I must mention the excellent paper *Exile in Practice*: The Alberti

Family In and Out of Florence 1401-1428 by Susannah Foster Baxendale

France

Prince Thomas's attempts to cross the English Channel in the summer of 1412 resulted in several failed expeditions. He was turned back on his second attempt and finally made landfall on August 10th at St-Vaast-La-Houge. His army moved inland to outsmart the proposed ambush at Cotentin. Not much is known of the battle, but mercenaries of Lord Douglas were there on the French side, and the English won a resounding victory before rampaging through France towards Orleans. My own contribution to the fiction was to have Jamie (and Forest) alert the prince to the treachery of the Armagnacs and the Scots.

The taking of Meung set the stage for similar events years later by Joan of Arc. The meetings at Blois and Buzancais took place in reality, and the letters from the French delegation that were addressed to the English king and Prince Henry rather than Thomas annoyed him a great deal. Diplomacy was obviously in its infancy then! James, 4th Earl of Ormond and Lieutenant of Ireland, is a real character, and was there throughout the French campaign before travelling back to London. The final agreements and the sums of money involved were enormous for the day; they totalled more than the entire GDP for England at that time. Then, as now, there was profit to be made in warfare.

I hope that you enjoyed A Knight and a Spy: 1412. Sir James de Grispere and his friends, companions and enemies will return in 1413 soon.

If you have not read Book 1 in the series, below is a synopsis

1410
Subterfuge or sword, which will save the kingdom?

Sir James de Grispere, squire in training, is thrown into a world of treachery, the Hundred Years' War, revolts, battles, the wool trade, piracy and pivotal events. Medieval history is brought to life in this story of fifteenth century England and the fight for the crown.

Please do write to me with any questions or comments as I love to hear from my readers:

simonfairfaxauthor@gmail.com

To obtain two free short stories of the backgrounds to Jamie- A Squire in Training & Contessa Alessandria - Florence 1401 got to my web site www.simonfairfax.com and sign up to my mailing list for news, competitions and new releases.

A message from Simon:

I know that you have over a million choices of books to read. I can't tell you how much it means to me that you choose time to read one of my books.

I really hope that you enjoyed it and that you found it entertaining. If you did, I would appreciate a few more minutes of your time, if I may humbly ask for you to leave a review for other readers who may be trying to select their next reading material.

If for any reason you weren't satisfied with this book please do let me know by emailing me at simonfairfaxauthor@gmail.com

The satisfaction of my readers and feedback are important

to me.

Best wishes,
Simon

About the Author

Simon Fairfax writes in two different genres: International financial thrillers and medieval fiction.

He is a former Chartered Surveyor, Editor of an online polo magazine (having played polo for a number of years) and has practiced martial arts, fencing and shooting. He now restores old classic sports cars for fun.

As a lover of crime thrillers and espionage, Simon turned what is seen by others as a dull 9 – 5 job into something that is exciting, and as close to real life as possible, with Rupert Brett, his unwilling hero.

His new medieval series now has three books released in a proposed 6 book series. The first, A Knight and a Spy 1410, is set in a tumultuous time at the English court. It tells the story of Jamie de Grispere, squire in training and his two companions as they fight the French to save Calais, Welsh treason and Scottish revolts. Details of all his books can be found at www.simonfairfax.com   or   email   him   at simonfairfaxauthor@gmail.com

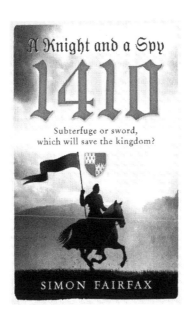

1410
Subterfuge or sword, which will save the kingdom?

Sir James de Grispere, squire in training, is thrown into a world of treachery, the Hundred Years' War, revolts, battles, the wool trade, piracy and pivotal events. Medieval history is brought to life in this story of fifteenth century England and the fight for the crown.

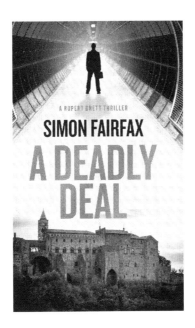

A Deadly Deal

If you like conflicted characters, rich period details, and complex plotting, then you'll love this historical financial thriller. Set in the 80s flowing from London to Italy it features Rupert Brett, a new kind of hero, an ordinary man thrown into extraordinary situations.

Acknowledgements

First of all my great thanks to my editor Perry Iles who helped so much in making my book come alive and my trusty BETA readers Deb, Patricia and Sarah. Also my new proof reader Kate Gallagher.

As always research has been the key to my work and it always surprises me how much went on in a single year in 1412.

To this end and in an effort to fully understand the events and people of the period I again read extensively, including Chris Given-Wilson's excellent book *HENRY IV* and Ian Mortimer's *THE FEARS OF HENRY IV.* Both give a brilliant insight to the events of the period. I would also recommend Ian Mortimer's *The time traveller's guide to medieval England* and I apologise if I have made any factual errors as a result. I would also mention Christopher Allmand's *HENRY V* which gave me such a fascinating view into this extraordinary King's life, events and personality.

Also, I would add to my bibliography this excellent book, that enabled me to understand fully the ships of the day, how they were constructed and used in warfare: *Medieval Maritime Warfare* by Charles D Stanton.

On sword fighting I also delved deeply into *The knightly art of battle by* Ken Mondeschien who explains the art as propounded by the brilliant Fiore dei Liberi. Also, Hans Talhoffer's *Medieval combat in colour* and *Armourers* by Matthias Pfaffenbichler. Also the excellent Youtube videos by

Modern History TV- Jason Kingsley, Scolagladatoria; Tod's workshop and to Mark of The Exiles

.

Finally, my thanks to all the horses and particularly polo ponies- including Richard- who taught me so much.

Made in the USA
Monee, IL
28 May 2024

59011874R00214